ERNNESTINE DE LACY;

OR,

THE ROBBER'S FOUNDLING.

AN OLD ENGLISH ROMANCE.

BY THOMAS PREST.

AUTHOR OF " ANGELINA," " GALLANT TOM," " THE DEATH GRASP,"

" EMILY FITZORMOND," ETC., ETC.

" If scenes of misery can entertain,
Woes I unfold—of woes a mighty train;
Prepare to hear of murder and of blood !"—POPE.

LONDON:

But he had scarcely given utterance to the words, when a terrific flash of lightning caught the tree,

But at that instant, Ernnestine uttered a loud scream, and darting between his lordship and her lover, she cried in frantic accents——

ERNNESTINE DE LACY;

OR,

THE ROBBERS' FOUNDLING.

CHAPTER I.

" Clouds burst, skies flash, oh, dreadful hour !
More fiercely pours the storm !—
Yet, here one thought has still the power
To keep my bosom warm."—BYRON.

THE fierce wind howled in hollow gusts ; the thunder rolled in tremendous peals ; the red lightning glared in the dark vault of heaven ; and the rain, in fierce torrents, descended upon the earth. The midnight hour had long since pealed, and the time, and all around, bespoke horror and gloom.

Accompanied by his faithful servant, Hugo, a gentleman was at this dreadful hour riding through an extensive wood, whose closely clustered trees rendered it almost impenetrable, and the thickly spread foliage made it nearly impervious to

No. 1.

the light of heaven, although it could not now keep out the fury of the elements, or resist the heavy shower of rain which forced its way through the leaves, and between the intertwining branches, and drenched the travellers to the skin.

The gentleman was a tall, powerful, fine-looking man, and his countenance might have been considered handsome, were it not for a certain expression of haughtiness and sternness which gave a forbidding cast to his features, and the contraction of his long, dark brows, which impressed the beholder with the idea that malevolence, revenge, and treachery, held a predominant sway over his mind. His complexion was pale ; and it required no very keen perception to discover that his breast was the abode of care mingled with other passions, sufficient to excite him to any deed of desperate power and anon, as the lightning darted across his face, there was a smile of contempt upon it, which was particularly repulsive, and he seemed to mark the ravaging of the tempest with the utmost indifference.

"Rage on, ye furious elements," he soliloquized, unheedful of the proximity of his domestic; "exhaust your wrath on me ;—I mind ye not. Ye cannot equal the tempest of my soul ! Howl ye winds !—roar ye thunders, more deafening than the yells and cries of a forest of wolves !—flash on ye forked lightnings !—descend ye overwhelming torrents !—I mock, I defy your utmost wrath ; my heart is adamant, and my mind callous of danger ! Black-visaged fate hath swept away every sentiment of feeling it once contained ; treachery hath made it torpid. I have no feeling now—I have no care—I have done with the world, and mind not how soon I am rid of it. But, no ;—there is one thought—one wish, which makes me cling to life !—that thought is vengeance ! Yes, vengeance ; not on those who have assisted to plunder me of my property, for that was occasioned by my own folly and mad infatuation, but upon him who has made a desert of my heart ; he who has robbed me of that which my soul more prized than all the riches the world could bestow. It is for that alone I wish not yet to die :—the time may come—it shall come !"

" It is a pity we left the inn at which we stopped in the evening, my lord," said Hugo, riding up to his master, and venturing to interrupt him in his meditations : " the sky then looked lowry, and I thought we should have a rough night of it. By the mass, an' we are in a pretty situation ; benighted in this dismal wood, where, doubtless, gentlemen of no very reputable description take up their abode, and may pounce upon us with a supper of cold steel before we are aware of them ; and with not the least signs of a house or shelter of any description."

" My faithful Hugo," said his master, somewhat relaxing the usual sternness of his looks as he spoke ;—" my faithful Hugo, it was folly in thee to persist in following the broken fortunes of thy master, and thus expose thyself to all the miseries that may attend him. Thou knowest full well that I am now a ruined man, and know not whither I am bound, or upon what purpose I am going : pr'thee turn thee back, and take with thee the gratitude of one whom paltry title now only distinguishes from the slowly station in which thou movest."

" Never, my lord," exclaimed Hugo, emphatically; " thou hast been a kind master to me ; I have lived with thee from childhood ; my father, and my father's father grew grey in the service of thy family, and never, never, while I have life, will I desert thee."

' Good, faithful fellow," ejaculated the other, as he pressed the hand of Hugo fervently, and seemed much moved by his manner; " be it even as thou wilt ; henceforth we are friends and equals :—forsooth, what do I now possess, that I should lord it over my fellows ? The haughty peer, deprived of that which brings him adulation, is but a man after all; and, oh, how much less than that man who has never mingled in the ostentatious world of pomp and vanity, and knows no luxury beyond those frugal necessaries which his own honest labour produces him, and renders doubly sweet."

" Nay, my lord, I do beseech thee give not way to these melancholy thoughts," said his domestic: " what if Fortune frowns to day, to-morrow she may once more beam upon thee her most radiant smiles."

The gentleman shook his head, and relapsed into his former state of apathy.

Still did the furious tempest continue its fierce battling, and its violence seemed rather to increase than abate. Ever and anon, trees that had stood the power of the elements for centuries were torn up by the roots, or split in twain by the lightning : the wind had risen to a perfect hurricane, and swept the rain in the faces of the travellers in a cloud, which completely blinded them. Altogether the scene was one of the most awful that the imagination could conceive. Still did the travellers pursue their way as well as they could ; but, instead of finding out a path, they appeared to become more and more entangled in the wood's intricate mazes.

" The blessed Virgin protect us !—it is a terrible night," exclaimed Hugo ; but he had scarcely given utterance to the words, when a terrific flash of lightning caught the tree near which he was, and split it to the root, striking him at the same time from his horse.

After recovering a little from the shock which this circumstance had given him, the gentleman went to the spot where Hugo had fallen, to see whether he was hurt. He called to him, he shook him, but all to no purpose ; and the next moment another flash of lightning revealed to him that the poor fellow was a blackened corpse, and by his side was the body of his horse, which the electric fluid had also killed.

" Poor fellow !" said his master, as he stooped over the disfigured body of his devoted vassal, " this, this is the reward thou meetest for following the fortunes of the abandoned of mankind ! Thus hath perished my only remaining friend !"

He stood for a second or two in melancholy contemplation of the sad spectacle ; then remounting his jaded horse, he once more proceeded as well as he was able, At length he broke through the more intricate portion of the wood, and was enabled to travel without so much difficulty. The storm also abated some of its violence, and the rain almost entirely subsided. By degrees the thunder ceased to roar ; the lightning no longer darted along the sky; and the wind seemed to have exhausted nearly all its violence, and only whistled in fitful gusts among the dark and heavily laden foliage.

The traveller spurred on his horse, and endeavoured to find out a path ; but all traces, if there had ever been one, were entirely obliterated. Shortly afterwards, however, he thought he beheld a large, dark object before him, which struck him as being a building of some description. Completely exhausted with fatigue, he urged on his tired steed, hoping his ideas would be realized, and that he might be able to obtain rest and shelter for a few hours.

He had not proceeded far when he beheld a light glimmering at a short distance from him, and which appeared to issue from a casement; he, therefore, felt certain that his first conjectures were true. The light, however, very shortly disappeared; but the traveller pursued his way in the direction in which he had seen it, and soon afterwards stopped at an ancient looking castle, surrounded with a moat, and which had, doubtless, formerly been nearly impregnable; but time had made sad ravages with it in many places: one wing was entirely in ruins, and the other part considerably delapidated. The drawbridge was down; and in all other respects it had the appearance of not being inhabited; yet was the traveller confidant that the light he had observed had proceeded from one of its casements.

" Perhaps robbers have made it their retreat," he reflected; " for who else would think of taking up their residence in such a gloomy, ruinous place? But, no matter," he added; " I have nothing that I care about losing—no, not even my life."

Having thus expressed himself, he tied his horse to a tree, and crossed the drawbridge. He was astonished to find the castle-gate standing wide open, and there was nothing whatever to obstruct his entrance. Reckless of danger, he did not hesitate a moment, but entered the silent court, which he crossed as well as he was able, his feet often coming in contact with the fragments of broken stone that had fallen from the building. As he advanced, and looking up towards the casement, he once more perceived the light, and was now, therefore, positive that his surmises as to the castle being inhabited were correct; he therefore hastened to the door he saw opposite to him, which immediately yielded to his touch, and he entered the building. The owl screeched dismally as he did so, and the bat flitted past him, as though warning him from the place as an intruder upon their territories. But, nothing daunted, he scrambled his way along, for it was pitch dark, and the floor was covered, like the court-yard, with broken fragments of masonry. Once he paused, as he thought he heard a distant sound as of loud laughter; but all being still, he once more groped his way, until his hand came in contact with the handle of a door, which was also ajar and pulling it open, he found himself at the foot of a flight of stairs. These he ascended, and when he had arrived at the top, he once more heard the sounds that had before vibrated on his ears, and which he was now certain was loud laughter in the voices of several men, and which strengthened his first idea, namely, that the old castle was the haunt of robbers.

Still, nothing daunted, he hastened along a gallery to which the stairs had conducted him, until he stopped at a door at the further end, from the interstices of which a glaring light streamed, and from the room to which it opened he had no doubt the sounds proceeded which he had heard. This supposition was speedily confirmed, for just as the traveller arrived at the door, he heard the following chorus sung, apparently with much glee, by a number of voices :—

> Round, merrily push the flask,
>   Bacchus, a god is, all own divine :
> Drink, drink, we in pleasure will bask,
>   The care of the robber's e'er drowned in wine !

SOLO.

Crusty old fools to our joys may be cold,
Let them preach while we handle their bright yellow gold ;
Those who are honest may meet fortune's frown—
Here we've a world and a mine of our own !

CHORUS.—Then round, &c

The voices ceased, and in a moment afterwards, at some order which appeared to be given by one of the party, but which the traveller could not catch, there was a great clattering as of mail and swords, and before he had time to endeavour to screen himself from observation, if such had been his wish, the door was thrown back on his hinges, and revealed him to a number of ferocious-looking men, all well armed, and who gazed upon the intruder with the most inexpressible astonishment.

Ah ! a spy ! a spy !" shouted several voices ; and the next instant a dozen swords were pointed at his breast, and he was completely surrounded.

" Hold !" cried a tall muscular man (who appeared to be the captain of the gang), and darting from the head of the table at which they had been carousing ; " I command ye to fall back and harm him not ; it is cowardly to murder one man in cold blood, and before ye are certain that he is what ye suspect him to be. If he be a spy, he will have to pay dearly for his temerity !"

In a moment the robbers returned their swords to their scabbards, and fell back at their captain's command ; the latter, after fixing a stern look upon the traveller, which he returned with equal firmness, said in a commanding tone :—

" Come forward, stranger !"

The traveller coolly folded his arms, and walking up to within a few paces of the captain, confronted him with a bold and steady look.

" Methinks thou dost carry a pretty brazen front, young man," said the captain ; " a very brazen front, considering the perilous situation thou art placed in."

" I and peril have become familiar," replied the traveller, firmly : " I know not why I should fear to meet it here."

" Humph !" said the robber, evidently astonished at the coolness of the individual he addressed, and whose tall and commanding figure, and the dignity of his demeanour, were sufficient to create admiration ;—" who, and what art thou ?"

" A man, as thou see'st," was the answer.

" What brought thee hither ?"

" I was benighted in the wood, and sought rest and shelter," answered the stranger.

" And knew ye not that this castle was the retreat of Black Ruthven and his brave and desperate associates ?"

" I did not ; and if I had, I should not have hesitated to enter it, just the same."

" Why ?"

" Because I have nothing to lose but my life, and of that I am weary, but for one thing."

" And what is that ?"

" The hope of vengeance against mine enemies."

" Thy dress is rich, thy bearing noble—art thou not a gentleman ?"

"I was what the world calls so, a short time since; but fortune and I have parted company for ever."

The captain eyed the traveller with more apparent interest than before; and the robbers seemed to look upon him no longer with feelings of suspicion, but of admiration.

"Thou seemest to speak with the candour of truth," observed the former;—"wilt thou join us?"

"He must, or never more quit this place alive!" exclaimed one of the ruffians.

"Hold thy peace, Ulric," said the captain;—"leave it to me, stranger," he continued; "thou sayest thou art unfortunate; that thou art reckless of danger; that the world hath wronged thee;—then what sayest thou, wilt thou not retaliate upon the world, and join as brave and jovial a set of fellows as there is in existence?"

The traveller paused and reflected: he traversed the apartment several times, and then turning to the captain, said,—

"I must have time to reflect on this proposition of thine; it hath taken me by surprise, and ——"

"Till the morning we will give thee," said the captain; "but remember that Ulric has spoken the truth. No person, who by accident wanders to our retreat, is ever suffered to leave it alive, and has no other alternative but to join us, or to perish through his mad attachment to what canting priests and idiots call honesty. It is our rule, and we never on any account depart from it.—Thou seemest weary; refresh thyself, and when thou hast done, Ulric will conduct thee to a chamber, where thou mayest repose comfortably as ever thou didst in thine own castle."

Having thus spoken, Ruthven motioned the stranger to be seated, who readily complied, after having first informed them where he had left his horse, which was immediately taken possession of. Before the traveller had finished his meal, the captain and most of the gang retired, leaving him only in the company of Ulric and four others. When he had concluded his repast, the latter asked him whether he wished to retire? and having replied in the affirmative, the robber took up a fresh trimmed lamp, after the traveller's sword had been taken from him, and beckoned him to follow. He led the way up two or three winding flights of stairs, and at last stopped before a ponderous iron door, which Ulric unlocked, giving him the lamp, and pointing to a bed in one corner of the room, departed, after having first secured the door on the outside, by lock, bolt, and bar.

The morning dawned, and at an early hour the traveller heard his door unfastened, and Ulric appeared to conduct him to the spacious apartment below, where he found the captain and the rest of the gang assembled the former of whom having motioned him to the end of the board, whereon the morning's repast was spread, thus addressed him,—

"Stranger, hast thou reflected on the proposition I made thee last night?"

"I have," replied the traveller, laconically.

"And to what determination hast thou come?"

"I am a ruined man," answered the stranger; "the bugbear honesty and I have done with each other, and ——"

"Thou dost consent to join us, then?"

"I do."

" And art ready to take the oath we always administer—to be faithful to the captain and his comrades?" demanded Ruthven.

" I am ready," replied the other.

In an instant he was surrounded by the gang, and being commanded to kneel, they crossed their swords over his head, while a goblet, containing a red looking liquid, was placed in his hand, and Ruthven in a loud and solemn voice, exclaimed,—

" Thou swearest eternal fidelity to Black Ruthven and his comrades; to keep faithful to them in every emergency, unto the death; to perform the commands of the captain, be it even the murder of thine own father, thy mother, or any of thy relations; and on the peril of their most deadly vengeance?"

" I swear," answered the stranger, in a firm voice.

" Thy name?"

" That do I wish to keep secret :—thou mayest call me, however, *Osmond, the Avenger!*"

" Be it so," said Ruthven. " Comrades, all hail to our new brother, *Osmond, the Avenger!*"

" All hail to our new brother, *Osmond, the Avenger!*" shook the vaulted roof, and the robbers brandished their glittering weapons above his head.

CHAPTER II.

" In truth she was a lovely babe,
    The stamp of innocence upon
    Her infant brow."—THE ORPHAN.

FOR many years the county of Northumberland had been infested with numerous bands of robbers, who bade defiance to the law, and in their intricate caverns, and strong castellated fastnesses, repelled every force that was sent against them, and excited an universal panic in the minds of the inhabitants for miles around. Innumerable were the depredations they committed, and their crimes of bloodshed created a feeling of universal horror and consternation.

Of all these marauders, none bore a more desperate character than *Black Ruthven*, a name which he had acquired from the darkness of his complexion, and always appearing in a sable dress, with a large black slouch hat, and waving feathers that fell upon his shoulders.

This man, with his ferocious gang, had taken possession of Alwyn Castle, and defied every power to make him abandon it. For many years he had carried on a triumphant career of villany, when he was at length slain in a desperate conflict with the retainers of a nobleman, on whom he had made at attack, and it was hoped, that the gang being thus deprived of their leader, would have dispersed; but this hope was soon found to be fallacious: he was succeeded by another equally as daring, although his nefarious deeds were not accompanied with that degree of savage cruelty which had characterised the actions of his predecessor.

This was no other than the man we have introduced to the reader in the previous chapter, as *Osmond, the Avenger.*

Many good traits, it was stated, accompanied the robber chief in his guilty practices ; for instance, he never committed murder, but when it was unavoidable for the accomplishment of his wishes, and to the poor and the fair sex, he always proved a friend.

One night, as Osmond and a portion of his gang was returning from one of his lawless expeditions, when they had reached that part of the wood near which the castle of Alwyn stood, he observed a bundle lying in his path, and, picking it up, he unfolded the mantle in which it was enveloped, and, to his utter astonishment, beheld one of the sweetest female infants his eyes had ever rested on.

" By the mass an' we have found a prize, Captain," exclaimed Arnold, the lieutenant of Osmond, as he knelt down and gazed in the little sleeping innocent's face, " an infant, and a beauteous one too ; poor brat, thou hast fallen from bad hands into worse I am fearful."

" How so?" answered Osmond, whose heart, as we have before mentioned was susceptible to some of the gentler feelings of nature, and who could not, as he gazed upon the unconscious babe, help admiring its beauty ;—" thinkest thou I would harm this little innocent? No! A murrian light upon he who could; Osmond, the robber chief, will prove that friend to it which its unnatural parents have not. I will take care of it."

As he spoke he took the infant in his arms, who awoke, and fixing its bright blue eyes upon the glittering mail which Osmond wore, smiled, as if in approbation of its future protector.

" In truth it is a fair babe," observed the robber, " and hard and inhuman must be the parent's heart who could abandon thee. The beast of the forest protect their young, but thy parents, poor little one, have left thee to the mercy of the world ; to perish,—for what other fate could they expect would attend thee? It is well attired too—this is no beggar's brat. Ah! what is this? A purse, well laden too, and with good gold pieces ; here is a letter also ; this perhaps may throw some light upon the business."

Osmond hastily broke open the seal, and as well as the light of the moon would allow him, perused the contents, while his dark and savage-looking associates watched him with astonishment, as they perceived the emotion he evinced, while he read the letter. One moment he became ghastly pale, and then his cheeks would become flushed, and he walked backwards and forwards with extreme agitation. A second and a third time he perused the letter, and his agitation increased rather than abated.

" Can it be possible?" he ejaculated, after a pause ;—" and this infant which has so miraculously fallen into my hands, is——Oh, revenge! revenge! Now. could I——" and he looked ferociously at the infant he had but a minute or two before caressed; " but no! It shall not be so; I will make this child the instrument of vengeance that shall bring misery upon the heads of mine enemies. Oh, Marian ; what a hell of torment would thy mind be, if thou didst know into whose power thy child had fallen. Take care of it, Arnold, and on with thee to our retreat."

" But what are we to do with the brat?" demanded the latter ; " a pretty

thing forsooth, and very fitting employment for a robber to turn nurse in his leisure hours."

"Hold thy peace, Arnold," said the captain, "and do my bidding. Old Beatrice can attend to it, and if not, I can soon make some arrangements about the business."

Arnold said no more, but folding the mantle round the child, carried it with much care, proceeding by the side of Osmond, and followed by the others, who made various remarks upon the singularity of the evening's adventure, and forming a variety of conjectures upon the conduct of their captain, and the agitation he had evinced on perusing the letter.

*　　*　　*　　*　　*　　*　　*　　*

It was near the midnight hour, and the guests had just departed from the snug hostelrie of Master Hubert Clencham, the proprietor of "The Flagon," which stood at the entrance to a wood, and was much frequented by the inhabitants of the neighbouring town. We say that the guests had departed, and to judge from the display of empty horns, pitchers, and flagons, Master Hubert had had a very goodly amount of customers on that evening, and the rosy, well-fed gills, ruby-tipped nose, blinking eyes, an occasional hiccup, and other demonstrations equally conclusive, would have led an observer to the supposition, that he had made himself perfectly agreeable and sociable with his guests; which he was accustomed to do, as his wife, who had never known him to retire to rest sober for one night in the week for the last twenty years, could fully testify. Master Hubert was, perhaps, a little too prone to doing ample justice to the juice of the grape; but

No. 2.

then withal he was so good tempered, and so merry, and so kind-hearted, that Maud, his better half, found it impossible to be cross with him long together. Moreover, his invariable argument was, that he admitted example was better than practice in most cases, consequently if he did not set the example of intoxication to his customers, they might not be inclined to drink, so that he should soon be ruined; whereas he was now enjoying himself in his own way, and saving a fortune by eschewing sobriety.

Of the force of these arguments, we cannot pretend to say much, but it is very evident they answered our host of " The Flagon's" purpose, inasmuch as he had saved a considerable sum of money, and had lately been able to purchase a valuable freehold, ground, &c., and the more he drank, the more did his business seem to increase.

Well, we have said that it was near midnight, and yet Master Hubert remained seated in his old arm chair in the chimney corner, with a flagon of sack before him, and deaf to all the entreaties of Maud for him to retire to bed. He was insisting, for about the sixth time that evening, that he should sing his favorite song, which was almost as long as the ballad of Chevy Chace, and generally took him rather better than an hour and ten minutes to accomplish. In vain did Maud expostulate with him on the absurdity and debauchery of his conduct; her remonstrances fell without the least effect upon his ears, and her arguments only served him for ridicule.

" Plague on thee, Hubert," said Maud, wrathfully,—" marry, an' thou get'st worse every day; here hast thou been at the flask since peep o' morn, and nothing, it seems, will persuade thee to leave it while there is a drop in the cellar."

" Thou sayest true, by the mass," returned Hubert, hiccuping, and taking a swig at the end of every half dozen words; " thou sayest true, Maud; I will never desert an old friend, and where shall I find a better one than the flask has been to me. Get thee to thy bed, and leave me to my enjoyment; thou knowest it is useless to attempt to persuade me; so put another log on the fire, and close to the shutters, for it is a rough night, and the wind blows keenly."

The night was indeed tempestuous, and the rain rattled violently against the casements; it was such a night when the bright blazing fire appears to have a double comfort, and Master Hubert seemed to think so, and it was a truly refreshing sight to see his jolly, rubicund countenance glittering like a new copper warming pan, in the reflection of the fire which burnt briskly on the hearth.

Finding all her persuasions were unavailable, Maud was about to retire to her chamber, when she was surprised and alarmed to hear a loud knocking at the door.

" Marry, good gracious! some one knocks!" said Maud, " who can it be at this unseasonable hour?"

> " More sack, more sack, 'tis the best of all drink,
> More sack, more sack, let us drink till we blink;"

sang Hubert, who had not heard the knocking.

" More sack, thou drunken idiot," said Maud, passionately, " will nothing bring thee to thy senses? Some one knocks, I tell thee, and there thou sittest, and takest no more notice than—there again!"

The knocks were repeated with more vehemence than before, and were followed by the voice of a man, but what he said they could not distinguish.

"By my troth thou art right, Maud," said Hubert, staggering on to his feet, "there certainly is some one knocking as thou sayest, and it is rather an unseasonable hour for travellers. But I suppose it is somebody who has been benighted in the wood."

"More likely it is that terrible fellow Osmond, or some of his gang;" said Maud, " and we shall perhaps be not only robbed but murdered."

"Out upon thee for a silly one as thou art," returned Hubert, " what, thinkest thou, Osmond wants with such as us?—He seeks higher game! besides, is he not always the friend of the poor?"

Once more was the knocking heard, and then the voice of the man imploring them to admit him from the inclemency of the weather.

"Aye, aye," said Hubert, aloud, " be not impatient, I must take the liberty of putting a few questions to thee first. Who art thou?"

"I am a traveller, and have walked far since the morning; I am wet and weary," was the answer, " and have one with me that requires the utmost care and attention; pr'ythee admit me, I have the means to remunerate your kindness."

"Oh, as for that matter," replied Hubert, " we can talk about that afterwards. But art thou sure thou art not deceiving me?"

"I swear I am not," answered the man, " for the love of heaven do not keep me standing here any longer, for I am already drenched to the skin and perished with cold."

"Well, well, tarry till I unbolt the door," said Hubert, " I will e'en venture to admit thee."

"Oh, no, no, not for the world!" cried Maud, with a look of terror, and who suffered her fears for a moment to overcome her natural kindness of heart.

"Nonsense, Maud;" observed her husband, " I feel certain that we have nothing to fear; and besides, this is not a night fit for a dog to be out in."

With that, humming his favourite song, the burthen of which we have quoted, he unfastened the bolts, and taking the lamp in his hand, opened the door, narrowly scrutinizing the person of the applicant without.

The man seemed to be very much fatigued, and was enveloped in a long dark mantle, folded in part of which he carried something with great care. He was a tall man, of commanding figure and handsome countenance, on which the lines of care and sorrow were strongly visible.

Hubert being satisfied, admitted him, and the stranger, with many expressions of thanks, took a seat in the chimney corner opposite to Hubert, and opening his mantle, the worthy host of the " Flagon," and his wife, were completely thunderstruck to behold that he carried in his arms a lovely female child, apparently not more than eighteen months old, who stretched forth its little limbs in apparent enjoyment, as it felt the genial warmth of the fire.

"What a little beauty!" exclaimed Maud, whose fears had now all vanished, as she gazed upon the interesting countenance of the infant; "and to be out on such a night as this, exposed to all the inclemency of the weather!"

"I see ye are surprised, my friends," quoth the stranger, as he observed the looks of curiosity with which Hubert and his wife were eyeing him, " and I do not marvel at it. Alas! you see in this smiling innocent, the victim of tyranny and cruelty, whom I am endeavouring to rescue from a dreadful fate. I have to travel some distance further yet before I shall reach the place of my destination, and where I can place the infant in security from her enemies. You see how exhausted I am, and I therefore beg of you to grant me a shelter for myself and my tender charge until the morning, and I will freely pay you what you may demand."

" As for that matter, master," replied Hubert, who was now getting quite sober again, " thou art welcome to all the accommodation I can give thee, which is this warm fire-side, until the morning, for my beds are all occupied. So sit thee down and take a cup of sack or two with me ;—and, I say, dame, get thee some milk, and warm it for this poor infant, who, doubtless, is hungry."

The stranger again expressed his thanks to Hubert and his wife, and she went readily to perform her husband's bidding, and kissing the infant, declared " it was one of the sweetest little cherubs she had ever seen."

The stranger seemed to be labouring under some heavy mental affliction, and frequently sighed deeply, and covered his face with his mantle, as if he was endeavouring to conceal his emotion from observation. He did not appear to be disposed to talk, and as it was now very late, Hubert and Maud prepared to retire to their chamber.

" But," said the kind-hearted hostess, " the child, surely thou wilt not leave her here ?—If thou art not afraid to entrust her to me, I will take care of the poor little thing till the morning."

The stranger seemed extremely grateful to her for this offer, but yet loth to part with his tender charge, but after some apparent struggle with his feelings he yielded, resigned the infant to Maud, and after bidding him good night, they retired to bed.

For a considerable time Hubert and his wife lay awake, and formed many speculations on the adventure of the night, and endeavouring to form some idea as to who the stranger could be, and in what manner he was related to the infant; but not being able to form any notion on the subject, they gave it up, and resigned themselves to the arms of Morpheus.

At an early hour on the following morning, (which was their invariable custom), Hubert and his wife arose. The infant had never cried during the night, and nestled in her nurse's bosom, slept calmly and soundly. Having descended to the parlour, they were surprised at the stillness which pervaded it, and opening the door, their astonishment was increased tenfold, when they discovered that the stranger was not in the room. In a minute afterwards, some object attracted Hubert's attention, lying on the table;—he approached and found it was a purse heavily laden, by the side of which was a letter addressed in an unknown hand, to him. Hastily he broke the seal, and to his infinite surprise, read as follows :—

" The child entrusted to thy care is of noble origin, but by a strange chain of events, which time may perhaps reveal, she is placed in thy charge, with a hope that thou wilt acquit thyself fairly, which thou art enjoined to do, or thou mayest repent thy refusal when it is too late.—Mark, the writer of this hath power to injure as well as to aid thee; he is disposed to do the latter, and for the same receive the purse of gold left behind ; a like sum shall also be forwarded thee on the same day of the month every year, for the trouble thou mayest be at. Thou art requested to bring her up with the most studious care and affection, and do not let her know to the contrary but that she is thine own relation, until such time as circumstances may render it necessary, or thou mayest receive instructions as to the same. Thou mayest call her Ernnestine. Remember these instructions and obey."

Hubert read the epistle two or three times, and first looked at his wife with amazement, and then turned his attention again to the letter. Its peremptory tone was far from pleasing him, but there was an interest and mystery in the whole affair, which deeply excited him. As for Maud, she seemed to be perfectly thunderstruck and bewildered by the adventure, and for some moments they were neither of them in a condition to give expression to their thoughts.

"The holy Virgin protect us !" at length Maud ejaculated, "here's a mysterious affair ; marry, and I can no more make it out than I can fly."

"Of one thing we are certain, that we have an addition to our family," returned Hubert, folding up the letter, and putting it carefully away—"unless we like to turn the poor little stranger adrift, which, forsooth, I could no more do than abandon thee, Maud."

"Turn the poor lamb adrift," said the kind-hearted hostess, pressing the little innocent closer to her bosom ; "the bare idea of that makes me shudder, Hubert ; it is such a lovely babe that my heart yearns towards it already, as if it were mine own flesh and blood. Yes, Providence has placed it under our protection, and we will never desert it, Hubert. The little cherub ; see, even now it smiles upon us, as if thanking us for the promise."

"It is indeed a fair child," observed her husband, "and as thou sayest, dame, it is the will of Providence that has placed her with us, and it is our duty to protect it. Besides, it is evidently the victim of cruelty and oppression, and should we abandon it, doubtless it would be left to perish, or fall beneath the dagger of an assassin."

"True," replied Maud ; "besides, the letter states that she is of noble origin, and who knows but that we may be the means of restoring her to those rights which some villain may have usurped from her ? Oh, there are a thousand reasons why we should not refuse the request of the stranger, and not one sufficiently cogent enough to prompt us to the contrary."

"And yet, Maud," said her husband, after a moment's reflection, "at our time of life, this is not only a strange, but an arduous task to impose upon us ; years are creeping on us apace, and who in its infant state, can bestow upon it those cares and attentions, which only a mother can give ?"

"Who ?—hark ye, Hubert," replied Maud, "is not our niece, Edith de Lacy, (who is as good a creature as ever lived,) now suckling her first child ? To her care for the present let the babe be consigned, who I know will bestow upon it the same motherly affection as if it were her own offspring."

"A good thought, Maud," said Hubert, "be it so, after our morning's repast, we will repair to Edith's house, and propose the same to her. But mind me,—I would caution you to keep the whole affair a profound secret, from every one but Edith and her husband, who is a worthy fellow and fit to be trusted, for who knows but that there may be those who seek her life. Come dame, place the child under the care of thy wench, Margaret, after enjoining her to silence, and then let us get our morning meal, and to business."

The good Maud obeyed the instructions of her husband, and never did she feel a lighter heart; (the never-failing reward for the performance of a good action,) and then placed the humble but plentiful morning's repast on the table, which although only for her husband and herself, was such a substantial meal as seemed more than sufficient for a large family to sit down to. During the intervals between eating and drinking, they continued to converse upon the adventure of the night before, to speculate upon who the stranger was that had brought the child, and to anticipate their plans for the future. They had had a large family themselves, but a strange fatality seemed to attend them, and their offspring had all died ere they arrived at years of maturity; and therefore were they the more disposed to welcome the little stranger, who had been brought to them in such a mysterious manner. Besides, in a pecuniary point of view, she would be no burthen to them, for, as has been before stated, Master Hubert, or as he was more commonly called, " the jovial host of the Flagon," possessed a goodly store of gold, &c., and had no relation that he knew of in the world, except the niece, who has been before mentioned, and to whom they purposed consigning the child.

" It is very evident," said Hubert, " that whoever this stranger is, he is no poor man, but whether he is any relation to the child, I cannot form any notion. At any rate, she shall be brought up with that respectability which may fit her for that station she is probably some time or the other destined to adorn. By the saints," he continued, turning the glittering contents of the purse out upon the table—" this is a large sum, and those who supply this must not have empty coffers. A portion of it I will allow Edith for her trouble, and the rest shall be carefully put by until she has grown up, when, if she finds not her parents, (if the writer of the letter keeps his word, and sends annually a like sum,) it will make a handsome wedding dower for her. But come, Maud, hasten thou with me, and let us despatch this business at once, for our guests will begin to gather speedily, and then we shall not have an opportunity of doing what we wish."

With these words, the worthy couple arose, and Maud, taking the infant from the arms of Margaret, covered it with her cloak to conceal it from observation, and accompanied by her husband, left the inn, and hastened on to the house of Edith de Lacy.

CHAPTER III.

" Rear'd by the same affectionate hand,
    Their hearts assimilated, until they
    Saw no other bliss but in each other's love."—Anon.

EDITH DE LACY resided at no great distance from the hostelrie of her uncle, and was comfortably circumstanced in life, she having married one Ranulph de Lacy, an honest bowyer, and who was descended from a noble family, the property of which had been entirely squandered, either by the folly and extravagance of his forefathers, or plundered in the conflicts that so often took place among the feudal lords. But Ranulph regretted not the loss of wealth or title; he was skilled in his business—he had a good home, a contented mind, and a virtuous and pretty wife, of whom he was doatingly fond, and a lovely child, a boy, their first born, who was suckling at its fond mother's breast, at the period of which we are now writing.

The neat and well-built house of Ranulph and his bride, which had been erected by Hubert, and made a present to them on the day of their nuptials, was situated in a romantic spot, and contained all the comforts, without any of the superfluous luxuries of the more ostentatious habitations of those who moved in a different sphere; and it was Edith's pride and delight to keep it in order, and to attend to the cultivation of the flowers with which their well-arranged garden was so amply stocked.

Combined to her natural intrinsic qualifications, Edith had received such instruction as few persons in her station, in those days, could acquire; in fact, it is well known that even among the nobility the most gross ignorance frequently prevailed. For this she was indebted to the pious sisterhood of the convent of Saint Mary's, in which she had passed the greater portion of her youth, being a great favourite with the Lady Abbess, and who had nearly persuaded her to take the veil.

In fact, Ranulph and his fair bride, (for extremely pretty she was,) might be truly said to be a worthy and happy couple, and Hubert and his wife were very much attached to them, as indeed were most persons who were acquainted with them. Who then could be more fit to rear the tender infant who had been placed in such a singular manner at the disposal of the host and hostess of " The Flagon ?"

The astonishment of Edith and her husband, when they were made acquainted with the adventure, may be imagined without any difficulty, and they very readily consented to do as Hubert and Maud requested.

" Yes," exclaimed Edith, as she took the little Ernnestine in her arms, and kissed it as fervently as if it had been her own offspring, " sweet innocent, in me thou shalt find a fond protector, that mother thou hast been deprived of ; thou shalt share my affections with mine own child, and be taught to love each other as brother and sister."

With these words she placed her fondly to her breast, and Ernnestine looked up in her face and smiled as if in gratitude, then nestled up to the little Godfrey, who was sleeping on his mother's bosom.

Ranulph watched the affectionate conduct of his wife with the most unbounded love and admiration, and kissed the cheek of the little stranger with much warmth and sincerity.

" The child shall never want a friend while it is in my power to protect her," he ejaculated; " she shall be to me as one of my own children, and I will not take any reward for my trouble, while I have the means of doing justice to her without !"

' Nobly said, Ranulph, my lad," said old Hubert, joyfully, and heartily pressing

his hand within his; " but this must not be ; a portion of this gold is only thy
due, and I insist that thou takest it; the remainder of this, and other monies
which I may receive from the person who has committed her to our care, as I before said, I intend to put by for her, and at some future period it may be of
service to her, and will, at any rate, save her from the terrors of want."

It was with the utmost difficulty Hubert could persuade Ranulph and his wife
to accede to the first part of this proposal, but at length the final arrangements
were completed, and Ernnestine became a member of the family of Ranulph de
Lacy, under the superintendence of the honest innkeeper and his wife.

" Well, i'faith," observed Hubert, when they had finally settled this point;
what happiness does the performance of a good action afford a person. My heart
now feels as buoyant and cheerful, as if I had just come into the possession of a
princely fortune, and something whispers to me that this poor child will be
the means of bringing us future felicity ; that she will prove an inestimable
blessing to us."

He was interrupted by a hollow laugh, and looking towards the casement of
the parlour in which they were seated, beheld staring in upon them a being of
peculiarly awful and unearthly appearance, with withered cheeks, wild ropes of
dark grey hair, sharp visage, and eyes of more than human fierceness.

" It is Hal., of the Glen," exclaimed Ranulph, " by my troth I like not his
coming hither, for his presence is always the harbinger of some evil. I will
speak to him."

The persons present trembled as Ranulph approached the casement to do as he
said, and even the sturdy host of " The Flagon" felt an irresistible sensation of
awe stealing over him, as he gazed upon the singular object which still continued
immoveable at the casement, and kept his piercing eyes fixed upon them.

Ranulph met his gaze undauntedly. " What wouldst thou here, Hal., of the
Glen?" was the interrogatory he put to him.

" I would open to thee the book of destiny," answered the latter, " and reveal
to thee that which is fated to come to pass."

" What canst thou tell me?" demanded Ranulph, in a firm voice.

" Wouldst know?"

" I would."

" Thou dost not scorn my power then ?"

" I would try it."

" Enough; wilt meet me at the midnight hour, in the Glen of Willows?
" asked Hal.

" I will," answered Ranulph, resolutely.

" Oh, forbear, forbear," interrupted the terrified Edith, looking with an expression of supplication in her husband's countenance.

" Art thou resolved to meet me ?" repeated the hollow voice of the hideous-
looking being, darting a ferocious look upon the horror-struck Edith.

" I am," was the fearless reply.

" Enough ! remember !" solemnly exclaimed Hal., and the next moment he had
vanished from the casement.

The strange being alluded to above, inhabited a deep cavern in a gloomy glen,
not far from the spot where this scene took place. He was commonly called Hal.,

hissing serpents, and other noxious reptiles obstructed his path. But yet did the bold bowyer courageously move forward, until a terrific peal of demoniac laughter, which seemed to come from the very bowels of the earth, and to convulse it beneath our adventurer's feet, caused him to stop. The next moment a blue cloud filled the cavern, which having gradually evaporated by the light that issued from a large circle of skulls, and the glare from the red fire that burned in a caldron which stood in the centre,—Ranulph beheld seated on a mound of earth, just outside the circle, the mysterious being he had come to meet, Hal of the Glen!

The awful-looking being was seated before a rude table, apparently formed out of human bones, and pondering over a massive volume, in which were inscribed a number of mystic characters. Before him stood a globe; above his head hung an aligator, and a skull and cross bones; while at his feet stood an immense black cat and a savage-looking dog, who growled fiercely as Ranulph entered the cavern.

The wizard removed his piercing eyes from the mystic volume when Ranulph appeared, and having fixed them on him for a moment or two, arose, took his wand in his hand, and stepped into the circle. No sooner had he done so, than Ranulph felt the earth tremble beneath him, and loud peals of thunder shook the vaulted roof.

"Advance, Ranulph de Lacy," said the wizard, "and fear not!"

"Fear!" repeated Ranulph scornfully, as he approached close to the magic circle, "what has he to fear, who sees no danger, and whose conscience is clear?—Hal of the Glen, I come at thy bidding; what wouldst thou of me?"

"Hast thou the courage to enter the magic circle?" demanded Hal.

In a moment Ranulph stepped into the ring, and advanced to within a few paces of the wizard, whose eyes seemed to gleam flashes of fire upon him. No sooner had he done so, than loud, terrific, and indescribable noises vibrated in his ears, the earth yawned at his feet, from which arose a number of hideous forms, who danced fantastically around him. The wizard waved his wand, and in an instant they vanished.

"Ranulph de Lacy," said the wizard, "beware; attempt not to move from the spot whereon thou art now standing until I command thee, or tremble for the consequences!"

"I obey;" answered Ranulph, firmly, "now, mysterious being, what wouldst thou with me, I repeat?"

"Ranulph, danger surrounds thee, woe and sorrow threaten thee, for the charge thou hast taken upon thee;" said Hal, in a solemn voice.

"How knowest thou that?"

"How know I, ha, ha, ha,—fool! what is there that I do not know?" returned the wizard, in a voice which made the spacious cavern re-echo again. "Hark ye, and believe, for it is I, Hal, the Wizard of the Glen, who tells thee; it is written in the book of destiny, that whoso taketh charge of the infant which thou hast undertaken to protect, until its real parents are discovered, shall be pursued with misfortune, and endure sorrow, misery, and disgrace!"

"I care not, humanity prompts me to the deed, and come what may, I will not desert the little innocent I have promised to protect!"

" Rash, fool ! wouldst bring misery upon thy wife, thy faithful Edith ?—wouldst entail anguish and disgrace upon thy son ?"

Ranulph started. At the mention of those so dear to him, his heart for the first time faltered, and he hesitated what reply to make. The wizard seemed to read his thoughts, and his eyes glared with exultation, as he exclaimed :—

" Pause, Ranulph de Lacy, while I disclose to thee a few pages from the Book of Fate. Art thou prepared to behold them ?"

" Proceed," said Ranulph, recovering his self-possession,—" proceed! 1 am prepared to encounter all the terrors thy magic art can raise."

" Enough ;—behold then ;" said Hal, and waving his wand, in an instant the cavern was involved in complete darkness, and Ranulph could not distinguish a single object around him. A dead silence also prevailed, which was uninter- rupted for several minutes. At length, however, a rumbling noise seemed to proceed from beneath the spot on which he stood, which sounded like distant thunder, and gradually a flickering light arose from the caldron, which increased, until the whole place was illumined by a deep red glare, and Ranulph beheld the wizard still standing in the same place as before, but the table on which was placed the mystic volume was before him, and on the latter his eyes seemed to be fixed with the most intense earnestness. At the back of the cavern also, Ranulph beheld an immense mirror, which was partially shadowed by a thin, vapoury mist.

Hal of the Glen did not change his attitude for several minutes, when suddenly he turned towards the caldron, and throwing himself into a variety of strange attitudes, he uttered the following words, at intervals, dropping something into the caldron :—

" By the power to which ye bend,
To me thy assistance lend ;—
By the charms which now I throw
In the caldron's burning glow ;—
The black blood of the poisonous snake,
The ring I from my finger take ;—
By the powers which all must fear,
Water, fire, earth, and air ;
By all the power which I boast,
By all hell's infernal host ;—
Whether evil, wrong, or right,
Quick reveal to mortal sight
That which either soon or late,
Is decreed to him by fate.
    Round the caldron now I go,
        And my mystic antics play ;
    In the mighty charm I throw,
        Powers of darkness then obey !

As the wizard uttered this incantation, he danced frantically around the cal- dron, continuing to throw something into the fire, and every time he did so, its blaze ascended to the roof; terrific shrieks rent the air, and the voice of thunder pealed more loudly than ever.

Completely paralyzed with astonishment, Ranulph stood transfixed to the spot, and watched anxiously all the awful proceedings. The wizard having ceased his wild antics, the cavern once more became completely dark, but it only lasted for a moment, when a bright cloud arose from the earth at the back of the cavern, and having gradually dispersed, revealed to the eyes of Ranulph the clear surface of the mirror, before which stood Hal of the Glen, slowly waving his wand as he uttered :—

> The charm's complete, my mandate hear,
> Phantoms, at my call appear!

Ranulph looked stedfastly towards the mirror, and was astonished to behold it reflect a complete representation of the interior of his own dwelling. His Edith was seated in the chimney-corner, and watching with looks of fondness and delight, the playful gambols of a lovely boy and girl, while a figure, the exact counterpart of himself, was leaning over the back of the tender mother's chair, and seemed to be wrapt in the same feelings of extacy as those Edith experienced. Ranulph was delighted with the picture ; but soon it changed, and the apartment now looked wretched and miserable ; his wife and himself, together with the little Godfrey and Ernnestine, were seated upon the floor before a fireless hearth, the pictures of poverty and squalid misery. Despair was in their eyes, and hunger depictured in their hollow and ghastly cheeks. Ranulph turned from the contemplation of this awful scene, with a shudder of horror, and when he once more fixed his eyes upon the magic mirror, it was again changed. He now beheld a beautiful garden, in which seemed to blossom all the loveliest of Nature's flowers ; a youth, who, by his likeness to himself, he knew to be his son, was kneeling at the feet of a beauteous damsel, in whose features he could clearly trace a likeness of the infant Ernnestine, and who was smiling upon him with all the ardour of impassioned fondness, and receiving with apparent pleasure a ring, which the young man was placing upon her finger, as a token of his love. But an instant, and this passed away, and Ranulph next beheld the dark and gloomy walls of a dungeon, to which he saw his son chained, and manacled hand and foot, while above his head glared, in characters of fire, the word "Murder!" Slowly this vanished, and in its place revealed to the astonished gazer a baronial hall of justice. Godfrey was standing in custody, apparently suffering all the agonies of horror and despair, and kneeling in supplication, he beheld a figure resembling himself, his wife, and Ernnestine ; but the stern judges averted their heads, and seemed deaf to the appeal. Once more the wizard waved his wand, and then Ranulph saw the representation of a woody glade, and Godfrey in the act of thrusting his sword through the body of his phantom likeness, while Ernnestine, with clasped hands, stood by, and seemed to be quite paralyzed with horror.

"Demon ! fiend ! I'll gaze no more !" exclaimed Ranulph, wound up to a pitch of frenzy, " it is but an accursed scheme, a damned delusion, to tempt me to swerve from my duty ! Avaunt ! I will no longer suffer myself to become the victim of thine infernal spells !"

The words had no sooner escaped his lips, than the horrible noises were renewed ; ghastly phantoms danced around him, and grinned upon and menaced him ; the magic mirror vanished ; total darkness ensued ; Ranulph felt himself felled to the earth by a powerful blow, and became insensible

The first red tint of the morning's sun was streaming upon the earth, and the feathered songsters had began to chaunt their mellifluous welcome to his golden presence, when Ranulph de Lacy regained his senses, and found himself stretched on the verdant earth, near the entrance to the cavern, in which the wizard performed his mystic rites.   The wet occasioned by the tempest of the night before soon dried up beneath the genial influence of Sol's scorching rays; and the air fresh and fragrant came reviving to the spirits of the bowyer.   He arose upon his feet, and gazing around him, at first had some difficulty in bringing to his recollection where he was, and what had brought him thither ; but soon the awful and mysterious occurrences in the wizard's cavern rushed upon his memory, and a momentary sensation of horror ran through his veins, as he dwelt upon what he had seen in the magic mirror, and the predictions of Hal of the Glen.—But this feeling was only momentary, and in a firm tone he soliloquized :—

" And shall I be tempted to swerve from my duty to my fellow-creatures, by the machinations of the powers of darkness ?   Shall the wild incantations of this fiend make me spurn the dictates of humanity, and cast the poor little stranger forth to perish, merely to——No !—by all my hopes of mercy here and hereafter, I swear, that whatever fate attend me, I will protect the poor child at the hazard of my life.   Hubert has exacted from me a promise to that effect, and my own heart sanctions it !"

A loud and unnatural peal of laughter, which seemed to proceed from the inmost recesses of the cavern, interrupted Ranulph in his meditations, and came so suddenly and unexpectedly upon him, that it made him start.   He looked around him, but he saw nothing to excite his curiosity, and all was now again silent as the dreary precincts of the tomb.   Ranulph looked into the cavern, but his eye could not penetrate the darkness beyond, and after a few minutes more passed in reflection, he determined to enter it, and see if he could unravel its mysteries.   He grasped his sword, (which he had found lying by his side,) firmly in his hand, and groped his way forward.   A suffocating effluvia filled this place, and Ranulph found considerable difficulty in breathing, and as he stretched forth his hands, he felt the cold and slimy toad crawling up the sides of the cavern. Finding that the darkness rather seemed to increase than disperse, and fearing that he should not be able to find his way out again, seeing, also, no chance of gratifying his curiosity, he made up his mind to give up his design, and turned back.   As he did so, the loud laughter, as if from a thousand voices, again shook the cavern, which had not subsided when he once more found himself in the Glen.

Ranulph sheathed his sword, and hastened on his return to his home, knowing that his gentle Edith, and her parents would feel unhappy at his protracted stay, especially when they were acquainted with the awful and mysterious business he was gone upon, and remembered the many wild legends that had been told of Hal of the Glen.

By the time he had emerged from the Glen, the sun was blazing forth in full splendour, and the green foliage seemed to receive a double freshness and beauty from his beams.

Charmed with the fineness of the morning, Ranulph walked slowly on, and gave up his thoughts to what had happened to him the night before, every circumstance of which was as deeply impressed upon his recollection, as if it had only occurred to him a few minutes previous. There were several passages in the visions which the wizard by his cabalistic art, had called up before him, which particularly struck him ; especially that scene, which shewed that a passion would spring up between his son and Ernnestine ; and the trial scene, where it seemed to prognosticate that Godfrey would be accused of murder. This certainly gave the fond father, for a few moments, some uneasiness ; but his natural good sense prevailed over the superstitious fears which the power of the wizard were sufficient to create in his bosom, and he endeavoured to divert his thoughts into some other channel, in which he succeeded.

Certain that if he related the truth to Edith of what he had seen and heard in his interview with Hal, of the Glen, it would not only render her miserable, but might prevent her from being so attentive to their little charge as she would otherwise be, Ranulph was not long in devising a tale, sufficiently horrible, certainly, but in no manner alluding to Godfrey or Ernnestine, and with which he doubted not she would be satisfied ; and having done so, he quickened his pace, and soon arrived at home, where he found Edith and her parents waiting in the utmost state of doubt and anxiety for his return. They greeted his return with the most unfeigned delight, and besieged him with questions about his adventure with the wizard.

" Marry," exclaimed Ranulph, laughing, " an' thou forgettest, Edith, that I have been out all night, methinks, and, by the saints, in none of the most agreeable of weather. I am both hungry and athirst, so pr'ythee bring forth some refreshment, or I shall have to make a meal of my russets, or some other portion of my ess."

Edith immediately bustled about, and placing a hearty meal before her husband, waited impatiently until he should have despatched it, so that her curiosity might be gratified. However, Ranulph seemed determined to tire her patience, for he not only ate what she had placed before him, but required a second allowance, which he consumed with equal relish, and as keen an appetite. At last, however, he did finish his meal, and then, Edith, Hubert, and his wife, gathered near him, while he related a most terrific story about what he had seen in the wizard's cavern, but which was completely foreign to the truth ; and so well, and so seriously did he detail it, that they shrugged up their shoulders, trembled, and believed every word of it.

Hubert and his wife having once more enjoined Ranulph and their daughter to secresy, pressed the beauteous infant to their bosoms, and kissing it affectionately, left the place.

*　　　*　　　*　　　*　　　*

We will now pass over a period of several years—nothing particular occurring to the characters in our narrative, during that time, deserving of attention. Faithfully had Ranulph and his wife performed their promise towards their little protegé, and the good Hubert and Maud looked upon her with all the same fondness as if she had been their grandchild,—and indeed in that character they viewed her, thinking that it was not very likely any one would ever come forward to dispute their claim upon her affections, as they had never seen the stranger who had brought her to " The Flagon," on the eventful night, and had but once received the promised allowance, which they found left for them in a most mysterious manner, in the very parlour in which they had given the stranger shelter; so that they concluded he was either dead, or, that—finding she had a good home, and those who would take care of her—he had deserted her. Neither Ranulph or Edith, in fact, wished for any person to come forward to claim her, for she was now as dear to them as their own child—the little Godfrey—who was the only one that survived out of the family they had had.

Ernnestine de Lacy, (by which name she was only known,) was a beauteous girl when ten summers had passed over her head, and at that early age she exhibited all those intrinsic and extrinsic charms, which, in riper years, were to expand into perfection. Her form was that of a little fairy, and her footstep was so light, that it seemed scarcely capable of dashing off the dew from the verdure beneath it. Her features were innocence and beauty combined; her eyes were a cerulean blue, beaming with intelligence and affection; and a smile continually played around the little twin chorals that formed her lips, which gave an irresistible sweetness to the expression of her countenance, which could not fail to rivet the attention of every beholder. Her skin was exquisitely fair, and her cheeks were flushed with the roseate bloom of health.—Her bright flaxen hair, fell in silken, natural ringlets over her neck and shoulders, in luxuriant profusion.

But it was not the extreme loveliness of the little foundling which drew forth most admiration, but the general sweetness of her disposition. Affectionate, gentle, obedient, and intelligent, she soon became the theme of conversation in the neighbourhood where she resided, and to every one she was always, even when a child, not only a welcome, but an honoured guest. If any of the old cottagers were sick, little Ernnestine was sure to be their frequent visitor, and she would bring with her such trifles for their relief as she had been able to obtain from Hubert, or Ranulph and his wife. Among the other children in the vicinity, she was an universal favourite; and if any quarrels took place among her little playmates, she was always the mediator between them, and never failed to bring about a reconciliation.

To Ranulph, and the affectionate Edith, she looked up with the same ardent attachment as if they had been her parents; indeed, she had never known any other, although, as soon as she could understand the meaning of it, they had, at the request of Hubert, told her that she was not their child, but the daughter of a distant relation, whom they highly regarded, but who had been dead ever since she was an infant. The sensitive heart of the lovely child frequently prompted many a tear to the memory of her supposed parents, but the unremitting affection of those who had adopted her, never failed to soothe her, and to draw her heart more closely, if possible, towards them. Of old Hubert and his wife she was doatingly fond, and frequently when they witnessed her innocent endearments, they mentally thanked the Almighty for rendering them the instruments of saving her from an untimely death, and for in so mysterious a manner bestowing upon them a being who promised to be a blessing to them in their declining days.

But if there was one that she was more ardently attached to than another, it was the little Godfrey; and he evinced for her an equal affection. In sweetness of disposition—in generosity of heart—in virtue—and every good quality, they assimilated, and from childhood, they were unhappy but when they were in each

other's society. Together they rambled over the green fields, climbed the steep hills, and gambolled down its sides ; or if anything prevented Ernnestine from being his companion, Godfrey never failed to gather for her a nosegay of the sweetest flowers, which she accepted with more sincere delight and gratification, than many in a higher rank would have felt at receiving a coronet of gems.

Godfrey was a noble boy, endowed with all the grace of his father, and his features expressive of every excellent quality. His disposition was open, free, candid, and generous, while, at the same time, although his manners were seldom ruffled by a storm, he evinced a proper spirit, that would not brook an insult, or truckle to oppression. Brought up in the hardy, healthful way which nature ordains, and not pampered by those luxuries, and ridiculous attentions in which the children of the wealthy are indulged, Godfrey early evinced uncommon strength, and a robust constitution. The glow of health was always upon his cheeks, and his vivacious eye shewed that his mind was the abode of content. He was ever at the head of the sports practised by the boys in those days, and was always the champion in everything they attempted to do. In racing, leaping, wrestling, none could equal him ; and as his father early taught him to bend the bow, as his strength increased with his years, he shewed great skill in the use of it, and it was one of his principal pleasures to ramble through the green forest with his " pretty sister," (as he called Ernnestine,) by his side, and indulge in this manly sport.

Such were Ernnestine and Godfrey when children, and is it any wonder that affection should spring up between two such kindred spirits ? Closely as two

No. 4.

fond hearts could be united, were their's, from childhood's earliest days, and
as they grew older, so did their love increase.—In childhood, they had known no
other passion but such as a brother and sister would feel for each other ; but as
years increased upon them, they both felt that their affection deserved a more em-
phatic name.   Godfrey approached her with more timidity, and when he saluted
her, she would blush, and hide her face, while a sensation shot through her
heart, which she was unable to understand.

But if to Godfrey and Ernnestine their feelings were inexplicable, not so were
they to their friends ; they soon discovered that they really loved each other
with all that ardent and impassioned fondness, which the heart is capable of
feeling.   This occasioned them all great uneasiness—for knowing their incapa-
bility of encouraging their love, and the almost utter hopelessness that they could
ever be united, unknowing who were the parents of Ernnestine—whether they
still lived—in what rank they might be—and if ever they might come forward to
claim her—they foresaw the misery this unfortunate passion was likely to bring
upon them.   But how were they to check it ?   Could they command them not
to love each other ?   Could they expect the summer's glow in their youthful
bosoms could be immediately frozen by the winter of indifference ?—No, it was
an affection implanted so deeply in their bosoms, that no earthly power could
eradicate.—It increased upon them, until it became a part of their very existence, and indeed to separate them from each other, must have been attended
by the death of one or both of them.

But it was necessary they should be warned of the hopelessness of their passion,
and the absolute necessity there was for their endeavouring to conquer it, and to
look upon each other only as a brother and sister should do, and that unpleasant task old Hubert took upon himself, and executed it with all the gentleness
and feeling that was possible.   Godfrey and Ernnestine listened to his words
with astonishment ; it was the first time they had been awakened to the reality
of their feelings, and the confusion of the former, and the blushes and tears of
the latter, convinced the old man that their surmises were verified.   After that
interview, Godfrey and Ernnestine, for the first time, knew what sorrow was.
But why should they be forbidden to love each other only as a brother and sister ?
Were they not worthy of each other ? were they not both alike virtuous ? and
were not their conditions the same ?—'Twas true she had been given to understand that her parents were no more, but she had not been informed whether or
not they had left her any property: and, indeed, she was stated to be the daughter
of a distant relation, and therefore, their birth was, doubtless, equal !—What objection then could they have to their being united together ? why should they tell
them their love was hopeless ? and if persisted in, could only be productive of
misery to themselves and their friends ?—Surely the opposition was unreasonable,
it was unjust, it was cruel.   But the misfortunes of the lovers were soon to commence in reality.   A cloud was in a short time about to burst, which would over-
whelm them in sorrow.

It was a melancholy day to' Godfrey and Ernnestine, when they were compelled to separate, for the former was growing apace, and his parents could not
think of his remaining always in a state of inactivity at home, neither did the
       bold and enterprising spirit wish it: yet at the thoughts of parting from

his beloved Ernnestine, even for the most brief space of time, he revolted. Bold, heroic, and aspiring, Godfrey longed to distinguish himself in the battle-field, and the crusade offered him every opportunity of gratifying his inclination; but the idea of being separated at such a distance from her who was the empress of his heart, and the uncertainty that they might ever meet again, made him abandon this idea, in spite of the solicitations of his father, to the contrary; and, instead, he accepted of a situation in the family of Sir Egbert de Courcy, who had taken a great fancy to him, and was anxious to retain him as the companion of his son, with whom Godfrey was also a great favourite.

The castle of Sir Egbert, was situated only a few miles from the residence of Ranulph de Lacy, so that Ernnestine and Godfrey had frequent opportunities of seeing each other, and absence only strengthened their affection, which they never failed to express to one another, notwithstanding their friends were averse to it: but true love cannot be restrained, even by the force of duty.

Not far from De Courcy Castle, stood the ancient castle of St. Aswolph, the residence of the lady of that name, whose urbanity and philanthropy, were greatly experienced by the poor on her wide domains, and for many miles around. She had been for many years a widow, and brought up her children (an only son and daughter,) in the same paths of virtue and benevolence as herself; and well did they profit by the excellent precepts she had instilled into their minds.

Lord Raymond St. Aswolph, the son of the estimable lady before named, was nearly forty years of age, but was still unmarried. He was a fine, handsome man, and possessed of all those accomplishments that constitute the gentleman. In manners, he was courteous, affable, and intelligent; treating the meanest of his dependants with respect, and never assuming that haughty and tyrannical demeanour, which was too common among the nobility of those days. In the battle-field, none had more nobly distinguished themselves than he had done; by which he had gained the favour of his sovereign, Richard Cœur de Lion, and the admiration of his chivalrous colleagues in arms.

Lord Raymond, from a youth, had been a considerable time abroad, and his mother and affectionate sister, the beauteous Marguerite, noticed with much surprise and concern, on his last return to England, that he was oppressed with a deep melancholy, which they in vain endeavoured to learn the cause of. Upon being questioned by his mother upon the subject, he earnestly desired her not to urge her questions, as the secret cause of his sorrow must ever remain an inviolable secret locked within his own breast.

Greatly afflicted was the venerable lady at this circumstance, but finding it was useless to question her son further, she dropped the subject, and endeavoured by every means in her power, to alleviate the melancholy under which he suffered.

Brought up in the family of this lady, was a lad called Reginald, whom Lord Raymond had promoted to the dignity of his Esquire, a station to which the natural good qualities and personal courage of the youth fully entitled him. He had been left an orphan in childhood, and his parents having been both in the service of the late Lord St. Aswolph, their child was brought up with the utmost care and attention, by the benevolent persons into whose hands he had so fortunately fallen.

Reginald was a remarkably fine youth, with a countenance expressive of every good and generous trait.   To an uncommon volatile disposition, he added a noble heart, and a courage which in early days, augured a distinguished future.

Hubert having formerly rendered some service to the father of Lord Raymond, whenever the latter came to England, he never failed to stop at " The Flagon" on the way, and Lady Celestine, his mother, also was frequently, for a short time, the worthy innkeeper's guest.   The beauty, the innocence, and intelligence of Ernnestine, greatly attracted the attention of Lady Celestine, and created her warmest admiration.   She would, indeed, have taken her under her patronage, but Hubert and her other friends refused to part with her; and Ernnestine herself, much as she esteemed the lady and her amiable daughter, could not bear the thoughts of leaving those by whom she had been so kindly brought up.   Ernnestine was now almost constantly at the inn, and was commonly called " The Fair Maid of the Flagon," and many were the persons who were attracted thither by her beauty and the sweetness of her disposition.

But there was one who viewed her with more admiration than all the rest ; who was more gay and jocund in her presence, and whose eyes sparkled with an expression of delight whenever they met, which called the blushes in her cheeks, and made her feel a sensation of confusion which she was at a loss to understand. The person we allude to was Reginald, who had been acquainted with them from childhood, and was frequently the companion of her and Godfrey.

Between Reginald and Godfrey, being alike in disposition and principles, an ardent friendship soon sprang up and they were as often together as circumstances would permit.   They endeavoured to outvie each other in the athletic sports that were common in those days, and by that means acquired that skill and superiority which obtained them such admiration afterwards.   Godfrey, however, had often noticed the marked attention which Reginald paid to Ernnestine, and sometimes a feeling of jealousy would spring up in his breast, which speedily vanished before the lively sallies of the former, whose continual good temper and flow of spirits, rendered it impossible for any person to be out of humour with him long.

As years passed away, however, the attention of Reginald increased, and Godfrey could no longer hesitate to conclude he loved her.   But Ernnestine encouraged not his passion ; and indeed, now that she was conscious of his real sentiments, avoided him as much as possible, and when in his presence, was more distant than she had been in the habit of behaving towards him.

The indignation of Godfrey, at what he considered the treachery of Reginald, was unbounded ; his mind was inflamed, and to such a state did his resentment carry him, that had it not been for the earnest persuasions of his lover, he would have accused Reginald of the fact, and demanded satisfaction.   However, with great difficulty, he stifled his feelings, and although they did not meet so often as they had done, Godfrey's behaviour towards him was very little changed.

Many a restless night—many a pang, did these thoughts occasion Godfrey ; but yet why should he fear ?—It was reproaching Ernnestine with inconstancy and deceit, if he suspected that she would encourage the passion of Reginald, and that she did not, and never would do so, he was convinced by the many affectionate assurances she made him.   But alas !—even allowing them to be faithful to each other, of what would it avail them ?   They had been told that they must not love; that they could never be united, and that harsh decree (for such they could not help thinking it,) filled their minds with despair.

How shall we describe the rage, the astonishment of Godfrey, when Ernnestine, with looks of distraction, informed him that Reginald, in the presence of Hubert, had acknowledged the love he entertained for her, and that the latter had, in spite of her prayers, her tears, and entreaties, with very little hesitation, given his consent to Reginald's paying his addresses to her, and had, (with a sternness and inflexibility which she could not have imagined he was capable of entertaining), commanded her to look upon him as her future husband.

Godfrey was thunderstruck;—he could scarcely believe the evidence of his senses;—could Reginald, whom he had ever thought generous, noble, and in fact, beyond all reproach, could he have been guilty of such base duplicity, such a cruel breach of friendship? It did not seem possible!—And then the conduct of Hubert;—that was even more strange and inexplicable than all! That he should so readily consent to sacrifice the happiness of Ernnestine to a man whom she could not love, when he had so peremptorily refused to sanction the affection of himself and her, and had turned a deaf ear to all that they could urge, seemed so cruel and unjust, that Godfrey was a long time before he could bring his mind to believe it. But he was soon convinced; Hubert and his parents made him acquainted with the determination of the former, and to his surprise, his father expressed his approbation of the same, and commanded him, on pain of his displeasure, to endeavour to forget Ernnestine, and to avoid her presence as much as possible. In vain, both Godfrey and Ernnestine threw themselves on their knees before them, and implored them to relent. They were inexorable, and neither tears or supplications could prevail with them.

We will not attempt to describe the agony of the lovers, but at length the grief of Godfrey subsided into rage against Reginald, whom he determined to seek out and wreak his vengeance upon his head. But Reginald avoided him, and they never met. Soon after this, he accompanied Lord Raymond to the Holy Land, and Ernnestine was informed by Hubert, that on his return, it was his intention that they should be united, and bade her forget the unfortunate passion she had imbibed for Godfrey, and to receive Reginald with that affection which was due to him who was to be her husband.

The reason of Hubert's mysterious conduct, in thus taking upon himself the disposal of Ernnestine's hand, and why his choice should be so obstinately fixed on Reginald, will be explained at a future period.

CHAPTER IV.

" Now murder, with his blood-stained hands,
Stalks forth at midnight dreary hour,
And pounces on the unconscious trav'ller."

Two years passed away—two years of bitter anguish to the lovers—when their friends prevented them from meeting each other as much as possible. But in spite of all their endeavours, they could not extinguish the flame in their bosoms; on the contrary, opposition only made it grow the fiercer, and they were certain that nothing but death could erase their sentiments. There were indeed intervals when hope entered their bosoms, but they were few and transient. Sometimes they thought on the probability of Reginald falling in the field of battle; or that long absence from the object of his affection, might change his sentiments; or that being brought to reflect upon the cruelty of endeavouring to thwart the wishes of those whose hearts were devoted to each other, and to whom he had ever pretended such ardent friendship, he would, with the generosity and nobility they had ever given him credit for, resign his claim to the hand of Ernnestine, and urge their suit with their friends. In spite of the circumstances that had taken place, they could not help encouraging, in preference to any of the others, the latter idea, and Godfrey was pleased that he had not seen Reginald before he had quitted England, which might have led to the most fatal consequences—as it was his determination on his return to appeal to him.

" Yes, Godfrey," exclaimed Ernnestine, " thou shalt appeal to Reginald, and my heart tells me it will not be in vain; Reginald is too good, too kind, to persist in pressing his suit, when he knows that my heart is another's. As a brother I can sincerely esteem him, and I know his noble nature will lead him to compassionate us; you shall describe to him the strength of our love; assure him of my warmest friendship, and implore him to forbear to solicit a hand, when the heart can sooner break than accompany it. I am certain he will not turn a deaf ear to us, and we shall yet be happy."

Godfrey pressed his lips to the lovely maiden's cheek, and smiled consent to her desires, and confidence in her surmises, and they parted happier than they had been for some time.

*   *   *   *   *

It was on a bitter cold night, in the month of December, when the snow was fast descending, and the wind howled without, making a cheerful fireside doubly welcome, that an unusual bustle was observed in " The Flagon," and Peter, mine host's serving man, and the other domestics of the establishment, seemed up to their eyes in business, making grand preparations as if in expectation of the arrival of some important guest.

Peter, who was a simple lad, had given full liberty to his garrulous tongue while at work in the parlour, and had soon furnished every guest present with the particulars of what was about to take place.

" So you expect Lord St. Aswolph to return this evening, and to call at your inn, on the way to his castle, do you?" demanded a strange, dark, fierce-looking man, enveloped in a huge mantle, who, with two others, equally unprepossessing in appearance, had been there for several hours, and had been drinking very freely.

Peter turned round very quickly, for the voice was none of the most musical, and the person who had addressed him, as well as his two companions, were anything but prepossessing; the fierce eye which met his, however, made him fearful of offending them by not returning any answer to the interrogatory, so he said,—

" Yes, his lordship always calls here on his way to his castle; so we must bustle about, and there must be no no skulkers here to day."

Pr'ythee, what kind of a man is Lord St. Aswolph, lad ?" inquired the man.

" Oh, as rich as a prince, as bold as a lion, and generosity itself," returned Peter.

" And will his lordship tarry here long, boy ?" asked the man who was seated next to the first speaker.

" Oh, no, his lordship will only remain here to-night, and will depart by break of day to St. Aswolph Castle."

" How far is St. Aswolph Castle from here ?"

" Humph," thought Peter, and he gave another suspicious look at the two, " marry, and you are rather inquisitive."

" About twelve miles," at length, he answered, " about twelve miles through the forest."

" True," said the stranger, " I had forgotten. He will have a dreary road to travel ; but I suppose he is well attended."

" No," replied Peter, " his lordship hates pomp and show, so he always sends his retainers on first, and is never attended by any one but his faithful Esquire, Reginald, who is betrothed to Miss Ernnestine."

The man exchanged glances of satisfaction with his companions, but Peter did not notice them, and after a pause, one of the other two said,—

" Methinks Lord St. Aswolph might have reason to be sorry that he did not have his retainers with him, if he should happen to be attacked by Osmond and his desperate gang, who infest the forest, and have for years past created such a panic in the country."

" Ah, that Osmond is certainly one of the most daring men I ever heard of," said Peter, " and seems to set all earthly power at defiance, though he is very good to the poor ; but Lord St. Aswolph is not to be so easily alarmed, and I dare say he would not be afraid to meet the robber-chief, although he is such a terrible fellow."

" That may some time or the other be put to the test," remarked the man who had first spoken, in an under tone, " but," he added, " the flask is empty, lad ; more wine."

Peter hurried away to do as the strange man required, and then the latter turning to his companions, exclaimed in tones of pleasure :—

" Joy, comrades, for with caution and determination, the money of this same Lord St. Aswolph shall be ours before the sun gilds the summits of the eastern hills to-morrow, and as our captain will know nothing of it, we can share the spoil among us, as we have often done before. We will lie in ambush for him and his Esquire, and only let us add resolution to the points of our trusty weapons, and a rich booty will doubtless be ours."

" By my troth, Rodolph," said the second speaker, " this is a fortunate job ; for of late our success has been upon the wane, and Osmond has behaved but badly to us, because, forsooth, he did not find us quite so ready to submit to his tyranny as our associates. I had almost began to despair of ever being able to replenish our exhausted coffers."

" And must our hands again be stained with innocent blood ?" exclaimed the third one, who, in spite of the efforts of his companions to arouse him, seemed imbued with a deep melancholy ; " is not the weight of our crimes already sufficient, but that we must still, like ravenous wolves, thirst for the blood of our fellow-creatures?"

"Fool!" cried Rodolph, "hast thou become a coward after all thy years of daring? What would repentance avail thee now? Is not thy life already forfeited to the offended laws of thy country, and thinkest thou an ignominious death upon the scaffold would acquit thee of the deeds thou hast already committed in the eyes of the world? 'Psha! Stephen, thou wert not wont to be so chicken-hearted. Leave conscience and remorse for monkish churls to prate about, we are men, and must have more substantial food to exist upon than religious cant. But here is wine."

At that moment Peter entered with the wine they had ordered.

Rodolph filled their horns, and raising his own to his lips, said,—

"Comrades, a toast :—Here's success to all daring undertakings."

"Bravo!" cried Gilbert, drinking off the contents of the horn, "Here's success to all daring undertakings."

"What, Stephen, wilt thou not drink that toast?" demanded Rodolph, seeing that the former's cup remained untouched upon the table; "it is a good one, methinks. Come, come, never droop, man. What if thou art a villain, is it not better to be a rich villain than a poor honest man? Money can purchase thee a good name, but your honest men starve on the quality they pride themselves upon, and are rewarded with the scorn of the world only."

"But," said Stephen, "can money drown the voice of conscience? Can lucre cleanse the hands imbrued in the blood of murder? Oh, no, I feel it cannot, and, by heaven, I would sooner be the most wretched, poor, and abject being that misfortune could create, and again be innocent as once I was, than I would become the possessor of the whole of the treasures of the earth."

"Since then thou art indeed so penitent," said Rodolph, smiling ironically, "pr'ythee assume the monk's cowl, confess thy crimes, purchase absolution, and betake thyself to the cloister, and no doubt, severe penance, with a mixture of hypocrisy and holy sophistry, will soon exalt thee to the mitre. Ha! ha! ha!"

"Nay, comrade," observed Gilbert, "no raillery, Stephen is not so foolish as to falter now, when he has already dared so much. Besides, this booty may be obtained without bloodshed. Come, let us retire for awhile, and talk the matter over. This is not a fit place for us to confer, there might be listeners; come, come."

With these words Rodolph and Gilbert departed, and Stephen very reluctantly followed them.

Godfrey and Ernnestine were particularly sad on this occasion, the former having, in spite of the objection of Hubert, persisted in being present. Hubert was, in fact, fearful of Godfrey and Reginald meeting, for well did he know the impetuosity of the former, and the equal readiness of the latter to resent an insult; and he was apprehensive that something serious would be the result of it. However, he made Godfrey promise that whatever might be his feelings, he would so far stifle them, as not to cause any disturbance.

This Godfrey did very readily, for he had made up his mind previously, that he would endeavour to meet Reginald the same as he had usually done, and with him to enter into a calm and dispassionate explanation of the strange conduct

which had caused him so many months of misery. Ernnestine had made him promise her that he would not meet Reginald with reproach, confident as she was, that when appealed to, the latter possessed too kind a heart not to forego his own claims, rather than see her unhappy. Indeed she was at a loss to account for his conduct in the affair altogether, which was so different to that he had previously shewn, and she could not persuade herself but that he had some stronger motive for his behaviour than at present appeared, or rather that he had some other object in view, than was at present known to anybody but himself. Still, although at intervals a ray of hope beamed upon her mind, Ernnestine could not divest herself of an impression that something of a painful nature was about to happen to her, that some melancholy event, some calamity, was on the eve of taking place, and which would be the occasion of much trouble to her and her friends.

As the time approached, Godfrey almost repented of the task which he had imposed upon himself, and shrunk from the idea of meeting as a friend, that man who had apparently acted with such deceit and treachery towards him. But he endeavoured to conquer his feelings as much as possible, and by the time that Lord St. Aswolph and Reginald did arrive, he had so far succeeded in his efforts, as to be able to meet the latter in a manner which would have led any one to suppose that nothing had happened to interrupt that friendship which had subsisted between them from their boyish days. As for Reginald, he was as gay, as candid, and as free as ever, and greeted his old friends with all that cordiality which had ever marked his character. Godfrey was thunderstruck ;—he had expected to see

No. 5

him certainly evince some confusion, but on the contrary, he was, anything, more free and volatile than ever.

Ernnestine trembled at the meeting, and, blushing, turned away her face from Reginald, whom time had greatly altered and improved in personal appearance. Reginald, however, did not appear to notice her emotion, and advancing towards her with gaiety of demeanour, gently took her hand within his, and in tones of delight, said :—

"Well, my pretty little Ernnestine, after fighting the battles of my country, here I am returned safe and sound, with a heavy purse, a light heart, and a bosom as full as—eh ?—How's this ? thou art dull, my love ; as dull as a November day."

Godfrey's bosom swelled with rage, and he was obliged to turn away to conceal his feelings, while Reginald, in the same strain of levity, continued—

"And thou, Master Godfrey, beshrew me, but thou dost also look as though thou wert in a fitting mood to commit suicide. Hast thou not a word for thine old friend, nor a hand to shake a welcome ?"

" *Friend !*" repeated Godfrey, bitterly, but recollecting himself, he said,—" Reginald, I trust that circumstances will prove that thou really art so, and that nothing shall ever give me cause to regret that I offered thee my hand as I do now, in friendship and welcome!"

As Godfrey thus spoke, he extended his hand, which Reginald shook most heartily, and continued—

" By my troth, this looks something like. And now Ernnestine, I must lay siege to the fortress of thy volubility, and, like a brave soldier, I shall not withdraw my forces, till we have entered into some negociation of friendship. Come —not a word ; well, this is indeed but a sorry greeting for one who expected to see thy face all sunshine, thy tongue teeming with love—fraught expressions— thine heart all gaiety—and thy bosom all tenderness and affection."

" Alas! is it then true ?" sighed Ernnestine, while crimson blushes covered her cheeks ; " oh, Reginald, in pity to me——"

" Reginald," interrupted Godfrey, with great emotion, " I had hoped that there never would have been any necessity for a scene like this ; I did really believe that thou wert my friend, and heaven knows that hadst thou been mine own brother, I could not have felt a greater regard for thee ; but now, when your own lips confirm the truth of——but I wish not to meet thee in anger ;—I plead for Ernnestine, for myself—hear me, and let thy tongue seal at once our happiness or eternal misery."

" Well then, my worthy proxy of love and beauty," ejaculated Reginald, by no means disconcerted by the manner in which Godfrey had spoke ; " pr'ythee, unfold all thou wouldst impart, and let me at once decide this important affair, for, by my conscience, Godfrey, thou art so serious that thy very looks give me the quinsy."

" Reginald," said Godfrey, after a brief pause, " thou surely must have known that me and Ernnestine have long loved each other with an ardour that nothing can ever abate ; and yet in spite of our friendship, thou didst press forward thy suit to her, and by some strange means, which have endeavoured but in vain to unravel, succeeded in winning the consen o my grandfather to become her husband ; surely this was not——"

"Oh, oh," laughingly interrupted Reginald, "the secret's out at last then, and at the very moment when I expected to hear my lovely little mistress, with an arch smile and an insinuating blush, give me a hint about the wedding ring, she sounds a retreat, and puts me and my forces to the rout. But you do me an injustice, Godfrey, to suppose that I would ever have acted in the base and hypocritical manner you have hinted at. 'Tis true, I love Ernnestine—'tis also true that I confessed my affection, and gained the consent of Master Hubert that she should become my bride—but at that time, although I will admit I entertained a suspicion to that effect, I knew not positively that you and Ernnestine were so fondly attached to one another; since then, however, I have had time to reflect more upon the matter; and I resolved on my return to England, to ascertain the truth, and if my ideas were confirmed, to make a sacrifice, which I must acknowledge, will cause me the greatest pain. But what sayest thou, my pretty Ernnestine; wilt thou quite discard me from thy bosom ?"

"Oh, no," exclaimed Ernnestine, fervently, and her beautiful eyes beaming with gratitude upon Reginald; "as a dear friend—a brother, thou shalt ever reign there, but I know thou art too generous to demand a heart which cannot grant thee more."

"Enough, fair damsel," said Reginald, "thou hast placed a fair valuation on my friendship and generosity, thou shalt now see whether I deserve those titles. Godfrey, thine hand." Godfrey eagerly extended his hand, and the young man placing it in that of Ernnestine, continued—"I resign her to thee; I relinquish in the name of Heaven, all claim upon her hand, and may Heaven bless and prosper your lives."

"Oh, Reginald," cried Godfrey, "how shall I ever sufficiently——"

"No more," interrupted the former,—"I have no more than done my duty, and require no thanks. I will also, if thou thinkest fit, plead thy cause with Hubert, and endeavour to persuade him to transfer that consent which he granted to me to thee."

Godfrey and Ernnestine both attempted to speak, but they had not the power; and looking more than words can express, they hurried out of the room.

"By my troth," exclaimed Reginald, when they had gone, "I feel more joy at heart this night, through what has transpired, than if I had been made King of England."

"Good evening to thee, my brave Esquire," at this moment exclaimed a voice behind him. The salute proceeded from Rodolph, who had returned to the inn alone, and had been seated for the last few minutes at a table behind where Reginald was standing.

"Ah," said the latter to himself, and starting,—"a stranger!—He's a black-looking one, however. Good evening," he added, aloud.

"It is a cold night, and the snow falls sharply down," said Rodolph; "however, I have some of our host's best sack here, and if that is not a good antidote for the inclemency of the weather, there are no choice spirits in England. Wilt drink with me ?"

"Aye," said Reginald, taking the horn from the robber's hand, "thou seemest a jovial fellow, and will not refuse thy request. Here's to that fickle dame, Fortune."

.‟ Marry, an excellent toast,” said Rodolph—“ here's Dame Fortune, and may she patronize all our undertakings.   And if I guess aright, thou art the esquire of Lord St. Aswolph ?”

“ The same,” replied Reginald

“ He is a noble gentleman.”

“ His country knows it.”

“ And a brave soldier !”

“ His enemies have ever found him so.”

“ Right; thou too has met the foe methinks ?”

“Aye, the camp, I may say, was my cradle, and the field of battle has since been my playground,” replied Reginald.

“ And a noble playground, too,” returned Rodolph.—“Thou art a brave lad!—drink. Dost tarry here long ?”

“ He is rather inquisitive,” thought Reginald, as he eyed more narrowly the robber's countenance.—“ Oh, no; we depart by the crow of the cock to-morrow morning, for St. Aswolph Castle,” replied he, aloud.

“ It is a noble edifice,” said Rodolph ; “ I know it well.   But it will be scarcely daylight, and the depredations committed by the robbers in the forest, render it prudent of every person to be on their guard.   Is not his lordship afraid to travel in that vicinity without being well attended ?”

“ Afraid !” repeated Reginald, with a smile of contempt. “ What, thinkest thou his lordship is so bad a soldier as to fear the lawless marauder ?—Oh, no: although there are only two of us, while we can boast of justice and courage on our side, we set at defiance the outrage of a robber.”

“ But thou mightest find a skilful sword wielded even by a villain's arm,” said Rodolph, in a significant tone.   “ But, come, the flask is empty.”

“ Then it must be replenished,” returned Reginald ; “ and, by my troth, here comes Master Hubert, just in time to fill it, and to take a cup with us.”

At this moment, mine host of “ The Flagon,” made his appearance.

“ Well, my old friend,” exclaimed the good-tempered youth, in a tone of vivacity, “ thou hast come at last.   I was afraid thou hadst forgotten there was such a being as Reginald at thine house.   Come, pr'ythee be seated, and we'll quaff a jovial cup or two together, or there are no saints in Christendom.”

“ I am sorry I cannot avail myself of thy offer, Reginald,” observed Hubert, “for it is a long time since we met before to night, and I had hoped to have passed a cheerful hour or two with thee.”

“ Marry ! and what shall hinder us ?” demanded the esquire.

“ Lord St. Aswolph,” answered the innkeeper, “ desired me to deliver to you this packet, which he should have left at the monastery of Saint Cuthbert, but forgot to do so.   It contains a valuable donation and letters of import, which it is necessary the Abbot should see this night: his lordship, therefore, requests that you will hasten with all possible speed.”

“ Ah ! a valuable donation !” said Rodolph, aside, and his eyes sparkling with pleasure.—“The monastery of Saint Cuthbert !—He must cross the forest, and if I depart immediately to my comrades, we can get there before him. A sure aim, and the booty is ours !”

Having thus spoken, Rodolph hastily arose, and left the house unperceived.

"This mission is, in good truth, rather unseasonable," remarked Reginald; however, it is but a short distance across the forest, and I shall be back time enough to pass a cheerful hour previous to retiring to rest. Give me the packet, Hubert."

The latter complied with his request, and then observed,—

" Now I think of it, Godfrey has to go part of the way on his return home, and he will, therefore, if you like, be your companion. It is a dreary journey, and it is a rough night; the wind blows tremendously, and the ground is covered with snow."

Reginald walked to the door and looked out.

"It is, indeed, a boisterous night," said he, "but I have a good mantle to shield me from the weather; and youth and activity will soon speed me on my journey."

" Wilt thou not ride?" inquired Hubert.

" Oh, no," answered Reginald; " my horse is jaded enough already, and Godfrey goes on foot, I presume: besides, for such a short journey it would be a pity to disturb the poor animal."

" Well, well, be it as thou wilt," replied Hubert; " but thou hadst better not delay—and, here comes Godfrey, already to depart."

Hubert briefly informed Godfrey what Reginald had got to do, and of the proposition he had made; and Godfrey was very well pleased at the circumstance, as he should have a companion the greater part of his way home, and he had a great deal to say to him, on the subject of the love between him and Ernnestine. Reginald, having wrapped his mantle close around him, him and Godfrey, without any more delay, left the inn, and proceeded on their way with all the haste they could.

The snow continued to descend rapidly, and the wind blew tremendously; but Rodolph, who had not lost a moment's time in putting his design into execution, awaited alone in the way which he knew Reginald must pass on his way to the monastery.

" My speed has outrun that of my comrades," said he, " for they have not arrived yet. This Reginald cannot be far off; so, I hope they will not tarry long. I know Gilbert is no laggard; but that conscience-stricken Stephen may slink off, if he does not keep close to him.—Hark! I hear footsteps approaching;—I will secrete myself behind this cluster of trees, and watch the person or persons approaching."

Before, however, he could do this, a shrill whistle vibrated in his ears, by which he was convinced his companions were close at hand. Almost immediately afterwards they came up with him.

" 'Tis well we are met," said Rodolph; " I do not think it is very likely that our victim will escape us."

" We have no time to lose," observed Gilbert, " even just now I caught the glimpse of a man who was coming in this direction,"

" Doubtless, it is he we seek," said Rodolph. " Hark! footsteps approach this way;—let us retire."

" I like not this business," remarked Stephen; " it is cowardly for three to attack a single man; and——"

" Psha!—out upon thee, fool!" hastily interrupted Rodolph; " this is no time for argument—away!"

The robbers retired; and, immediately afterwards, Reginald (who had just parted with Godfrey, he having to go in a contrary direction,) approached the spot.

" By the mass! the snow peppers down rarely, and the wind whistles rather unmusically," said he, shaking his mantle; " this is certainly not a very agreeable spot, and likely enough to be infested with the desperate characters that Osmond and his gang are represented to be. But I have got my trusty servant by my side, and I will therefore push on my way without fear."

Just at that moment he started back in amazement, when he beheld Rodolph standing in his path, with an evident determination to obstruct it.

" Who art thou?—and why dost thou cross my path?" demanded Reginald.

" My business is very brief, my bold squire," replied the robber, " and thy compliance must be as prompt.—An' please thee, I'll just take charge of the packet thou hast about thee, to bear to the monastery of Saint Cuthbert."

" Very civil and obliging, certainly," returned Reginald, with the utmost coolness; but, let me pass!"

" No hesitation," said Rodolph, resolutely; " thou shalt not pass until thou hast given me the packet."

" Hark ye, my fine fellow," replied Reginald, " I am a soldier, and unused to be treated so caverlierly; so, let me pass, or by the saints this trusty weapon shall soon put thee beyond the power of disobedience!"

" Nay, then, since thou art so obstinate," cried the robber, " take the consequences!"

With these words, he rushed upon Reginald with great fury; but the latter met his attack with cool intrepidity, and would, undoubtedly, soon have overcome Rodolph, had not Gilbert at that critical moment started behind him, and plunging his dagger into his side, the unfortunate Reginald sunk to the earth a corpse.

No sooner was the atrocious deed committed, than the fury of the tempest seemed to increase: the wind howled frightfully, and the snow was driven before it like a funeral shroud. Nature seemed to express its indignation at the crime. Stephen turned away from the corpse with a shudder, and covered his face with his hands while Rodolph knelt down and proceeded to take from the vest of the unfortunate Reginald the packet which had been entrusted to him to convey to the monastery of Saint Cuthbert.

" The booty is ours!" exclaimed the assassin, as he held up the packet to the eyes of his companions; " fortune has smiled upon us, and the deed has been well done."

" It is a hideous crime—a hellish deed!" returned Stephen, " and justice will most assuredly overtake us."

" Silence, fool!" cried Rodolph; " thou art always ready with thy cowardl fears and surmises.—Nature must have been in a sorry mood when she made thee a robber, forsooth."

" Cursed be the hour when villany made me a monster!" said Stephen, with a shudder of horror, as he gazed upon the pallid and blood-stained features of that unfortunate youth, who, but a few minutes before, had been imbued with health, vigour, and vivacity. "Oh, what years of misery, what days and nights of horror and remorse have I not endured since! The torments of hell have haunted my pillow; sleep has been a misery to me, for then it has brought the mangled, bleeding forms of my victims before my scared eyes. I have seen their ghastly, piteous looks, as they glared upon me in the agonies of death. Their dying curses have reverberated in my ears; and myriads of exulting fiends standing by, have shouted, 'Behold the bloody work of thine hands, murderer! Go on, and reap thy reward,—endless torment, everlasting damnation!' Oh, Rodolph, what gain, what money, can compensate us for an earthly hell like this?"

" 'Psha!" ejaculated Rodolph, impatiently, "this is the mere cant of children and priestcraft.—Away with conscience! The true heart of a robber is as firm as a rock; freedom is his friend, and honesty his football. But, let us away! —Hark!—By my troth, some persons are coming this way; if we are not careful we shall be discovered.—Quick, quick—this way, this way!"

Thus speaking, Rodolph hastily fled from the spot, followed by his comrades.

On separating from Reginald, Godfrey turned into the way which led to the place of his destination, his mind too fully occupied with the occurrences of the day, for him to heed the inclemency of the weather; but, suddenly, a strange foreboding of something wrong about to happen, darted across his brain, and he regretted that he had suffered Reginald to go on his errand by himself, knowing that the place was infested with robbers, and that his single arm could not effect anything, probably, against numbers. So strongly was this idea stamped upon his mind, that he turned back into the path which the esquire had taken, thinking to overtake him, and being resolved to accompany him to the monastery and back to the inn, knowing that his absence from the castle, on such a stormy night would be excused, and that he could be accommodated with a bed at the residence of his parents.

With as much speed as he could, he hurried in the direction which he knew Reginald must pursue, and at length reached the fatal spot where the murder had been committed. Not noticing the corpse of his ill-fated friend, he stumbled over it; and, what was his horror upon raising himself up, to behold the blood-stained form of a human being. Shuddering with apprehension, he lifted it up, and looked narrowly into the ghastly features of the murdered man, and his blood seemed frozen in his veins with terror, when he recognised the features of his friend.

" God of Heaven!" he exclaimed, "who has done this frightful deed?—Reginald, my friend!—alas! alas! why did I leave thee? Had I been present, my aid might have rescued you from the assassin's murderous blow!"

While he was still leaning over the corpse in intense agony, the sound of voices vibrated on the air, and the next moment several villagers came to the spot, one of them bearing a lantern. They started back in amazement and horror, when they beheld the blood upon the snow, and saw Godfrey supporting the body of the murdered man.

" Ah!" cried one of them, who seemed to be a little more courageous than his fellows, " what is the meaning of this?—A foul deed has been committed; let us secure the murderer!"

" The murderer !" exclaimed Godfrey, with the most inexpressible horror, and, turning towards the men, who, urged on by the speaker, now advanced to seize him; " no, no, ye are mistaken ; I have but this moment discovered his bleeding corse ; he was my friend ; unfortunate that I was, not to be present to arrest the assassin's arm !"

" Never mind what he says," said the first speaker; " this story he must tell somewhere else ; but it is our duty not to let the assassin escape. Behold, here is a sword stained with blood, which no doubt belongs to this man, and with which the infernal deed has most probably been perpetrated. Seize him, comrades !"

Godfrey had drawn his sword to be on his defence, in case he should be suddenly surprised, when he turned back after Reginald, and upon discovering his mangled body, it had fallen from his hand, and become stained with the blood of the unfortunate man ; and now, so horror struck was he at the charge which had been so unexpectedly brought against him, that he was completely petrified to the spot, and had not the power to utter a syllable. Urged on by the words of the man who had spoken, they rushed simultaneously upon him, and while some of them secured him, the others raised the corpse of Reginald in their arms, and moved hurriedly towards the nearest town.

CHAPTER V.

" When I repose beneath the sod,
    Unheeded in the clay,
Where once my youthful footsteps trod,
    Where now my head must lay ;
The meed of pity will be shed
In dew-drops o'er my narrow bed."—BYRON.

AN universal dullness seemed to reign over the guests of The Flagon, (nothwithstanding that the noble and esteemed Lord St. Aswolph honoured it by being its inmate), for which no person was able to account, unless it was the dreariness of the weather, and the inclemency, for the wind blew a complete hurricane, and the fast drifting snow quite blocked up the doors and casements. Yet were Hubert and his dame, Ranulph and Edith, together with Ernnestine, seated around one of the most cheerful-looking fires that fuel could make, and each did their best to shake off the gloom which pervaded their bosoms, but the effort was a singular failure. Hubert, whose jest was always ready at the tip of his tongue, made several ineffectual attempts to be funny, but his mirth was most dismal indeed, if we may judge from the expression of the countenances of those around him, upon which the most heavy clouds of melancholy foreboding seemed to hang. A dead weight appeared to hang upon the heart of the generally contented and happy Ranulph, which he tried, but in vain to banish, and it was very evident, from the looks and manner of his wife, that she partook of his feelings. As for

Ernnestine, she seemed to be restless, and anxious to be alone, and, notwithstanding the explanation which had that day taken place between her, Godfrey, and Reginald, she felt completely wretched. Horrible presentiments of, she knew not what, in spite of her reason, had taken possession of her brain, and the forms of Godfrey and Reginald kept rising to her mind's eye, in characters which excited only anguish and suspense. Her parting with Godfrey that night had been characterised by that sorrow and unwillingness which they had never before experienced, and which, under all the circumstances was the more remarkable. Long had the sad word " adieu" hung upon their lips, and many were the times they embraced before they could make up their minds to separate, and when they did part, Ernnestine felt as if they had parted never to meet again. Fain would she have retired, and in the solitude of her own chamber given vent to those feelings which weighed her spirits down, but she could not make any reasonable excuse to her kind friends, and therefore did she continue, although the frequent attempts at conversation only disturbed her.

" Holy Virgin," at length observed Maud, as a gust of wind drove the snow iolently against the casement, and howled in dismal gusts down the chimney; —" What a terrible night ; indeed those are best off who are safely housed."

" True, Maud," answered her husband, " and yet one might be inclined to doubt it, seeing the gloom under which we all seem to suffer here, in spite of the crackling of the cheerful fire, which appears to reproach us for our feelings. We much need the presence of Reginald, forsooth, whose mind is never sad, and

No. 6

whose ready wit, and incessant buoyancy of spirits, is a never-failing antidote for the horrors."

"Aye," said Ranulph, "it was unfortunate that he should have had to gone upon this errand on such a night, and when we so much needed his society; Godfrey too, for the purpose of being his companion on the road, has left us sooner than he otherwise would have done, and thus our little party has lost two of its best members."

"It is a night not fit to turn a dog out in," said Edith, "and the lads will be frozen to death, or lost in the snow. I cannot but acknowledge that I feel very sad."

"Which, by the mass, seems to be a complaint which is general amongst us," returned Hubert; "but a murrian to melancholy.—Fear not, Reginald and Godfrey will take no harm; they are young and hearty, and the inclemency of the weather will have very little effect upon them. What are frosty nights, or drifting snows, when opposed to their young blood? 'Psha, when I was their age, it was not a rough night that would damp my spirits. No, no;—but see, I declare Ernnestine is the saddest of us all, and sits there as gloomy and as silent as if some heavy calamity had befallen her. This will not do; I must see what effect my old son will have upon ye :—

> "Let care ne'er appear
>   Where good fellowship meets
> 'Tis mirth that gives birth
>   To all life's choicest sweets.
> The gloom of the tomb
>   Suits no temper of mine,
> With joy we'll destroy
>   It in rich sparkling wine!
> More sack! more sack! 'tis the best of all drink,
> More sack! more sack! let us drink till we blink!"

Honest old Hubert sang his favourite bacchanalian song with all his accustomed hilarity, and seemed inclined to follow the advice given in the last two lines, but it failed to have that effect upon the persons present that he wished it should, and finding that nothing appeared to be likely to have the power to dissipate the ennui which prevailed he gave up the attempt, and paid his respects to the flask himself so frequently, that his rubicund nose at length glowed like a red-hot coal.

Another hour passed away, and there was very little change to be observed in the behaviour of the persons present, unless it was indeed that their depression of spirits seemed to increase.

"Reginald tarries," at length observed Hubert, "he ought to have returned long ere this, for the distance is no great deal from hence, and it is not the sort of night for a person to loiter much on the road."

"Thou art right, Hubert," said Ranulph, "but perhaps something may have detained him at the Monastery of Saint Cuthbert, or he may have stopped there until the storm has abated."

"Alas!" said Edith, "that forest is a dreadful place, and should Reginald or Godfrey be attacked by any of the robbers——"

"Psha! niece," interrupted Hubert, impatiently, "thou talkest foolishly;—

thinkest thou Osmond, or any of his gang, would interrupt them? Oh, no, they look for higher game, where they may expect to be rewarded by a rich booty for their trouble. Now, if they were any of them aware that Reginald is the bearer of something valuable to the Monastery of Saint Cuthbert, why, I might be inclined to participate in thy fears; but that they should gain such knowledge is not very likely. Ah! what is that?"

Every person started on their feet, and looked around them with amazement, as a loud and unnatural laugh vibrated in their ears, which seemed to proceed from immediately outside the inn, and the next moment a strange light illumined the spot, and the astonished gazers could distinguish a dark, shadowy form, which appeared gradually to dilate itself, until it arose above the human stature. By degrees, the countenance, which before had been concealed from observation, was revealed, and the persons present beheld, with astonishment and horror, the frightful features of Hal of the Glen. His large and fiercely gleaming eyes were intently fixed upon Ranulph de Lacy, who had immediately recognized him, and having raised his long, thin, bony fingers, he motioned him to leave the inn and follow him.

"Mysterious being, I come," exclaimed Ranulph, as he drew his sword, and rushed out, before any of his friends, who were petrified to the spot, had the power to offer to prevent him.

As soon as he left the inn, the supernatural form of the wizard fled from the spot, once or twice turning round to Ranulph, and waving his hand for him to follow. Onward went the wild, mysterious being, as though carried away on the blast, which still swept wildly o'er the earth, although the snow had ceased to descend, and the moon burst forth with uncommon brilliancy, giving a ghastly and singular appearance to the snow-covered trees and the scenery around. Ranulph could not keep pace with his mysterious conductor, and sometimes he was almost entirely lost to his view, when the wizard would stop until he had come within a short distance of him, and then off again he would start, with the velocity of the whirlwind, and laughing hollowly as he proceeded.

Still, with the utmost courage and intrepidity, Ranulph continued to follow, and perceived that the wizard led the way towards the glen, from which he knew they could not now be at any great distance, and at length they arrived at the entrance, which the rays of the moon, however bright, could never penetrate. Hal of the Glen, immediately vanished into the interior, and Ranulph was left in the midst of the dense darkness by which he was surrounded; but still undaunted, he endeavoured to grope his way, and to reach the wizard's cavern, where so many years before, he had been a spectator of the awful and mysterious scene, conjured up by the power of Hal. As he advanced, strange murmuring sounds appeared to fill the place, and sometimes an indistinct laugh would vibrate in his ear, which made him start, and expect to see himself surrounded by the appalling forms which the cabalistic art of the wizard had before exhibited to his eyes; but all remained the same as before, and Ranulph proceeded, with even increased courage, until his attention was arrested by the following words, which were sang in a strange and supernatural voice, every tone of which made a powerful impression upon the astonished listener:—

" Who comes here, 'mid darkness and gloom,
    Who comes in the silence that reigns in the tomb ;
    Who comes where the wizard his power doth show,
    And prognosticates weal, or sorrow, or woe ?
        Would he read the Book of Fate ?
            Would he the dread future scan ?
        Let him quick his wishes state,
        Though to escape it be too late,
            From dread Destiny's fell ban !
    Advance, advance, this way, this way,
        In the magic circle stand,
        Ere he doth from this cavern stray,
        Ere the sun shall summon day,
            By him shall Destiny's book be scanned !"

The voice ceased, and all remained in the same impenetrable darkness as when
Ranulph had first entered, but still some secret impulse seemed to urge him
forward, and at length, after having advanced some distance farther, suddenly, a
loud peal of thunder shook the earth beneath him, a supernatural light illumined
the place, and revealed to Ranulph exactly the same scene as he had witnessed
eighteen years before; and there, in the centre of the magic circle, stood Hal of
the Glen, with his eyes fixed with a searching glance upon his countenance, and
pointing with his wand to the magic volume, on which were inscribed a number
of mystic characters.

" Ranulph de Lacy," said the wizard, " wouldst know the fate of thy son ?"

" Ah ! what meanest thou, strange and awful being ?" hastily demanded Ranulph, while an icy chill ran through his veins, when he reflected upon what
might have happened to Godfrey and to Reginald, which seemed the more probable, as the absence of the latter was so protracted from the inn.

" Before I can answer thee," said the wizard, " thou must step into the magic
circle.   Wilt thou obey ?"

Ranulph made no answer, but immediately stepped into the circle, and as he
did so, the thunder pealed with redoubled violence, and he experienced a repetition of all the horrors which we have described in the early part of this tale.

" Now, then, strange being," exclaimed Ranulph, firmly, but with much
eagerness, " what of my boy ? Speak, I adjure thee !"

" Ranulph de Lacy," returned Hal, while a fiendish look of exultation passed
over his features as he spoke, " Ranulph de Lacy, once before did I read thee
a page from the book of thy destiny, and shewed thee the means by which thou
mightest escape from it ; but thou didst scorn my prognostications, and mocked
my power ;—the first of these predictions is now fulfilled."

" Demon ! fiend !" cried Ranulph, frantically, " do not torture me by a suspense, more terrible than certainty ; if, indeed, thou knowest, at once convince
me of thy power, by revealing to me that of which thou pretendest to have the
knowledge ;—my boy, my Godfrey —"

" Is accused of murder !" was the reply.

" Of murder !" gasped forth Ranulph, while cold drops of perspiration began
to gather upon his temples, " my boy accused of murder ; impossible !—But he is
not guilty, Ah !—thou didst not say he was guilty ?"

A sardon grin passed over the hideous features of the wizard, but he made no answer.

"By the power you pretend to possess, and which I now believe you do," added Ranulph, "tell me, whom is my unfortunate son accused of murdering?"

"Behold!" answered the wizard, waving his wand, and immediately there appeared upon the surface of the mirror, an exact representation of that scene, where Godfrey, after having discovered the mangled remains of his friend, is about to raise him in his arms, when the villagers rush in, and the foremost one accuses him of being the assassin.

"Reginald!—Godfrey, my boy, the murderer of his dearest friend!" cried Ranulph, as he gazed with straining eye-balls upon the vision; "oh, impossible!—Away with it!—Avaunt, and seek not to distract me with such base delusions!"

"Presumptuous fool!" exclaimed the loud voice of the wizard, "again dost thou dare to doubt my power?—Away then, and awake to all the horrors of the truth!"

As the wizard spoke, loud peals of thunder shook the place, the lightning glared in at every aperture with awful fury,—a complete hurricane seemed to convulse the spot, and even above the noise occasioned by this elemental warfare, terrific and unearthly sounds, like the cries of a thousand demons rent the air, while hideous phantoms danced around with threatening and wrathful gestures directed towards Ranulph.

The wizard of the Glen still remained standing in the magic circle, while his form appeared to dilate itself to more than its usual size, and his eyes glared upon Ranulph De Lacy with the most frightful expression.—A deep horror fell upon the usually undaunted heart of the bowyer, and he was paralyzed to the spot, and unable to move even a muscle.

"What infernal spell surrounds me?" he at length found power to exclaim, "fiend, wizard, if such thou art, do not rack me to madness, but tell me, why am I selected the victim of thy diabolical arts, and what wouldst thou with me?"

"I would shew thee that which is in store for thee, so that thou mightest be prepared for it, and probably, by caution, avert the arm of Fate," answered Hal of the Glen; "but thou affectest to despise my power! Even now I tell thee, thy son is the inmate of a dungeon, charged with the crime of murder!"

"Great God——" exclaimed the agonized Ranulph, but no sooner had he given utterance to that sacred and Almighty name, than the wizard turned away with an expression of horror, and dreadful groans reverberated through the glen, accompanied by thunder, and all the horrors that had before filled the breast of Ranulph with such alarm, and it was several minutes before it ceased. At length, however, the wizard once more turned towards Ranulph, and in tones of solemnity, said :—

"Mention that word again, and not only is my will to serve thee at an end, but thou mayest tremble for the consequences that will accrue to thyself. Wouldst know more of Hal of the Glen?"

"I would," replied Ranulph.

"Hast thou courage to hear?"

"The courage," repeated Ranulph, scornfully, "he must indeed be a coward who has not fortitude to contemplate misfortune, when, by so doing, his prudence may suggest to him the means of evading it; thou art no wizard if thou dost thus estimate the sentiments of Ranulph de Lacy."

"Enough! I will e'en try thy boasted courage," returned the wizard, "bare thine arm."

Ranulph in a moment pulled up the sleeve of his tunic, and the wizard grasping his wrist, held his arm over the cauldron, and immediately pierced a vein with the point of a dagger. The red blood spirted forth, and dropped into the cauldron, and as it did so, a loud burst of supernatural laughter shook the place, the flames blazed up to a tremendous height, and myriads of snakes appeared to be twisting fantastically among them; at the same time, the wizard might be seen amid the blue vapoury smoke by which he was surrounded, performing a variety of mysterious antics around the cauldron, until at length the noises ceased, and Hal no longer continued to indulge in the mysterious ceremony we have been describing, but turning towards Ranulph, leant upon his wand, and fixed his looks earnestly upon his countenance. Ranulph never for an instant evinced the least terror, but withstood the piercing glance of the wizard with the utmost firmness and indifference. At length, the wizard again removed his eyes from Ranulph, and after waving his wand several times above his head, he appeared to be dropping something in the cauldron, and at last gave vent to the following incantation :—

> "Spawn of adder here I take,
>   Poison from the envenom'd snake,
>   A murderer's heart, a dragon's blood,
>   Hissing snake and poisonous toad!
>   A splinter from the gibbet tree,
>   Where hang the mouldering bones of three;
>   In the cauldron mix and burn,
>   So that we by the charm may learn
>   What by Destiny's decreed,
>   To he who doth our answer need!
>   Sisters wild, who read his doom,
>   Hither, hither, hither come;
>   From the realms of darkness, here
>   At my summons quick appear!

In a moment the glen became involved in impenetrable darkness, and for a few seconds Ranulph felt a sensation as if the earth was yawning and shaking beneath him;—then forked lightning flashed fiercely around him, and appalling shrieks vibrated in his ears;—directly afterwards, the light returned to the glen, and Ranulph beheld a number of frightful looking hags dancing around him,—and their fiery eyes glaring upon him with gestures sufficient to fill the stoutest heart with horror. Still did Ranulph, however, firmly stand his ground, and unflinchingly prepared himself to hear the result of this mysterious and awful adventure.

The wizard remained in the same position as when he commenced the incantation, and waving his wand, as the witches performed their mystic dance, he thus exclaimed :—

" Hail sisters of the mystic art,
　Ere from hence ye all depart,
　By the power which ye possess,
　A power which mortals must confess ;
　Tell what fortunes shall accrue,
　To he who does thy knowledge sue."

No sooner had the wizard given utterance to these words, than one of the witches rushed forward towards the cauldron with a wild cry, and performing several mysterious antics around it, in a voice harsh and disgusting as a croaking raven's, she gave expression to the following words :—

" He's doom'd, he's doom'd
　For sorrow and care,
His peace shall be broken,
　His heart know despair.
He shall weep, he shall weep,
　There's a curse o'er his head,
Oh, well may his breast
　The abode be of dread.
'Tis begun, 'tis begun,
　There's much anguish in store,
And many's the day
　Ere his grief shall be o'er !"

When the witch had concluded, she uttered a piercing shriek, and immediately vanished, and the wizard again waving his magic wand, turned to the other frightful hags, and said :

" Let it be gladness, let it be woe,
All that shall befal him let him know !"

The second witch now left her companions, and after performing the same ceremony round the cauldron, shrieked forth the following, in tones of appalling impressiveness :—

" E'en now in dungeon dark secured,
Godfrey, his son, is safe immured ;
Accused of shedding human blood,
Joy, sisters, this to us is food !
Human anguish, human woe,
Is the greatest bliss we know ;
Shall he die ? shall he die ?
That I'll not tell ——

THIRD WITCH. 　　　　　Nor I,

FOURTH WITCH. 　　　　　Nor I !

The whole of the witches now shouted in chorus,
" Shall he die ? shall he die ?
That I'll not tell,—nor I,—nor I !"

Many demoniacal voices laughed exultingly, and then the frightful forms gradually faded from the view of Ranulph de Lacy, and he was left in total darkness.

At length, completely overpowerd by what he had seen and heard, he endeavoured to find his way out of the glen as quickly as possible, and after considerable difficulty succeeded. The morning air burst upon him fresh and reviving, and tended, in a great measure, to calm the agitation which racked his mind.   After what he had seen and heard in the glen, he could no longer indulge in scepticism, as regarded the supernatural character of the beings he had seen, and when he reflected upon their awful prognostications, his horror was so great, that he could scarcely support himself.   Anxious to gain a confirmation or a contradiction of his worst fears, he hurried on towards the inn, thinking that probably Edith had not left there all the night, and that he was more likely to have his doubts and his fears satisfied than at his own residence.

In the meantime, while these strange and appalling events were going forward in the wizard's glen, the agitation and alarm of the individuals at " The Flagon," at the protracted absence of Reginald, and the mysterious appearance of Hai of the Glen, and the departure of Ranulph with him, increased to an almost insupportable degree.   Lord St. Aswolph had made several inquiries after the former, and when Hubert informed him of his not having yet returned, and of the apprehensions he and the others entertained, he paused for a few moments,— and after apparently weighing the circumstances over in his mind, said .—

" After all, I do not think that anything has happened to my faithful Squire, and I do not marvel at his continued absence, when we consider what a terrible night it is, and the improbability that the good Prior of Saint Cuthbert's would suffer him to return till the morning.   Rest thyself contented, Master Hubert, he is safe enough, I do believe me, and will be with us by the break of day, for he knows it is my wish to leave here early, and I always like to be punctual."

Hubert could not make any reasonable objection to this opinion, and he, therefore, bowed and retired ; and, on returning to the parlour, he found his wife, Edith, and Ernnestine, exhibiting the utmost symptoms of uneasiness, and, apparently, in no mood to be consoled by the observations that had been made by Lord St. Aswolph.

Edith's emotion, since the departure of her husband in the company of Hal of the Glen, was even more violent than the others, and she resisted all the persuasions of her uncle to retire to bed, until he should return, and set her doubts at rest.

Hubert, Maud, and Ernnestine, however, at length, retired to their chambers, leaving Edith seated by the fire-side below, and listening with the most intense anxiety to the pauses between the blast, thinking to hear the footsteps of Ranulph approaching the house ; and frequently she went to the door and looked out, but the fast-falling snow rendered all attempts to distinguish any object abortive, and she returned to her seat in despair.

We would fain do adequate justice to the state of Ernnestine's feelings during this painful period, but we find it impossible : in her breast, the most terrible apprehension of some approaching evil had taken such deep root, that she found it quite impossible to conquer them, and a hundred frightful images flitted before her fevered imagination.   She retired to her couch 'tis true, but sleep was for some time a stranger to her, and she lay tossing about, unable to find the least consolation or ease.

" Almighty God !" she ejaculated, as with clasped hands, she raised her eyes towards Heaven, " I beseech Thee, in Thine infinite goodness and mercy, to avert that danger which I apprehend, and to bring both Reginald and Godfrey safely here again."

Feeling rather more tranquillized after offering up this prayer, Ernnestine at length sunk to sleep, but not to rest; no, visions of the most tormenting description haunted her pillow, and harrassed her. She beheld Godfrey and Reginald fall, covered with blood beneath the murderous poniards of several ruffians; and their looks of dying agony were intensely fixed upon her as they closed their eyes in death. Then the scene changed, and she saw Godfrey still alive, but his face was pale, his eyes beamed forth a wild expression, and his limbs were manacled with heavy fetters. She tried to rush forward and embrace him, but in an instant the walls seemed to close, and he was hidden from her view. The terror created by this dream awoke her, and she started up in the bed, while cold drops of perspiration stood upon her temples, and her limbs trembled violently. Suddenly, a strange noise, which seemed to proceed from the room below, smote her ears. It sounded like the murmuring of several voices, and she thought she could distinguish the moans of a person as if in deep distress.

"Good God!" exclaimed Ernnestine, as she sprang from her couch, and proceeded to dress herself hastily.—"What can have happened?

Her heart sank with apprehension as the sounds increased, and with trembling steps she began to descend the stairs.

As she descended, the sounds of grief were repeated, and she heard Edith give utterance to the most distracted expressions, and certain that something particular had taken place—at the same time having a slight presentiment of the facts—she hurried as well as her trembling limbs would allow her, into the

No.7

parlour of the inn, where, in addition to Hubert, his wife, Ranulph, and his Edith, she found several strange men. Lord St. Aswolph was also present, and seemed to be violently agitated, and the whole scene presented the greatest confusion. Edith, Hubert, and Maud were wringing their hands with the most violent demonstrations of grief.

Ernnestine was so astonished and alarmed, that for a moment or two she was deprived of the use of speech or motion, and stood gazing upon all around her in stupified amazement and consternation.

"For Heaven's sake," she at last found strength to articulate, "what is the meaning of this? Oh, tell me, I pray you, what has happened?"

"For the present, my love," said Ranulph, who was more firm than any of the rest, although his cheek was pale and his lips quivered, "do not, I implore thee, urge the question, but retire again to thy chamber, until this general agitation is somewhat abated. It may not be so bad as we at present apprehend."

"Oh, no, no," ejaculated Ernnestine, with increased eagerness, "suspense is far more horrible than certainty! I beg of thee to let me know the worst; something dreadful has occurred, of that I am convinced, or why all these blanched countenances—these expressions of bitter grief? If thou really lovest me, dear father—for such I must always consider thee—oh, instantly reveal to me the truth."

Ranulph was too much bewildered and agitated to make any immediate reply, and the others could only give further expression by sobs and groans, to the anguish which distracted their bosoms.

Lord St. Aswolph, in the midst of the affliction which evidently tormented his mind, could not help gazing upon the trembling damsel with looks of the most unbounded admiration. Her beauty, and the innocence and simplicity of her manners, had made a powerful impression upon him from the first moment he had beheld her since she had sprang into womanhood. Never, he thought, had he seen so lovely a being before, and now, as she appealed to her friends, with the chrystal tears glistening like pearls in her expressive eyes, and her exquisitely moulded bosom throbbing and heaving with the violence of her emotion, he felt a sensation dart through his heart, which he had never before experienced, and which he was at a loss to understand.

"Sweet maiden," he said, addressing her in a tone of the utmost kindness, "pr'ythee do as De Lacy hath requested thee, until thou hast sufficiently calmed thy apprehensions to hear with fortitude the painful news."

"My lord," returned Ernnestine, with a look of offended pride, "and thinkest thou so poorly of my courage as to suppose that I would not have the fortitude to hear the truth? This suspense requires a far greater portion of resolution. But thou refusest to tell me, Ranulph—Hubert—Maud?—Oh, surely this is cruel."

One of the strange men who had been hitherto conversing with his companions in an under tone, and being more officious and less scrupulous than the rest, overhearing Ernnestine's last words, in spite of the significant looks of Lord St. Aswolph, said—

"Marry, young lady, and there has been a deed of blood committed; Reginald, the 'squire of his lordship, has been barbarously murdered!"

"Murdered!" screamed the horror-struck maiden; surely it cannot be!"

"Alas! it is too true," chimed in the fellow's companions all together.

Ernnestine cast her eyes round upon the different persons in the room, as if she would read in their looks a contradiction of this shocking assertion ; but in the expression of every person's countenance, she saw too plainly a confirmation of the dreadful truth.

She caught at a chair to prevent herself from falling, such was the effect this intelligence had upon her, and then in a voice of indescribable grief, she cried—

"Reginald murdered !—Unfortunate youth !—Oh, God! who has done this awful deed ?"

"By the mass, young lady," observed the same garrulous individual, who had spoken before, "we have got the murderer safe enough ; me and my companions found the body of the unfortunate man in the forest, and took his blood-thirsty assassin on the spot. It is——'

"Hold, fellow !" interrupted his lordship, hastily,—"speak not another word, I command thee, Ernnestine ; again I entreat thee to calm the agony which fills thy bosom, and to wait another time for the information thou askest. Thou canst begone," he continued, turning to the villagers, "remove the corpse of the unfortunate youth to my castle, and I will attend to this dreadful, this painful business anon. Away."

At this moment, Edith recovered, and looking with a vacant stare around the room, she shrieked forth in accents of madness.

"Where is he ?—Where is my boy, my son, my Godfrey ?—Wretches, why have ye dragged him from his wretched mother ?—Who dare accuse him of mur, der ?—Nay, I heed not your menaces ; the voice of innocence will be heard !— Who dare, I repeat, accuse my son of shedding the blood of his fellow-creature ! —Monsters 'tis false ! But fool that I am to appeal to wretches whose hearts are unacquainted with pity ? The sport is the misery of their fellow-creatures —their food, the blood of the innocent !—Do not hold me !—Let me fly to him !— They would murder him ; they would rob the parents of their only son ! Where is he?—Ah! see they have dragged him to a dungeon, they have loaded his limbs with fetters. They will not listen to his protestations of innocence ;—they will try-him for this frightful crime ; they will magnify trifles into facts, and triumph in spilling the blood of one whose nobleness of soul they cannot equal !"

"Bear her hence, good Ranulph," said Lord St. Aswolph, "thou seest that the intensity of her feelings has affected her senses. Alas! it is indeed a sad job, but fear not, Justice will prevail, and whoever is the actual perpetrator of this fiendish deed, an all-merciful Providence will not suffer them to escape retribution, or fail to throw His protecting shield over he that is accused, and make his innocence manifest, if he is not guilty of the dreadful crime with which he is charged."

"My son, my wretched, my unfortunate son," ejaculated Ranulph, with a burst of agony, "thy father would answer for thine innocence with his life. The name of De Lacy never yet was tarnished, and cannot be now in the person of my noble Godfrey."

With these words the distracted Ranulph removed his wife, who, again overpowered by the strength of her feelings, had once more fainted.

In the meantime Ernnestine, who, the moment the dreadful intelligence was

imparted to her, had felt as though she had been struck by a thunderbolt, remained paralyzed to the spot, a living statue of horror and astonishment. Nor
had she been able to utter a sentence, so violent was the effect that the accusation
of Godfrey of the murder of the unfortunate and ill-fated Reginald had had upon
her. This stupefaction—this silence—was more alarming than the most phren-
zied exclamations would have been, and the horror of every one present was increased when she suffered poor old Maud to take her arm, and lead her away, as
passive as an infant, as though she was unconscious of what was taking place, and
her eyes still fixed upon vacancy. She was removed to her chamber, where she
remained in the same melancholy state of apathy the whole of the day.

Shortly afterwards, Lord St. Aswolph quitted the inn, and, at his request,
Ranulph accompanied him, leaving poor old Hubert and his wife to give free vent
to the heavy sorrows which filled their bosoms, and to look after Edith and
Ernnestine, who both remained in a state of insensibility, notwithstanding the
chirurgical skill of one of the pious monks, who attended from the Monastery of
Saint Cuthbert.

CHAPTER VI.

" Who dare accuse me of this hellish crime,
    Which even fiends would shrink from doing?
    Where are your proofs?—Are they on my brow?
    Move they in my actions before or since?
    You cannot bring forward a single scrap—
    A particle—nay, not an atom of evidence,
    That shall prove me guilty. By Heaven!
    (The guilty wretch hath not the courage to appeal
    To that tribunal.)—I am innocent!"

IT was midnight, and there were none of the robbers in the large vaulted apartment under the castle of St. Alwyn, where these lawless men usually assembled, but Rodolph, and the other two ruffians, who had been concerned with him
in the murder of the unfortunate Reginald. Osmond and the rest of the gang
had gone upon one of their predatory excursions, and left them in charge of
the place.

Rodolph and Gilbert pushed the flask merrily round, and seemed to be much
elated, but Stephen sat apart from them, and was burried in the same gloom and
thoughtfulness, which had lately characterised him. He seemed to pay no attention to the noisy revelry and coarse ribaldry of his associates, but was evidently
entirely absorbed by the painfulness and intensity of his own thoughts.

" Well, by my troth," at length observed Rodolph,—" did ever any one see
such a dull, effeminate fellow as Stephen, in this world? Here have we lately
met with a booty that ought to make any one rejoice, and although it certainly
cost us a little more trouble than we at first calculated upon, we have managed
it so well that we are safe from all suspicion even, and our captain is also igno-

ant of our guilt, and is likely to remain so, as Godfrey de Lacy is accused of perpetrating the crime, and strong evidences of his guilt are likely to be brought against him ; and yet, forsooth here is Stephen fretting and alarming himself as much as if he were already under the hands of the executioner."

" It is not the fear of punishment in this world, Rodolph," said Stephen, "but the goading, the racking torments of a guilty conscience. And this last dreadful deed, has added to it a weight which appears to bear me down. I try to fly from thoughts, but try in vain ;—I seek to shut out the image of the murdered man—but no, his blood-stained form pursues me wherever I go—his pale and distorted features are ever before mine eyes."

" Idiot !" cried Rodolph, " this cowardice will betray us, if we do not adopt means to put and end to it. Hark ye,—if thou persistest in this sickening weakness, thou mayst surely repent."

"Nay, Rodolph, if thou dost not thyself fear that an all-searching Power above will make known thy guilt, and bring thee to punishment, thou hast nothing to fear from me. I feel how dreadful it is to live, with all this weight of guilt upon my soul, but yet it is even still more terrible to die. But this youth, this unfortunate Godfrey—surely thou canst not, thou wilt not suffer him to perish on the scaffold, the innocent cause of our crime ?"

" That must be as his judges decree, and as his evil star prevails," returned Rodolph, " it shall not, at any rate, be my task to tell his accusers that he is innocent, and that we are the guilty persons."

Stephen groaned, and turned away his head with an expression of horror.

" For my part," observed Gilbert, " I think as Rodolph does, that it is very lucky for us that the suspicion has fallen upon this Godfrey, as thou callest him, for should we be discovered, we should stand very little chance of escaping the hands of justice; our captain, as we have done the deed in secret, and kept the booty to ourselves, would not protect us, but on the contrary, would be more likely himself to deliver us up for our treachery."

" Villain! thou sayest right," exclaimed a loud voice from behind, where the ruffians were seated. They started with terror at its well-known tones, and looking up, beheld Osmond, their captain, surrounded by the other portion of the gang, standing behind them, and gazing upon them with an expression of the greatest indignation.

"Miscreants !" continued Osmond, after a pause, " I have overheard every sentence you have uttered ; comrades, say, what punishment do those merit, who turn traitors to our cause, and deceive their captain ?"

" Death !" was the loud and universal reply from the robbers.

" Away with them to confinement," commanded Osmond.

Rodolph and Gilbert now fell upon their knees before their captain, and abjectly prayed for mercy, while Stephen covered his face with his hands, and seemed to be suffering more from the horrors of guilt, than terror at the discovery which had been made by their captain.

" Base, cowardly wretches," exclaimed Osmond, as he looked scornfully upon the robbers ; " and dare ye beg for mercy, who have thus so shamefully broken through our rules. The shedding of human blood at any time, unless it is unavoidable, I have strictly prohibited, yet ye not only disregard this, but, moreover, commit the deed without my sanction, and appropriate the wages of your crime to your own use. Away with them, their portion is death!"

"Oh, mercy, mercy, captain," cried the trembling Rodolph and Gilbert, looking ghastly pale, as their comrades, fearful of disobeying Osmond's orders, came forward to seize them; as for Stephen, he exhibited no signs of fear, save that which his own guilty conscience excited, and with clasped hands, stood apparently composed, and awaiting his fate.

"Dastardly churls," exclaimed the indignant Osmond, "for thy craven hearts, thou dost more richly merit death, than even for thy treachery. Away with them to the Hall of Torture, there punish them for their present cowardice, afterwards, away with them to separate dungeons, and in the meantime, I will consider in what manner it would be meet to dispose of them for their former offence. But hold!—The booty they took from the murdered man, where is it?—Answer me, knaves, or by my hopes of vengeance on mine enemies, in five minutes more, ye shall hang like dogs from the first tree in the forest!"

Rodolph and Gilbert answered not, but with sullen looks and livid lips, they looked fearfully at each other, and in a hesitating manner, as if they were tenacious of parting with that which had cost them so much to obtain, and yet shrunk appalled at the death which they were certain Osmond would not fail to inflict upon them. What cowards are the guilty at the prospect of death; how do the most ferocious ruffians quail at the sight of danger.

"Ah! miscreants!" cried the robber-chief, while his dark brows became contracted, and every feature was distorted with rage, "dare ye disobey? To the forest with them!"

Another moment, and the trembling wretches fate would have been irrevocable, when Rodolph, overcame by his excessive terrors, implored the forbearance of Osmond, and promised to reveal the place where the booty was concealed.

He did so, and the captain took the packet, which the ruffians had unfastened, and gazed with apparent astonishment and delight upon the valuable contents.

"Away with them," he said, turning to the ruffians who had the charge of Rodolph and his companions, "away with them, and do my bidding."

The three wretches looked at each other with blanched cheeks, but they knew it was useless to appeal to Osmond for mercy, and they were forced into the Torture-room, a large stone chamber adjoining that in which the robbers were assembled, and soon their loud and piteous cries were sufficient to convince the robber-captain that his orders had been strictly complied with.

For some time Osmond seemed completely absorbed in the contemplation of the contents of the packet, of which the murderers had plundered the unfortunate Reginald; after which he traversed the room with hasty steps, and muttered some sentences in so low a tone, that they were perfectly undistinguishable to his comrades. But they took no notice of his behaviour, as he was frequently in the habit of indulging in such fits, and had always strictly enjoined them at the peril of their lives, never to offer to interrupt him, or to ask any questions as to the cause. It was very clear, however, that some heavy grief hung upon Osmond's mind, and that it had been misfortune alone, and the hard and unendurable buffetings of Fate, that had induced him to take to the predatory life which he now led.

Of Ulric, however, Osmond had made a confidant, and had imparted to him all the events of his early history. They were seldom apart, and the captain had made so great a friend of Ulric, that he had delegated to him almost as much power over the gang, as he himself possessed. The lawless and desperate ruffians looked upon Osmond and his lieutenant with dread, and never offered, by word or look, to disobey their orders, for well did they know that for such disobedience, their lives would be certain to pay the forfeit.

"Ah, Ulric," suddenly exclaimed Osmond, as the former, who had been upon business to another part of the country, entered the place, "marry, an thou hast returned in good time, I have much to impart to thee, and greatly need thy counsel and advice."

The robber-chief drew Ulric aside, and shewed him the packet, and they stood conferring together in suppressed tones for several minutes, when, at length, Ulric observed :—

" 'Tis well, captain, I much approve thy plans ; but the girl ?"

"Forsooth, she is now a comely damsel, as thou knowest," answered Osmond, "but it is not against her my deadly vengeance is excited ; no, Ulric, I would not harm her, although those that gave her being, have brought sorrow and disgrace upon me, and made that world to me a desert, which once to me was a world of sweets and flowers. I do confess me, Ulric, that my heart yearns towards her, and many a time have I watched with looks of admiration, and unaccountable delight, her light and sylph-like form, as she bounded in innocent sport up the steep hills, or gambolled in the old green- wood, unconscious of danger, and a stranger to fear. Ah, Ulric, there is something in her form and features, which so strangely bring to my recollection the image of her who—— but, psha ! I am getting weak as a child at the time when I should be most firm."

"But art thou certain that he of whom thou hast been speaking," said Ulric, "is the same that——"

"The same that robbed me of peace, of happiness, of name, of all that I once possessed," added Osmond eagerly, while he appeared to undergo the greatest emotion ; "yes, he it was who forced the poisoned chalice to my lips, and rested not until I had drained it to the dregs ! He it was who planted ten thousand daggers in my heart, and made that heart cold as marble. No doubt he thinks that I have long since slumbered with the dead, and that he is now secure from danger ; but he shall find that he is deceived ; he shall, ere long, learn that the man he has so deeply injured, still lives for vengeance, aye, deadly and implacable vengeance. This night, I shall leave here, Ulric, in furtherance of the scheme I have already imparted to thee, and should I not return at the time I have stated, thou mayest conclude that something has happened to me, and wilt know how to act. Now to our nightly repast, and when our comrades have betook themselves to their rest, I will away."

With these words Osmond, the robber-chief, and his favourite, Ulric, joined their companions at the festive board, and the coarse revelry was kept up in the same manner as usual till a late hour, when the robbers at length slowly departed to the different apartments appropriated to them, and Osmond having bade farewell to Ulric, and repeated his injunctions, buckled on his trusty sword, slung his horn across his shoulder, and wrapping his mantle around him, strode forth from the castle, and bent his steps across the forest.

We will now return to Godfrey de Lacy, who, having been conveyed to prison by the persons who had discovered him standing over the body of the murdered man, in the narrow confines of his dungeon, had time to reflect upon the unfortunate and dangerous situation in which he was placed; but firm in the consciousness of his own innocence, and confident that he could without much difficulty, repudiate the charge brought against him, he suffered not so much for himself as for his parents and Ernnestine, on whom he feared the event would have the most dangerous effect, and the shock so alarm them, that fatal results might be the consequence.

With disordered steps, he paced the gloomy cell, and gave free indulgence to the agonising thoughts which tormented his bosom.

"Alas!" he soliloquized, "my beloved parents, what will be your anguish, when you hear of the dreadful crime with which your son is accused? And Ernnestine, my dearest Ernnestine, oh, how will her feelings be harrowed up; what indescribable horror will torture her gentle bosom, when she becomes acquainted with the situation of her to whom she is so devotedly attached?—The Holy Virgin protect her, and give her fortitude to support this heavy trial, for I fear the intelligence will break her heart!"

He beat his breast and sighed heavily, as these reflections crossed his mind, and traversed the dungeon to and fro, in a state of the utmost mental excitement. The terrible fate of Reginald filled his mind with the greatest horror:—

"Oh, who could have done this hellish deed?" he soliloquised. "Who can the heartless, the blood-thirsty wretches be? And by what strange fatality is it, that I, who was his dearest friend, and who had so much reason to admire him for his generosity towards me and Ernnestine, should be suspected of being his murderer? Alas! it seems as if some infernal spell was upon me, and that sorrow had marked me for one of her victims!"

Once more the wretched youth groaned with the intensity of his agony, and throwing himself upon the straw, which was placed as a substitute for a pallet, in one corner of his cell, he gave himself up entirely to the horror of the thoughts that crowded rapidly upon his brain.

Again and again did he upbraid himself for having left Reginald to pursue his way alone, after having walked with him so far on the way to Saint Cuthbert's Monastery; and the impression was strong upon his mind, that had he not done so, the dreadful catastrophe would never have taken place. Not being aware whether the packet with which Reginald had been entrusted, was taken from him, he was unable to judge what had been the object of the murderers; but he had no doubt that it had been plunder, and that the crime was perpetrated by some of the wretches who infested that part of the country: and, as this idea occurred to him, he became more and more confident of his innocence being quickly and clearly established, for nothing had been found upon his person to criminate him, and his character was too well known, for it to be supposed for a moment, that he would have any connection with the miscreants above alluded to. But the bare

idea of his being taken upon suspicion of committing so foul a deed, filled his bosom with horror and shame, and he had a severe struggle with his feelings to enable him to retain anything like his usual equanimity.

Hour after hour passed away in this horrible state of agony and suspense, and morning brought with it no change. But he could only guess the lapse of time, for there was not even a ray of light could enter his dreary cell, and it was so cold and damp, that his limbs trembled as if he had been suffering under a violent fit of the ague.

At length he was aroused by seeing a light glimmering from the crevices of the door, and soon afterwards he heard the bolts withdrawn; the key turned in the lock; the heavy door fell back on its hinges, and, in a moment, the gaoler entered, followed by Ranulph, who rushed frantically into the arms of his son, and was so overcome by his emotions, that he was unable to utter a syllable.

"My son! my son!" at last exclaimed Ranulph, in a voice which sufficiently evinced the agony of his feelings. "Alas! what dreadful fate has brought thee into this situation? Oh, never did Ranulph de Lacy, whose name was never sullied yet, and whose forefathers were noble and great,—never did he, I say, expect a trial so severe as this!"

"Father!" said Godfrey, withdrawing himself from his embrace, and looking at him with a mingled expression of astonishment and reproach,—"father, can you believe me guilty of this cruel, this horrible crime?"

"Think you guilty, my son," replied the agitated father; "believe my noble-minded boy capable of imbruing his hands in the blood of his fellow-creature, and

No. 8

that fellow-creature his friend, the companion of his youth?—never! never! Oh, Godfrey, pardon me if my words appeared to convey such an idea; indeed, my emotion is so great, that I scarcely know what I say. Yes, my son, well do I know thine innocence, and that Providence will enable thee to make it manifest on the day of thy trial. The Lord St. Aswolph believes thee guiltless, and fain would use his influence to release thee from confinement; but justice and thine own character, demand the strictest investigation into this awful affair."

"My poor mother and Ernnestine," said Godfrey,—"alas! what will be their suffering at my wretched, my disgraceful situation? Oh, I care not for myself, but for you, my dear parents, and that sweet maiden, on whom my heart's affections are placed. I am ready to meet my trial with firmness, for the Great Judge above, who knows my innocence, will not desert me in the hour of need. Alas! what will be the anguish of them to see me arraigned at the bar, for a crime at which Nature revolts? Tell me, father, are they not distracted? Oh, do not disguise anything from me, for to deceive me, would only be to add to my anguish."

"I will not deceive thee, Godfrey," said Ranulph; "but, pr'ythee endeavour to sustain thy fortitude under this heavy misfortune, for thy grief, of course, would increase the agony of those for whom thou expressest so much concern."

Ranulph then, with as much composure as possible, related to his unfortunate son all that had taken place, and did not disguise from him the violent effect it had upon the feelings of his mother and Ernnestine. When Godfrey heard of the anguish endured by his mother, and the heart-rending situation of Ernnestine, he smote his breast, and traversed his cell in a state of mind which may be easily imagined; but at length the arguments of his father prevailed, and he became gradually more calm, and, at the request of Ranulph, related all that he knew to have taken place the night before his separation from the ill-fated Reginald, and his subsequent return and discovery of the body.

Ranulph listened to him with the most breathless attention, and when he had concluded, he exclaimed in a tone of delight,—

"Thank Heaven! my son, everything is so clear, that there cannot be the least doubt of thine innocence being quickly established. There is not the slightest evidence to criminate thee! Thou must be acquitted, and not even the breath of suspicion shall dare to contaminate thy name. Bear with it, then, my son, and all will soon again be well."

Ranulph de Lacy remained as long as they would permit him in the cell with Godfrey, and when at last they were compelled to separate, they were both more tranquil and sanguine as to the fortunate issue of the fatal affair, and the latter, having breathed a prayer for his mother, Ernnestine, and his other dear friends, felt more happy and resigned.

Ranulph de Lacy had not departed many minutes, when the gaoler entered the cell, and informed Godfrey that a holy monk wished to speak with him.

"Admit him," said Godfrey; and the gaoler departed, and quickly returned, followed by the tall figure of a monk, whose features were almost entirely concealed beneath his cowl.

"Pr'ythee, leave us, son," said the friar, addressing the gaoler in a deep and sonorous tone, which Godfrey listened to with an astonishment, which added to the unaccountable interest the monk had excited in his bosom the moment he beheld him. The gaoler bowed, and obeyed the command of the holy man.

After the gaoler had quitted the dungeon, and the monk had listened to the sound of his receding footsteps, as he retired along the subterraneous passage, he turned round towards Godfrey, and folding his arms across his breast, stood for a few minutes silently contemplating the astonished youth, while his eyes, which were all that Godfrey could distinguish from beneath his cowl, were fixed upon his countenance with an earnestness which seemed as if it could read his most inmost thoughts.

The prisoner felt a strange awe stealing over his senses, in the presence of the mysterious friar, and he waited with the greatest impatience to hear what he had to say to him, or whether he had merely visited him to perform the offices of religion. At length, the monk broke the silence which he had hitherto maintained—

"We are now alone," said he; "there are no listeners at hand to overhear us."

"Why shouldst thou fear them, holy father?" demanded Godfrey in a tone of surprise.

The monk returned no answer, but drawing closer to Godfrey, he took his hand, and throwing back his cowl, he discovered the determined, but handsome features of a man, apparently about forty years of age, who gazed upon the youth with an earnestness which excited his utmost interest and amazement.

"Ah!" exclaimed Godfrey, drawing back, "thou art no monk?"

"Be cautious," said the stranger, in an under tone,—"thou guessest right."

"Who art thou, then?"

"No matter; I am thy friend."

"How am I to know that?"

"I will prove myself to be so anon," was the stranger's answer.

"What wouldst thou with me?" inquired Godfrey, whose astonishment creased at the singular words and manner of the stranger.

"I would serve thee."

"How?"

"Thou art charged with murder, Godfrey de Lacy," said the man.

"True; but I am innocent."

"I know it."

"Thou?" repeated the youth, in a tone of the most unqualified surprise; how canst *thou* know me guiltless of this atrocious crime?"

"It matters not," returned the stranger, "let it suffice that I speak not erroneously."

"For what purpose didst thou come hither?" asked Godfrey, eagerly.

"To offer thee liberty!"

Godfrey shook his head.

"Thou mockest me, stranger," said Godfrey. "What power hast thou to offer me freedom?"

"More than thou dost imagine," was the answer.

"I cannot solve this mystery," observed Godfrey;—"why shouldst thou interest thyself in my fate? I know thee not."

" But I know thee. Thou art the son of Ranulph de Lacy, the bowyer; many a good yew bow, the work of his hands, have I bent ere now. He once did me a service; he saved my life, and I would repay the debt by saving the life of his son."

" Alas! thou talkest wildly, stranger," remarked Godfrey; "yet do I thank thee for thy good wishes and designs, however impracticable they may be."

" Thou shalt find that they are not impracticable, if thou wilt agree to make the trial," remarked the man.

" What wouldst thou propose?"

" Thou shalt know," answered the other, and in a moment, throwing off his monkish dress, Godfrey beheld, with astonishment, the tall and muscular person of a man, attired in a handsome dress, with daggers in his belt, and a ponderous sword by his side. Godfrey started back with amazement at this sudden and unexpected metamorphoses, while the stranger beheld the sensation he had excited with apparent indifference.

" Dost thou know me now?" demanded he.

" I do not," replied Godfrey—" tell me thy name?"

" Osmond the Avenger!"

" Ah! the robber?"

" The same, and thy friend. Nay, thou needst not turn away with such disdain; thou mightest have many a worse friend than Osmond, the robber chief; well may those tremble who have made him their enemy."

" Again I ask thee," said the youth, " how thou wouldst serve me?"

" Have I not told thee?—By effecting thy liberation. But come, there is no time to lose; the gaoler will be surprised at the length of our conference, and return ere we can put my project into execution. Quick, attire thee in this monkish garb, and thou mayst pass out of this prison without suspicion."

" And thou——" demanded the astonished Godfrey.

" I will remain here until I think thou hast had time to escape, when fear not but that my good sword will shew my passage through all who are daring enough to obstruct me. Quick! quick!—the disguise, while it is yet in thy power to avail thyself of it."

" No, no, I will not do so," said Godfrey, after a moment or two's reflection; " were I to fly from hence, I should quickly be retaken, and to do so, would be like an acknowledgment that I am guilty of the foul crime of which I am suspected."

" Bethink thee," said Osmond, "shouldst thou leave ere I will shelter and protect thee, and take steps to establish thine innocence beyond a doubt, so that thou mayst again fearlessly mingle with the world without the slightest imputation upon thy character. Be quick and decide."

" Would not my conduct appear weak, cowardly, and would not every one condemn me, did I act as thou dost advise me?" asked Godfrey.

" Psha!—Could they condemn thee when thine innocence was made manifest, and the real assassins brought to light?"

" Ah . canst thou do as thou sayest?"

" I pledge myself that the real murderers of Reginald shall be delivered up to justice," answered the robber chief.

"Enough!" cried Godfrey; "I will avail myself of thine offer, and as thou art sincere, so will my gratitude be due to thee."

"What interest could I have in deceiving *thee?*" demanded Osmond; "thinkest thou I would run the risk I am now prepared to do, were it not with a wish to serve thee? But we are wasting time. Thou wilt pass easily out of the prison in this disguise. Outside thou wilt find some of my brave fellows waiting to receive thee; commit thyself to their care, and fear not.'

While Osmond was thus speaking, he had assisted Godfrey on with the disguise, and drew the cowl over his face, to conceal his features from observation.

"But, then," said Godfrey, hesitating, "how wilt thou escape?"

"Again, I tell thee, to fear not for me," replied Osmond; "nothing can prevent my escape from hence; I will quickly follow thee—away, away.—Hark! the gaoler approaches!—silence—caution."

At that moment, the door of the dungeon was opened, and the gaoler made his appearance. Osmond had got into a dark corner of the cell, so that his person could not be distinguished directly, and Godfrey, after having apparently invoked a blessing on the head of the prisoner, turned to pass out.

The gaoler looked at him stedfastly, but did not appear to have any suspicion; and Godfrey, with a solemn step, in keeping with the holy character he had assumed, walked out into the passage beyond.

"Holy father," observed the gaoler, "thou wilt pass the sentinels as thou didst on thine entrance, and thou canst not miss thy way; I have business with the prisoner, or I would guide thee."

"Thanks, my son," said Godfrey, attempting to disguise his voice. The gaoler started.—

"Ah! what voice is that?" he exclaimed, in a tone of astonishment; "it is not that of the monk's! Hold! thou goest not hence, until I am satisfied."

As the gaoler uttered these words, he opened the small lantern he carried with him, and the light streamed full upon the robber chief.

"Ah! by the infernal host," cried the gaoler, "there s treason abroad!" and he sprang towards Godfrey, with an intention of detaining him; but, scarcely had he given utterance to the words mentioned above, when Osmond rushed upon him, and plunging the dagger to his heart, the unfortunate wretch gave but one groan, and sunk a corpse at the feet of his murderer.

"Fly, Godfrey, fly!" he exclaimed; "thou canst pass on now without any danger; and leave me to work my way to liberty!—I will rejoin thee anon."

Godfrey, horror-struck at what had taken place, and scarcely knowing what he did, obeyed the injunctions of the robber chief, and traversed the gloomy passage with hasty steps, until he reached the first sentinel, who, seeing his holy garb, asked no questions, but suffered him to pass on. In like manner he passed every sentinel, until he at last gained the exterior of the prison, where he beheld several men lurking about, whom he suspected to be the robbers whom Osmond had mentioned to him. He soon found that he was perfectly right in his conjectures, for they no sooner saw him, than the principal one, who seemed to take the lead of the rest, made a sign to him to follow; and, turning round an angle of the prison, him and his companions were soon hidden from sight.

Godfrey did follow the men as quick as possible; and when he had come up to the man who had given him the sign, and who was Ulric, the lieutenant, and confidant of Osmond, he threw back his cowl and revealed himself.

"'Ah! 'tis all right," said Ulric; " but, our captain ?"

" He bade me tell thee, he would rejoin thee anon," returned Godfrey ;— " ah! see, even now he approaches this way !"

At that moment, Osmond, in a perturbed state, and with his hands covered with blood, came running towards them, with the greatest precipitation.

" Quick! quick! where are our horses ?" he cried : "I have been compelled to murder all the sentinels as I came up to them, and I have not left a soul that can tell who is the perpetrator of all which has taken place. Away with ye !— for should the escape of Godfrey de Lacy be discovered immediately, a pursuit would take place, and we might have to fight hard to effect our escape !"

The horses were standing just at the entrance to the forest, in the charge of two of the robbers, and they had brought one with them for the use of Godfrey. They were soon mounted, and, clapping their spurs into the sides of their fleet steeds, they were soon far away from the place in which Godfrey had so lately been confined, and in a short time, the lofty towers of St. Alwyn Castle, the impregnable retreat of Osmond and his daring band, appeared in sight.

Having crossed the moat, the drawbridge was almost immediately raised, and Osmond put his horn to his mouth, and blew a loud blast three times, upon which the door was opened by a ferocious-looking man, and the robbers and Godfrey passed into the hall of the castle.

Godfrey had hitherto had little time to reflect upon the course he had adopted; but it now, suddenly, came upon his mind the construction it was most likely that would be put upon his escape from prison ; it would, he thought, appear to the generality of people like a confirmation of his guilt, because, had he been really innocent, (at least, so it would appear to mere superficial observers,) he would not have feared the evidence which might be adduced against him on his trial, and would have risked anything sooner than have fled, and thus lay himself under the stigma of cowardice, if not of the actual guilt of the dreadful crime with which he stood charged. Besides, what a sacrifice of life—of the lives of innocent persons, and who were only doing their duty—had it caused, and what would be the opinion of the public on the subject? They would suppose him to be the actual perpetrator of the several murders, and eternal obloquy and detestation would rest upon his name; and, innocent as he was of the assassination of the unfortunate men, was he not the indirect cause of their fate ?—for had he not in a moment of weakness accepted of the services of the bandit chief, the lives of the ill-fated beings would have been saved, and he would, in the consciousness of his own innocence, have passed triumphantly through the painful ordeal, to which it was his ill-starred fortune to be subjected. Again, if ultimately it was proved that he was not guilty of the murder of Reginald, would not a suspicion of his integrity attach itself to him, since he had connected himself with the robbers, the terror of the country, to effect his release from incarceration? Alas! it would ; and he feared his reputation was ruined for ever! And what would be the agony, the distraction of his family—of Ernnestine, when the news of his flight, and the horrible circumstances that had attended it, reached their ears ?— What dreadful doubts, surmises, and apprehensions would torment their minds ?

What accursed infatuation,—what strange weakness could ever have induced him to yield to the insidious persuasions of Osmond, and what could ever have induced the latter to run the risk of rescuing him from confinement, if he had not some sinister design in view? He knew him not, no more than from what report had spread of his desperate deeds, and why should he, therefore, take any interest in his fate? True, he had told him, that his father had once rendered him a service, but he had only his bare assertion to satisfy him of that being a fact, and his father had never mentioned such a circumstance to him, nor had he ever alluded to it, even in the most remote manner. Osmond had promised to make his innocence manifest, and to bring the real assassins to light; but, if he even did so, what could ever remove from him the stigma of having accepted of the services of a robber, an outlaw, to effect that object? And would he not ever afterwards be looked upon as a friend and associate of the lawless chief? Alas! he had acted very imprudently—very rashly; and he feared that the result would prove an everlasting source of unhappiness and disgrace to him and his family, and destroy the good, the irreproachable name he had hitherto borne in the world.

These were the thoughts that rushed rapidly on the brain of Godfrey de Lacy, the moment he entered the robbers' retreat, and most poignant was the anguish they occasioned him. He paused, and struck his forehead in the bitterness of his agony, and Osmond, observing his emotion, turned suddenly from his companions, and looked stedfastly at the former, said,—

"What now?—Why dost thou hesitate? Has childish fear taken possession of thy faculties? Dost thou repent thee of availing thyself of the liberty which I have taken so much trouble to obtain thee?"

"Would to Heaven," answered the young man—"would to Heaven that I had never seen thee; what an effusion of blood would it have saved, and have prevented the foul calumny and opprobrium that will attach themselves to my once unsullied name. Let me return to my dungeon, and meet, as a man, conscious of his innocence, ought to do, the dreadful charge which is brought against me!"

"Psha!" exclaimed Osmond, "what childish weakness has now taken possession of thy faculties? Return, and thy fate is sealed; remain here, under my protection, and, as I have before assured thee, thine entire innocence shall be made known to the world; and, moreover, thou shalt be entirely exculpated from any share in the bloodshed which subsequently occurred. The fools were obstinate, or their lives would have been spared;—Osmond likes not the unnecessary effusion of blood. Come, come—this way; this way."

Scarcely knowing what he did, Godfrey suffered himself to be conducted by the robbers along the hall, which had lost nothing of its feudal grandeur, and presented the same magnificent *coup d'eil*, as it had done during the period of the ancient possessors of the castle. They passed into a place which had formerly been the chapel of the gothic pile, and Ulric, proceeding to the alter, stamped several times upon a marble slab immediately before it, and at length a secret door flew open in the front of the altar, and exhibited a flight of stone steps. These he immediately began to descend, and was followed by the robber, Osmond keeping close by the side of Godfrey, and taking great pains to point out to him the way. At the bottom of these steps, they found themselves in a long, arched passage, to the extremity of which they proceeded, and, opening a door, they entered immediately upon the spacious underground apartments, or rather caverns—for they resembled them more than anything else—which were occupied by the robbers.

The novelty of the scene which burst upon his view, engaged the attention of Godfrey, and for a few moments estranged his thoughts from the painful subjects that had before occupied them. The first apartment they entered was a very spacious place, and was hung around, on all sides, with arms of every description. From the roof which was vaulted, depended several lamps, that served to make it sufficiently light, and cast a glaring reflection upon the swords and coats of mail which hung around, and gave it the appearance of a baronial hall. In the centre was an immense table, at which the robbers always assembled to take their meals, and indulge in their rude revelry. At the head of the board was a chair raised considerably higher than any of the rest, having a canopy over it. This was appropriated to the use of the captain. On the right of this was another chair, rather lower, in which Ulric, the lieutenant of the daring gang, always took his seat.

When they entered, there were about forty dark, powerful, and determined-looking men, seated at the table, who immediately arose, and shouted in tones of welcome,—"All hail to our noble captain, Osmond, the Avenger !"

" And to the man whom I have taken under my protection, Godfrey de Lacy !" exclaimed Osmond, taking the hand of the former, and leading him towards the table.

" Welcome to Godfrey de Lacy !" shouted the robbers, simultaneously, and the captain and Ulric immediately took their seats, Osmond placing Godfrey in a seat on his left hand, after which the robbers resumed theirs, and silence prevailed.

Godfrey could not help feeling a degree of interest at the novelty of the scene to which he was thus introduced, which he had never experienced before ; but, yet, amidst it all, his thoughts still dwelt upon the danger of his situation, and the misery his friends would be enduring, when the news of his flight became known ; and he reproached himself for the temporary weakness which had tempted him to yield to the persuasions of the robber chief.

Osmond immediately noticed the depresssion of spirits under which he laboured, and, he as quickly read his thoughts, but did not for a while offer to interrupt him,—suffering him to give free indulgence to all which was passing within his mind.

A plenteous repast was soon placed upon the table, of which Godfrey was invited to partake ; but his thoughts were too busily occupied to suffer him to assent. The wine cup was circulated freely, and the robbers soon became excessively merry, making " the welkin ring again" with their rude and boisterous revelry.

At length, Osmond, having by a motion of his hand commanded silence, gave the shoulder of Godfrey a hearty smack, and in a tone of assumed gaiety, observed,—

" Come, come, Godfrey, arouse thyself, and let not needless apprehensions torment thy bosom ; beshrew me, but thou art as dull as one who has inhabited the solemn walls of a cloister all his days. Here thou art as safe as if thou wert at the other end of the globe. This is our territory, and no one yet has been found fool-hardy enough to dispute our right of possession. Here, in our strong fastnesses, we may be truly said to be impregnable. We bid defiance to

any force, and there is not a man amongst us who would not die sooner than yield."

Godfrey shook his head and sighed ;—

" I fear me," said he, " that thine is a life of care—of sorrow, and of crime."

" It is a life of freedom," exclaimed Osmond. " We are not the lowly serfs of lordly tyrants, nor own we the power of monarchy. We hold the maxim good, that the good things of this life were sent for the enjoyment of us all ; and when we see others monopolizing more than is their share, we think we have an undoubted right to take it from them and appropriate it to our own uses. Why should others' coffers contain abundance of the bright yellow gold, and ours go empty ?—The poor are our friends, for we relieve their wants. Bloodshed is our abhorrence, and sincerely do we regret when necessity compels us to it. We have laws of our own, which maintain proper order and subordination, and we do not fail to punish those who break them. Upon the world we look with contempt—for we are all men who have been so buffeted about by misfortune, as to become disgusted with it and the hollow minds of its votaries. This impregnable castle is our palace—this bonny green-wood our kingdom. What sayest thou ?—Thinkest thou the robber's life is altogether to be laughed to scorn ?"

Godfrey returned no immediate answer.

" Surely it must have been some great misfortune, indeed," said he, " which could have induced thee to take to this lawless course of life ; for, (I pray thee pardon me for my boldness,) an I am not much mistaken, thou art not of lowly origin, and wert born to higher and happier expectations."

No. 9

" Thou conjecturest right," replied Osmond, with a sigh, " I have known what it is to mingle with the riches and the noble—to receive the smile of adulation—and command subservience. I have lorded it in my prosperity with the most powerful, and basked in the courteous smiles of my sovereign's favour: But treachery, oppression, and hypocrisy hurled me from my proud estate, and now you see me as I am!—Oh, woman, woman, thou wert born to deceive; to link man in thy golden fetters; to sport with his feelings, and break the heart thou hast enfettered !"

Osmond paused, and seemed to be so violently agitated as to be unable to give utterance to his feelings. The dark and hardy-looking men appeared to pay his feelings the utmost respect, and to sympathise with the sorrow that oppressed his mind, and which was known only to Ulric, the lieutenant. Osmond arose from his seat, folded his arms, and traversed the cavern with hasty and agitated steps. At length, he returned to his seat, and looking more composed, said to Godfrey, who had watched his conduct with much interest—

" Pardon me, Godfrey; it is a weakness which time nor circumstances can ever conquer. Oh, Marian !—too beautiful, yet too false!—What anguish hast thou cost me! What pangs—what torments hast thou inflicted in this bosom! What thinkest thou of this, Godfrey?"

As the robber-chief thus spoke, he took from his bosom a miniature, in a gold frame, set round with pearls, and presented it to Godfrey, who gazed with astonishment and delight upon one of the most beauteous countenances he had ever contemplated. It was that of a female, apparently about the age of Ernnestine, and the remarkable likeness to whom was the most surprising. As he looked intently upon it, his sorrows came fresh upon him, and when he recollected the agony which Ernnestine and his parents were most likely at that time suffering, he could scarcely support himself.

Osmond had been scrutinizing the expression of Godfrey's countenance narrowly, and seemed to penetrate his thoughts.

" What thinkest thou of it, young man ?" said he. " Is it not surpassingly lovely ?—Thinkest thou, her who looks so beautiful—so innocent—could harbour deceit?"

" Deceit; never !" exclaimed Godfrey. " By Heaven, it is a gross libel upon one of the most beauteous of Nature's works !—But the likeness !—I could almost imagine she was before me !"

" Of whom dost thou speak ?" demanded Osmond, eagerly.

" Of her to whom are devoted my heart's warmest affections," replied Godfrey, hastily.

" Of Ernnestine !" added the robber.

" The same," observed Godfrey, " by the saints I never beheld so great a likeness !—Tell me, who is the original of this?"

" For the present I must not tell thee," answered Osmond, " although I marvel not at thy question. But, enough of this, we will to the business which more immediately interests us at the present moment."

" Alas !" ejaculated Godfrey, as the full horror of his situation came fresh upon his memory, " would that I had never yielded to thy persuasions, Osmond: what torturing pangs would it have saved those dear to me, and myself."

"Psha!" uttered Osmond, impatiently, "this weakness surprises me, Godfrey de Lacy; thou, the son of Ranulph, the stalwart bowyer, whose deeds with the stout yew bow are so well known; and thou thyself an esquire, and hitherto celebrated for thy prowess. Arouse thee, I say; I promise thee—and Osmond was never known to' break his word—that thou shalt come off unscathed and free. Even now I go to put my plans into execution; and, in the meantime, rest assured that I am thy friend, and that thou needest not tear the result of this painful event.

CHAPTER VII.

"Sorrow upon sorrow thickens,
As clouds obscure the brightness of a summer's sky
All, all around is black despair,
And misery sits and triumphs o'er his victims."

EDWIN AND ELFRIDA.

We left the inmates of "The Flagon" in a most pitiable condition, when Ranulph de Lacy and Lord St. Aswolph quitted the inn to make their way to the castle of the latter, that they might there consult together on the best means to bring the actual murderers to light, and save Godfrey from the fate with which, under present circumstances, he was threatened.

Lord St. Aswolph took a most lively interest in the fate of Godfrey, which was probably increased from the respect which he felt for Ranulph, his father, and the rest of the family, but more especially owing to the extraordinary admiration which the beauteous, the all-ravishing, Ernnestine had excited in his bosom. His lordship was not more than eight-and-thirty, and was, as we have before stated, a remarkably handsome and accomplished man. His amiable qualities, and the elegancies of his mind, were also equal to those of his person, and he immediately gained the esteem of all who beheld him. When many years younger, he had been a good deal on the continent, and it was supposed by many that he had met with some disappointment in love, for, when he returned to England, his manners were strangely altered, and his cheeks, which were once ruddy with the glow of youth and health, had become pale and careworn; and his spirits, that were once remarkable for their vivaciousness, were oppressed with an air of gloom, which rendered him quite a different being. But as to the real cause of this melancholy, no one knew anything, not even his lady mother, who, as might be expected, was exceedingly aggrieved to witness the sorrow under which he laboured, and was anxious to afford him all the consolation and alleviation which her affection could suggest. Whenever she questioned him upon the subject, he made some evasive reply, in fact, he seemed greatly distressed, and it would be a considerable time before he could regain his equanimity.

"Dearest mother," he would say, "pardon me if I decline to impart to thee that painful secret, which could only render thee unhappy, and make me more wretched than I am. I pray thee, urge me not, or think me wanting in love or duty to thee, my honoured parent, that I thus decline. Time, which effects all things, may ameliorate my grief, and for thy sake I will endeavour to conquer it."

But it was some time ere the sorrow of the young man evinced any signs of being abated, and many were the wretched days and nights that the amiable Lady Celestine passed, when she observed the melancholy state of mind under which her son laboured, and his sister Marguerite, whose soul was the abode of virtue, gentleness, and affection, tried every effort that her love for her brother could suggest, to elicit from his bosom the cause of his heavy affliction, so that she might impart to him that comfort and sympathy which she knew so well how to bestow. But all her efforts, like those of her mother, failed, and, at length, seeing how greatly their importunities appeared to add to his anguish, they abandoned the attempt, and mentally uttered their fervent prayers to heaven that time might reduce and ultimately banish the trouble under which he at present suffered, and make them acquainted with the cause.

This hope was somewhat realized ; the bustle and excitement of war soon engaged his attention, and gradually appeased, if it did not entirely triumph, over his secret sorrow ; it settled into a calm but unshaken seriousness which gave a deeper interest to his character, and excited the most fervent commiseration of all who knew him.

Although Lord Raymond had had many advantageous opportunities of marrying, he had invariably declined, and seemed, indeed, to have abandoned all thoughts of matrimony, and to have wedded himself entirely to the battle-field. Gallant indeed, were the deeds he had there performed, and many a stalwart Saracen had felt the weight of his arm. On the plains of Palestine he had performed prodigies of valour, and no one stood higher in the favour of his sovereign Richard the First, than Lord Raymond St. Aswolph. He had received many distinguished marks of his esteem, and many were his proud compeers in arms who envied that skill and bravery they could not equal.

As we have before mentioned, Lord Raymond had frequently been a visitor, when he was in England, at "The Flagon," and had often opportunities of seeing Ernnestine; but then she was a child, and although he could not but admire the sweetness and beauty which so deeply interested all who beheld her, it was a very different feeling which now inhabited his breast, when he beheld her spring up into all the full bloom and freshness of womanhood ; possessed of every endowment, natural and acquired, and with that delicacy and purity of mind which are woman's greatest charms. He felt at the moment that it was love which she had inspired in his breast; but when he recalled to his mind every lineament of her countenance, and remembered the strange resemblance which had so forcibly struck him, something far stronger than that passion he was convinced inhabited his bosom.

With sentiments such as these, it may easily be conjectured what was the emotion of his lordship at the awful catastrophe which had lately occurred, and which had placed Godfrey in such imminent peril; although, of his innocence of the murder of the unfortunate Esquire Reginald, he had the most perfect conviction. With the particulars of the circumstances which had placed Ernnestine under the protection of Ranulph de Lacy, he was unacquainted, but he believed that she was closely related to them, and he knew that she had been brought up with Godfrey; that she was his foster sister, and he could not but suppose that she entertained the utmost affection for him; therefore, the shock this event would in all probability give to her feelings, he feared might be attended with the most fatal consequences. Of the actual passion which subsisted between them, he had not any suspicion. These thoughts, independent of the common feelings of humanity, prompted him to exert himself to the very utmost to establish the innocence of Godfrey, and to bring to punishment the assassins of Reginald.

Ranulph and his lordship conversed some time upon this painful subject, and at length, Lord Raymond advised the former to see his son with all possible expedition, and to advise with him to bear up against the misfortunes that had so suddenly come upon him, and that in the meantime, he would use all his exertions to gain his liberation and exculpation from the frightful crime of which he was accused. He also promised to visit the young man in his dungeon as soon as he had returned from Sir Egbert de Courcy's, with whom he was going to consult as to the best way it would be prudent to proceed to attain the object of their wishes.

Ranulph de Lacy, on leaving the prison of his son, slowly wended his way, in a gloomy mood, towards the inn, meditating in what manner it would be best for him to endeavour to soften the anguish of his wife and Ernnestine. Completely abstracted from all that was passing around him, he had proceeded to some distance on his road, when, by the reflection of the sun, he, all at once, beheld the shadow of some object on the grass, and suddenly pausing, he raised his eyes, and was astonished and somewhat startled, to behold, leaning against the withered trunk of a tree, and with his fierce-looking eyes fixed stedfastly upon him, the Wizard of the Glen.

"Avaunt! fiend, devil!" exclaimed Ranulph, "obstruct not my path, thy sight strikes horror and disgust into my soul! Wherever thou approachest, despair and misery follow; even now, I feel that I am suffering under thine infernal spells! Avaunt, I say!"

"Ha! ha! ha! Ranulph de Lacy, then thou feelest at last that power which thou didst venture to despise?" said the wizard, in that peculiar tone of voice which could not fail to impart horror to the minds of all those who heard it, at the same time a demoniacal smile overspread his terrific features. "'Tis well, 'tis well, all must acknowledge and fear the power of Hal of the Glen!—Did I not tell thee that the girl Ernnestine would be the cause of misery to thee?"

"Thou didst, dread being," replied the bowyer, "but innocent and guiltless as is that beauteous maiden, how is it possible?"

"Thou wilt see anon. Did I not prognosticate all which has now happened to thy son?"

"True, too true," answered Ranulph, "but why torture me?"

"Thou hast yet much more to suffer, Ranulph de Lacy," said the wizard. "Godfrey is no longer the inmate of the dungeon in which thou so lately beheld him."

" Ah! gasped forth Ranulph, while his whole frame evinced the powerful emotion which the words of the wizard excited, " what meanest thou ?"

" That Godfrey, thy son, has purchased his present liberty at the price of human blood, and become the associate of infamy and crime !"

" Liar !" shouted Ranulph, hoarsely, " thou mockest me !"

" Incredulous fool !" cried the wizard, his eyes appearing to flash fire, " again thou presumest to doubt me ! Return, then, to the prison, and learn the truth of what I say !"

And without saying another word, the wizard fixed upon him a grin of malicious triumph, and turning from him, almost immediately disappeared from sight, leaving Ranulph in a state of complete stupefaction.

When Ranulph had in some measure recovered from the horror and amazement into which the appearance of the wizard, and the words he had given utterance to, had thrown him, he clasped his hands to his forehead with intense agony, and in a voice of the most powerful emotion, cried :—

" Good God ! what have I heard?—Can the assertions of this awful being be true ?—Impossible! and yet have not one portion of his terrible predictions been already fulfilled, and why should I longer doubt him ?—Alas ! there is a curse upon me and mine, and nothing but misery appears to be allotted to us !—Oh, let me back to the prison and learn at once the worst !"

With an agitated step he turned from the spot, and with the most horrible apprehensions retraced his way to the prison. He had not proceeded far when he perceived Lord Raymond running towards him with a wild air, and the utmost agitation expressed in his countenance. On beholding De Lacy approaching him, he started, and in a voice which bespoke the anguish of his mind, exclaimed,—

" Ah! De Lacy, thou returned? Hast thou, then, heard of the terrible catastrophe ?"

" What catastrophe, what has occurred ? Oh, speak, my lord, and end at once this horrible state of suspense !" frantically cried Ranulph.

" Godfrey has escaped from confinement," replied his ordship, " and the gaoler and three of the sentinels have been found cruelly murdered at their posts."

" Horror ! horror !" gasped forth Ranulph, while the blood seemed all at once to freeze in his veins, " do not mine ears deceive me ? Who hath been at work to do this? Who can have committed these bloody deeds for the purpose of bringing disgrace upon my name, and to break the hearts of his distracted parents?"

" I beseech thee," said Lord St. Aswolph, repressing as much as possible his real feelings, " I beseech thee to compose thyself, good Ranulph, and walk with me to the castle, where we may consult together on this dreadful circumstance, and I will tell thee everything as far as has come within my knowledge."

" My God ! surely cannot be awake," cried the distracted De Lacy, almost unconscious of what St. Aswolph had last said to him ; " it must be some frightful delusion that I am labouring under; Godfrey, my son, my poor boy, stain his hands in human blood, rather than meet the foul charge which had been brought against him?—Impossible ! No, no, I cannot, I dare not believe it !—This is the bloody work of others, and not of him. But to think of it is madness!—Let us to the prison, where I can at once ascertain the truth!"

"No, no, with me, with me, De Lacy," answered Lord Raymond, taking his arm, and forcibly leading him in the direction of the castle of St. Aswolph.

In the meantime, the condition of the inmates of "The Flagon," as may be expected, were in a state of great distress, although they were at present ignorant of Godfrey having escaped from prison, and the dreadful circumstances that had followed. His mother's anguish was almost past endurance, and she was for hours in a state of utter insensibility, and Ernnestine was deaf to all the remonstrances and expostulations of old Hubert Clensham, who, to tell the truth, as well as his dame, was in a very little better condition, and much needed that fortitude and resignation with which he sought to inspire others. They waited most anxiously the return of Ranulph, and it was with the utmost difficulty that Hubert could prevent his niece (when she had regained her sensibility), from hastening herself to the prison, and rushing into the presence of her unfortunate son, so insupportable was the anxiety which she felt to see him. Ernnestine too, she would freely, readily have accompanied her, and it required all the firmness and resolution the innkeeper could muster, to prevent them from putting their wishes into effect, which, in their then agitated and frantic state, would, most likely, have been productive of the most painful results, and could have rendered them no good, but on the contrary, only serve to shake the nerves of Godfrey, and to increase their own misery.

"It is useless to give way to this overwhelming affliction, since sorrowing will not mend it," observed old Hubert, "we should not, conscious as we all are of Godfrey's innocence, despair. He must be able triumphantly to rebut this hideous charge, and, for I see my part, not the slightest evidence against him, except the fact of his being found standing over the body of the unfortunately murdered youth, and his weapon stained with blood, which could easily have been done by accident. To be sure, many knowing his love for Ernnestine, might suspect him of having been excited to do such a deed, by jealousy, he being rejected, and Reginald affianced to Ernnestine."

"Oh, no, no," exclaimed Ernnestine, the deep red blushes of maiden modesty mounting to her cheeks, "they were friends, the best of friends, and it was not long before Godfrey and Reginald left the inn together, that the latter forfeited all claim to my hand, and abandoned his suit in favour of him who has ever had possession of my heart. This day, it had been Reginald's intention to have urged our passion to thee, and to have endeavoured to persuade thee to consent to our nuptials. Oh, Reginald, generous, kind-hearted youth, little didst thou think of the dreadful, the untimely fate which was so soon to befall thee!"

"Is this true?" asked Hubert, eagerly.

"Thinkest thou that I would give utterance to that which was otherwise than true?" demanded Ernnestine, with a look of astonishment at the observations that the innkeeper had made use of.

"Nay, nay, pardon me, child," said Hubert, "I meant not to say so, but my mind is so distracted, that I scarcely know what I am giving utterance to. But, pr'thee seek to compose thyself, my poor girl, and all may yet be well.

Providence will not suffer the innocent to fall a victim, and that he is guiltless, who that has known Godfrey de Lacy, will attempt to deny?"

Ernnestine sighed heavily, without making any reply, and running towards Edith, who was weeping violently, she sufficiently stifled her own emotions to endeavour to impart consolation to her, who had been to her more than a mother.

Hour after hour waned away, and evening advanced, but still Rauulph de Lacy did not return, and their anxiety to know the reason of his protracted absence, exceeded all bounds. Hubert and the others frequently went to the window, to see whether he could behold him approaching, but every time he was more and more disappointed.

" Give me my cloak, dame," at length he said, " I will go forth, and see if I can meet him ; something particular must have taken place, or he would never have tarried thus."

Old Maud reached down her husband's cloak, which hung upon a peg in the parlour, and having put it on, he was about to sally forth, when an exclamation of astonishment, not unmixed with terror, from Ernnestine, arrested his attention, and drew the observation of himself and Edith towards her.

" What ails thee, child?" inquired Hubert, as he advanced towards the spot where he was standing, " what has alarmed thee?"

" There, dost thou not see those men approaching so hurriedly this way?" said Ernnestine, pointing in the direction on which her attention was rivetted ; " they are certainly coming hither, and now they advance nearer, they look agitated, and—what can have happened?"

Hubert had immediately fixed his eyes upon a mob of soldiers and others, who were hurrying towards the inn, and although he pretended not to be so, he was very little less alarmed than Ernnestine, and instantly foreboded some additional calamity. However, it would not do to let his wife or the two other females notice his agitation, or it would have increased theirs, and have rendered it a scene of confusion, which might not have been easily overcome, and in as firm a voice as he had the power to assume, he observed :—

" Nay, my love, do not agitate thyself; why should we fear? We are innocent of any crime, and ——"

A loud knocking at the outer door interrupted Hubert's speech, and it not being opened immediately, it was followed by a series of kicks from numerous feet, intermingled with the sound of several voices.

Hubert, leaving Ernnestine in the care of his wife, went to the door, which he opened, and he had no sooner done so than the room was half filled with people.

" Marry, and what is the reason of this abrupt entrance into my house?" demanded old Hubert, mustering up more firmness than might have been expected.—" By the mass, and it does appear as if thou wert bent to take it by storm."

" By'r Lady," answered one of the men, who seemed to be the head of the party, " an' I am much mistaken if thou dost not deserve to have thine house pulled about thine ears. But I have no time to bandy words with thee here.

Guard the outer doors, and see to the casements. Hubert Clensham, in the name of the king, I demand to search, well, thy premises."

"For what?" sternly demanded Hubert.

"For a villain!" was the laconic reply.

"Of whom dost thou speak? Master Hubert Clensham is not in the habit of harbouring villains in his house, knave!"

"We seek Godfrey de Lacy, who stands charged with the murder of Lord St. Aswolph's Esquire;" said the man.

"What meanest thou?" asked the astonished Hubert, and looking eagerly in the countenance of the officer as he demanded the question.

"By Saint Paul!" cried the officer, "and thou art not indeed unconscious of the circumstance, old man, thou actest thy part to a miracle. But thou art not so ignorant as not to know that supposed murderer has made his escape from prison this day, and, in order to effect his object, hath shed the blood of the gaoler and the sentinels who obstructed him."

A loud and piercing shriek from Edith followed this speech, and she sank, apparently lifeless, upon the floor, while Ernnestine seemed completely transfixed to the spot in stupified amazement and horror, and did not appear to move a muscle of her countenance.

Such was the agitation which the shock caused in the mind of Hubert, that he was unable to speak, while the officer, giving some hasty instructions to his men, turned to him and said :—

"Come, come, old man, it is useless for thee to pretend to all this ignorance

No. 10

of the matter; thou knowest full well that the assassin is either concealed in thy house, or thou knowest the place where he is secreted. He cannot escape the hands of justice, and all those who connive at his concealment, will not fail to meet with that punishment which such an offence deserves."

" It cannot be true," at length ejaculated Hubert, wildly, " it is some base fabrication of the brain, to torture an innocent family. Godfrey de Lacy fled,— impossible !"

" I tell thee it is true," replied the officer, " but this pretended astonishment will not avail thee; thou knowest full well, old man, all about it, and probably thinkest to detain me in converse, while the murderer is effecting his escape from hence. Guard well every entrance, comrades, and see that no person quits the house, while I prosecute a strict search after the fugitive."

His orders were promptly obeyed, and the officer and two others, left the apartment and retired up-stairs, while those below examined every nook and corner, in which it was likely that a human being could be concealed; but of course, it was without success. In the meantime, poor old Hubert paced the room in a state of the utmost distraction, and could scarcely believe but that all he had heard was a mere delusion, whichever way it was, however, it seemed that they were doomed to heavy trials, and he shuddered when he reflected upon the shocking effect it would have upon his parents and Ernnestine.

Edith was still insensible, and was being supported in the arms of Maud, while Ernnestine remained transfixed to the spot, the emblem of horror and despair.

In a few minutes the officer and his companions returned to the parlour.

" Well," said the former, " at any rate, the fellow is not there, and it appears that thou hast been no more successful in thy search down stairs. They have managed the business well, but still, I am resolved that he shall not elude our vigilance. I know not whether I ought not to take these people into custody, at any rate, two of ye shall remain behind here, and take up your quarters for awhile, until such times as the fugitive is retaken, or some clue discovered to the place of his conceealment. The rest of you follow me."

With these words, the officer and his companions left the inn, with the exception of the two men whom he had chosen to remain behind, in order that they might keep watch.

While this was going on, Maud had removed the insensible form of her niece into an inner chamber, and Ernnestine was, by the order of Master Hubert, consigned to the care of a female servant, who led her from the apartment into the chamber which was appropriated to her use, where every thing that humanity could suggest was done to tranquillize her feelings, after the severe shock they had received.

As soon as the females were taken care of, and the two men who had been left at the inn, had been served with an excellent sack-posset, the good qualities of which they seemed capable of discussing with no small ability, Hubert, unable to endure the state of suspense and horror which the assertions of the officer had excited, put on his cloak, and left the house, determined to make the best of his way to the prison, to ascertain the particulars of the shocking affair, and, if possible, to learn the cause of the protracted absence of Ranulph. As he walked along, the most dismal thoughts and apprehensions crossed his mind, and his worst fears were soon confirmed by the persons he met, who were all full of the wonderful escape of Godfrey de Lacy, and horror-struck at the dreadful crimes he was supposed to have perpetrated to effect his design. The feelings of the poor old man, incapable as he knew Godfrey to be of the awful crimes imputed to him, may be easily imagined, and he tottered on towards the prison, amid the commiseration of some, and the brutal remarks of others, who had been the foremost to express their horror and detestation of the crimes committed, and the last to lean to the side of mercy, and not condemn the unfortunate young man, until his guilt was made fully manifest.

The interview between Lord St. Aswolph and the unhappy Ranulph de Lacy, was a long one; and, in vain, they sought to hit upon some plan to bring about the developement of this strange and awful affair, and to account for the disappearance of Godfrey under the circumstances related; but the more they conversed upon the subject, the more did they become bewildered, and, at length, they separated, without having come to any satisfactory conclusion, only being resolved to use the most indefatigable exertions to discover the retreat of the unfortunate youth, which was the only chance they had of solving the mystery. Certainly suspicion was now stronger than ever against Godfrey, for if he had fled from the prison on his own accord, it had a great appearance of the consciousness of guilt, or he would otherwise have met his trial with that firmness which ever characterizes the person accused wrongfully. But it was very evident that he must have had some assistance, and the most probable idea they could form was, that Godfrey had been made the dupe of some villains who had some sinister design in view, the nature of which they were utterly at a loss to form the least conjecture of.

At length, unable to come to any decided satisfactory conclusion, Ranulph de Lacy quitted the castle of St. Aswolph, Lord Raymond having previously assured him of the deep interest he took in the painful affair, and of his determination to do all that was in his power to unravel the mystery in which it was at present enveloped, and in spite of the recent circumstances, to do all that he could to make the innocence of Godfrey apparent.

It was late in the evening when Ranulph de Lacy reached the inn, for he had been to his own residence first, not knowing whether or not his wife was there, and he was afterwards in too violent a state of agitation to venture to the first-named place. How could he ever impart the horrible intelligence of Godfrey's flight, and the several murders he was supposed to have committed in effecting the same, to Edith and Ernnestine? They would never be able to support the knowledge of this shocking event;—it would certainly kill them, or bereave them of their senses, and when he remembered the lamentable state in which he had left his wife and Ernnestine, when he quitted the inn in the morning, he saw nothing but despair around him.

He wandered for some time in the wood, reflecting upon these circumstances, and seeking in vain to remember anything which might impart a single ray of hope or comfort to them, but all his efforts were unavailable. Again the predictions of the wizard recurred to his memory, and the manner in which they had been so far realized, impressed itself most powerfully upon his mind. But why should Fate pursue him with troubles so severe?—What had he ever done that he should thus incur the wrath of the Almighty?—It seemed as though some infernal spell was upon him, and Ranulph de Lacy, who had hitherto scorned to give way to the weakness of grief, sunk beneath these accumulated troubles, and became truly wretched.

But, that Godfrey was guiltless of the crimes imputed to him, he was confident; his noble, his virtuous nature would revolt at the bare idea of such atrocity. By what means his escape from the prison had been effected, and by whom, (for he was certain he could not have done it himself,) he was the most at a loss to conjecture. But what could ever induce any one to run such a risk, and how could they have persuaded Godfrey to their wishes, and thus to cast upon himself the stigma of being guilty of the crimes of which he was accused?—In vain he sought to solve the terrible mystery; the more he ruminated upon it, the deeper did he become involved in perplexity.

Tired of wandering, in this dismal mood, he had placed his back against the trunk of a tree, and with his arms folded across his chest, was indulging in these gloomy reflections, when he was startled by hearing some one pronounce his name. He looked up, and beheld standing before him the tall and muscular form of a man, enveloped in a huge mantle, who was gazing earnestly upon him. His features were regular and handsome, and although Ranulph could not recollect where and under what circumstances he had seen him before, the countenance of the man was perfectly familiar to him.

"Ranulph de Lacy," repeated the stranger.

"Who art thou, and how knowest thou my name?" demanded the bowyer.

"It matters not," returned the other, "I am thy friend."

"How am I to discover that?"

"By the services I shall render thee."

"Methinks thou boastest vainly, stranger," said Ranulph, with an incredulous shake of the head, "why shouldst thou wish to serve me?"

"In return for the good thou once did me," was the reply.

"Ah!" exclaimed Ranulph, looking earnestly in the man's face, but still he could not recal to his memory where he had seen him before, although he was firmly convinced that this was not the first time they had met. "To what dost thou allude?—What good have I ever done thee?"

"That thou mayest know at some future time," replied the man, "at present, it is enough for thee to know that I can and will serve thee."

"How?"

"By saving the life of thy son!"

"Ah!" cried Ranulph, "what knowest thou of him?"

"That he is safe, and will shortly be restored to thee, when his innocence of the crimes of which he is unjustly accused, can be clearly established."

"Liar!" ejaculated Ranulph, "thou comest here to sport with the feelings of a broken-hearted father, and to endeavour to excite hopes in his bosom which thou hast not the power to realize."

"Not so warm, Ranulph de Lacy," said the stranger, dispassionately, "thou dost me wrong by thy suspicions. "I tell thee again, Godfrey, thy son, is safe, and under my protection!"

"Impossible!" said De Lacy, " and who and what art thou?"

" One whose name is feared by all.'

, " I would know it."

" Osmond, the Avenger !" was the answer, and without waiting to say another word, the robber-captain turned upon his heel, and before Ranulph could recover from his astonishment, was out of sight.

" Can what I have heard be true ?" ejaculated Ranulph, when he was restored to a consciousness of what had happened to him. " Ah! the words of the wizard, they are corroborated ;—did he not tell me that my poor boy had become the associate of the votaries of crime and infamy ?—Good God ! how could my son in a moment of weakness thus degrade himself, and bring misery and disgrace upon his unhappy family ?—But I will seek him out ;—1 will to this robber's retreat, and insist upon seeing him."

He turned to go towards St. Alwyn Castle, when he suddenly bethought himself, that, as it was now getting late, and his absence from the inn had been protracted beyond the time they had expected him back, a considerable deal, and that they would be alarmed lest anything should have happened to him, he resolved to defer his visit to the robber's retreat until the following morning, when he would at all risks go, and ascertain whether or not the robber-chief had spoken the truth ; but, still he considered it would be best for him not to say anything to them about what had occured to him, and that would save them a considerable deal of care and anxiety, at the resolution which he had formed.

Having come to this determination, Ranulph de Lacy slowly directed his footsteps towards " The Flagon," meditating with terror upon the misery which the recent dreadful events would cause them.

Old Hubert having been unsuccessful in seeking for Ranulph, had returned to the inn, and right glad was he when he saw him come back ; but the gloom, the heavy care which was settled upon his brow, told him how deeply the barbed arrow of sorrow had entered his heart. Edith was still in a very melancholy condition, but somewhat more composed than she had been in the morning. Ernnestine, too, was better, or rather she had made a powerful effort to stifle her own feelings, for the purpose of endeavouring to impart consolation to Edith, and in which she had succeeded much better than could have been expected. The consciousness of Godfrey's innocence, and the certainty which she felt that Omnipotence would not permit him to suffer for the guilty, tended to arouse her from the afflicting state of despondency and despair under which she had at first suffered, and Ranulph felt much relieved when he beheld her.

The return of De Lacy added to the composure of Edith and her foster-daughter, and he exerted himself to the utmost to add to the good work which Ernnestine had begun, in which he succeeded beyond his most sanguine expect-taions.

" The will of the Almighty be done," piously exclaimed Edith, raising her eyes towards heaven, " He knows the innocence of my poor boy, and will in His infinite mercy and justice, rescue him from the danger which now threatens him."

" He will, He will, dearest Edith," said her husband, " let us pray to Him, and although such heavy clouds of grief now hang over us, He will quickly disperse them, and render us once more happy !"

The eyes of the beauteous Ernnestine once more brightened up with renewed hope. They all knelt down, and with fervour and sincerity, devoutly offered a prayer to the Most High. After this they felt more calm and collected, and could more coolly converse upon their sorrows, and form conjectures as to the cause of Godfrey's mysterious disappearance. At length, they retired to their separate chambers for the night, where they could give free indulgence to their thoughts without any fear of being interrupted.

At an early hour in the morning, Ranulph having informed his wife that he had some business of importance to go upon, left the inn, and proceeded through the deep green-wood towards that spot where the strong castle of St. Alwyn stood, its lofty towers being seen at a considerable distance, far o'ertopping the summits of the trees. This place was carefully avoided by the most courageous, for the robbers were such desperate ruffians, that the vulgar and the superstitious imagined they were invulnerable, and that each possessed a charmed life.—But De Lacy was an entire stranger to fear, and if there might be any confidence placed in the words of Osmond, (who had told him he was his friend, and that it was his intention to serve him), he had never less cause for apprehension than on the present occasion.

It was not long before he arrived at the castle, whose black and flinty walls seemed to frown defiance upon invasion. But here he was placed in a difficulty he had not thought upon before he started. The castle was surrounded by a deep moat, and the drawbridge was drawn up, so that it was impossible for him to gain an entrance. He was quite bewildered, and at a loss how to act, but to return home without accomplishing his object, he could not bear even to think upon for a moment; for nothing could exceed the anxiety which he felt to be satisfied whether Osmond had indeed spoken the truth, and if his unfortunate son was really under his protection. He walked round the moat, with the hope of seeing some other part where he might gain an entrance to the castle, but he was unsuccessful, and returned again to the place where the drawbridge was fixed, uncertain how to act. He had not stood there long, however, when the drawbridge was let down, and, the next minute, several of the robbers came forth, and crossing it, reached the very spot where Ranulph was standing.

They started back with no little astonishment when they beheld De Lacy, and the intrepid air with which he stood and gazed upon them.

"Ah! a stranger?" cried the foremost of the robbers, "what dost thou here?"

"Doubtless he would pry into our secrets," said another, "he is a spy, away with him to our captain."

"He it is I seek," answered Ranulph, firmly, "yet I am no spy."

"Thy wish shall be gratified," said the first speaker,—"but remember thou must give a good account of thyself, or thou wilt have reason to repent thy boldness in coming hither. This way, follow me."

Ranulph De Lacy folded his arms in his mantle, and without making any reply to the robber, followed him across the drawbridge, and entered the castle. After traversing the different apartments and passages, which we have before described, they at length arrived at the cavern or vault, in which Osmond and his comrades were accustomed to assemble, and Ranulph could not help wondering at all he beheld, and the systematic manner in which everything appeared to be conducted, but the apartment above mentioned, created his especial astonishment. He was not, however, suffered to indulge in these thoughts long, for a familiar voice called upon him by name, and looking up, he beheld Osmond seated at the head of the long board whereon the robbers conducted their revels. About sixty determined looking men were seated around the table, who arose when he entered, but immediately resumed their seats when they heard the captain mention his name.

Ranulph cast an eager glance around, thinking to behold Godfrey, but he was not there.

"Welcome, Ranulph De Lacy," observed Osmond, beckoning the former to approach. "Hast thou then ventured to the retreat of the daring robber chief, who bids defiance to those laws, which only the foolish and the servile obey?"

"An thou speakest the truth, yesterday," returned Ranulph, "thou art my friend, therefore, were I even so disposed, I have no cause to fear thee."

"Truly spoken," said Osmond, "I am thy friend;—but thou needst not look so anxiously around; he thou seekest is not here!"

"I see he is not," observed Ranulph, sternly, "thou hast deceived me. I was a fool to place any reliance in thy word."

"Nay, not so fast, Ranulph De Lacy," returned the robber, "Osmond's word was never yet broken; Godfrey De Lacy, thy son, is in my keeping, but it is yet early, and he has not arisen. Ulric, hie thee to the chamber of the youth and bring him hither."

Ulric bowed and left the room, and De Lacy stood in trembling suspense until his return, and the robber chief did not offer to interrupt him. Soon, Ulric came back, but alone, and alarm and confusion were depicted on his features.

"How now!" exclaimed Osmond, starting up, "what means this? where is the young man?"

"He is not in the room, which was allotted to him to repose in," answered Ulric, "he has fled."

"Fled?" cried the robber chief, in a tone of the most indescribable astonishment; "impossible!"

"Marry and I speak the truth, captain," answered Ulric, "if thou doubtest me, thou canst speedily satisfy thyself."

"It is a mere cheat, a juggle!" exclaimed Ranulph de Lacy, in accents of wrath, "thou hast trepanned me hither for some sinister purpose, my son was never in thy power."

"Ranulph de Lacy," replied Osmond, in a calm manner, "this is no time to bandy words; but I tell thee again that thou dost me wrong by the suppositions thou dost entertain of the motives of my conduct. What sinister design thinkest thou I could have against thee?—Besides, thou camest here of thine own free will; I invited thee not. Follow me, I request thee."

Ranulph laid his hand on his sword, and without making another observation at that time, followed the robber chief in haste through the several caverns and passages, until they reached the apartment which had been allotted to Godfrey to repose in. It was entirely vacated, and no traces of its late occupier were left behind.

"S'death!" exclaimed Osmond, "but the bird is flown to a certainty; what could have induced him to have done so? The foolish boy will frustrate the schemes I have formed to save his life, and to rescue his character from reproach!"

"And what proof hast thou to convince me my son has ever been here?" demanded Ranulph, who being incredulous, expressed no astonishment at the circumstance, which he thought had merely been invented by the robber-chief, to further some design or the other.

"Still art thou doubtful?" said Osmond. "Forsooth, I thought better of thee, Ranulph de Lacy. Proof I have none, if thou wilt not believe me and my comrades;—ah! what is this?—A letter!—Yes, and addressed to me."

Osmond picked up the letter, which, having fallen off the table on which it had been placed, was not at first noticed. He unfolded it, and having hastily glanced over the contents, he turned to Ranulph, and placing it in his hand, said—

"There, marry, an' thou wantest proof, methinks thou wilt consider that sufficient; knowest thou that hand-writing?"

"Ah! by the mass! it is my son's!" exclaimed the bowyer, recognizing the characters in a moment; "here is his name, too; I cannot doubt any longer."

Eagerly the father of Godfrey perused the contents, which were addressed to Osmond, and ran as follows:—

"I cannot reconcile my mind to the course thou wouldst I should pursue to gain the establishment of my innocence, although I do heartily thank thee for the interest thou hast taken in my fate, and the risk thou hast run, with no other motives I feel assured than a wish to serve me. I go to resign myself into the hands of the officers of the law, and depend upon the consciousness of mine own innocence and the goodness of the Almighty to get an acquittal.

"GODFREY DE LACY."

"Gracious Heaven!" ejaculated Ranulph, "then, by this time, my unhappy son is once more incarcerated in that dark and loathsome dungeon, and believed to be the perpetrator of all those dreadful crimes!"

"Nay," observed Osmond, "it may not yet be too late to save him. Ranulph de Lacy, wilt thou entrust thyself in my company?"

"Thou meanest me no harm?" remarked Ranulph.

"On the contrary, I would serve thee; I would save the life of thy son.

"I _will_ entrust myself with thee," said the bowyer.

"Let us away then," observed Osmond; "Ulric, follow with fifty of our men at a short distance, so that thou mayest be ready in case we should need thy assistance."

"What wouldst thou do?" demanded Ranulph.

"Thou shalt see anon," replied the robber-chief, "at present we have not a moment to lose. Come, come, we must not tarry longer, or it will be useless going at all."

The robbers hastily buckled on their swords, and prepared to follow the lieutenant, while Osmond and Ranulph hastened from the cavern, by the same way they had entered it, and the drawbridge being let down, in a few moments they were in the forest, and wending their way with rapid steps towards the prison, from whence, by the aid of the robber-chief, Godfrey had so recently made his escape.

CHAPTER VIII.

" Hold, slaves !
By the Gods, the first whose murderous hand
Shall be raised to harm him, dies !
He is innocent of the crime !—I say he is innocent !"

IN the meantime the persons we left at the hostelrie of Hubert Clensham, as
may be supposed, were in a state of the most painful anxiety and suspense as regarded the fate of the unfortunate Godfrey, and what would be the result of this
horrible affair. Still did both Edith and Ernnestine behave with far greater
composure than could possibly have been expected, and tried to await the issue
of these very melancholy and perplexing circumstances with patience. The
excitement which had been caused in the neighbourhood, by the murder of
Reginald, and the others, hourly increased, and the inn was surrounded by a
crowd of persons, who expressed their indignation against the supposed guilty
person in language of no very measured description. The evidences of Godfrey's
guilt appeared so strong, that the effect it had upon the minds of the idle rabble
was too powerful to be eradicated, and, notwithstanding the high character
which the unfortunate youth had borne previously, they all pronounced him
guilty, and but for the high esteem in which they held Hubert Clensham, they
would have broken into the inn, and probably have committed some outrage
upon the inmates.

No. 11

The brutal conduct of the ignorant mob had a most painful effect upon the minds of Ernnestine and Edith; and Hubert, who was fearful that it would be productive of some fatal consequences, at length, went forth, and, addressing some words to the crowd assembled, intreated them to disperse. His words had the desired effect; they gradually departed, only two or three stragglers remained for a short time behind, and they having exhausted their stock of information and speculation upon the dreadful affair, at length became tired, and slinked off also, leaving the coast clear.

We have before stated that Ranulph had not informed them whither he was going on the morning when he left early, with the design of hastening to the retreat of the robbers; but his absence caused no surprise in the bosoms of his friends, as it was only natural to suppose that until some explanation of the mysterious affair, which at present engrossed their whole attention, and excited their deepest interest, was obtained, he would not be able to rest, and that he would make all the inquiry he possibly could. As hour after hour passed away, and still he did not return, they began to feel somewhat uneasy, and it required all the arguments that it was in the power of Hubert to make use of, to quiet their apprehensions.

The two fellows who had been left at the inn by the officer, enjoyed their quarters amazingly, for the refreshments disposed of by mine host of the "Flagon," were of the finest quality, and they did not forget to pay their respects to them as frequently as they had an opportunity. In this respect, Master Hubert was no churl, and often treated them, for which they repaid him by behaving with less insolence than men of their class were in the habit of doing.

On the day of which we have been writing, they were seated in the back parlour of the inn, with a stiff sack-posset before them, which was the fourth they had already had, and so much did they seem to relish it, that it did not appear likely that they would be disposed to leave off drinking it in a hurry. The effects of this goodly fare had imparted an unusual glow to their countenances, and as they tumbled off dose after dose, their noses became more rubicund, and their tongues wagged more flippantly.

" By the mass! our host sells some excellent stuff, Maurice," ejaculated one of them, smacking his lips, and then taking another hearty swig, " this it is that nourishes a man, makes him happy, and opens his heart!"

" Forsooth, Henric, and it does as thou sayest—that is, if it opens a man's heart, what a generous, good soul thou ought to be," answered Maurice, with a grin, " for I never saw a man that could better play his part with it than thou canst."

" Ha! ha! ha!" laughed Henric, " why, I do confess me that I am no flincher from the good things of this life, and i'faith thou hast thyself a most thirsty throat, as methinks Master Hubert will find out before we leave."

" 'Psha! Henric, thou dost scandalize my character," said the other, with an ominous hiccup, " thou knowest full well that I cannot bear to see any intoxicating beverages before me."

" And therefore dost thou put them out of sight as speedily as thou canst," quoth Henric; " I must say, though, that it is no unpleasant thing to have plenty to eat and drink when it costs nothing for the same. Our host is a good fellow."

"Thou sayest right, and sorry am I that he has got this trouble in his family," said Maurice.

"Aye, it is bad for Master Hubert," observed Henric, "but his grand-daughter, as I trow it is, must feel it more severely, for Reginald was to have been married to her."

"By the saints! she is a beauteous girl," said Maurice, "and I would not mind——but, what noise was that?"

Maurice jumped upon his feet as he spoke, and looked around him.

"I heard no noise," remarked Henric.

"It sounded like the closing of a door."

"Likely enough," replied Henric, "blown to by the wind, which whistles pretty sharply. Come, sit thee down again, and let us toast the fair maid of the inn."

At that moment a scream smote their ears, which seemed to proceed from the room up stairs.

"Hearest thou that?" demanded Maurice; "perhaps thou wilt say that that is the wind also?"

"Something has happened, it is very plain," said Henric; and arising from his seat, he accompanied Maurice up stairs. The room door was closed, but there were voices of lamentation to be heard. Not waiting for any ceremony, Maurice threw open the door, and a scene presented itself which filled them with astonishment.—Clasping the forms of the distracted Ernnestine and his mother to his bosom, was Godfrey de Lacy, while poor old Hubert and Maud stood by, the very images of despair and horror.

"By the mass! it is the murderer," exclaimed Maurice.

"'Tis false," ejaculated Ernnestine, in a firm tone, and turning a look of indignation upon the man; "he is no murderer; his hands were never yet stained with the blood of his fellow-creatures, and thou shalt not tear him from us. I will cling to him, and if he must die, we will perish together!"

"Godfrey de Lacy, thou art our prisoner," said Henric, advancing towards him, and attempting to remove Ernnestine from his embrace.

"Bold, presumptuous varlet," exclaimed Godfrey, his cheeks glowing with resentment, as he pushed the man away, "lay but a finger upon this afflicted damsel, and I will strike thee a corpse at my feet!—Nay, stand back, but a few moments, and I will attend ye; I do not wish to escape."

The men drew back, and gazed on the melancholy scene with some expression of pity.

"Mother—Ernnestine," ejaculated Godfrey, in a voice almost choked with emotion, and kissing the cheeks and foreheads of both alternately, as they clung with frenzied eagerness to him, and sobbed upon his bosom, "I implore ye to calm your feelings, and believe me when I tell ye, that all will yet be well, and that I shall shortly be restored to ye, without the slightest stain upon my character!—Mother, release me, I pray;—oh, to see thee suffer thus, unmans me;—Ernnestine, for the love of heaven! endeavour to restrain thine anguish; I racks my brain to madness to see thee suffer thus! Our evil star will not always preside!—No, no, my sweetest, there are yet happier days in store for us, so pray thee compose thyself, and rest assured that we shall be restored to each other, when sorrow shall no longer attend us, and when I shall have fully rebutted the foul charge which is brought against me! Take them from me, my uncle, and endeavour to impart to them that consolation of which they stand so much in need."

"Oh, God! my heart will burst," sobbed the agonised Edith, throwing her arms round the neck of Godfrey, and hugging him yet more closely to her bosom ; "my son, my son, they shall not separate us; they shall not again bear thee to their frightful dungeons!—I will cling to thee with the power of a giant, and defy them to tear me from thee !—Ernnestine, hold him, do not let them approach him !—Villains, have ye no feeling for a wretched mother ?—Stand off, I say—ye shall not touch him !—Hubert—Maud—ye surely will not let them take him from us, and drag him to certain death?"

"Edith," observed Hubert, approaching her, and endeavouring to remove her from the arms of her son, " I beseech thee to appease the violence of thy grief, which can effect no good, and will but add to the sufferings of thy unfortunate son."

"Yes, Hubert says aright," said Godfrey, gently withdrawing himself from the close embraces of his mother and Ernnestine, upon whose cheeks he pressed a fervent and farewell kiss; " bless thee, bless thee both!—There, there, take them, Hubert; farewell, and may all good angels watch over and protect them."

Edith and Ernnestine, who seemed to be unconscious of what was passing, suffered themselves to be led into another room, and Godfrey then clasping his forehead, and covering his face with his hands for a few moments, turned to Hubert and Maud, with a look of manly fortitude, and said,—

"My dearest friends, farewell; remember me in your prayers, and believe me that I shall be able clearly to remove the dreadful suspicion which at present rests upon me."

The old man and woman embraced him ; they tried to speak, but the power of their grief choked their utterance. At length, releasing himself from their arms, he turned to the two men, and in accents of firmness and resignation, said,—

"I am ready to attend ye ; lead on."

Before Hubert or his wife had power to speak, Godfrey de Lacy had left the inn, and was on his way to the prison.

Osmond, the robber-chief, and Ranulph de Lacy, followed at a short distance by Ulric and the robbers, who had been odered to attend, pursued their way with all the haste they could, and hitherto the bowyer was so confused with what he had heard, and at the singular interest which the robber seemed to take in the fate of his son, that he had not thought to inquire even what Osmond purposed doing; but when they had got some distance from the Castle of St. Alwyn, he suddenly stopped and interrogated him on the subject.

"There is no time for words upon the subject at present," replied Osmond ; "let it content thee that I am resolved at all hazards that Godfrey shall be free. If we hasten on we may overtake him before he reaches the prison, and then thou canst easily persuade him to return to the castle, where he would have secure enough now, had he not so foolishly rejected the good offices I intended him."

" But suppose he should have reached the prison ?"

"Why, then we must force an entrance, and drag him from the place," returned Osmond; "it is not so well guarded, and were it ever so, Osmond and his bold comrades would not fear but that they would meet with success."

"The thought is madness," said Ranulph, " and I will not be a party to any such scheme. It will but increase the prejudice against my unfortunate son, and can effect no ultimate good ; for, should we for the present rescue him, there cannot be a doubt but that he would soon fall into their hands again, and then his judges would be more ready to condemn him, although innocent of the crimes with which he is charged. Besides, should he even be acquitted, would not his name be contaminated for ever when it should appear that he was the friend and associate of robbers ?"

" Thou talkest madly, Ranulph de Lacy," said Osmond, " and if thou wouldst be guided by me, all would be well; I pledge my troth, that Godfrey shall be restored to liberty, and that not the least discredit shall attach itself to his name. Ere long thou mayest be inclined to trust the robber-chief, the outlaw, and to court that friendship which thou now seemest afraid to accept."

Before Ranulph could make any answer to this, their attention was arrested by a loud noise, which rent the air, and which appeared to be at a little distance from them. It was a loud shouting from a number of voices, and between the pauses that ensued, they could distinguish such exclamations as " Hang the Villain !" " Kill him !" and many others, of an equally savage character.

They hastily passed through an opening in the wood, and immediately a dense mass of people advancing in the direction they were pursuing, burst upon their sight.—Missiles were flying about in all directions, and they seemed to be aimed at some wretched individual in the centre of them, who, several soldiers were endeavouring to protect from their fury, but evidently with little success. The mob came nearer; Osmond and Ranulph instinctively rushed forward to meet it, and forced their way into the centre of it—but who shall describe the horror and agitation of the latter, when he found that the object of their wrath was his unfortunate son. Yes, it was Godfrey, who was pale and bleeding, through the wounds he had already received by the missiles that had been thrown at him.

The excitement created by the circumstance of so many murders, and all supposed to have been perpetrated by one man, had increased to an almost indescribable degree, and as Henric and Maurice proceeded with their charge from the " Flagon," a mob of persons surrounded them, and assailed the wretched Godfrey with every epithet of detestation they could make use of. In vain the officers remonstrated with them—in vain the unhappy youth himself appealed to them ; they were deaf to everything, and would certainly have forced him from the custody of the officers, and put their threats into execution, had it not been for the timely arrival of some soldiers upon the spot, who flew to the aid of the two men who were endeavouring to convey Godfrey to prison. Every step they proceeded the crowd increased, and they seemed determined to force him from the custody of the soldiers, and to inflict a summary punishment upon him.

"Down ! down ! brutal knaves !" cried the enraged and distracted Ranulph, when he discovered that it was his son, and rushing, sword in hand, in amongst them, followed by Osmond.   Two of the mob were instantly stretched upon the earth, and such was the astonishment and confusion their sudden and desperate conduct occasioned, that the men fell back in consternation at their approach, and they had nearly worked their way up to the side of the prisoner, ere the soldiers or the crowd seemed to recollect themselves ; but the moment afterwards Ranulph was recognized, and several voices exclaimed—

"It is de Lacy, the bowyer !—death to the whole family of the murderer !"

Again the attack was renewed with redoubled fury, the soldiers and the mob pressing upon Ranulph and Osmond, and it appeared to be not at all improbable that they would indeed put their threats into execution, when the robber-chief suddenly raised his horn to his lips, and blew a blast which made the wood re-echo again, and immediately afterwards, Ulric, and the other robbers, who had been close upon the spot, came pouring in among them, dealing destruction on all sides, and filling those they attacked with amazement and terror.   They made but a feeble resistance, and the soldiers being unable to stand against the desperate attack of the robbers, gave way, and, as well as the mob, fled in all directions, and Godfrey was left in the power of his friends.

For a minute or two the confusion caused by this unexpected event, rendered Godfrey and his father incapable of moving or speaking, but, at length, when they found that the coast was clear, they rushed into each other's arms, and embraced one another with a fervour which the circumstance will account for.

"There is no time to be lost," said Osmond, "let us away to St. Alwyn Castle ; for, doubtless, we shall, if we remain here, be surrounded by such numbers that we shall find it impossible to resist, and Godfrey will then once more fall into their power."

"I seek not to escape," said the latter—"nay, it is my wish that I should submit to the trial to which I must be subjected ere I can prove my innocence."

"'Psha !" cried Osmond, "and thinkest thou they will give thee an impartial trial ?—No ; they would condemn thee unheard, and hang thee like a dog.   Even now the infuriated wretches, but for our timely arrival to thy rescue, would have hung thee to the branch of one of the loftiest trees in the wood !—Come, come let us away !"

Ere either Godfrey or Ranulph could make any reply to this, they beheld a large party of soldiers, headed by the officer who had been sent in search of Godfrey to "The Flagon," approaching rapidly towards them.

"Curses on thy tardiness," cried Osmond, "we are now placed in another dilemma through it.   We must have a severe struggle for it, or we shall be overpowered ; they far outnumber us.   Stand to, comrades, and fight your hardest.   Osmond, and his brave fellows, have had to fight against far more fearful odds than these, and yet come off conquerors.   On with ye ! we will make the attack, and try to throw them into confusion, or, at any rate, to keep them engaged, while Godfrey and his father make the best of their way to the castle. Ranulph de Lacy, with thy son, hasten away, and fear not, we shall soon follow ye."

"It is useless," urged Godfrey, "I cannot long escape them, and should I do as thou wishest, I should involve my father in the same danger as myself.   I will not offer any resistance, and I charge thee not to attempt it. I am not unmindful of what I owe thee for thy good intentions towards me, but——"

"Nay, then," interrupted Osmond, "since thou art thus obstinately bent or thine own destruction, I must take more determined steps to prevent thee Surround him, comrades, and shield him and his father from danger with your last drop of blood!"

In an instant, the robbers completely enclosed Godfrey and Ranulph, so that they could not possibly escape, and then, with determined looks, awaited the approach of the soldiers. No sooner had the latter got within reach of their arrows, than the robbers bent their bows, and so certain was their aim, that several of the soldiers were slain; but still, nothing daunted, and resolved to secure their prisoner, at all hazards, they rushed on, and the robbers having thrown aside their bows and arrows, the conflict that ensued, sword-in-hand, was dreadful. Long did it continue, and for some time fortune seemed to be on the side of Osmond and his companions; but, at length, the soldiers contrived to divide them, and, then, Godfrey and his father were completely left alone, and the robbers beginning to fall fast, their desperate spirits became daunted, and they fled in all directions, leaving the former entirely to the mercy of the soldiers, who, of course, immediately secured them.

"Cowards! dastards! traitors!" shouted the robber-chief, completely mad with rage, as he saw his fellows hastening away. But his words were useless, for they were soon out of hearing, and finding that it was to no purpose for him to attempt to go to the aid of Godfrey or his father, he made the best of his way towards his impregnable castle.

In the meantime, Godfrey and Ranulph were hurried away by the soldiers to the prison, where, after being heavily manacled, they were thrown into separate dungeons.

CHAPTER IX.

" Oh, let me only breathe the air,—
  The blessed air that's breath'd by thee ;
And whether on its wings it bear
  Healing or death, 'tis sweet to me!"

LALLA ROOKH.

DURING the time that these events were being enacted, the mind of Lord Raymond St. Aswolph was busily occupied in endeavouring to devise some means to develope the awful mystery which attended the death of his favorite esquire, the unfortunate Reginald, and in seeking to find out some clue to establish the innocence of Godfrey. But this he found to be a task attended with the utmost difficulty; for recent circumstances tended to involve the dreadful affair in still greater ambiguity, and to increase the public excitement against the supposed villain. The escape of Godfrey from the prison, attended as it was with so many dreadful crimes, was an event of such horror, that he endeavoured, but in vain, to solve it, or to find any clue to exonerate the accused. " Had the latter been conscious of his own innocence," reflected Lord Raymond, " would he have shrunk from a public investigation, or have fled from a trial, in which he must have felt confident of being able to disprove the dreadful charge brought against him ?—No ;" common reason told him he would not ! But here there were not only damning proofs that he had fled like a dastard from the said investigation, but in effecting that escape, the murder of three other individuals had been added to that fearful crime of which he was before suspected. And yet, the irreproachable character which Godfrey had hitherto borne, and the high opinion which Lord Raymond had always entertained of him, rendered such a suspicion repugnant to him. Still had the circumstance of the flight of the young man rendered it almost impossible for him to do anything in the affair :—how could he, in fact, advance anything in proof of the innocence of one who had, if really not guilty, apparently taken the very steps to establish his guilt beyond a doubt ? —Besides, how could he do so, with any appearance of reason, when the unfortunate man, of whom he was suspected to be the assassin, was his favourite esquire ;—one on whom he had lavished the greatest favours, and whom he had ever noticed with marked distinction ? It would appear as though he was endeavouring to defeat the ends of justice ; and the only power he could with reason exercise, was to cause a thorough investigation into the circumstances, which the flight of Godfrey had thwarted ; and however guiltless he might be (which he could not help feeling assured he was), the conduct of the accused was fully calculated to prejudice the judges against him.

These thoughts completely distracted the mind of Lord St, Aswolph after Ranulph de Lacy had quitted him. Deep as was the interest he felt in the bowyer's son, yet were his feelings aroused to a tenfold degree, when he reflected upon the anguish it would cause to the beauteous Ernnestine, who, since he had last seen her at the inn, had never for a moment been absent from his thoughts. Her image had haunted him during his waking and sleeping moments, and he could not but acknowledge to himself that the feeling he felt towards her was that of unbounded love ;—of love so powerful, that all that he had heard of the sentiment before, except for *one*, fell far short of it.

" Oh, Ernnestine, lovely and amiable maiden," he soliloquised, " how happy must that individual be, who shall be blest with thine affections ! What a mine of incalculable worth, humble as thou art, art thou in thyself ! What an inestimable treasure !—a treasure beyond all price ! What fortune, what wealth could add charms to thine intrinsic worth ? Methinks it would be Heaven to be assured of thy love, if the next moment were to close the eyes of the happy object of thine affection in death ! Never but once hath mine eyes gazed upon such peerless beauty ; such a concentration of unspeakable worth !—And that one is now——but, let me not think upon the painful subject let me endeavour to erase it from my memory altogether ! But, then, the features of this lovely girl ;—so like her, that I could almost imagine when I gaze upon her that she stood once more before me, in all the ripeness and surpassing beauty of youth ! Methought that another so fair could not exist !—but, here I behold her counterpart.—Her counterpart, say I ?—By Heaven ! she is by far more beauteous

than even that angelic being, upon whom my memory still dwells with such unbounded adoration. But of what use is it my entertaining this passion for one who can never be mine? No; in spite of my rank and wealth, how can I ever hope to win the heart of one whose virtues and whose beauties render her a treasure beyond all price? But, then, to know the misery, the bitter anguish, the shame that she will have to undergo, at the disgrace which will be brought upon her family, should not the innocence of the unfortunate youth, Godfrey, be clearly proved? The dreadful suffering she must now be enduring, tortures my brain to madness! By my soul's welfare, there is no sacrifice I would consider too great, to spare that gentle bosom one moment's respite from grief!—But I waste time. I must see her, and endeavour to impart that consolation and hope to her bosom, which the melancholy situation in which she is placed requires: then to adopt some means to elucidate the dreadful mystery of Reginald's assassination; to seek to unravel the cause of the flight of Godfrey; to discover the real perpetrators of the appalling crimes laid to his charge; and to make the world acquainted with the entire innocence of the accused."

Lord Raymond was about to leave the castle, with the intention of hastening to the " Flagon," when, at that moment, a miniature fell from his bosom and he picked it up with much agitation expressed in his demeanour; as his eyes became rivetted upon it, heavy sighs escaped his bosom, and his lips were compressed with emotion. It was the likeness of a lady, young, and exquisitely lovely; such a one as is but seldom seen; and who appear like angels sent from Heaven for a while, to entrance mankind, and to show how weak in comparison are the inmates of this sublunary world.

No. 12

As Lord Raymond continued to gaze upon this miniaure, his interest appeared to increase, and at length he exclaimed,—

" Wonderful !—As I gaze upon the likeness, my amazement and admiration increases. By Heaven ! every feature, every lineament is the same !—The eyes beaming forth the same gentle expression ;—the same roseate glow upon the cheeks; — the same twin corals, — and fair and graceful neck, and beautifully rounded bosom : Can it be?—Or, is it the effect of enchantment? I could feast my eyes for ever upon it. Ernnestine, beauteous prototype of her who first engaged my affections, thou hast gained that ascendancy over my heart, which nothing on earth can ever destroy !"

As he thus spoke, Lord Raymond pressed the miniature to his lips in a paroxysm of transport, and then replacing it in his bosom, hastened from the apartment and quitted the castle. He had scarcely got beyond the moat, by which the Gothic building was surrounded, when he beheld the tall figure of a grey friar approaching towards him; and when he had got within a few paces of him, he stopped immediately in his path, and folding his arms across his chest, waited to address him.

Lord Raymond, astonished at the singular behaviour of the monk, paused, and gazed at him for a few moments with earnest attention. The monk, however, did not offer to alter his position ; and, as far as his lordship could judge, for his cowl was drawn close around his head, leaving scarcely more than his eyes visible, he seemed to be looking upon him with the deepest interest. At length, seeing that the monk did not seem likely to move, he advanced, and having come close to him, greeted him with due reverence to his sacred character, and said :—

" The grace of the blessed virgin be upon thee, holy father ; why gazest thou so earnestly at me ?"

" Because," replied the monk, in a harsh voice, and the deep tones of which startled Lord Raymond,—" because it is some years since we have before met, and mine eyes would fain feast themselves upon the man I so mortally hate."

" Hate !" repeated Lord Raymond, in a tone of astonishment—" this, from one of thy sacred form, father ;—whose actions should be those only of charity and love ?—But who art thou, and how have I incurred thine enmity ?"

" Wouldst know, Lord Raymond St. Aswolph ?"

" I would."

" Take, then, my answer at my dagger's point," exclaimed the supposed monk, taking one from beneath his garb, " and with it the name of——But no," he added, drawing suddenly back ; " the time is not come yet—the scheme is not yet ripe for execution !—Live, proud Lord St. Aswolph, but rest assured that the time is not far distant when the deadly vengeance of him thou hast so deeply injured, shall descend upon thine head !"

" Insolent hypocrite ; tear off this holy garb, which thy words convince me thou hast no right to wear, and——"

" Nay, nay," interrupted the apparent friar, " put up thy weapon, it would be of little avail opposed against me. One word of mine could freeze thee into ice, and unnerve thine arm."

" Liar !" exclaimed Lord Raymond, whose feelings were unusually excited ; " I dare thee to the test—thou knowest me not."

" Know thee not," reiterated the other, scornfully—" fool !—Thine ear !"

As the mysterious stranger thus spoke, he laid hold of the arm of Lord Raymond, and whispered a few words in his ear. The latter turned deadly pale in a moment ; his limbs trembled violently—he staggered from the hold of the monk, and became fixed and immoveable as a statue For a few minutes he continued in this condition, and seemed to have lost the power of all his faculties, but when he did somewhat recover himself and looked round him, the stranger was gone.

So overcome was he by the words which the monk had uttered to him, that it was sometime before he could proceed on his way ; but not far had he gone, when he beheld a female form running with frantic haste towards him, and immediately his thoughts were averted from what had so recently occurred to him, and his whole attention directed to the female who was now approaching him. As she came nearer, it struck him that he knew her, and in a moment afterwards, his surmises were confirmed. It was Ernnestine, pale, breathless, and nearly exhausted, who, with the air of a maniac, had rushed unseen from the " Flagon," immediately on being made acquainted with the sorrowful particulars of the combat which had taken place between the robbers and the mob, and the consequent imprisonment of Ranulph de Lacy, as well as his unfortunate son, Godfrey. Unable longer calmly to remain at home, she had determined, at all hazards, to gain an interview with her lover and her father in the prison. When she beheld the astonished Lord Raymond, she uttered a faint scream, and completely overpowered by her emotions, and the exertion she had undergone, she became insensible in his arms.

· How shall we describe the mingled feelings of transport, anguish, and astonishment of Lord Raymond, as he held the insensible damsel to his bosom, and gazed with intense ardour upon her pale but lovely features ?—With what rapture did he gaze upon that maiden, who the most eloquent language must fail to do adequate justice to.

> " Light as the angel shapes that bless
>   An infant's dream, yet not the less
>   Rich in all woman's loveliness ;—
>   With eyes so pure, that from their ray
>   Dark Vice would turn abashed away,
>   Blinded, like serpents, when they gaze
>   Upon the emerald's virgin blaze !
>   Yet, fill'd with all youth's sweet desires;
>   Mingling the meek and vestal fires
>   Of other worlds, with all the bliss,
>   The fond, weak tenderness of this !
>   A soul, too, more than half divine,
>   Where, through shades of earthly feeling,
>   Religion's soften'd glories shine,
>   Like light through summer foliage stealing—
>   Shedding a glow of such mild hue,
>   So warm, and yet so shadowy, too,
>   As makes the very darkness there
>   More beautifu than light elsewhere !"*

* The Fire Worshippers

How did he long to breathe upon her lips the kiss—the fervent kiss of love; but, yet, a feeling of delicacy restrained him, and, raising her in his arms, he hastened with her back to the castle, and placing her under the care of two female domestics, went to make his mother, the amiable Lady Celestine, acquainted with the circumstance.

Lady Celestine had always felt a most lively interest in the fate of Ernnestine; her uncommon beauty had excited her admiration, and the sweetness of her disposition, and the simplicity, yet intelligence of her deportment, had charmed her. Frequently had she watched her when a child at her innocent gambols, when she has been going near Ranulph de Lacy's residence, and her heart yearned towards her with a sentiment far more powerful than mere esteem. She envied Ranulph and his wife the lovely charge which had been entrusted to them, and would, with pleasure, have taken her under her protection. What a charming companion would she have made for her daughter, Marguerite, and what delight would it have afforded her to have seen them become the partakers of each other's studies, and striving to emulate each other's virtues. Many handsome presents had she sent her, and she was a frequent visitor at St. Alwyn Castle, which ever afforded the amiable lady the most infinite gratification, and was looked forward to with impatience and delight by the little Marguerite. Several times had she endeavoured to persuade Hubert Clensham (who it appeared had more authority over her than her foster-parents,) to permit her to take her altogether under her protection, but, although mine host of " The Flagon," expressed his gratitude to her ladyship for her kind wishes, in the warmest manner, of course, he declined the honour.

Feeling so great an attachment as she did towards Ernnestine, therefore, it is not to be wondered at that her ladyship should be very much hurt at the melancholy circumstances that had recently taken place, to afflict the bosom of the poor girl, and those of her friends, and she was likewise very much distressed at the awful and perilous position in which the unfortunate young man, Godfrey, was placed, who, notwithstanding, suspicion was so strong against him, she firmly believed was innocent of the foul crime laid to his charge. When her son, therefore, so soon returned to the castle and informed her of what had taken place, she felt a mingled feeling of pain, and yet pleasure, (since the object she had formed such an attachment to, was thus accidentally placed under her care,) and, attended by her daughter, Marguerite, she hastened to the chamber to which Ernnestine had been taken.

With what feelings of indescribable rapture and anguish did Lord Raymond St. Aswolph hang over the senseless form of the beauteous Ernnestine, after he had borne her into the castle, while his mother and sister affectionately sought to restore her to sensibility. So powerful were his emotions, that Lady Celestine and Marguerite observed them, and could not help feeling some surprise, although they were not at all astonished that the uncommon loveliness of Ernnestine should make an impression upon the most insensible heart, much more the warm and passionate nature of Lord Raymond.

It was evidently with much reluctance that he retired from the chamber, and he would not leave the castle until he was assured that Ernnestine had so far recovered as to be able to relate to Lady Celestine and her daughters, such of the afflicting circumstances as had come to her knowledge.

Lord St. Aswolph was not less grieved than surprised at the events. What could be the meaning of the attempt at rescue which had been made in behalf of Godfrey?—Who could the men have been who had been engaged in the affair, and why should they take any interest in the fate of the young man?—Under what infatuation, too, could Ranulph have been acting, thus to involve himself in danger, in so fruitless a task as endeavouring to release his son from the hands of the officers, a course to which he had previously seemed to be so much opposed, and which could have no other effect than that of increasing the suspicion which was attached to Godfrey? These circumstances passed rapidly over in the mind of Lord Raymond as he quitted the castle, and wending his way towards the prison, being resolved to seek an interview with Ranulph de Lacy and his son, and to endeavour to elicit from them an explanation of that which at present was involved in so much mystery; but it was in vain that he tried to conjecture the real cause of the events that had been related by Ernnestine. The misery, however, which the latter was suffering, and that which he feared she was still doomed to undergo, racked his brain and tormented his mind more than anything else; and he was apprehensive that it would have such an effect upon her constitution, and cause such a shock to her feelings, that she would never be able to recover from.

"Beloved maiden," soliloquized Lord Raymond as he proceeded towards the place in which Ranulph de Lacy and his son were confined, "what would I not give—what sacrifice could I consider too great, if it could save thee from the anguish which will rack thy gentle bosom? By Heaven! I could be content to endure the greatest misery that could fall to the lot of mortal, if, by so doing, I could do away with, or ameliorate the pangs that corrode thine heart! Oh, Ernnestine, till I beheld thee, I thought that no other woman could ever inspire my bosom with love, than her who once reigned the empress of my heart! But how much more powerful is the affection—the uncontrollable affection—I must acknowledge I now feel for thee, and which nothing can conquer while the blood of life flows within my veins! But alas! what hope is there for me?—Dare I hope to raise a reciprocal feeling in the bosom of the too-lovely Ernnestine? I feel myself unworthy of such a treasure; and humble as her circumstances are, she is by far too inestimable a prize for me ever to hope to obtain. But I talk madly! How know I that her heart is not already possessed by some more fortunate individual? It is not likely that one so fair can be indifferent—can be insensible to the tender passion!"

For the first time the idea of Godfrey darted across his brain, and the uncommon agitation which Ernnestine evinced, seemed by far too powerful for any person to experience, who merely felt an ordinary affection. This, coupled with what he had before heard, that a jealousy had existed between Godfrey and the unfortunate Reginald, in consequence of the latter being accepted by Hubert Clensham, as the suitor of Ernnestine, and which was one of the most powerful causes of suspicion against Godfrey, as being guilty of the murder of the Esquire, raised a tumult of passions in his breast that were quite new to him

The prevailing feeling which agitated his bosom, was one so nearly approximating to jealousy, that it was difficult to find any other name for it. He hurried on towards the prison, with his mind in a state of the greatest uneasiness, but fully determined, by some means or the other, to elicit from Godfrey the truth.

" But," he ejaculated, as he proceeded, " how could it be otherwise ?—Is it at all likely that a young man, endowed with the natural qualifications, both personal and intrinsic, that Godfrey de Lacy possesses, could fail to interest a heart so susceptible as Ernnestine's, or that he should be insensible to the power of her charms ? Besides, have they not been brought up together from infancy ? —Have they not been the constant companions of one another, and so thoroughly acquainted with each other's dispositions, having such an opportunity of being constantly together, and giving utterance without restraint to their sentiments, would it not have been a matter of astonishment if they had not imbibed the effervescent passion of love for one another ? It would !—it would ! and I must be a fool not to have discovered the truth in a moment. Besides, did not the maiden freely acknowledge in my presence, and in that of her relations, that she loved Godfrey, and that Reginald, convinced of the mutual affection they entertained for each other, had generously resigned his claim to the hand of Ernnestine, in favour of his rival, and had, moreover, promised to use his influence with Hubert, to give his sanction to their union ? Yes, yes, and fool, idiot, I must have been, not to have thought of this before ! What hope, then, is there for me ? Can I ever expect to estrange her affections from that favored youth on whom they are so firmly fixed ? And should I not be acting the part of a villain to endeavour to do so ?—Yes, I should ; and it would have no other effect than that of rendering two beings, whom I believe to be so worthy of each other, for ever miserable. Alas ! there is no hope for me, and I must endeavour to stifle a passion which can never be gratified, although my heart break in the attempt."

With these distracting thoughts Lord Raymond hurried on towards the prison, and was soon ushered into the dungeon in which Ranulph de Lacy was confined. He found the bowyer more composed than he could have imagined he would have been, and to his urgent inquiries as to the cause of his rashly endeavouring to rescue his son from the custody of the officers, Ranulph replied,—

" Thou art not rightly informed, my lord ;—I sought not to release Godfrey from the custody of the officers, but to save him from the fury of a brutal rabble who would have slain him."

" But who were those who aided thee ?" inquired Lord Raymond.

Ranulph hesitated for a minute or two, and then answered ;—

" Pardon me, my lord, but upon that point I cannot at present satisfy thee."

" No," ejaculated his lordship, with much surprise ; " and why not, forsooth ?"

" Because it might be to the injury of those whom I firmly believe are our friends," returned the bowyer.

" I like not this mystery," said Lord Raymond, with evident marks of dissatisfaction ; " if they are good men, and true, surely thou wouldst not hesitate to make me acquainted, who am one of thy best friends, with their real names and characters, and their motives for taking so deep an interest in thy affairs, and those of thy son."

" My conduct may appear strange, my lord," returned Ranulph, " which, doubtless, it is; but time will, most likely, unravel all that which at present seems so mysterious. More at present I cannot say; but of this I can assure thee, that of the real motives for their conduct, 1 am as ignorant as thyself, although I firmly believe that their friendship is sincere. But pr'ythee, my lord, what of my wife,—of Ernnestine? Alas! are they not distracted at my situation ?"

Lord Raymond informed him of all he knew, and Ranulph's anguish was most excessive when he heard it.

" I tremble for thee, Ranulph," said Lord St. Aswolph, " for thou hast placed thyself in a most awkward predicament, and prejudiced the case against thine unfortunate son."

" Oh, I fear not for myself or Godfrey," replied Ranulph, " for I feel confident that we shall come off triumphant;—it is only for the dreadful sufferings which my wife and Ernnestine will undergo in the interim. Alas! I fear that it will break their hearts !"

" Endeavour to compose thyself upon that point," observed Lord Raymond, " there shall be nothing wanting on my part, {and that of my honoured mother, to appease their anguish, and ——"

" I know thy goodness, my lord," interrupted Ranulph, " and never shall I be able to repay the debt of gratitude which I owe thee. But Ernnestine, who loves my poor boy so fondly, who ——"

" Loves him !" reiterated his lordship, colouring, " as a brother, doubtless, she does.

" As a brother," returned Ranulph, " oh, how weak is that name for the passion which Ernnestine feels for my son, and which he so ardently returns. They adore each other, and although I have deemed it prudent to endeavour to eradicate it from their hearts, nothing, I am certain, will ever be able to conquer it."

Lord Raymond made no reply, but he sighed deeply. Here, if any had before been wanting, was a confirmation of his surmises, which he could no longer doubt. Promising again to use all his best endeavours in the cause of Ranulph and his son, he soon afterwards quitted the dungeon, and hastened to that in which Godfrey was confined. Nothing materially different to that which had transpired in the interview between Lord Raymond and Ranulph de Lacy, took place upon this occasion, Godfrey, like his father, most firmly refusing to satisfy him upon the subject of the robbers; who had been the cause of aiding him in the escape he had made from the prison, and the subsequent events that had taken place; and at length Lord Raymond, not at all satisfied with the mystery which they both maintained, left the prison.

He had not got many paces on his way home, when his arm was suddenly grasped by a powerful hand, and turning round, he beheld Hal of the Glen.

Lord Raymond, albeit he was unused to fear, could not help gazing upon the awful and mysterious-looking being, by whom his progress was thus arrested, with feelings of astonishment and consternation : and, no wonder, for Hal of the Glen was a frightful object, and, in those days of superstition, was well cal-culated to inspire the beholder with sentiments of disgust and horror. He held the arm of his lordship with an iron gripe ; and his wildly flashing eyes were fixed upon his countenance with an intensity which seemed as if it would pene-trate to the inmost recesses of his heart, and read his every thought. Lord Ray-mond, although he had often heard talk of the magician, had never before seen him, and his sudden appearance bewildered and dumb-founded him for a few minutes. All this time, the magician retained the hold of his arm, and never for an instant removed his eyes from him ; at the same time, a sardonic grin over-spread his hideous features, which was appalling to look upon.

"All hail to thee, Lord Raymond St. Aswolph !" at length Hal of the Glen broke silence. "Wouldst know thy future destiny ?"

"Aroynt thee, hideous being !" cried Lord Raymond ; "who art thou, that thus accosteth me ?"

"One, whose name few can hear without dread," was the reply :—"one who knowest thy most secret thoughts, and can tell thee all thou wishest to know."

"Leave go thine hold, and let me pass ;—thou art some vile impostor !"

"Impostor !" reiterated the magician, and his fiendish laugh seemed to shake the forest. "Wouldst have proof that thou liest ?—I would tell thee whether the love thou entertainest for the fair Ernnestine de Lacy will ever be returned !"

"Ah !" exclaimed the wonder-stricken St. Aswolph ; "how knowest thou that which I have never yet whispered to mortal being ?"

"Did I not tell thee I could read thy thoughts ?" returned the magician. "Thinkest thou now that I am an impostor ?"

"Mysterious being, who art thou ?"

"Hal of the Glen !"

Lord Raymond started at the mention of that name, and looked aghast at the magician.

"Thou hast heard of me ?" said Hal.

"Aye, oft have I heard of thee, and thy damned sorcerles," replied Lord Ray-mond. "Avaunt, fiend ; I will not listen to thee :—the souls of those who are tempted by thee, are in jeopardy !"

Again, the loud and supernatural laugh of Hal shook the air, and his eyes seemed to flash with more than mortal lustre.

"And, art thou, then, the bold and stalwart Lord Raymond St. Aswolph ?" demanded the sorcerer,—"he, who fain would make the world believe that he feareth neither man nor devil ?—Thou art afraid to hear what I can tell thee, and that which would be the means of saving thee from sorrow and crime ?"

"Crime !" repeated St. Aswolph, his bosom heaving with indignation : "crime associated with the unsullied name of St. Aswolph ! By——"

"Hold !" interrupted Hal of the Glen ; "thou mayest e'en spare thine oaths ; they are useless mockery to me. I tell thee, that I alone can point out thy future destiny, and save thee from misery, shame, and guilt !—But thou rejectest my offers ?"

"I do !"

"Obstinate fool! go, then, thine own course, and remain ignorant of the

yawning gulph upon whose brink thou now standest, until it is too late to save thee. Begone! and live but to endure all——"

"Hold! hold!" interrupted Lord Raymond, terrified by the words of the magician; "I do repent me of what I said, and would fain avail me of thy boasted skill in divination."

"Then, follow me."

"Whither?"

"Thou'lt see."

"How know I that thou mayest not mean me harm?"

"If thou doubtest, go thy way."

"Lead on, I will trust thee."

The magician laughed exultingly, turned round, and proceeded into the deepest recesses of the wood with great rapidity, and Lord Raymond, wrapping his mantle around, followed him.

They were not long in reaching the Glen, in which the sorcerer held his mystic orgies; but Lord Raymond, several times on the way, repented having complied with the wishes of Hal; and two or three times he was half inclined to turn back. However, whenever these thoughts occurred to him, the magician turned round, and looked fiercely upon him, as though he could tell what was passing in his mind: and an inscrutable power seemed to urge him on, which he could not resist.

Arrived in the cave of the sorcerer, Lord Raymond felt the blood run cold in

No. 13

his veins with horror at all that met his gaze, while the magician proceeded to form the magic circle, and to go through similar awful preliminaries to those which we have previously described. Thinking it was now too late to retreat, St. Aswolph aroused all his energy, and prepared to see the result of this awful and mysterious event with firmness.

The magician went through the whole of his cabalistic ceremonies and incantations; and, after the lapse of a few minutes, during which interval a number of frightful and shadowy forms danced around Lord Raymond, and the impressive and supernatural voice of the magician was heard to speak as follows :—

> " Lord Raymond, thou hast hither come,
> To learn from me thy future doom :
> Darest thou brave the magic spell,
> And hear the facts that I can tell ?"

" Proceed !" returned St. Aswolph; " I will listen to thee, and fear not to learn all that by thy mystic arts thou mayest be able to impart to me."

The magician waved his wand, and uttered some unintelligible words, after which, he fixed his eyes intently on the magic volume before him, and remained unmoved and silent for several minutes. At length, he once more turned to St. Aswolph, and in the same tones, ejaculated,—

> " Many sorrows hast thou known,
> And thou shalt meet with many more :—
> Ere twice two years have flown,
> Thou'lt have cause to grieve full sore.

> " Beware ! for thou may'st shun thy fate;
> Beware the dread avenger's hate :
> Beware of one who seeks thy blood,
> Whose lair is in the tangled wood !
> Beware of one who thou shalt meet
> Mounted upon a charger fleet,
> In sable mail accoutred—
> Oh, well may'st thou his vengeance dread !
> When thou dost the gauntlet throw,
> His power thou shalt quickly know.
> Of the robbers haunt beware !
> For one who hates thee lurketh there."

As the magician gave utterance to the last lines, waving his wand all the while, there suddenly appeared in the magic mirror, at the back of the cavern, the figure of a grey friar, exactly like the mysterious monk whom Lord Raymond had encountered in the wood. But an instant, and the monkish garb fell off, and he beheld the tall figure of a man encased completely in black armour, with his vizor down, and from his casque waved a plume of feathers of the same sable hue.

" Sorcerer," exclaimed Lord Raymond, gazing with astonishment at the phantom, "if thou would'st warn me against my secret foe, reveal to me his features."

" It is forbidden," replied the magician; " seek not to know more than my power can disclose to thee !"

Again the magician waved his wand, and the phantom vanished.

" But, what of Godfrey de Lacy?"

" He shall be saved!" answered Hal of the Glen.

" Enough," ejaculated Lord Raymond ; " I am satisfied !"

" And the fair Ernnestine," continued the magician.

" Ah ! what of her?" eagerly demanded St. Aswolph. " Godfrey loves her!"

" He does ;—and, so dost thou !"

" But, does she return his passion ?"

" She does."

" Then, there is no hope for me ?"

" She will love thee, also."

" Ah !" cried Raymond, in a tone of rapture;—" blest assurance; sorcerer, for that, I thank thee."

" Beware, Lord Raymond St. Aswolph," said the magician, in deep and solemn accents :—

" If thou takest her to thy nuptial bed,
(Though her thou art decreed to wed,)
A curse upon thine head shall light,
That shall pursue thee day and night.—

Behold !"

Solemn music was now heard, which gradually died away; and, quick, at the summons of the magician, Raymond beheld in the mirror the interior of a chapel, and, kneeling at the altar, he saw two forms, the exact resemblance of himself and Ernnestine. The priest was just about to join their hands, when, suddenly, loud peals of thunder shook the cavern, the priest vanished, and the figure of a female, of lovely countenance, in long robes of white, rushed in between them, and a sepulchral voice was heard to exclaim,—

" Forbear !"

As Lord Raymond gazed upon the countenance of this phantom, his blood ran icy cold through his veins: cold drops of perspiration " stood upon his quivering temples," and, with extended arms, rushing towards the magic mirror, he cried in delirious accents,—

" Image of my sainted Marian, why appearest thou to me ?—Oh, speak to me, and let me once more hear those heavenly tones that have so often charmed my ravished senses !"

Terrific shrieks rent the air as Lord Raymond thus spoke ;—the vision disappeared, the cavern became involved in impenetrable darkness, and the following words, in the voice of the sorcerer, met his ears :—

" Thou hast broken the charm;—away, I cannot reveal to thee more !"

Lord Raymond paused a few moments, stupified and bewildered by all he had seen and heard ; but, at length finding that he was alone in the magician's cavern, and an irresistible terror creeping through his veins, he groped his way out, and, after great difficulty, found himself once more in the open air.

He paused to take breath ; and, leaning against a tree, he became completely absorbed in the recollection of the strange events that had occurred to him within the last two hours, the awful things he had seen, and the singular and awful predictions of the magician. The warning he had given him of the sable knight, his prognostications as regarded Ernnestine, and the curse that he had foretold should descend upon his head should he bed with the beauteous damsel, although he had said that he should wed her, all rushed upon his memory in rapid succession, and involved him in a train of ideas that only served to perplex him more. But, what had made a deeper impression upon him than any other circumstance, was the last vision which Hal of the Glen had conjured up to his view ; and, as he thought upon it, and remembered the words that the phantom had uttered, a sensation of horror shot through his frame, which he sought in vain to resist.

At length, arousing himself, he was about to proceed on his way, when, raising his eyes, he beheld standing before him, with his arms folded across his chest, and his cowl down, the gaunt figure of the grey friar, who had before crossed his path, and the exact form which Hal of the Glen had exhibited to him in the vision, and which had afterwards been metamorphosed into the black knight !

Raymond placed his hand on his sword in an instant, as he remembered the mysterious words that the grey friar had formerly uttered to him, and the warning which he had received from the magician ; and the supposed monk, observing his action, uttered a hoarse laugh of scorn, which resounded through the wood, and filled Lord Raymond with confusion and dread.

" Fool !" exclaimed the supposed monk, " put up thy sword ; it would avail but little against me. Even now, I could trample thee in the earth, and gloat upon thy blood; but I shall spare thee for a while ;—the hour of my vengeance is not yet come ! Tremble ! Lord Raymond St. Aswolph : I have sworn to be thy bane—thy curse !—to devise such tortures for thee that thou canst not shun ; and to bring upon thee misery and shame, by such secret insidious, and unavoidable means, that the blow shall fall upon thee when thou art least prepared for it ;— that the storm shall burst on thee so suddenly, that thou must sink beneath its violence.—Tremble !"

" Vain, boasting miscreant, I will not be bearded and threatened thus by thee, without resenting it ! Off with thy cowardly disguise, fell ruffian, and, if thou art a man, boldly meet in fair and equal contest, he thou hast sworn to wreak thy vengeance upon. Nay, dastard, knave, thou mockest me ;—thus, then, do I force thee to——"

As Lord Raymond was thus speaking, he rushed with great fury upon the grey friar, who stood calm and unmoved, until he had got him within his reach, when he grasped him by the throat, with the same ease as he would do an infant, and hurling him from him to the earth, with Herculean might, he uttered in a loud voice,—

" Idiot ! think not that thou canst cope with me !—This moment thy life is in my hands ; but I will lend it thee for the present. Remember the Grey Friar ! Remember the Black Knight ! Think of Marian, and tremble !"

He said no more, but leaving Lord Raymond prostrate on the earth, he hurried into the deepest recesses of the wood, and was almost immediately lost to view.

Bursting with rage, and filled with astonishment, not unmingled with dread, Raymond, in a few moments, gathered himself up, and reflecting with anguish upon all that had occurred to him, he slowly bent his way to St. Aswolph Castle.

CHAPTER X.

" Oh, love ! most sacred passion,
    What bounds, what limits are there
    To thy power ?   The human heart
    Is thy territory and thy slave.
    In youth or age alike dost thou
    Hold thine empire !"   CLEOPATRA.

DISTRACTING and perplexing were the thoughts that occupied the bosom of Lord Raymond after the awful and mysterious events we have been describing. Every word the magician had given utterance to had gone to his heart, stamped as it was with every appearance of truth ;—all that he had seen had made a forcible and indelible impression upon his mind. The appalling vision which had been conjured up before his wandering eyes,—the phantom of Marian,—the prognostications uttered by Hal of the Glen,—the words he had spoken as regarded Ernnestine, and the warning he had given him against encouraging that love which her charms had engendered in his breast, all conspired to bewilder and torment him. Then, again, the strange predictions that had been uttered about the black knight, and his singular meeting with the mysterious being immediately after his quitting the glen, filled him with strange doubt and apprehension. " Who could this man be ?" he reflected ; " and, why should he fear him ? How could he have incurred his enmity ?" He endeavoured to recal to his memory from amongst the number of his former acquaintances any one to whom he had given sufficient cause to excite his hatred and revenge. There was one,—but he had every reason to believe that he was long since dead ; and, therefore, who could the present man be ?

" Ah !" he suddenly exclaimed, as the thought rushed upon his brain, " did he not mention the name of Marian ?—and, who else but he could it be ? But, no ; I could not have been wrongly informed from the source whence I obtained the information, and I have nothing, therefore, to fear from him.—Who, then, can it be ?"

He was unable to come to any satisfactory conclusion, and proceeded on towards St. Aswolph Castle, still revolving in his mind all the mysterious and bewildering circumstances that had taken place.

" Would that I had not yielded to the persuasions of the sorcerer," he soliloquized ; " what many painful and tormenting thoughts would it have saved me ! But, Ernnestine, why should my love for her be forbidden ?—And why, if I unite my fate with her's, should it entail misery upon me ?—Misery with Ernnestine ! By the mass, the prognostication is as false as hell ! What a heaven of bliss must she bestow upon that happy being who is destined by fate to possess her hand and heart ! But the magician said that she would be mine,—that I should wed her ! Oh, entrancing thought ! Were I certain that this would be realized, what felicity would be mine ! But, no ; he said—he, the sorcercer— that I should be miserable and accursed for ever, should that even take place ! I am distracted with doubt, hope, uncertainty, and dread.! The shade of my Marian, too !—that forbade the nuptials !—and shall I fly in the face of Heaven?—No, no, Ernnestine, too lovely girl, thou must never be mine !—But, can I ever forget her ? Can I ever become indifferent to her ?—No, no ; though distance may divide us; though other forms, gentle and beauteous as thine, may meet my sight, thine image is so firmly stamped upon my heart, that it can only be erased with death. But, yet, how strange and unaccountable is the passion I feel towards her ! It is something more than love—it is a sentiment more powerful than adoration ! It is a feeling which to me is inscrutable ! In her presence I feel a kind of sacred awe; and, methinks I could—but, where are my thoughts wandering ? Oh, how I wrong the unfortunate Godfrey (whom I am at this time professing to befriend) by entertaining such ideas ! Have I not been assured that he loves the maiden, and that she returns his passion ; and why, then, should I seek to torture two fond hearts that have already been so deeply lacerated by the misfortunes that have attended them ? Raymond, arouse thyself, and struggle against this weakness. Yes, whatever may be the consequences, whatever anguish I may endure, I will endeavour to forget Ernnestine in any other character than that of a dear friend—a beloved sister."

As Lord Raymond came to the conclusion of this soliloquy, he reached the castle, where his first inquiries were after the beauteous object who occupied his thoughts. He learnt with much grief that, although by the joint efforts of Lady Celestine and his sister Marguerite she was restored to sensibility, she was in such a state of agony, owing to the many dreadful events that had followed so rapidly one upon the other, that the most serious apprehensions might justly be entertained. We need not seek to describe the pain this caused Lord Raymond, and his agitation was particularly observed by his mother and Marguerite, who although they well knew the urbanity and humanity of his mind, and the deep commiseration he always felt in the misfortunes of his fellow-creatures, could not help remarking the unusual emotion he evinced upon this occasion, with some feelings of surprise. But they soon thought more lightly of the subject, and did not so much wonder that Lord Raymond should feel a deep interest in the sorrows of so young and beauteous a maiden, more especially as Ernnestine had made so powerful an impression upon their own hearts.

In spite of the melancholy circumstance that had brought it about, both Lady Celestine and her daughter could not help experiencing a feeling of pleasure that Ernnestine had thus accidentally become an inmate of the castle, and fallen under their protection ; and they entertained a fervent hope that her friends might be persuaded to suffer her to remain with them.

All the affectionate attention that humanity could prompt, was paid to Ernnestine by these amiable beings; and they exerted themselves to their utmost endeavours to soothe her anguish ; but, alas ! what arguments could they make use of to alleviate the sufferings of the poor girl, under such heavily afflicting circumstances ? They sought to inspire her with hope that there would be a fortunate issue to the dreadful affair which now agonized their minds ; but, alas ! this was a task too difficult to be easily accomplished ; and the more the poor maiden reflected upon it, the greater cause for despair did she see. Indeed, what cause for hope was there ? What evidence had the unfortunate Godfrey of his innocence to offer any more than his own?—and, prejudiced as the public were against him, and which they, in truth, had such good reason to be, from the many suspicious circumstances that had occurred to fix the guilt upon him, what could he offer in excuse for his having escaped from the gaol, and the blood which had been spilt in effecting it? And, did not the attempt which his father had made to rescue him from the custody of the officers, more than ever stamp the appearance of guilt upon him? Alas! yes; fate seemed to have conspired against them, and nothing but horror surrounded them.

The distraction of Hubert Clensham, Maud, and Edith, when they heard of the critical situation of Ranulph, as well as his son, could only be equalled by that which raged within the bosom of Ernnestine; and, like her—although they were certain that Lord Raymond St. Aswolph would exert himself all that was in his power to save them from the fate which threatened them—like her they believed that the circumstantial evidence which would be adduced would be too readily believed; and that there was very little chance of Godfrey and his father escaping, condemned, as they already were, apparently, in the minds of their judges. Besides, in those days, justice was but rarely awarded in cases of this description, and especially where the accused happened to be a plebeian. Rude and barbarous as were the times, the sacrifice of the life of a menial was considered of very little importance; law was guided by vengeance; and the most trifling circumstances were brought forward and suffered to weigh as evidences of the criminality of the accused. What hope had they then that Godfrey would be enabled to substantiate his innocence of the crimes alleged against him; or that his father would be able to escape punishment for having attempted to effect his escape?—None, none; and which ever way they turned their thoughts, nothing but misery presented itself to their imagination.

Soon after Ernnestine had left the 'Flagon,' in that state bordering upon frenzy, in which we have described her to have been met by Lord Raymond, Hubert, his wife, and Edith, unable to remain at home, made their way also to the prison; but they were refused an interview with the prisoners; and they were treated so brutally by the ignorant mob, that they were glad to seek refuge in the Castle of St. Aswolph, where they had ascertained Ernnestine had been taken. The Lady Celestine and her daughter expressed the greatest sympathy in the distress of the unfortunate family, and endeavoured all they possibly could to alleviate their anguish. As it was uncertain when Ernnestine would be sufficiently restored to convalescence to be removed, it was proposed by Lady Celestine they should remain at the castle until after the trial, which was to take place in a week. To this, Hubert and the others readily assented, more particularly as it would enable them to attend the couch of Ernnestine, and having partially succeeded in conquering the violence of their own grief, to ameliorate that of her's.

Lord Raymond had been unremitting in his endeavours to procure evidence to establish the innocence of Godfrey, but he had made little or no progress, and, notwithstanding the predictions of Hal of the Glen, who had told him that Godfrey would be saved, he began at last to entertain but very little hopes of such a result taking place. He had had several interviews with the prisoners, and found them both calm and firm,—Godfrey, in particular, shewing in his conduct all the confidence that conscious innocence could inspire. The principal anguish which tormented his mind, was caused by the suffering which he was convinced Ernnestine must be enduring at his awful situation, and at the misery which must lacerate the heart of his mother.

Lord Raymond read his thoughts, and, as he beheld the power of the love which filled his bosom towards Ernnestine, in spite of the sympathy he felt for the misfortunes of Godfrey, he found it impossible entirely to conquer a sentiment of jealousy, which, in spite of his endeavours to the contrary, would steal over him.

At length the important morning arrived,—the morning of that day which was to decide the fate of Godfrey de Lacy and his father; and, contrary to all expectation, Ernnestine had so far recovered her strength and equanimity, as not only to be able to quit her chamber, but to form a resolution to attend the Hall of Justice, and give what evidence she could of the guiltlessness of the accused.

The trial excited the deepest interest, and as soon as the court was opened, it was crowded to excess in every part. Lord Raymond St. Aswolph was seated by the side of the Justiciary, and on the bench were many other noblemen of distinction, among whom was the master of Godfrey de Lacy. We must, however, make the trial the subject of our next chapter.

CHAPTER XI.

"Look at me—mark well my countenance,—
Note well each sentence that I utter;
Annalyze my every action, and thou'lt own
If I am guilty of this foul crime,
Then is the child just born a murderer!"

LORD RAYMOND ST. ASWOLPH had waited in the most painful suspense the arrival of the day of trial, and he trembled for the result, for on it, he was confident, depended not only the life of the accused, but also of Ernnestine. It would be superfluous to say that she had been attended upon, as also had Edith, with the utmost solicitude by Lady Celestine and her daughter; and, contrary to all expectations, when the morning arrived, Ernnestine evinced more fortitude and resignation then she had ever done before, and talked with perfect calmness on the probable issue of the agonizing event. But even at that time he passed a few of the most delightful moments he had ever experienced in the society of the beauteous damsel, when she thanked him in her usual sweet and fascinating style, for his kindness to her and her dear friends, and more especially for the interest he had taken in the fate of the unfortunate Godfrey, and the exertions he had made in his behalf. For ages could he have dwelt upon every word that fell from her lips; every sentence she uttered was transport to his ravished senses. He earnestly, however, implored both her and Edith not to persist in the design

they had formed to be present at the trial; but all the arguments that himself and his mother could make use of, were unavailing; they were determined, and Lord Raymond, mentally uttering a prayer to heaven to sustain them throughout so painful an event, quitted the castle and bent his way towards the Hall of Justice.

On his way thither, he could not help noticing several very strange and suspicious-looking men lurking about, some in groups, and who seemed to be strongly armed; but imagining that they were only going upon the same errand as many more, namely, to witness the proceedings, he did not suffer the circumstance to occupy his mind many minutes, but went on his way.

As we have before stated, the hall was densely crowded; for in those days of barbarism, the trial of a plebeian was rather an unusual occurrence; it was enough for them to be accused of crime, and their execution immediately followed.

The despotic noble had a license, in a manner of speaking, to do with his vassals what he thought proper, and upon the slightest offence or caprice murdered them with impunity. In this instance, however, the interest excited was so great, both the murdered man and the accused being so well known, and Lord Raymond had so exerted himself with a firm belief that he should be able to remove all shadow of imputation even, from Godfrey, that there were no means, had there even have been any desire, to have prevented the trial from taking place; and, indeed, it had been the universal theme of conversation ever since the murder of the ill-fated Reginald had been discovered

No. 14

And now the awful moment approached,—Lord Raymond looked around the Hall, but he did not perceive either Ernnestine or Edith, and he began to hope that they had abandoned their former resolution and would not attend. There was a pause, and all was silent as death in the hall, when the Justiciary ordered Godfrey de Lacy to be brought forward. No sooner had he given the order, than a piercing shriek rang through the hall, and Ernnestine and Edith, with pale cheeks and wild demeanour, rushed from the place where they had till this moment been concealed, and threw themselves at the feet of the Justiciary, and the other officers of the law, who surrounded them. Their appearance caused a great sensation in the hall, and Lord Raymond descended from his seat, and instantly went to their assistance; but they heeded him not, and seemed to be unconscious of every thing but the awful errand upon which they had come.

"Oh, my lord," ejaculated Ernnestine, with clasped hands, and her eyes fixed with the most vehement expression of supplication upon the countenance of the Justiciary, "let mercy predominate in thy breast towards an innocent and injured youth. He is guiltless!—By Heaven! he is guiltless!—Oh, thou knowest not the noble soul of Godfrey de Lacy, or thou wouldst be well convinced that his heart would recoil from the bare idea of the horrible crime of which he is accused!—Oh, spare him! I beseech thee!"

"By all thy hopes of mercy do not bereave a mother of her only son, upon so foul, and so dreadful a charge as that which is brought against him;" cried Edith, "If thou dost, his blood will assuredly be upon thine head, and the curse of Heaven will pursue thee."

"Woman," said the Justiciary, sternly, "thou talkest wildly; but I can pardon thee for the boldness of thy speech. I am here to administer justice, and by the guidance of the Judge of Judges, I will do so."

"Be calm,—be calm, I beseech ye both," said Hubert Clensham, who was in the hall, and had placed himself by their side, as soon as they made this appeal to the Justiciary, "and place a firm reliance upon the goodness and clemency of the Almighty, before whom we must all one time appear. He will not fail to protect the innocent, and bring the guilty to punishment."

"The business of the court must not be delayed," said the Justiciary, in reply to some few words that had been addressed to him by Lord Raymond, imploring him to bear with the unfortunate women;—"bring hither the accused, I say!"

Lord Raymond drew his breath short, and was in scarcely a state of less agitation than Ernnestine and Edith. With looks of the most intense anxiety and agony, he watched the countenance of Ernnestine, as she fixed her eyes upon the door through which the prisoner must pass, and ere a moment had elapsed the clanking of heavy fetters was heard, and Godfrey was led in by the officers. His step was firm, and although his cheeks were pale, yet did his eyes beam with an expression of conscious innocence.—A frantic scream from Ernnestine and Edith drew his attention towards them, and the next instant they sprang towards him, and threw themselves upon his neck.

"Mother!—Ernnestine, sweet innocent, to meet thee thus!" cried Godfrey, with a burst of agony;—"Oh, God! surely Thy decrees are too severe!—my heart will burst—I—I—but, no; let me be firm;—it is only the guilty that should tremble or give way to weakness ;—dear Hubert, take them from me, lest my brain should be bewildered !"

Poor old Hubert·Clensham, who evinced the most remarkable self-possession and fortitude on that awful occasion, did as Godfrey desired ; and directly afterwards they fainted, and were borne out of the hall into an adjoining apartment.

In the meantime the trial commenced, and proceeded ; and before it had concluded, Ernnestine was sufficiently recovered to give her evidence, which she did in so clear, so explicit, and so earnest a manner, that it made a great impression upon the judges; and, stern and callous almost to feeling as they were, they could not help being touched by the beauty and anguish of the hapless damsel. Who could doubt for a moment that aught but truth could fall from lips like her's ?—But, yet all that could be adduced in confirmation of the innocence of Godfrey, failed to convince his stern and inflexible judges ; and after all the witnesses had been examined, the Justiciary arose, and addressing himself to the unfortunate youth, said,—

" Prisoner ; thou hast heard the evidence adduced against thee ; if thou hast anything to say to avert thy fate, speak it ; and Heaven aid thee as thou mayest deserve !"

Godfrey turned his gaze for an instant upon Ernnestine and his mother, who seemed petrified to the spot with horror, and then in a firm and manly tone, he thus spoke :—

" My lord, thou callest on me in vain, if what has already been advanced in proof of my innocence has failed to convince thee. That I am not guilty, I solemnly again, in the face of Heaven, repeat ; but, if thou art resolved that I shall fall a victim to this dreadful charge, I must e'en submit with the consolation of an unsullied conscience, and a firm reliance on that mercy from a Supreme Judge, which man denies me here. I would, if it would avail me implore thy mercy for the sake of my poor mother. I would ask of thee my life, that the lives of my unhappy parents might be prolonged. I would ask thy mercy for the sake of yon trembling innocent, whose heart will be broken for ever, should I die a death of shame.—I would ask thee to spare my life for these :—for my innocence, I have nothing further to urge !—I may appear guilty ;—I may be thought a monster, which I should be were I guilty of the dreadful crimes with which I have been charged ; and gazing multitudes may behold my death with exultation, and ring their curses in my ears ; but there is one truth,—one consolation will uphold me through every horror,—it is, that *I am innocent !"*

The manner in which Godfrey spoke seemed to make a great impression upon the judges and every person in the hall ; but still there were so many condemnatory circumstances in the evidence which had been brought against him, they saw no reason why mercy should be shewn him.

He had firmly disavowed having acted of his own free will in his escape from the prison, and of being the murderer of the gaolers, yet had he as firmly refused to reveal the names of the person or persons who had assisted him, and perpetrated the crimes, solemnly, however, declaring that his father (who it was intended to put upon his trial afterwards) was entirely innocent of any participation in that deed ; and that circumstance weighed more than all against him ; the Justiciary therefore pronounced him 'guilty,' and was proceeding to pass upon him the sentence of death, when suddenly a loud voice from a distant part of the hall was heard to exclaim :—

"Godfrey de Lacy is innocent of the crimes alleged against him, and those who condemn him, will be guilty of his murder !"

Lord Raymond started at the well-remembered tones of the voice, and directing his gaze to that part of the hall from whence they issued, his astonishment may be well imagined when he beheld standing confronting the judges, the tall figure of the mysterious grey friar, whom he had twice encountered under such singular circumstances.

The attention of the court was immediately rivetted on the speaker, and astonishment pervaded every bosom, while Lord Raymond, as his eyes became fixed upon the figure of the mysterious monk, whose face was still covered with his cowl, felt an involuntary shudder of horror rush through his veins, for which he could not account, but found it impossible to resist. So great was the surprise and confusion the abrupt appearance and address of the stranger had caused in the court, that it was several minutes before any one could speak, until at length the chief Justiciary, arising, said,—

"Stranger, who art thou, and what hast thou to say respecting the guilt or innocence of the prisoner?"

"Who I am it boots not," replied the monk ; "I repeat my assertion, that you have convicted an innocent man; Godfrey de Lacy is not the murderer of Reginald, or the two other persons ;—and this I am ready to prove."

"How, sayest thou so, stranger?" demanded the Justiciary; "and to judge by thine holy garb, thou wouldst not speak an untruth. Tell me, who thou art, and what knowest thou of this dreadful affair ?"

"I tell thee again, my lord Justiciary," returned the supposed friar, in a stern voice, "that my name it matters thee not to know; if I prove to thee the innocence of Godfrey, and produce the real assassins, surely that should be deemed sufficient."

"Not so, holy father," observed the Justiciary; "thou mayest accuse others of these bloody deeds for the purpose of rescuing the prisoner; and it is but fair that those thou chargest with the perpetration of the same, should behold and know their accuser. If justice is thine aim, and thou art no false monk, thou wilt not hesitate to remove thy cowl and comply with my request."

"I do object me to do as thou desirest, my lord Justiciary," replied the mysterious monk ; "but I will not play thee false."

"My lord Justiciary," ejaculated Lord Raymond, "trust him not, I beseech thee, but insist upon knowing who he is.—Well assured am I that he is no monk, and that——"

"Beware! Lord Raymond," interrupted the stranger, "if thou wouldst not prevent the innocence of Godfrey de Lacy, whose cause thou pretendest to espouse being made manifest, thou wilt hold thy peace !—Thou and I have much to settle with each other at some future day, but not now, and——"

"Hearest thou not, my lord, he threatens me?" said Lord St. Aswolph. "Am I to sit here and be bearded thus by an insolent braggart as this is? I demand that he be seized and compelled to reveal who he is !"

"Stand back ! at thy peril touch me not!" cried the stranger, boldly, and waving his arm, as the Justiciary gave instructions to the officers of the court to seize him, and they advanced for that purpose; "mark me! I came for the furtherance of justice; the life of an innocent man is periled upon it, while if thou followest the advice of this headstrong noble, the real murderers will be suffered to escape punishment. By the mass an' a finger is laid upon me with an intent to harm me, I will have terrible satisfaction !"

"Ah! darest threaten ?" said the Justiciary, sternly.

"I dare more than thou art probably aware of, my lord Justicary," replied the stranger firmly, " but I do besech thee hear me with patience, and hold me harmless while I proceed to do what justice prompts."

"Hold ! touch him not;" ordered the Justiciary addressing the officers. — "Prisoner, knowest thou this man ?"

Godfrey looked earnestly at the supposed monk for a moment, and remained silent.

"Why dost thou not answer ?" demanded the Justiciary, peremptorily.

Godfrey still made no reply.

"This silence is a strong proof of guilt," observed the Justiciary; "the prisoner and this man are conniving together to deceive the court and baffle the ends of justice !"

"I tell thee, judge, 'tis false!" cried the mysterious stranger, " give me fair chance and I will prove the truth of what I have asserted to thy satisfaction."

"How ?"

"At one word the real assassins shall be produced before thee !"

"Fulfil, then, thy promise," said the Justiciary, who seemed strongly impressed with the manner of the stranger, and was somewhat awed by the boldness and determination of his words.

"Behold the assassins of Reginald before ye!" exclaimed the accuser, and, in an instant, the three robbers whom Osmond had doomed to die by the law of the land, for the crime they had committed, came tremblingly forward, and seemed to shrink appalled at the stern glance of their captain, whose eyes, from beneath his cowl, were fixed sternly upon them. A murmur of astonishment ran through the court at this unexpected incident, while the eyes of the Justiciary and the spectators wandered first to Osmond and then to the accused, who had resigned themselves into the hands of the officers, and seemed fully prepared to meet that fate from which they had no means of escaping. Rodolph alone appeared to hesitate, and to be uncertain how to act; but when he encountered the stern glance of Osmond, he turned away his head, and stood trembling by the side of his companions. It would be impossible to describe the feelings of astonishment, hope, suspense, and doubt that pervaded the minds of Godfrey and the others so deeply interested in this painful and tedious affair, and they awaited the result in a state of the most torturing anxiety.

"How ! what means this ?" demanded the Justiciary, at length.

"That we are rightly charged, my lord Justiciary," said Stephen, in firm accents, for tired of a life which the poignant agony of a guilty conscience had long rendered insupportable to him, he viewed the probability of his fate with the greatest calmness and even satisfaction ;—" we are the murderers of the unfortunate man, of slaying whom, Godfrey de Lacy is most wrongfully accused and condemned !"

The surprise of all who heard this gratuitous confession, was increased ten-fold, and they looked upon the robbers with breathless attention, and upon Osmond, who had folded his arms across his chest, and was standing, with form erect, by the side of the three trembling wretches.

"Babbling idiot !" exclaimed Rodolph, hoarsely.

"But who is he that hath accused thee ?" hastily demanded the Justiciary.

Rodolph advanced a few paces, and looking at the Justiciary, was evidently about to speak, but Osmond, who noticed his action, and read his intention, rushed to him, and grasping his arm fiercely, exclaimed, at the same time placing the point of a poniard to his breast :—

"Villain ! Remember thine oath !"

Rodolph shrunk back, and cowered beneath the gaze of the robber chief, but offered not to say another word.

"This trifling with the patience of the court," said the Justiciary, "I cannot permit longer; seize this stranger, who, if what he has stated be true, is, doubt-less, equally guilty with those he accuses !"

"My lord, I crave thy pardon," said Lord Raymond, "but I would suggest that ere thou proceedest to such an extremity, thou wilt hear any confession that these men may think proper to make. Remember, that the life of Godfrey de Lacy,—whom I firmly believe guiltless, although he has been condemned for this dreadful crime,—hangs upon that slender tenure."

"Be it so, my lord," said the chief Justiciary, after reflecting for a minute or two, then addressing himself to the prisoners, he demanded whether they either of them wished to say anything. Rodolph and Gilbert turned sullenly away, and made no reply, but Stephen immediately entered into a minute detail of the dreadful circumstance exactly as it took place, and has been described, and produced the packet exactly as Lord Raymond had entrusted it to the ill-fated man to convey to the Monastery of Saint Cuthbert, and the unfortunate Esquire's ring which they had taken from his finger. These, Lord Raymond was able to swear to in a moment, and the innocence of Godfrey de Lacy now began to be apparent.

Ernnestine, Edith, and Hubert clasped their hands, and raised their eyes to-wards heaven, in speechless gratitude, while Godfrey awaited, with the utmost firmness and composure, the result.

"But, yet it would seem that Godfrey de Lacy is colleagued with these men," said the Justiciary, after a pause; "for, if he knew himself to be entirely in-nocent, why should he seek to escape ?"

"That was my action, and he knew not either me or the purpose for which I had come upon, when, in the disguise that I now wear, I gained access to his dungeon," said Osmond ; "he acted on my persuasions alone."

"Ah !" observed the Justiciary, hastily, "thou acknowledgest thyself to have been the cause of his escape, and, doubtless, thou art the murderer of the two unfortunate men who were slain on that occasion ?"

"That, too, do I confess," replied the robber-chief, boldly. "I entirely ex-onerate Godfrey de Lacy from any participation in those deeds ;—but I warn ye to let me depart unscathed and unmolested, or be the consequences on thine own heads.—I have performed an act of justice, and——"

" Who art thou, for the last time, I demand ?" exclaimed the Justiciary.

" Osmond, the Avenger !" returned Rodolph, in a moment, and fixing a look of exultation upon the robber-chief.

" Traitor !" ejaculated Osmond, springing towards the robber, and, grasping him by the throat, he plunged his poniard several times into his body, and the ruffian fell a bleeding corpse at his feet !

So completely paralized were the whole of the spectators at what had so suddenly and unexpectedly taken place, that they had not the power to move or speak ; but at length the Justiciary arose, and again ordered the officers to seize upon Osmond. In a moment, however, his sword was unsheathed, and he stood in the attitude of defence, at the same time placing his horn to his lips, he blew three shrill blasts, which re-echoed through the spacious and lofty hall !—Instantly the robbers came pouring into the hall in every direction, and surrounding their captain, with their good yew-bows bent to their shoulders, prepared at a word from Osmond to deal destruction around.

" Stand back all of ye," said Osmond, " suffer me to depart from hence without interruption, and we will harm ye not, but destruction to those who madly seek to molest us !"

Universal astonishment prevailed in the court ; the Justiciaries and the spectators were astounded, and Osmond and his comrades, laughing triumphantly, slowly retreated from the place, leaving Gilbert and Stephen, together with the body of Rodolph behind them ; and they had got far away from the court before those who had been witnesses of what had taken place had sufficiently recovered from the surprise and confusion into which it had thrown them to offer any resistance.

CHAPTER XII.

" Try me as thou wilt,
I am so strong in innocence, that I
Laugh proudly to scorn each ordeal
Thou mayest test me with."

By the time the excitement the events we have just been describing had caused in the court had subsided, and the Justiciary and those who had heard the trial of the prisoner, had somewhat recovered from the state of astonishment into which the singular and daring conduct of the robber-chief had thrown them, the court was cleared of spectators, and such was the desperate character of Osmond and his gang, at the same time so far had he gained upon the esteem of the poor people, to whom, as we have before stated, he was a generous friend, assisting those in distress out of the booty he made in his predatory exactions from the wealthy, that no one thought for a moment of opposing their departure, and they had regained their strong hold, the Castle of St. Alwyn, before the sensation their appearance had excited at the Hall of Justice had disappeared.   At length, however, the chief Justiciary, having aroused himself, turned to the other noblemen seated by his side, and said,—

"This daring circumstance must be promptly attended to.—Too long has this desperate robber and his gang been suffered to carry on their lawless schemes with impunity, and to set every power at defiance ; but I am resolved that some steps shall immediately be taken to put an end to his guilty career, and to exterminate him and his guilty associates. Let the two prisoners be conveyed to safe custody, and, to-morrow, we will commence their trial. I am not yet satisfied that Godfrey de Lacy is innocent, or that he is not an accomplice of these wretches, and——"

A loud scream from Ernnestine interrupted the speech of the Justiciary, and, rushing forward, she threw herself on her knees at the feet of the nobleman, and in frantic accents, ejaculated,—

"Oh, my lord, spare him !—in mercy, spare him !—do not again tear him from me ! Ah ! I see thou art bent to take his life ! Thou art determined to murder him, although such unquestionable proofs of his innocence have been established. Godfrey, dear, much injured Godfrey, they shall not separate us :— if they are resolved against all reason and justice to detain thee a prisoner, I will share the same dungeon with thee, and——"

"Ernnestine, dearest maiden," interrupted Godfrey, with the utmost emotion, "if thou wouldst not drive me to madness,—if thou wouldst not see me unman yself, thou wilt endeavour to compose thy feelings, and to await with patience the issue of this painful affair. For myself, I fear not the result. I am so confident of mine own innocence, that I know ere many days I shall be restored to thee, my love, and without the slightest blemish or suspicion upon my character. Come, come,—cheer thee, cheer thee, sweetest, and trust me that all will be well."

During the time that Godfrey was speaking, the mind of Lord Raymond St. Aswolph was racked with the most distressing agony ;—in the first instance, to see the torture which the mind of Ernnestine was undergoing, was quite sufficient to occasion him the most poignant regret, and then the tender words that were exchanged between her and Godfrey, convinced him of the intensity of the passion which subsisted between them, and shewed him, in a more glaring point of view, the utter hopelessness of the love with which the beauteous damsel had inspired him. He, notwithstanding, appealed to the humanity of the chief Justiciary and Godfrey and our heroine, with the mother of the former, were permitted to embrace each other ; after which the feelings of the poor girl having overpowered her, she fainted, and by the orders of Lord Raymond was given into the care of Hubert and Edith and taken to the Castle of St. Aswolph, while Godfrey was removed to his dungeon, there to await the final decision which his judges might come to after the trial of Stephen and Gilbert.

Ernnestine remained in a state bordering on frenzy during the whole of that night, and the bosom of Lord Raymond underwent scarcely less misery than that which the unfortunate damsel was enduring. Every hour but served to add to the strength of that affection with which her innumerable charms and intrinsi*

qualities had inspired him ; and when he weighed every circumstance of the love
which her and Godfrey felt for each other, and the injustice of which he was
guilty to that unfortunate youth by indulging in an affection which he felt assured
could never be returned by the object who had given rise to it, he began to place
but very little reliance upon the prognostications to which Hal of the Glen had
given utterance, and saw the absolute necessity, for the sake of his own peace of
mind, of endeavouring to eradicate it from his heart. But, alas ! this was more
easily thought of than done ; and Lord Raymond passed a sleepless night,
ruminating upon every painful circumstance, and totally at a loss to think of any
plan by which he might be able to accomplish that which his generous nature
prompted.

Early the following day, Lord Raymond sought an interview with the chief
Justiciary, and endeavoured to convince him of the injustice he was doing to Godfrey, by longer detaining him in prison, or putting him to further trouble or
anxiety, after the acknowledged assassins were in custody ; but his lordship, who
was a stern judge, and a bigot in his way, was deaf to all the expostulations of
Lord Raymond, and expressed his determination that the whole affair should
undergo the most minute investigation, his opinion being unchanged as regarded Godfrey being an accomplice of the robbers, against whom he had formed
the resolution of sending a strong body of men after the trials were at an end.

One subject had particularly occupied the thoughts of Lord Raymond, since
the day before, and that was in discovering that the enemy who had inspired
him with so much dread, and who had two or three times threatened him with

No. 15

his vengeance, was the robber-chief, Osmond, the Avenger, who had for some years past spread such an universal panic all over the country; but how it was he had excited his hatred and revenge, he was at a perfect loss to imagine; for, although he had looked narrowly into his countenance during the time he had removed his monkish disguise, notwithstanding his features were somewhat familiar to him, he had not the slightest recollection of where he had seen him before; and he could not recal any circumstance to his mind which was at all calculated to assist his memory. He could not help thinking, however, upon him with a feeling of unaccountable dread, and neither could he divest his mind of an idea that he was destined to experience from him some annoyances of a dangerous and afflicting description, which he would find it impossible to avert.

The trial of Gilbert and Stephen proceeded that day, and they were condemned to die; but in spite of the innocence of Godfrey being established beyond the power of any reasonable person to doubt, the chief Justiciary and several other officers of the law did not think proper to be satisfied, and it was resolved that Godfrey should undergo the test of boiling water. It was in vain that Lord Raymond protested against this brutal and superstitious ordeal; the Justiciary and the others had made up their minds, and they would not hear of anything in opposition to their decision; and it was resolved that the ring which had been taken off the murdered man's finger, should be placed in a bowl of boiling water, and that if Godfrey could take it thence without receiving any injury, he should be pronounced guiltless, and himself and his father acquitted; but if, on the contrary, he should not be able to take it forth without being scalded, or refused to pass through the ordeal, they should both be considered guilty, and suffer death with the two robbers.

It was with sentiments of the utmost disgust, abhorrence, and indignation, that Lord Raymond heard this resolution, and he felt gratified to think that neither Ernnestine nor Edith were in the hall, they both being too ill, from the previous day's trial, to be able to attend; but such was the state of brutal ignorance and superstition of those unenlightened days, that many who were present felt gratified at the decision, and commended the impartiality and skill of the chief Justiciary for the idea. As for Godfrey himself, when he was asked whether he was willing to submit to the test, he replied, with a look of ineffable contempt and pity for the arbitrary and merciless feeling of his judges,—

" Willingly !—I place a firm reliance in Heaven, which will not suffer me to fall a victim to gross superstition, and shameless persecution."

He then breathed a prayer to Omnipotence, and invoking a blessing on the head of Ernnestine, he awaited with firmness, the most undaunted, the moment when he was to pass through the ordeal. The bowl was prepared, and the boiling contents poured into it from a cauldron. Then the ring of the late Reginald having been thrown into the bowl, the right arm of the young man was bared, and he was left to choose his own moment for the performance of this dreadful task. The most breathless suspense pervaded the whole court, and the actions of the young man were watched with the most profound attention. Once more he prayed the protection of Heaven,—then with a fearless expression of countenance he plunged his arm into the bowl of boiling water, and to the wonder of every one present, brought forth the ring without receiving any more injury than as if the water had been entirely cold ! A murmur of satisfaction passed through the hall, and then the chief Justiciary exclaimed,—

" Godfrey de Lacy has passed through the ordeal, and brought forth the ring uninjured ; he is, therefore, pronounced innocent of the foul and bloody charge of which he had previously been convicted, and together with his father, Ranulph de Lacy, is discharged from custody."

The fetters were removed from the limbs of the young man, and the next moment he rushed to the arms of his father, and both falling on their knees, poured forth their gratitude to the Most High for their miraculous delivery from the awful fate which had not many minutes before threatened them.

The first ebullitions of their joy having exhausted themselves, Lord Raymond descended from the seat which he had occupied, and in the warmest terms congratulated Godfrey de Lacy and his father upon their acquittal; after which the court broke up and the spectators soon dispersed ; those who had been most violent in condemning Godfrey de Lacy, being now the most noisy in their applause at the decision which had been given by the judges, and the miraculous manner in which he had passed through the ordeal.

Lord Raymond invited Ranulph and his son to his castle, and the delirious extacy with which the lovers embraced each other, and the frantic transport with which Edith clasped him to her bosom, and wept tears of gratitude and unfounded delight, needs no description. The joy of Ernnestine was so great, that it overcame her, and she became insensible.

At the same time that Lord Raymond felt the most sincere pleasure at the restoration of Godfrey to liberty, it was not unmingled with a sentiment approaching to jealousy, when he beheld the fond endearments the lovers bestowed upon each other, and the encouragement which Ranulph and Edith now seemed to give to their passion ; and while he reproached himself for the sentiment, he felt it was utterly impossible for him to conquer it, and every hour, every minute, served to increase the love which had gained such ascendancy in his bosom. It was a remarkable thing, that so strong as were his determinations, and when it is considered how quick-sighted jealous love is generally, Godfrey did not mark the emotions of his lordship, but so fully occupied was his mind with other thoughts, which the late exciting circumstances had created in it, that the former could give no thought to anything else but them and Ernnestine.

Lord Raymond, his mother, and Marguerite, treated them all with the most marked attention and kindness, and so much had Lady Celestine's love for Ernnestine increased, that she again expressed a wish to take her under her protection.

Hubert expressed his sense of her ladyship's kindness and condescension in the most fervent terms, but, at the same time, most respectfully declined this offer, stating, more particularly, as his reason for so doing, that he had been so long accustomed to her presence and the sweetness of her society, that now he was sinking into the vale of life, he could not dare to think upon depriving himself of her affectionate attentions. This argument was so forcible that Lady Celestine could not offer any opposition to it, but she felt very much disturbed at the circumstance, the interest, as we have before stated, which

Ernnestine had excited in her bosom, being of the most extraordinary and unaccountable description. But if her disappointment and vexation were great, how much more powerful were the same feelings created in the mind of Lord Raymond, who now felt that to live out of the presence of that beauteous damsel, was to be consigned to the greatest misery; but he stifled his emotions as well as he was able, lest they should be noticed by their guests.

Ernnestine, too, who could not be insensible of the kindness of Lady Celestine, sincerely regretted that her duty, and other circumstances, would not allow her to consent to the request she had made so urgently, but she felt that the honor her ladyship intended her, was far more than she had any right to expect, and received it with sentiments of the utmost gratitude, sweetly expressing herself to that effect, in a manner which excited the admiration of her listeners.

To the gentle and beauteous Marguerite, who had evinced so much affection towards her, her heart warmed with all the tenderness of a sister, and she felt that in her society she could have been supremely happy; and she was fearful, that by her declining the offers of Lady Celestine, it might appear to them that she was unmindful of the distinguished deference with which they had behaved to her and her friends, of the deep interest they had taken in their affairs, and the troubles that had lately afflicted them.

After some time passed in conversation upon other topics, a sudden thought seemed to occur to Lady Celestine, and addressing the friends of our heroine, she said,—

That, notwithstanding they had thought proper to decline the offer she had made them, of taking Ernnestine under her protection, and she could not but approve of the motives that prompted them to do so, she did not imagine that they could have any objection to her becoming her guest for a few weeks, until the late painful affair had entirely blown over in the public mind.

This invitation Hubert Clensham would also, had he consulted his own will, have declined, but admitting that it was most reasonable, and fearing that he should offend their best friends, he gave his assent to this proposition, and left it entirely to Ernnestine to decide.

The eyes of Godfrey de Lacy wandered to the countenance of his lover, and by their expression shewed the anxiety with which he awaited her answer. She easily read his thoughts, and by a sweet smile of encouragement, convinced him that, although she felt it to be her duty to give her assent, it should not be the means of preventing them from often meeting each other.

We need not seek to pourtray the feelings of extacy that prevailed in the bosom of Lord Raymond, when he heard the charming object of his admiration agree to become their guest, and never did he feel more sincerely grateful to his mother than he did for making this proposition.

The day passed away in the most agreeable manner, and in the evening Hubert and his wife returned home, after a most affectionate separation from Ernnestine, and evincing as much emotion as if they were about to be divided by miles, and without any prospect of seeing each other again; while Ranulph, Godfrey, and Edith, remained at the castle for the night.

Amidst the pleasure which Lord Raymond experienced at his being so near to

Ernnestine, his mind was strongly harassed and perplexed when he reflected upon all the events connected with the recent trial, but more especially upon the behaviour of the robber-chief towards himself—the several times he had appeared to him, under such mysterious circumstances, and the threats he had held out to him; not that he feared his power, (although his daring deeds had caused much consternation in the country, and it was thought to be so hazardous a task to seek to rout him and his desperate companions from their stronghold, that the attempt had but seldom been made, and then it was always attended with unsuccess,) but there was another and indefinite feeling crossed his mind whenever he thought upon him, which, in spite of all his efforts to the contrary, he found it utterly impossible to shake off.

From Godfrey and his father he had now received every particular concerning the late events, and the deep interest which Osmond had taken in the fate of the former, and the risk he had run, and that for one who, it would seem, was a stranger to him, more astonished him than all. He very much regretted that a man who had shown such disinterested friendship for Godfrey and his father, should not only be his (Lord Raymond's), declared most bitter foe, but the enemy to, and an alien from his country.

CHAPTER XIII.

"Although I am a bandit bold,
And plunder is my aim;
I never did my help withhold,
When pity made the claim."

OSMOND and his daring associates reached the impregnable castle of St. Alwyn in safety, and were hailed with the loudest cheers by the robbers, their companions, who had been anxiously awaiting their return.

"All hail! to our gallant chief, Osmond, the Avenger!" they shouted, and the lofty subterranean retreat, wherein they usually assembled, resounded again with their deafening shouts of delight and exultation, when their captain briefly informed them what had taken place.

"By this time, most likely, the dastard traitors who dared to disobey their captain's injunctions, have paid the penalty with their lives," said Osmond. "Comrades, remember their fate, and beware how ye keep the oath which binds us in unity together; a terrible punishment shall inevitably be the lot of those who break our laws. Say—is there any one among ye who disapproves of the manner in which your captain has behaved on this occasion?"

"None! none!" was the simultaneous answer, and again loud demonstrations of admiration shook the vaulted cavern.

"Enough!" said Osmond; "then are ye all prepared to stand by your captain while ye have life, should any attack be made upon us?"

"All! all! with the last drop of our blood," cried the robbers, unsheathing their swords, and crossing them; "death and destruction to the hated foes of Osmond, the Avenger!"

"'Tis well, my brave comrades," said Osmond. "I thank ye for your zeal, and shall not be unmindful to repay it. Ulric, see them to the castle, and be careful every thing be in readiness, so that in case of an attack from those whom we have just cause to expect will make one, we may be prepared to give them a warm reception, as we have done ere now."

"I will obey thee, captain," answered the lieutenant of the robbers, "but here in this strong fortress we may bid defiance to all the force they can bring against us."

"Thou sayest true, Ulric," observed the robber-chief; "but now would I draw thine, and the attention of our brave comrades to another subject. Ye all know this Ernnestine, the fair maid of the inn?"

"We do."

"Then, mark me; death is the portion of he who molests her, or does not protect her when she may require it! Dost hear?"

"We do, captain, and swear to obey."

Enough; know ye also the lady Marguerite, the sister of Lord Raymond St. Aswolph?"

The robbers replied in the affirmative.

"Then I charge ye,—any of ye, that may meet her, make her your prisoner; but, as ye fear my vengeance, use no more violence than may be found necessary to convey her to our retreat."

The men swore to obey; and these matters being adjusted, and Ulric having seen that the castle was secure from any danger of a surprise, they gathered around the festive board and commenced their usual revelry.

"Yes," cried the robber-chief, when he retired to rest, "the fair Marguerite, the sister of the man I have the greatest cause to detest, shall become the mistress of Osmond, the Avenger!—Long have mine eyes beheld her with the warm glances of desire, and never will I rest until she has become mine!—Oh, this will be glorious revenge for the wrongs I have received at the hands of Lord Raymond, and will torture him more than if I were at once to sacrifice his life, which I have the power to do. But no, he shall live to see me triumph and exult over his sufferings, and to ring my curses in his ears!"

As Osmond thus spoke, he clenched his fist, and, with a look of determination, quitted the cavern.

The chief Justiciary, who, for some unaccountable reason, had become prejudiced against Godfrey de Lacy, was resolved, at once, to put into execution his design upon the robber-chief and his companions, and to endeavour to destroy those who had been so long the terror of the country, more especially as they had been the means of rescuing from the iron fangs of the law those individuals he had most unaccountably and unjustly condemned, unheard, in his own mind, and upon whom he felt a sanguinary regret, that he had not had an opportunity of inflicting that punishment for the crimes of which they had been accused. The chief Justiciary was notorious for his brutal severity and partiality, and, in private life, he was haughty, tyrannical, despotic, and overbearing; yet, there were those who said they remembered him when his character was widely different, and when he was as much esteemed for his general urbane and benevolent conduct, as he was now hated, dreaded, and despised.

This extraordinary change could only be accounted for through some severe domestic calamity which had attended him, and which will shortly be more fully explained.

Lord Randolph de Mowbray, (the chief Justiciary), had formerly, as we have before stated, been held in the highest esteem, and for the remarkable metamorphosis that his character had so suddenly undergone, no other reason could be assigned than that his wife had proved faithless to him, at least, so it was suspected, for the truth could never be fully ascertained, his lordship thinking proper to keep his private sorrows confined to his own bosom. It was well known, that she had very suddenly disappeared, and it was currently rumoured at the time, that she had eloped with one of his lordship's menials. Lord Randolph had been summoned to the field of battle, and, during his absence, had left his lady under the protection of his cousin, Sir Wilfred Martingale; after enduring all the dangers and horrors of the strife;—after encountering every difficulty, Lord Randolph de Mowbray returned to England, fully expecting to clasp again to his throbbing bosom, a wife whom he worshipped. Sir Wilfred hurried to meet him; deep melancholy darkened his brow;—he asked for his wife. A tale of maddening horror was his answer;—she had blasted her fair name for ever, and yielded to the lascivious desires of one of his vassals; at least, such was the account given by Sir Wilfred. Yes, that woman he had loved; nay, adored; whose mildly beaming eye glowing upon him with innocence and affection, had chased every care from his mind;—that woman was an adultress!

Such was the tale related to Lord Randolph, and which had not only embittered his future days, but had been the cause of effecting such a marvellous change in his disposition; but, yet the severity and injustice with which he treated most of the cases that came before him, was perfectly unpardonable, only as the act of a madman; and many persons firmly believed that the severe blow we have been describing, had been the means of overturning his reason.

Fully satisfied of the power possessed by Osmond, and of the many futile attempts that had been made to apprehend him, the Justiciary felt convinced that nothing whatever could be hoped to be effected, unless it was by stratagem, and with that view, he bethought him, that, if he could prevail upon one of the two prisoners under sentence of death, by the promise of a free pardon, to assist them in taking the robbers by surprise, (for he was well aware that there were many secret entrances to the castle), they might secure the daring chief and his gang without bloodshed.

Filled with this resolution, his lordship sought an interview with the two men;

but, in spite of the offers that were made them, such was the regard in which they held the oath which had been administered to them when they joined the robbers, that they refused to divulge a syllable which might be the means of endangering the safety of Osmond and his comrades, who was held in such respect, a respect almost amounting to awe, by all those under his command. Stephen, in particular, evinced much emotion when his lordship made the proposal; and it had been noticed on the trial that he was very much agitated whenever Lord Randolph addressed him, and frequently turned very pale. Several times he seemed as if he wished to address something to the Justiciary, but had not the courage to do so; but, on the present occasion, after his lordship had made use of all the persuasions and arguments he could think of, to induce one of them to accede to his wishes, and was about to quit the dungeon in which the robbers were confined together, Stephen, in a voice of much emotion, called him back, and requested him to listen to him for a minute or two only. His lordship most readily complied with his request, thinking, that, in all probability, he had relented, and was ready to give him all the information in his power.

"Now, prisoner," said the latter, "what wouldst thou of me?"

"Pardon me, my lord," replied the penitent robber;—"but, (although by so doing, I shall, doubtless, harrow up thy feelings), I would ask thee, whether thou hadst not once, one whom thou didst consider to be thy friend?"

"1 had,—1 had," hastily answered the Justiciary; his manner being very much agitated, "but why ask me such a question?"

"The name of this *friend!*" hastily demanded Stephen.

"Sir Wilfred Martingale."

"Thou hadst a wife?"

"Prisoner, thou seemest resolved to madden me!—Oh! I had indeed, a wife."

"Thou didst believe her false to thee?—Thou thoughtest she fled with one of thy menials?"

"Thought she fled!—Alas! had I not too terrible confirmation of the truth?"

"Thy supposed friend told thee so?"

"He did."

"And, two years after the circumstance of which thou hast just spoken, that *friend* disappeared, and has never been heard of since?"

"He did;—but tell me,—what knowest thou of him?"

"I am that villain!—I am that treacherous friend, to whom thou didst entrust the honour of thine injured wife,—in me thou beholdest Sir Wilfred Martingale!"

"Thou Sir Wilfred Martingale!" exclaimed the Justiciary, with astonishment; —impossible!"

"Alas! my lord," returned the robber, "it is too true; years may have changed my features; dissipation may have altered and attenuated my form; but —oh, the damning voice of a guilty conscience defies me to forget myself. My Lord Randolph, look at me more narrowly;—dost thou not recollect me now?"

The Justiciary did look more closely than before into the countenance of Stephen for a few minutes, and then observed :—

"Thy words astonish me ;—the Sir Wilfred Martingale I called my friend, had a scar on his right wrist."

"Behold, 'tis here !" ejaculated the prisoner, turning up the sleeve of his doublet, and exhibiting the scar mentioned. When the Justiciary beheld it, he started back in the most indescribable state of agitation, and his countenance became very pale, then clasping his hands to his forehead, he exclaimed :—

"Almighty Father ! thy ways are, indeed, wonderful ; but say, unhappy man, hew canst thou prove the innocence of my wife ?"

"In a few words, I doubt not that I shall be able to convince thee, my lord," replied the other, " and then thou wilt see how infinitely wise are the decrees of Omnipotence ; and, however slow it may be, that a just and terrible retribution is sure to overtake the guilty. Long before the circumstances took place, which called your lordship to the field of battle, I had beheld her ladyship with the eyes of sinful desire, and when thou didst confide to me her honour, and left me to protect her during thine absence from her arms, I was so elated, that it is won-derful I did not betray myself. Not many days after thou hadst quitted thy native land, I made the most bold advances to the Lady Constance, and I need not say that she not only indignantly repulsed me, but that she severely reproached me for my treacherous conduct. I scornfully laughed at her observations, and determined that I would not abandon my designs until I had ultimately accomplished my wishes, let the consequences be what they might. But the virtue of Lady Constance was proof against all my deep laid schemes, and I found that I had no chance whatever, unless it was by using violence. In that also I failed, and Lady Constance contrived to escape from my power. I had my spies about in all directions, and soon succeeded in discovering the place of her retreat ; and, one night, when she was not at all aware that the place of her concealment was found out, she was seized, by my orders, and conveyed to a place of security, in a remote part of the country, where I was resolved that nothing should again prevent me from gratifying the wishes that had entered my bosom. In vain the unfortunate lady endeavoured by every means in her power to render my base schemes abortive ;—I, at last, succeeded in accomplishing my wishes ; Lady Constance, thy wife became the victim of my unlawful desires."

" Gracious Heaven !" exclaimed the Justiciary, his countenance becoming ghastly pale, and every limb trembling with convulsive emotion ; " to what a dreadful tale have I been listening ; but it cannot be true !—Wretched man, thou art mad, or wouldst deceive me !"

" Would to God thy words were true, my lord," replied the prisoner, " but, alas ! what interest can I have in attempting to deceive thee, when I am already condemned by the laws of my country to die ?—I repeat, and my blood freezes with horror when I recal the same to my mind, that thy unfortunate wife was violated by me. In order to drown the voice of suspicion, I had contrived to persuade, by the offer of a rich reward, Orlando, her favourite page, to leave the castle in a secret manner, and raised a report that she had eloped with him. My diabolical scheme succeeded too well. The world, I believe, generally thought her guilty, and for awhile, I triumphed in my iniquity. I kept the Lady Constance confined ; but, it was soon evident that she was rapidly sinking under the horrors of the situation in which she was placed ; and that the indignities I had offered her, and the shame and dishonour I had been the means of heaping upon her, were fast preying upon her constitution, and that she was gradually sinking of a broken heart. In the meantime, however, thou didst return home, and thou knowest the story which I told thee, and which thou, unfortunately, wert too ready to believe. For months after thou hadst come back, Lady Constance continued to be the victim of my guilt and treachery, and imagined thou wert no more, for I had told her that thou hadst perished on the battle-field. At length, however, she sunk beneath the weight of her sorrows. She breathed her last, and in what other character could I view myself than as the murderer of the unfortunate lady ?"

" Oh, villain ! villain !" cried the Justiciary, in tones of the most acute agony ; " to what a recital of horror have I been listening ;—and this from thee ; from one in whom I confided, as if thou hadst been mine own brother ?"

" Ah ! well do I merit thy reproaches, thy curses, said the prisoner, " I am, indeed, a guilty wretch, without hope of mercy from offended Heaven ; but, deeply have I suffered for the crimes I have committed. In about two years after thy return to England, unable to bear the reproaches of my conscience, and yet, coward like, afraid to confess my guilt, and to make all the atonement in my power,—I suddenly quitted the country, and it was supposed by you, and many others, no doubt, that I was dead. On the continent, I entered into those scenes of folly, dissipation, and vice, that were soon the means of squandering away my once ample fortune. 1 became a beggar, and had not a friend in the world. I returned to my native land so altered in my personal appearance that it would have been scarcely possible for any of my former acquaintances to recognize me. I accidentally encountered Osmond, the Avenger, and some of his comrades in the wood. I had no money, and knew not in what way to exist;—Osmond seeing me a desperate man, made me an offer to become one of their gang. Reckless entirely to the course I might in future pursue, I readily yielded my compliance with his request, and have ever since continued to be one of his associates, and never, but in the instance of that awful crime, for which I and Gilbert are justly doomed to suffer, did I break through the rules prescribed by us. This is the simple statement of the facts, my lord, and thou beholdest in me a terrible example of the retribution, which, sooner or later, is sure to overtake the guilty.'

"Wretched man, murderer of my unfortunate Constance," ejaculated the distracted nobleman, "what unspeakable agony has thy dreadful tale inflicted upon my mind. Heaven pardon thee, for I feel that I cannot."

Having thus given expression to his sentiments, the Justiciary covered his face with his hands and rushed out of the cell.

Stephen and his companion suffered the penalty of death for the murderous crimes they had committed, on the following day, and, with the termination of the trial, and their execution, the excitement which had prevailed in such an extraordinary degree began to abate. Godfrey, however, felt far from happy, the visit of Ernnestine to the Castle of St. Aswolph, although it was for a limited period, filled his mind with a variety of conflicting ideas that caused him the utmost uneasiness. Notwithstanding, he had frequent—nay, daily interviews with her, her conduct was unchanged; was as warm, as ardently affectionate as it had ever been towards him; and his parents, and Hubert Clensham, did not seem to view it with the same repugnance that they had previously done; but, yet, when he noticed the attentions of Lord Raymond towards Ernnestine, and remembered many words that he had promiscuously dropped, he could not help thinking that his conduct was rather remarkable, and far more particular than the difference of their stations, and the circumstances called for. That he loved her, never for a moment entered his thoughts,—at least he could not satisfy himself that such an idea had taken possession of his mind; yet, there was a certain familiarity in his behaviour towards her—at least, so he imagined,—that he viewed with anything but sentiments of satisfaction, and he longed for the time when her visit to the castle would be at an end, and she again became the inmate of 'The Flagon,' where he 'might hope to become her companion again, without any restraint upon their conduct.

True love is naturally selfish; it is tenacious of losing the smallest iota of affection, which it considers it has a right to monopolize from the object of its choice, and so it was with Godfrey de Lacy.

Filled with these thoughts, a few days after the important trial, Godfrey, after he had had an interview with his lover, walked forth, almost unconscious whither he was going, into the dark recesses of the forest; and so fully occupied was his mind with the chain of ideas we have been attempting to describe, that he wandered on, without noticing what direction he was going, until the shades of evening had descended upon the earth, and he had become so deeply entangled in the mazes of the forest, that he was at a loss to know in what manner he should extricate himself.

The spot he was in was one of the deepest gloom, and such a place as seemed to be seldom, if ever, traversed by the foot of man, and the branches of the trees were so thickly interwoven with each other, that their foliage forming a deep canopy over his head, almost entirely excluded the light of Heaven. Before him was a long vista of trees, which seemed interminable, and the appearance of which was of the most awful description.

Godfrey never remembered to have seen this place before; but recollecting the different accounts he had heard, he, after contemplating it for a few seconds, said,—

" This must be the entrance to that awful place, occupied by that mysterious being, Hal of the Glen, believed, by most persons, to be a sorcerer. Let me hasten from this place. But stay," (he added, as a sudden thought darted across his brain,) " what should I fear ?—I never wilfully harmed mortal, and why, then, should I ?—Besides, if this strange being possesses the power he pretends to, I may learn something from him which I wish to know. Shall I seek his presence ?"

" Seek his presence?" re-echoed a hollow voice, which vibrated awfully along the dreary avenue.

" Ah! that voice," cried Godfrey; ' was it only the echo of mine own, or that of the power I seek ?"

" The power thou seekest !" responded the same voice.

" This is no deception," exclaimed Godfrey, looking with astonishment around him; " but, yet, I do not see anything. Mysterious being, where art thou ?"

" Behold !" was the answer.

Godfrey once more looked up, and beheld a pair of fierce eyes fixed upon him ; Hal of the Glen stood in his presence, though how he had come there he knew not, unless he had arisen out of the earth.

Godfrey gazed upon him with a mixture of wonder and awe, and then, in a firm tone, demanded,—

"What wouldst thou with me?"

"Didst thou not invoke me?" said Hal.

"No."

"But thou didst wish to see me?"

"How knowest thou that?"

"Ha! ha! ha!—What is there that is hidden from Hal of the Glen?— Follow me."

"Whither?"

"To where thou shalt learn all that thou desirest to know, although the knowledge may cause thee much unhappiness!"

"Ha!"

"Dost fear to make the trial?"

"Fear!" returned Godfrey, proudly ; "what is there that I should fear? —Lead on ; I will follow thee, and test the power of thy sorceries."

"Enough!" exclaimed Hal of the Glen—"this way, and gain thy wishes."

Godfrey drew forth his sword from his scabbard, at which the wizard fixed upon him a demoniacal grin of contempt, and walked on, without saying another word. Or, rather, he seemed to glide along, for he proceeded with the greatest velocity, so that Godfrey found it a very difficult matter to keep up with him, and his feet did not appear to touch the ground. As they thus pursued their way, the mysterious and incoherent mutterings of numerous voices seemed to diz in the ears of Godfrey; and ever and anon, a strange, and scarcely distinct phantom would flit with the speed of thought before his eyes, and would then immediately become invisible. Occasionally, too, the wizard would turn back, apparently, to see whether or not he was following him, and his eyes would glare upon him like balls of fire.

Godfrey felt an icy chill running through his veins, but yet he was completely undaunted, and was determined, let whatever might be the consequences, to see the result of this adventure. He had heard many wonderful stories about the power of the magician, and he was now, therefore, resolved to know how far they were to be depended upon.

After threading their way along this dismal avenue for some distance, they, at length, reached the glen, in which the wizard held his awful and mysterious power, and here the magician went through the same ceremony, and Godfrey was witness to the same kind of horrors that we have described on two or three previous occasions. The magic circle was formed, and Hal of the Glen, after giving him the same precautions as he had formerly done to his father, and to Lord Raymond, commenced his incantation, throwing various ingredients into the cauldron, dancing round it with frantic gestures, and giving utterance to the following words, that were, at intervals, accompanied by loud peals of thunder and flashes of lightning, that revealed the horrors of the place in a more ghastly point of view :—

> " Spirits from charnel house just broke,
> Thy mighty power I now invoke ;
> Aid me, then, to tell this youth,
> What he seeks to know—the truth !
> Spirits of darkness and of air,
> What I would know, now quick declare ;
> His fate has it been to inspire
> A maiden's heart with Cupid's fire ?"

A brief pause ensued, and then a hundred awful voices thundered forth the following answer :—

> " Godfrey bends low at beauty's shrine,
> And is beloved by Ernnestine !"

A feeling of extacy, of unbounded delight, took possession of the bosom of Godfrey when he heard this, and he could scarcely restrain the expression of his joy ; notwithstanding, the sincerity of Ernnestine's love required no confirmation with him.   The wizard once more danced around the mystic cauldron, and shortly afterwards broke forth in the following strain :—

> " Is the maiden to him true ?
> Smiles she on no one but he ?—

The voices replied,—

> " Another her with love doth view,
> And she his bride's destined to be !"

Again the voice of the wizard demanded,—

> " His name, who loves this maiden fair,
> To whom, the bride, is doomed to be ?
> Quickly, spirits, now declare."

Spirits.—" St. Aswolph's, noble lord is he !"

" Horror ! horror!—Lord St. Aswolph, the destined busand of my Ernnestine," cried Godfrey, in tones of distraction ; fiends of darkness, I will hear no more!—It is a base mockery !—Avaunt, demons, to thy native hell !"

Instantaneously the glen became enshrouded in deep and impenetrable darkness, and the words of Godfrey being followed by the most terrific yells, and bursts of supernatural laughter, he found himself alone.

Bewildered—paralyzed—horrorstruck, by all he had seen and heard, Godfrey de Lacy, remained for a few minutes completely transfixed to the spot, and could scarcely believe that what he had seen and heard was not a delusion; but, at length, having partially recovered himself, he called upon Hal of the Glen, and commanded him to appear once before him. A loud burst of demoniacal laughter was the only reply he met with and feeling an irresistible sensation of horror creeping through his veins—which he found it would be impossible for him to conquer at that moment—he groped his way back to the spot, at which he had encountered the wizard, as speedily as possible.

The moon had arisen when he arrived at the open space immediately before the dark avenue which led to the glen, in which he had lately witnessed so many horrors; and the brightness with which it beamed upon the surrounding scenery, strongly contrasted with the unearthly gloom he had just emerged from, His mind was racked to distraction, and his brain burned, as with a fever.

"Ernnestine, the bride of Lord Raymond!" he cried.—" Impossible!—It cannot be !—It must not—it shall not be !—What fiends are at work to distract my mind ?—I am the victim of some infernal spell !—Ernnestine, the bride of another! and that man the proud and wealthy St. Aswolph!—'Psha! I will not believe it!"

"But thou mayest believe it!" exclaimed a voice close to his ear, and turning round quickly with amazement, he beheld the tall and commanding figure of Osmond, the robber-chief, standing at his elbow. "Godfrey," continued Osmond, "thou hast visited Hal of the Glen ?"

"He has appeared to me," answered Godfrey, "and prevailed upon me to listen to his infernal predictions."

"They will be verified."

"Ha!"

"Who dares to dispute his power," returned Osmond; "I tell thee, Godfrey, that Lord Raymond views the beauteous Ernnestine with the eyes of affection !"

"Confusion!" cried the youth; "have my senses left me; or am I made the sport of some inscrutable power ?—Osmond, thou hast proved thyself to be my friend; do not, therefore, I beseech thee, deceive me, on the present occasion; how knowest thou that Lord St. Aswolph has dared to raise his thoughts to Ernnestine ?"

"No matter," answered Osmond, " I tell thee again it is so, and——"

"Then, by hell! he dies!" exclaimed Godfrey, in a tone of desperation, and taking a dagger from his bosom as he spoke.

"Nay, not so," coolly returned Osmond, " Lord Raymond must not fall by thy hand. I have a much more satisfactory method of revenge in store for thee."

"But the wizard has prognosticated that he shall become the husband of my Ernnestine."

"And e'en let him be so," answered the robber-chief, "that very circumstance will but add to the vengeance which will at one period or the other, descend upon his head with destructive violence."

"I do not understand thee," said Godfrey; "for the love of Heaven, do not rack me, but at once explain to me thy meaning!"

"Not now—not now," returned Osmond, "for the present thou must remain ignorant of my designs; let it suffice that I am thy friend, and the mortal foe of Lord Raymond St. Aswolph; and do not give way to despair; Ernnestine sincerely loves thee, and in spite of whatever circumstances may intervene, she shall ultimately become thy bride!"

"Mystery upon mystery," ejaculated Godfrey,—"when will this be unravelled?"

"Wait patiently, and thou wilt see," replied the robber-chief; "for the present, farewell; we shall anon meet again!"

Thus speaking, Osmond hastened into the deep recesses of the wood, towards the Castle of St. Alwyn, and was soon lost to the sight.

Godfrey paused, and meditated for an instant, but his brain was so bewildered by what had taken place, that he scarcely was conscious of what he was doing, and, with disordered steps, he bent his way towards the Castle of St. Aswolph.

CHAPTER XIV.

"There is a mystery about him, lady,
    An air of ambiguity, I can't unravel.
    He should be noble from his demeanour,
    Yet the fierce name he bears inspires terror."

ELATED by the happy change in their circumstances, and the favourable result of the painful and alarming events that had long caused them so much anxiety; also sincerely grateful for the manner in which she was treated by the noble family of St. Aswolph, and which she had no right to expect, considering the difference of their stations, Ernnestine soon recovered her former spirits, and, delighted to see that her friends no longer seemed to be so averse to the addresses of herself and Godfrey, she began to look forward to happier days.

Lady Celestine seemed to make it her study to see in which manner she could best contribute to her pleasure and enjoyment, and the beauteous Marguerite appeared to be completely miserable when out of her society. Our heroine,

therefore, it need not be wondered, experienced a feeling of regret as the time approached for her to leave the castle; and were it not that she was fearful of causing pain to her dear friends, and seem forgetful of the unbounded affection with which they had ever behaved towards her, she could have been content to have remained an inmate of St. Aswolph for the rest of her days.

The Castle of St. Aswolph, as we believe we have before mentioned, was, in truth, a most magnificent and venerable structure, not more remarkable for its gothic architectural beauties, than the picturesque scenery amid which it stood. Its spacious halls and chambers abounded with all that feudal grandeur could imagine; and the romantic grounds by which it was surrounded, displayed the consummate taste of its fair occupants, to whose judgment their arrangement was due.

No two minds could better assimilate in virtues and accomplishments than did those of our heroine and the Lady Marguerite; they, in fact, seemed by nature formed to be companions and friends. Enthusiastic admirers of the wonderful works of Omnipotence, it was their delight to wander in the forest dell, or by the margin of the pellucid streamlet, which meandered its silvery course through the gardens of the castle; where Marguerite, taking her lute, upon which instrument she was a most accomplished performer, she would strike its chords to notes of simple melody, while Ernnestine would, probably, accompany its tones to some pathetic ballad, making the bonny green wood resound with notes of harmony and gladness.

No 17

It was upon one of these occasions, when Ernnestine had been an inmate of the castle about a month, that herself and Marguerite walked forth into the forest, and took their seats on a green knoll in one of the most beautiful and secluded spots of that delightful place. It was a lovely day, the peaceful shade to which they had betaken themselves was sufficiently secluded from the scorching rays of the noon-day sun, to render it peculiarly pleasant and refreshing. The feathered songsters were warbling forth their sweetest carols, and everything was calculated to soothe the mind oppressed with care into calm tranquillity. The fair companions were quite enraptured with all around them, and, at length, Marguerite, striking the chords of her lute to a favourite melody, Ernnestine, in tones of sufficient sweetness to enchant the most insensible being, sang the following

SONG.

A song to the wood, the bonny green wood,
Whose sons have for ages so sturdily stood ;
Braving the tempest, which erst has been driv'n,
With terrible wrath through the high vault of Heaven !
With their branches so stout, that the wild blasts defy,
And their emerald heads, that soar to the sky;
Whose trunks have been hewn for the ocean's wide flood,
Then a song to the sons of the bonny green wood,
A song to the bonny green wood.

Oh ! what can compare with the wood's peaceful shade,
Its bird-cluster'd oak trees, its calm, silent glade,
Where the wild deer are bounding so joyous and free,
The emblems of glorious liberty ?
When Sol in bright splendour awakens the morn,
And is heard the loud notes of the forester's horn ;
Then find me the churl, among life's human brood,
Who would not a song for the bonny green wood.
A song to the bonny green wood.

"Charming! exquisite! my sweet Ernnestine," ejaculated Marguerite, in accents of admiration, when our heroine had finished the above song; "by the blessed Virgin, thou dost improve daily, and begin to make me quite ashamed of my poor skill on this instrument."

"Thou art disposed to flatter my humble abilities lady, methinks," replied Ernnestine, blushing deeply at the compliment which Marguerite had paid her; "I deserve not such praise."

"Nay, say not so, my dear girl," said Marguerite, sweetly, "for thou dost thyself an injustice; thou art deserving of far greater eulogiums than any I can bestow upon thee. My brother has lost a treat, which he will much regret, orsooth, when I inform him of it."

"Thy brother! lady," said our heroine, in accents of timidity, and as a feeling came over her which she had never experienced before.

"Yes, Ernnestine," answered her companion, "thou knowest Raymond is a very great admirer of thy vocal powers, and that was the first song he heard thee sing. I have frequently heard him speak in terms of rapture at the manner in which thou didst execute it on that occasion. Thou knowest my brother has a most refined taste."

" I know it, lady," returned Ernnestine, again blushing and trembling; " but I am fearful that Lord Raymond has suffered his natural generous and kind-hearted disposition to prejudice him in this instance. Praise from such a source is, indeed, highly flattering to me."

" I am delighted to hear thee speak thus, my charming Ernnestine," observed Marguerite, her bright eyes sparkling with additional lustre, with pleasure and vivacity; " I feel myself equally honoured with my brother for the compliment thou hast bestowed upon him, a compliment, it would be complete affectation in me to seek to deny that he fully deserves."

" Oh, I am confident he does," said Ernnestine, in tones of ardent sincerity ; " and never shall I cease to remember him with the utmost regard, for the——"

" Too generous and beauteous Ernnestine," at that moment exclaimed a voice immediately behind them, and the next moment Lord Raymond stood before them, his eyes beaming an expression of the most unbounded admiration upon our deeply-blushing and confused heroine. " Alas!" he continued, " how shall I ever be able to evince that proper sense of gratitude, which such an opinion, and uttered by thee, deserves. Permit me, as a small proof of the sentiments with which thou hast inspired me, on my knee thus to press my lips upon thine hand, and to assure thee —"

" Hold! audacious noble!" cried an enraged voice, and in an instant Godfrey rushed between Ernnestine and Lord Raymond, as the latter was about to kneel, and frowning fiercely upon him, grasped the arm of his lover with a determined air. The group formed a tableau of astonishment and confusion.

" How now, sirrah!" cried Lord Raymond, when he had partially recovered himself, and in indignant tones;—" methinks thou dost forget thyself."

" Methinks *thou* dost forget *thyself*, my Lord Raymond St. Aswolph," replied the young man, with a bold and undaunted air; " methinks thou dost forget thyself, thus boldly to advance thy suit towards one who is the affianced of another."

" Insolent!" ejaculated his lordship, who was unable to controul his anger within those bounds which reason usually dictated to him; " were it not that the difference of our rank protects thee, thou shouldst repent this."

" Were my Lord Raymond sincere in his threats," returned Godfrey, with equal spirit, " he would not endeavour to shield himself behind the bulwark of his rank !"

" By all my hopes, I cannot tamely brook this !" exclaimed Lord Raymond, passionately drawing his sword, and rushing impetuously on Godfrey ; but at that instant Ernnestine uttered a loud scream, and darting in between his lordship and her lover, she cried, in frantic accents,—

"Oh, hold! hold! my lord; for the love of Heaven!—for my sake, put up thy sword!—Godfrey, art thou mad?"

"Mad!—Mad!" repeated the latter. "Confusion!—surely my senses deceive me!—Can this be my Ernnestine, and pleading for my titled rival?"

"Godfrey!" ejaculated Ernnestine, reproachfully, and bursting into tears, "canst *thou* think so basely of me?—Alas! how have I deserved this?"

"Fairest lady," said Lord Raymond, "appeal not to this headstrong youth; he will have good reason, methinks, to repent his rashness; such behaviour, forsooth, but ill-becomes the wooer of one of the most gentle of her sex."

"Brother," interrupted Lady Marguerite, in persuasive tones, "pr'ythee let us retire, and leave Godfrey and Ernnestine to themselves; an explanation from her lips, I am convinced, will shew him how unjust have been his suspicions, and needs no assurance from me. Come, Raymond."

"Sweet sister," replied Lord Raymond, "I will yield compliance with thy wishes, for the sake of Ernnestine, to whom, the saints forbid, that I should be the cause of one moment's anguish. Godfrey de Lacy, I do advise thee to endeavour to controul thy passions with the bounds of prudence, and remember that modesty best becomes thy humble rank."

"Godfrey de Lacy needs no tutor in Lord Raymond St. Aswolph," haughtily replied the young man, "neither, though humble be his rank, will he tamely brook an injury from any man, however noble may be the blood which flows within his veins, or lofty the station he hold in society."

"Godfrey," ejaculated Ernnestine, with much emotion, "if thou valuest my love, cease this offensive tone, which——"

"Oh, fear not, lady," interrupted his lordship, "for thy sake I will not heed his words. Fare thee well."

Thus speaking, Lord Raymond kissed his hand to our heroine; Marguerite smiled sweetly upon her, and taking the arm of her brother, they walked on towards the castle, leaving the lovers to themselves.

For some minutes after Lord Raymond and his sister had quitted the spot, neither Godfrey or Ernnestine were able to speak to each other; and the former, with folded arms and contracted brow, walked backwards and forwards with uneven and agitated steps, while his heaving chest, and the sighs that frequently escaped his bosom, told at once the mental anguish he was enduring. Ernnestine, too, evinced the greatest emotion, while, at length, her feelings completely overpowered her, the burst into tears, and placing her long fair fingers on her lover's arm, she looked up reproachfully in his face, and in a voice of deep agitation, said,—

"Alas! Godfrey, what strange infatuation has taken possession of thy reason; how has thine Ernnestine deserved this?"

"My Ernnestine," repeated the young man, pausing, and looking at her stedfastly, while he in vain struggled to repress the powerful feelings of jealousy that racked his mind, "say not so; the name is mockery: thou art no longer *my* Ernnestine—thou hast deceived me—cruelly, heartlessly deceived me!"

"Godfrey," ejaculated Ernnestine, as a mingled sentiment of offended pride and resentment filled her bosom, " this from thee ! But no, no—my ears must have deceived me ! Thou couldst not be so unjust—thou must be labouring under some unfortunate delusion; otherwise, I must still think too well of Godfrey de Lacy, to suppose him capable of entertaining such ideas of her who has ever shewn how sincerely, how fondly, how unchangeably she loves him."

" Ernnestine," ejaculated Godfrey, clasping his forehead, " thou torturest, hou distractest me ! Leave me ! Oh, no, no; there was a time, and but a few short hours since, when I fondly believed that no woman could love man more fervently, more sincerely, than thou didst me; but the delusion is fled—the spell is past—the mist is removed from before mine eyes : Ernnestine's heart belongs not to Godfrey de Lacy !"

" Godfrey," said Ernnestine, in a voice half stifled by sobs, and turning away her head, " I will not reproach thee, for I feel assured that thy mind must be disordered, or never couldst thou give utterance to language such as this, to her who has ever been ready to make any sacrifice for thy sake. Alas ! alas ! what a cruel fate is mine, to meet the suspicions of him for whom every fibre of my soul throbs with woman's most ardent affection."

" Ernnestine," returned Godfrey, " canst thou deny that I caught this titled wooer on his knee at thy feet, pressing thine hand to his lips, and breathing forth in accents of eloquence, the protestations of his love and admiration ?— Did not mine eyes behold this maddening sight, I say ? Deny this, and I will acknowledge how much I have wronged thee, and make thee all the atonement in my power."

" I cannot deny—I will not attempt to disown, Godfrey," said the beauteous maiden, " that thou caught Lord Raymond in the position thou hast described; but he had that moment only made his appearance to me, and the words he gave utterance to, were only such as the ardent nature of his sentiments and friendship, I feel confident, prompted."

" Friendship !" reiterated the impetuous youth, with a bitter smile; " bah ! it is the libertine's mask—the villain's shield ! Well do I know the base schemes these noble sycophants make use of, in order to further their guilty views. Ernnestine, canst thou, wilt thou solemnly declare that thou hast never encouraged by word, by thought, or by deed, the passion which, 1 am certain, Lord Raymond St. Aswolph hath imbibed for thee."

" Godfrey de Lacy," solemnly returned our heroine, and in accents that for a moment or two abashed the youth, " if thou canst think so basely of Ernnestine, she is unworthy of thy love; and though her peace of mind be destroyed for ever—though her heart be broken in the attempt, she will release thee from the vows thou hast so often made to her, and —"

" Hear me, Ernnestine, for the love of Heaven," interrupted Godfrey, moved to agony by the alteration in her manner, and the solemnity of her tones, " If I have been prompted by the fervour of my love for thee, to do thee wrong, I implore thee to forgive me; but answer me two or three questions. Nay, thou must."

" What wouldst thou of me, Godfrey ?" asked the damsel, timidly.

" Tell me, has Lord Raymond ever before made any advances towards thee ?"

" He has never, by word or deed, given me reason to believe that he felt for me any other sentiment than that of friendship."

"And thou lovest him not?"

"Godfrey,—Godfrey, thou distractest me," sobbed Ernnestine; "I have ever—shall ever esteem the noble Lord St. Aswolph, for the services he hath rendered to thee and thy father; but to love any other man than Godfrey; —alas! alas! I am an unhappy wretch, thus undeservedly to be suspected of faithlessness by he whom I thought could sooner have perished than doubt my troth!"

She turned away in bitter anguish, and her tears fell fast and unrestrained. Godfrey looked at her for a moment with all that intensity of agony which racked his breast, and then exclaimed,—

"Should I have wronged her, oh, how can I hope for her forgiveness or pardon myself? It cannot be; Ernnestine false to me! love another, after all the tender asseverations she hath so often made to me—impossible! To believe that would be to suspect that there is no purity in heaven. Some accursed spell has taken possession of my senses. I am mad! Why do I take such pains to torture myself? Wretch that I must be to accuse this beauteous innocent of harbouring a thought which truth and virtue would blush at! But, no, no; my brain wanders—I know not what I am uttering!—She is innocent, or virtue itself is guilty!—But then the prognostications of the magician!—Ah! the recollection of them again maddens me!—The position, too, in which I caught Lord Raymond, which seemed so well to corroborate them! Distracting thoughts; worse than the torments of perdition!—I shall go mad!

"Godfrey," sobbed forth the deeply-agitated Ernnestine, while the expression of her sparkling eyes beamed reproach and innocence upon him, " I did not deem that thou couldst do the too-fond Ernnestine the injustice to doubt her constancy; but it appears I imagined wrong, and since it is so, and thou suspectest her of faithlessness, she must be unworthy of thy love, and therefore does she struggle against the strongest passions of her heart, and resign thee, sincerely hoping thou mayest find some other girl, who will love thee with the sincerity, the fervour, that she does!"

"Ernnestine," exclaimed the young man, with the most intense, the most ungovernable emotion; " thou no longer lovest me, if ever thou didst, and now only seeketh an excuse to cast me off for another!"

"By the Blessed Virgin thou wrongest me, Godfrey; deeply, cruelly, wrongest me!—Have I not ever proved by my conduct that thou, and thou only, wert the possessor of my heart, and that, even, should Fate ordain that we might never be united, now, in the face of Heaven, I swear, that no other man shall receive my love—my hand!"

"Ah! sayest thou so ?—Then, why continue to remain beneath this roof?"

"And thinkest thou, Godfrey, that thy groundless jealousy would ever induce me to behave with ingratitude towards those to whom we are all so largely indebted?" demanded Ernnestine; " No; to Lord Raymond—his amiable mother and sister, we are greatly indebted; they have thought fit to treat us with that marked distinction, which the difference of our station would not have led us to expect; they have honoured us with their friendship; and shall I gratuitously insult them, by rejecting their hospitality upon mere caprice?—No, Godfrey, in thy unfounded jealousy thou dost forget those sentiments of reason and generosity that have hitherto distinguished thy character."

Godfrey paused, and remained silent for a few minutes, traversing the place with hasty and uneven footsteps. He was evidently buried in deep rumination, and was engaged in a painful struggle with his feelings. Ernnestine, in the meantime, was enduring all the poignant anguish which the circumstances had given rise to, and covering her face with her hands, her grief found vent in deep and convulsive sobs. Godfrey turned his eyes towards her; and, after a moment's hesitation, he approached, with an air of gentleness, and in subdued accents, as he took her hand, ejaculated,—

"Ernnestine, dearest Ernnestine, I feel that I have been wrong; but the strength of my affection for thee hath been the sole cause; say, canst thou, wilt thou pardon me?"

Our heroine looked up with an expression of the most unbounded tenderness through her tears, and, after struggling for a moment with her feelings, she replied, sweetly,—

"Forgive thee, Godfrey!—oh, canst thou doubt me for a moment?—But," she added with the most bewitching archness and simplicity, "I cannot yield my pardon, without exacting certain conditions from thee."

"Name them, sweetest Ernnestine," said Godfrey,—"there is nothing thou canst request of me that I will refuse thee."

"Never to repeat these unjust suspicions; that is all I would demand!" returned Ernnestine.

"And that do I solemnly promise thee, my love," said Godfrey, as he pressed the blushing maiden to his heart, and they sealed their reconciliation in the most fervent kisses. At that moment a loud and hollow laugh resounded through the wood, and made the lovers both start, and look fearfully around them; but nothing at all met their gaze, and Ernnestine trembled violently and turned very pale, at the singularity of the circumstance. Godfrey drew his sword, and rushed towards the spot from whence the sounds appeared to issue, exclaiming,—

"Some insolent churl hath been watching us, and listening to our converse; but, by my troth, he shall pay dearly for his boldness and curiosity."

He reached the place, and looked around him, but no object met his gaze, and after a minute scrutiny, he sheathed his glittering weapon, and returned to Ernnestine in a state of the most indescribable astonishment.

"Who can it have been?" he cried, "I am certain I was not mistaken."

"Oh, doubtless, it was only some rustic passing along, and joking with his companion," said Ernnestine, who had quickly recovered from the alarm into which the circumstance had thrown her.

"Aye, likely it was so," answered Godfrey, endeavouring to regain his composure, but succeeding very indifferently; and after many other tender asseverations, and embraces, they parted, and Godfrey bent his steps from the castle towards the residence of his father. In spite of the vows he had made to Ernnestine, he did not feel at all satisfied with the conduct of Lord Raymond, especially after the circumstance he had witnessed, and the prognostications of Hal of the Glen, and his mind was distracted with a variety of conflicting thoughts, when, suddenly, he felt his arm arrested, and turning round, he was thunderstruck at beholding the awful and mysterious subject of his thoughts, the magician, standing before him, and gazing upon him with a look of demoniacal exultation.

Godfrey was startled by his sudden and unexpected appearance, and Hal of the Glen appeared to notice his confusion with a look of satisfaction, and again a loud laugh of supernatural exultation escaped him, and made the wood resound.

"Fiend! sorcerer!" at length cried Godfrey, worked up to a pitch bordering upon madness, what with his own feelings, as regarded the incident we have just been relating, and the wild mirth which the magician exhibited; "for what comest thou here? To mock me in my misery?"

"To tell thee that thou art an easy dupe,—a fool;" replied Hal.

"What meanest thou?"

"That thou deceivest thyself, if thou thinkest that Lord Raymond loves not the fair Ernnestine, or that she will not become his bride."

"Lying sorcerer! has she not sworn to love none other; to have none other but me?"

"She hath; but she cannot evade her fate; Ernnestine shall become the bride of Lord Raymond St. Aswolph:"

"No more! demon, thou mockest me!—Thou seekest to drive me to madness; I will no longer listen to thee! Avaunt!"

"Ha! ha! ha!" laughed the magician, as he gradually vanished, "thou wilt be glad to seek me anon, Godfrey de Lacy!"

The young man clasped his forehead in a delirium of agony, and for some time after Hal of the Glen had disappeared, he stood in a bewildered state, uncertain in what manner to act. The words of the magician had thrown him into a state of the utmost agitation, and a burning fever seemed to rage within his brain. At one moment, he determined to return to the castle, and once more seeking an interview with Ernnestine, accuse her of deceiving him, and insist upon her immediately returning home, or to acknowledge her hypocrisy, and confess to him at once that he was no longer dear to her. Then, again, he would upbraid himself for doubting the truth of that fair maiden, who had made every. sacrifice for his sake, and reproached himself for placing any belief in the words of a fiend, who seemed to delight in working the misery of mankind. But the more he reflected, in spite of all his efforts to the contrary, his indignation against Lord Raymond increased, until it reached an almost ungovernable pitch, and his soul began to thirst for vengeance. In a state of mind he had never before experienced, he walked on, with his eyes bent to the earth, and in profound thought, and he had not proceeded far, when his arm was arrested and his name being pronounced, he looked up, and beheld Osmond, the robber-chief, standing before him. He looked at him earnestly for a few minutes, and then, in a careless tone, ejaculated:—

"So,—Godfrey de Lacy; so gloomy and thoughtful? What hath occurred to disturb thee? Hath not thy mistress, the fair Ernnestine, pleased thee?"

"Confusion!" exclaimed Godfrey, with resentment. "comest thou here also to mock me?"

"Nay, thou dost me wrong, young man," answered Osmond, "methinks thou hast hitherto found the robber-chief thy friend, although thou mayest not consider thyself much honoured by the acquaintance. But I see how it is, thou doubtest the fidelity of Ernnestine."

"I do."

"Thou wrongest her!"

"But Lord Raymond loves her."

"He does, and she will become his bride."

"Agony unbearable!" ejaculated Godfrey, "but how knowest thou that?"

"Because I am determined to do all in my power to effect that object;" was the answer of the robber-chief.

"Thou, Osmond,—thou?" cried Godfrey, in amazement.

"Yes, I repeat, that I will do all in my power to bring about a union with Lord Raymond St. Aswolph, and Ernnestine."

"This from thee, Osmond,' exclaimed Godfrey; "thou who hast but a minute since assured me of thy friendship towards me!"

"And I told thee only the truth;—as thou wilt find."

"Thou speakest in problems, robber; how canst thou be my friend, when thou declarest thine intention to endeavour to bring about a union between Ernnestine and Lord Raymond?"

"Though she weds Lord Raymond, it will not prevent her nuptials with thee; and will be the means of my amply avenging myself on him I have so much reason to hate."

"This mystery is agonizing; Osmond, if there is anything serious in thy words, for Heaven's sake, explain them to me."

"Not at present," returned Osmond, "it might be the means of defeating my purpose; once more, I tell thee, that thou hast not a more sincere friend, or one that will do more to serve thee, than Osmond the robber-chief. But I must begone, I have business of importance to attend to. Thou canst tell Lord Raymond St. Aswolph, and the others that have dared to threaten me, that I defy and despise them all, and that, if they attempt to disturb me in my retreat, I will give them such a reception as they will not easily forget. Tell them that Osmond and his brave comrades laugh to scorn, and bid defiance to all the force they can bring against them, and with their good yew bows, and trusty blades, will deal destruction among them, nor yield while a man of them hath a spark of life remaining. Tell them this ; and, moreover, that the robber-chief is waiting impatiently for the sport. Now, fare thee well, Godfrey de Lacy, and be of good cheer, for whilst thou hast a friend in Osmond, thou hast nought to fear.''

Having given utterance to these words, before Godfrey had time to return any answer, Osmond left the spot, and in an instant was out of sight.

" The fates have conspired to torture me to madness," exclaimed Godfrey, after a pause,—" what can all this mean ? What can I conclude from the words and mysterious behaviour of Osmond, or has he only done this to increase my anguish and suspense ? By Heaven ! I shall go wild ! I cannot endure this ! Oh, Ernnestine, didst thou but know the suffering I am undergoing, even though thine heart is no longer mine, I am certain thou wouldst pity me. Pity ! and from Ernnestine, too ;—alas ! there is something so degrading in that word, that methinks even her scorn would be preferable to it. Fierce thoughts take possession of my brain ;—let me endeavour to fly from myself."

With these words, Godfrey clasped his hands to his forehead with the most indescribable agony, and rushed with wild and disordered steps towards the deepest recesses of the forest, there to give vent to the anguish which filled his bosom. Arrived at a spot which was seldom trodden by the foot of man, he threw himself upon the earth, and covering his face with his hands, gave indulgence to a passionate burst of emotion, in which one moment he blamed the conduct of Ernnestine, and, at another, reproached himself for the strange infatuation he had suffered to take possession of his senses, to believe her unfaithful. Then he reprobated, in the most violent terms, the conduct of Lord Raymond, and, forgetting the disparity of their rank, vowed the most signal, the most terrible vengeance against him. Time but added to, instead of decreasing the agony of his thoughts, and when he arose to return home, he was in a state bordering upon distraction.

In the meantime Ernnestine was in a state of mind far from enviable, after the circumstances we have recently related ; and notwithstanding her and Godfrey had come to a reconciliation, she could readily perceive that the subject would not drop where it was, and that it was but the forerunner to many sorrows, the nature of which she could not exactly understand for the present. She felt deeply hurt that Godfrey should so readily have suspected her truth, and, yet she could not help admitting to herself, that the singular situation in which he had beheld Lord Raymond was sufficient to excite his jealousy. She also considered that Lord Raymond had acted imprudently, and that his behaviour was, certainly, more ardent than mere friendship should dictate ; and now, for the first time, she recalled to her memory circumstances in the behaviour of Lord Raymond towards her, which, although they had not excited any surprise at the time, now inspired her with a feeling which caused her much uneasiness. She determined to avoid his presence as much as she possibly could, and had it not been for fear of offending his amiable mother and Lady Marguerite, she would have quitted the castle immediately. But then, again, she upbraided herself for blaming the conduct of his lordship, and for believing him capable of doing anything wrong. If his lordship had imbibed a passion for her, she was certain that the difference of their stations in the world would preclude the possibility of his ever paying his addresses to her, and to entertain an idea of dishonour, she felt convinced he was perfectly incapable. Altogether she much regretted that the circumstance had taken place, and was fearful that it would be the cause of much uneasiness to all parties.

On retiring to her chamber at night she did not feel inclined to go to rest, she therefore took up a book, and soon became absorbed in the interest of its contents. She was suddenly, however, aroused, and somewhat alarmed, by imagining she heard the sound of a footstep outside the door. She listened, but all was still; and thinking it had only been fancy, or probably occasioned by the manuscript she was perusing, which was a legendary tale, of the most terrific description, she once more began to read. She had not, however, proceeded far, when she again heard the noise; and being confident that she was not this time mistaken, she hastily arose from her chair, and had no sooner done so, than her chamber-door was gently opened, and the tall figure of a man, his face covered with a black mask, presented itself to her terrified view. He no sooner beheld her, than muttering some inarticulate words to himself, he shrank back, and closed the door again, and Ernnestine could hear him retreating along the gallery.

Horrorstruck; petrified to the spot, our heroine could not move, neither could she give utterance to the least cry. All her faculties seemed for the moment to be suspended. Suddenly, however, she was aroused by hearing a piercing shriek, which proceeded from the direction of the chamber in which Lady Marguerite slept. With a courage with which persons are sometimes inspired in moments such as these, Ernnestine took up her lamp, and hurried along the gallery towards Lady Marguerite's chamber.

Once more as our heroine proceeded along the gallery, a dismal shriek, fainter than before, sounded in her ears, and then all became again silent as death. With unabated courage Ernnestine bent her footsteps to the chamber of Lady Marguerite, and her worst fears were confirmed, when she found the chamber door wide open; and on entering the room, she was struck with horror when she perceived that it was vacated, that it was quite evident, from the appearance of the bed, that the unfortunate lady had never retired to rest. It was now clear that the cries that had met the ears of Ernnestine had proceeded from Lady Marguerite, and that she was borne forcibly away from the castle by the man who had so much alarmed her but a few minutes before; but who he was, or how he had contrived to gain access to the building, she was completely at a loss to conjecture, and, in fact, was, at that moment, in too great a state of agitation, to reflect with coolness upon the subject.

She was so completely horrorstruck by what had taken place, that, for a few [minutes, she was rivetted to the spot, and was unable to move, or to give utterance to the least outcry; but, at length, she screamed frantically for help, and rushed wildly to the chamber in which Lady Celestine slept, and arousing her, informed her of the circumstance which had taken place. The distracted lady could scarcely believe the evidence of her ears, but when she, at last, became convinced of the truth, she uttered a loud scream of horror, and became insensible. The domestics were now aroused, and, with Lord Raymond, came to the spot to ascertain what was the cause of the alarm. When made acquainted with what had happened, a scene ensued which baffles all description. Lord Raymond immediately questioned all the servants narrowly; but they most positively declared that they had not seen any stranger about the castle, and certainly no one had given him admittance. He then immediately dispatched one party of them to search every part of the castle, and the vaults and subterraneous passages underneath; a second, in one direction of the forest,—while he, with another portion of his [vassals, took a different route, he being determined to scour the country in all directions, and an immense reward was offered to any one who should be fortunate enough to gain any clue to Marguerite's discovery, or the man who [had borne her away. While they were gone, the state of distraction to which Lady Celestine was reduced, was truly distressing to behold; she no sooner recovered from one fit than she fell into another, and for some time, the most serious apprehensions were entertained that the result would prove fatal. Our heroine attended upon her with the utmost care and affection, and it was to her that she was indebted, principally, for her ultimate recovery. So brief was the time which Ernnestine had been allowed to gaze upon the man, who had, doubtless, come to her chamber in a mistake, and he being also masked, that she did not think it at all likely she should be able to recognize him; and conjecture was exhausted, in vain, to endeavour to find out who the villain could possibly be who had committed this outrage. In vain had been the researches of the persons in the castle, and the vaults and passages underneath: they could see nothing of the objects of their search, although it was very evident the man had effected his escape that way, from the circumstance of all the doors being open, and they having been known to be all secure on the evening before. But how had the man become acquainted with the secret passage?—How have gained the means of untastening the doors, if there had been no treachery among the domestics?—It did not seem to be at all feasible. The servants were all again closely examined, but they were not enabled to elicit anything more than they had before done, neither by threats, persuasions, or promises of reward; and thus the painful affair remained involved in the most impenetrable mystery.

The search of Lord Raymond and the others, had been attended with no better success; and his grief and anxiety may be very readily conceived. In vain he racked his brain to endeavour to imagine into whose power his unfortunate sister had fallen; although she had many admirers—as might be expected, from her numerous charms, accomplishments, and virtues—there was not one among them whom he could for a moment believe to be capable of committing such an act; and this state of suspense and uncertainty, was more torturing than even the knowledge of the place of her retreat and positive misery, when he would have it in his power to rescue her. Notwithstanding his own agony of mind, he stifled his feelings as much as possible, and endeavoured all that was in his power to appease the anguish of his mother. In this he was ably assisted by the gentle and kind-hearted Ernnestine; but for some time their exertions were of no avail—Lady Celestine remained for a while completely inconsolable, and at times her intellect was deranged, and, altogether, she was brought to a most pitiable condition.

At the earnest solicitations of Lord Raymond and his mother, and with the sanction of her friends, Ernnestine consented to prolong her stay at the castle for a few weeks longer, in order that she might by her affectionate soothings, endeavour to abate the sufferings which the mysterious disappearance, and the uncertainty of the fate which had attended her daughter, occasioned Lady Celestine.

Although Godfrey sincerely sympathized with Lord Raymond and his mother, in the melancholy loss they had recently sustained, the prolonged visit of Ernnestine, especially after what he had heard from Hal of the Glen, and Osmond, the robber-chief, as may be expected, occasioned him the greatest uneasiness; it seemed as though fate had conspired to render him truly miserable, and what made him still more so, was, that he was compelled to keep his thoughts confined to his own breast, for how could he attempt to reproach Ernnestine with her conduct, without bringing upon himself a suspicion of inhumanity?—Incapable of concealing his real thoughts—although he tried hard to do so—Godfrey avoided the presence of Ernnestine, for the present, as much as possible, and passed all his leisure hours in the forest, brooding gloomily upon the prognostications of the magician, and the singular observations which Osmond had made use of on their last meeting. In vain he had endeavoured to stifle the feelings of jealousy that had taken possession of his bosom, and he, every day, became more unhappy.—Ernnestine noticed his anguish, and well read his most secret thoughts, and the misery it caused her gentle bosom may be very well imagined; she could not help accusing Godfrey of cruelty, thus to continue to encourage a suspicion of her fidelity towards him, and there were moments when her woman's pride almost tempted her to resent it in the most marked manner; but she conquered this passion, and mentally breathed a hope that time would effect a change, and convince him of the injustice he was doing her by entertaining such suspicions.

The most vigilant search was continued to be made in all parts of the country, after Lady Marguerite, and the villain who had torn her from her friends in so clandestine a manner, and a fortune was offered to any person who could furnish them with such information as might bring about the desired object; and as day after day, and week after week, passed, still without bringing them the least intelligence, the distress of Lady Celestine and her son became almost insupportable. Alas! what might not have been her fate?—They shuddered with horror to think of it, and again the madness of their despair was increased tenfold.

At length, after more than a month had passed away from the time of Lady Marguerite's abduction, and Lord Raymond and his mother had tried by every means in their power to gain a clue to the place where Marguerite was confined, a sudden thought rushed upon the mind of the former, the probability of which struck him most forcibly.

"Ah !" he exclaimed, as this idea flashed across his brain, " Osmond, the robber-chief; did he not threaten me with vengeance ?—He is, doubtless, the villain who hath forced Marguerite away, and who now holds her in his power, with some guilty design, if she hath not already fallen a victim to the base passions of the miscreant. Fool! that I did not think of this before; I might have saved her: but even now it may not be too late, and by all my hopes, I will hunt him and his lawless companions from their retreat, or perish in the attempt !"

With these words, Lord Raymond, without saying anything to his mother upon the subject, hastily quitted the castle, and made his way towards the ancient Baronial Hall of the Chief Justiciary, whom he had seen but seldom since the trial —that nobleman having been confined to his bed for several weeks, after the confession which he had received from the lips of Stephen. To him he made known the suspicions that had just crossed his mind, and the resolution he had come to, having made up his mind to collect together all his numerous retainers, and requested the assistance of his lordship, to destroy that desperate gang which had been so long a terror to the country.

The Chief Justiciary expressed his readiness to do all in his power to aid Lord Raymond in his project, but made him acquainted with his own doubts upon the subject, especially after what Stephen had informed him of the security which the robbers possessed. To this, however Lord Raymond paid but little attention, and it did not in the least alter his determination. Steps were, therefore, immediately taken to put their designs into execution, but it was conducted with the utmost secresy—that being considered by far the most prudent, as, if they made known their intentions, the robbers would take good care to make preparations to repel them.

Lady Celestine trembled when she became acquainted with the determination of her son—for, notwithstanding she was inclined to believe that the suspicions of Lord Raymond were not erroneous, so well did she know the desperate character of Osmond and his gang, that she felt certain they would sooner die than yield.; and it was not at all likely, if Marguerite really was in their power, that they would fall without wreaking their vengeance on her. Lord Raymond combatted those arguments as ably as he could, but still he could not deny the reason of them. However, to run any risk was preferable to the state of suspense and mystery in which they were involved at present ; and nothing, consequently, could move him from the determination he had come to. In two or three days all the arrangements were completed, and Lord Raymond and the Justiciary set about putting their designs into execution. The vassals and retainers of Lord Raymond St. Aswolph, at midnight, passed from the castle through the secret passage, and were joined by those of the Justiciary in the forest. They then pursued their way by circuitous, but unfrequented routes, until at length the lofty turrets of St. Alwyn Castle burst upon their view.

CHAPTER XV.

" These ancient halls, of feudal grandeur once the seat,
Are now the haunt of lawless men, whose crimes
Have made them aliens from society."

LEGEND OF THE ABBEY.

ON the night that the event we have been describing,—and which had created so much pain and anxiety in the noble family of St. Aswolph,—took place, the beauteous Lady Marguerite had retired at an earlier hour than usual to her chamber, not that she felt inclined for repose, for, on the contrary, her mind was tormented with strange and dismal forebodings, and which rendered her totally unfit for society. In vain she sought to shake them off, for the more she endeavoured to do so, the more powerful did they come, and yet she was at a loss to account for them, for hitherto Marguerite's days had been those of unruffled calm, and sorrow was unknown to her, but now a sensation had come over her mind, which served to make her truly wretched, the impression fast gained greater strength, that she was about to experience some heavy misfortune, which it would be utterly impossible for her to avoid.

" And yet," she ruminated, " surely this is silly; it is childish weakness, and I should not encourage it. What have I to fear, while I put my trust in the Blessed Virgin, and do nothing to violate the laws of God or man ?—Enemies I cannot have, for with the world I have hitherto but little associated, and I know not that being to whom I have ever intentionally given offence. I will not give way to such folly; I will arouse myself from this state of unwarrantable weakness. I am ashamed of myself for having for a moment given way to it."

She took up an ancient legendary manuscript she had found in one of the old apartments of the castle, and endeavoured to divert her mind from the gloomy thoughts that beset it, in the perusal of its contents. In this she succeeded better than might have been imagined, and soon became totally absorbed in reading the wild and terrific legend it related. In this manner the time passed unheeded away, and it was getting late, when suddenly she was aroused by hearing a noise, as if some person was walking along the gallery upon which her chamber opened. She was terribly alarmed, and remembering that she had not secured the room-door, she arose for that purpose, but before she could reach it, it was opened, and to her extreme terror, a man with his features partly concealed by a black mask, and whose person was covered with a huge dark mantle, presented himself to her sight. Marguerite was so overcome by her terrors, that she was unable to move or to utter the least sound, and the stranger advancing towards her, threw his arms around her, and in a low and solemn tone, ejaculated :—

"Silence, maiden, on thy life; thou must with me; resistance is in vain, and the least outcry may bring destruction upon thyself and those most dear to thee. I have plenty at hand, who, at the least signal, will fly to my aid. Thou art mine !—Come !"

In spite of the threats of the man, Marguerite did scream aloud, as the man raised her in his arms and bore her from the apartment, until at length, completely exhausted by her struggles and her fears, she became insensible.

When she recovered, she found herself alone, laid upon an elegant couch, and in a handsomely furnished apartment. A light was burning on the table, and all around her was as silent as death. She gazed around her with amazement, and then her recollection returning, and remembering the manner in which she had been seized, she became very much alarmed, and rising from the couch, hastened to the door and the casements, which she tried, but found them secure. She next screamed aloud, but the dismal echo of her own voice was the only answer she received, and she wrung her hands in frantic despair !—

"Holy Virgin!" she exclaimed, " where am I, and what will become of me?—Oh, help! help!"

Still no answer did she receive, and once more she scrutinized the room narrowly, to see if she had any recollection of the place, but she had none whatever, although she was confident that she was not in the Castle of St. Aswolph, and that wherever she was, she was in the power of the villain who had borne her away, for what purpose she was at a loss to conceive, or who and what he was.

The apartment, as we have before stated, was very handsomely furnished, and everything around seemed to denote the magnificence of the building to which it belonged. It was hung around with richly embroidered arras, and vases of flowers, which filled the room with a delightful fragrance, rested on richly carved standings in each corner. The hangings of the bed were in corresponding taste, and appeared to be almost new, and as if fitted up expressly for her reception. Everything she beheld, filled Marguerite with astonishment, yet her fears were equal to it, and the mystery in which the whole affair was involved was almost insupportable. On one side of the room, was a painting of he Virgin, before which Marguerite immediately prostrated herself, and implored her protection from any of the snares and dangers by which she was doubtless surrounded. She then arose, somewhat more composed, and endeavoured to await with patience the result of this ambiguous affair.

Day beginning to peep, she extinguished the light, and seating herself at the table, and leaning her head upon her hand, gave way to the dismal thoughts her strange situation naturally created. Conjecture, however, she exhausted in vain, to discover who the man was that had borne her away, and what could be his designs in so doing. In this manner about three hours passed away, when Marguerite was startled by hearing some one unlocking the room-door, and the next moment it was thrown back on its hinges, and the tall figure of a man stood before her. Immediately upon beholding his features, (for he was now unmasked,) she screamed and ejaculated in accents of horror :—

"Oh, God! is it possible?—Am I then in the power of——"

"Osmond, the robber-chief," added the man, in a mild voice, and bowing respectfully.

No sooner did the distracted damsel hear this than she covered her face with her hands, and groaned with horror.

" Nay, lady," said Osmond, approaching her, " I prithee give not way to unnecessary grief; Osmond is not half so terrible as the voice of calumny hath reported him. To the fair sex he can behave with gentleness and love, but especially to the fair Lady Marguerite."

"Lawless man," ejaculated Marguerite, "for what purpose hast thou torn me from my friends?—Why am I brought hither?"

"In the first place, beauteous maiden," replied Osmond, "I was prompted by love; nay, start not, I repeat that thy numerous charms have inspired me with a passion as warm as ever glowed within the human breast. But fear not; though I have thee securely in my power, and nothing could prevent me from obtaining the gratification of my wishes, here, thou shalt be as safe as if thou wert within the proud walls of St. Aswolph. Lady, think not, that although Osmond hath been driven by misfortune and treachery, to the lawless course of life which he now pursues, that he possesses a heart insensible to feeling, or the more tender passions; there was a time when—but no matter, now, it is sufficient that I love thee, and hope to be enabled to inspire thee with reciprocal sentiments."

A deadly sickness came over Marguerite as she listened to the boldness of the robber's words, and it was several seconds before she was sufficiently composed to return any answer; but at length, turning upon Osmond a look of gentle reproach and supplication, she said,—

"Oh, Osmond, if as thou sayest thou wert once noble, once guiltless, thou wilt pity me, and restore me to my friends, and best evince your esteem for me by no longer detaining me against my will. For such an act I might not only be grateful, but learn to sympathize with thy misfortunes."

"Restore thee to thy friends!" reiterated the robber-chief; "oh, no, no, no, lady, that canst never be; Osmond will not resign the glorious opportunity of revenge which is now afforded him."

No. 19

"Revenge!" cried Marguerite, with a look of terror; "against whom?"

"Thy brother, lady; the proud Lord Raymond St. Aswolph, whom I have such ample cause to detest, to despise!"

"Impossible! my dear brother could never have injured thee!"

"Never injured me, fair damsel!—Oh, he hath been the bitterest foe I have ever known; from him have I to date my ruin—all my misery— the many bitter pangs I have for years endured—the curse of blighted hopes, ruined fortune, name, and high estate!"

"Blessed Virgin!" ejaculated the alarmed Marguerite; "this can never be; my brother so kind, so amiable, so noble, so generous;—it is some base fabrication, or thou labourest under some strange and painful delusion."

"Nay, lady, it is as I have told thee; and so will Lord Raymond discover ere long. It is well for him that his memory is so shallow; or that he can so easily bury in oblivion the deeds of other days;—but it will be my task, and the day is not far distant, to remind him of his vices and demand retribution."

"Robber," exclaimed Marguerite, proudly, "my brother may defy thy weak threats, and treat them only as they merit, with scorn and utter contempt. But rest assured he will discover in whose power I am detained, and have ample vengeance for this outrage."

Osmond smiled scornfully, and after a short pause, said,—

"Lady, thou knowest not the power of Osmond, or thou wouldst not talk thus; but it is useless to bandy words with thee upon the subject. Time will show. Thou wilt do well to consider what I have told thee, and endeavour to view me with other sentiments than those of hatred and disgust. Rest assured, however, that here thou shalt suffer no insult; Osmond will protect thee from it, and treat thee with that profound respect thy sex, and the deep interest thou hast inspired him with, prompt. Every enjoyment but that of liberty shall be thine here. Thou wilt, therefore, act wisely by well considering what I have said to thee; and by endeavouring to act in accordance with my wishes. Do this, and I solemnly declare that I will forgive thy brother all the injuries he hath done to me; and blot out from the tablet of my memory the sorrows and degradations I have experienced from him. I will now leave thee, lady, and give thee full time to prepare thine answer. Farewell!"

Thus saying, Osmond kissed his hand respectfully to Lady Marguerite, and quitted her presence.

Left to herself, Lady Marguerite give herself up entirely to the most painful reflection, which her critical situation fully justified, and paced the chamber with hurried and uneven footsteps. Now her thoughts wandered to St. Aswolph, and the bitter agony and suspense her mother and Lord Raymond would be in at her mysterious disappearance, and the uncertainty as to her fate; then she would reflect with the most unbounded astonishment upon the mysterious observation which Osmond had made use of, and in vain endeavoured to elucidate them. By what means her brother had ever offended the robber-chief, so as to excite his revenge to such an implacable degree, she was at a loss to imagine; and by what strange circumstance he had become connected with him, was equally mysterious to her. She was one moment disposed to place no confidence in it, and to believe it to be merely a fabrication of Osmond's; but then the total absence of any motive for such an invention occurred to her, and again caused, her mind to waver. She had always looked upon Lord Raymond as a being of a superior order, and one totally incapable of harming by word, thought, or deed, his fellow-creatures; consequently, in what manner he could by any possibility have given Osmond cause for the deadly hatred he confessed towards him, she was at a loss to conceive. Then, the melancholy which had beset the mind of her brother for so long a time, and, in fact, although not now so powerful as it was, had become settled upon him, darted upon her recollection, and filled her bosom with strange doubts, ideas, and apprehensions. The impenetrable mystery which her brother had ever maintained upon that subject, and the anguish and impatience which he ever evinced when questioned concerning it, all came vividly to her recollection, and involved her still further in fruitless and conflicting conjectures, and she feared that the business would not terminate without considerable trouble to them all.

But, how intense was her agony, how powerful her fears, when she thought upon the situation she was placed in; the prisoner of Osmond, the Avenger, the desperate robber-chief, whose very name inspired terror in the bosoms of those who heard it; surrounded by wretches to whom every species of crime was familiar and insulted by the loathsome passion of Osmond, who had so boldly and openly avowed his sentiments towards her, and proclaimed his intentions,—intentions which she knew full well he would not fail to carry into effect, unless something should occur to rescue her from his power, for of what avail would be any resistance she might offer to his villany? Her destruction seemed to be inevitable; and yet there was something so noble and generous in the demeanour of Osmond at times, which led her, in spite of his threats, to hope that he would relent, and perhaps abandon his evil designs altogether, and, yielding to her tears and entreaties, restore her to her friends.

She was interrupted in these reflections by the sweet and plaintive voice of a female singing a song, in tones of the most bewitching melody, and which completely rivetted her attention, and excited her warmest admiration. The voice seemed to proceed from an apartment immediately contiguous to the one she occupied, and she listened with intense interest to the words of the ballad, which were simple, but possessing all the charms of poetry.

"Thank Heaven!" ejaculated Marguerite, when the female had ceased,— "thank Heaven, there is another of my own sex near me. Oh, if she is as gentle in her nature as the delicacy of her tones would augur her to be, what consolation would it afford me, if she were permitted to be my companion. Should she possess a heart of sympathy, my situation would be lightened of half its terrors."

She had scarcely given utterance to these words, when she was startled by hearing a noise at the wainscot on one side of the room, and directing her eyes that way, she was thunderstruck at beholding the arras slowly raised, a pannel in the wainscot had been slid back, and in an instant the graceful form of a young woman of a gentle and beauteous countenance, stepped lightly into the apartment, and advanced towards her.

"Fair Lady," said the young woman, in accents of sweetness, "be not surprised at seeing me; I have ome to ask you whether you feel disposed to take your morning's repast now, and I am deputed to be your companion, while you remain here, if you think me worthy of that honour."

" A female here !" remarked Marguerite, continuing to gaze with the most unfeigned astonishment upon the speaker, " so fair, and apparently, so amiable too. Surely, thou art some poor unfortunate, like myself, detained here against thy will ?"

" Alas ! lady," replied the female, with a sigh, " it is not so ; I am a willing inmate of these walls ; my husband is one of the gang."

" Impossible !" exclaimed Marguerite ; " one like thou art can never have so degraded herself as to become the voluntary associate of robbers—of lawless men, whose crimes have rendered them a terror to their country."

" Thou wrongest Osmond and his gang, lady," returned the other, " they are not half so fierce, so cruel as they are by many represented to be. Ask their characters of the humble and the distressed, and they will tell thee, that—but, no matter; we will drop this subject for the present. Say, lady, shall I bring thee refreshment, or is there anything particular that you desire ?"

Marguerite answered in the negative ; but feeling faint, she assented to partake slightly of some refreshment. The female then left her by the same means she had entered, closing the secret pannel after her.

Marguerite was so surprised at what had taken place, that for a minute or two she was transfixed to the spot, and could scarcely believe that what had taken place was real ; but at length, recovering herself, she hastened to the secret pannel, and endeavoured to find out the way to open it, but without succeeding ; the spring was on the other side, by touching or pressing upon which alone it could be opened.

She left it with disappointment, and awaited the return of the female with some impatience. She was not kept in this manner long, for presently the secret pannel was again slid back, and the object of her thoughts again reappeared, bringing in refreshments with her, which she spread upon the table, and then invited Marguerite to partake.

The viands were of the most delicate description, and Marguerite did slightly taste of them, while the female took a seat at the further end of the table, and seemed to view her with looks of warm admiration and compassion.

" Fair lady," at length she said, " thou didst not answer me before,—say, wilt thou accept of my humble services as a companion, while thou art an inmate of this old castle ?"

" Oh ! gladly," replied Lady Marguerite ; " but, Heaven send that my stay here may be short. Alas! the anguish my friends must endure at my mysterious disappearance, racks my brain to distraction."

" I am sorry for thee, lady," answered the female, " and fain would assist thee, were it in my power ; but, rest assured, that however strong may be thine apprehensions, thou wilt be treated with the most profound respect while thou art here. Death would be certain to be the portion of any one who should dare to offer thee the slightest insult."

" Strange inconsistencies !" ejaculated Marguerite, " but alas ! how little cause have I to hope that it will be as thou sayest, after the open avowal which the robber-chief hath made to me. But say, who art thou, and what is thy name ?"

"I have already informed thee, lady," said the young woman, "that I am a robber's bride; I am the wife of Ulric, and my name is Blanche."

"And what could ever have induced thee to link thy fate to one of these lawless and desperate men?"

"Ah! lady," replied Blanche, and a deep sigh escaped her bosom; "I united my fate to that of Ulric, because I loved him; and, at the time that I did so, virtue and integrity stamped his character."

"Thou interestest me," said Marguerite, who, for awhile, forgot her own sorrows, and painful situation, in the excitement occasioned by the words of the robber's bride; "what could have driven him to this hazardous and degrading course of life?"

"Tyranny and oppression; misfortunes under which some persons would have sunk altogether," answered Blanche.

"Indeed! and thou didst accompany him to this place, and resolved to share with him in his misfortunes?"

"Lady," replied Blanche, with a look of surprise, "wouldst thou that I should have deserted my husband, he whom at the altar I had vowed to love, and who had been so kind and attentive to me? wouldst thou, I repeat, have had me desert him in his adversity?—Oh, no, no, we have shared each other's happiness; each other's affections; and whatever may be the consequences, I will be the partaker of his misfortunes."

"Noble, heroic, devoted woman!" cried Lady Marguerite, with admiration; "the sentiments thou hast expressed, fill my breast with the warmest esteem towards thee; and adds to the deep regret I feel that either thou or thine husband should be placed in a situation which daily exposes ye to the retributive hands of the law. I am convinced thou art of no plebeian race; both thy language and manners show that thou hast formerly moved in no mean rank of society."

Blanche again sighed, and a tear glistened in her eye.

"Thou judgest rightly, lady," she replied, "I once moved among the gayest of the children of rank and splendour; had every luxury and enjoyment that wealth could purchase, and—— but it is past now;—it is like a dream to me;—and let me endeavour to bury the remembrance of it for ever in oblivion."

"Pardon me, Blanche," observed Marguerite, affectionately taking her hand, and looking in her countenance with an expression of the deepest sympathy;—"I would not appear impertinently inquisitive, neither would I wish to revive the sorrows that have apparently so deeply afflicted thee; but I cannot conquer the interest thy words hath excited, and if thou thinkest me worthy of being entrusted with thine history, believe me thou shalt receive from me all the commisseration and consolation it may be in my power to impart."

Blanche paused, and looked earnestly in the countenance of Lady Marguerite, and after wiping away the tears that the reminiscences of her sorrows had excited, she said:—

"Thou dost possess a gentle heart, lady, and I am certain of the motive by which thou art stimulated;—I—I—will confide in thee."

Lady Marguerite drew her chair closer to Blanche, and after a short time had elapsed, during which she was endeavouring to compose her feelings for the task, the latter commenced as follows:—

" My father, Sir Willoughby de Mortimer, was one of the bravest knights the British army could boast of, and was much esteemed for his many noble and virtuous qualities. He had large estates, and particularly a fine old Gothic castle, in a part of the country there is no occasion for me to mention. Of my mother, I fain would not say anything, for, alas !—but, no matter; suffice it to say that the marriage between her and my father was an unfortunate one. I was their only offspring, and when I was not more than twelve years of age, my mother abandoned her husband and me, and eloped with another man whom Sir Willoughby had imagined was his friend, and we heard no more of them. This melancholy event my father took so much to heart, that he never recovered from the effects of it; he shut himself and me almost entirely up in his castle; we saw no company; seldom walked further than the grounds that extended around the castle; and, in fact, he became, I might almost venture to say, a perfect misanthrope; so that thus early in life did my troubles begin. But use soon familiarised me to this melancholy course of life, and I envied not the pleasures of the world ; my chief delight was in endeavouring to soften the severity of my poor father's anguish; and if I could but win a smile from him, oh, what happiness was mine ! —Then I would sing to him, and those were the only moments when his mind seemed to be transitorily diverted from the bitter sorrows that oppressed it; and he would kiss my lips, and look into my face with such fondness, that I shall never forget.

" The pleasures usually known to young persons of my own age, were at at that time not experienced by me ; but yet with it all, could I but soothe the sorrows of my father, I felt a happiness far beyond that which worldly and evanescent pleasures can supply.

" The only persons who visited us was the Earl Harlingwood and his son, Alfred, who was several years older than myself. Lord Harlingwood was a nobleman, whom, I must say, I never could thoroughly like, for there was something peculiarly haughty and stern in his behaviour ; but between him and my father there subsisted the greatest friendship; and, indeed, to such an extent that he had entrusted him with the arrangement of most of his affairs, and had appointed him my guardian, in case that he should die. Lady Harlingwood had been an invalid for several years, and was unable to leave her chamber. Lord Harlingwood was a young man of the most amiable qualities ; and of prepossessing person and manners. He had ever shewn me the most marked attention, and it was soon evident that he had imbibed an ardent passion for me, and I must acknowledge that my heart beat responsive to his sentiments ; we confessed our love for each other, and anticipated every happiness in our passion, for we never for a moment imagined that our parents would object to our nuptials, but, on the contrary, that an alliance between the two families would afford them the utmost satisfaction ; we, therefore, never thought of acknowledging to them our sentiments, at least, not for the present, believing that they must discover it by our manners ; moreover, I advised Alfred not to press his suit, at present, to my father, fearing that he might imagine I was tired of the solitary life I was leading, and wished to leave him to himself.

"Time passed on, and at length the melancholy hour approached, when I was fated to become an orphan; the heavy affliction my poor father had experienced, had so preyed upon his mind, that his constitution entirely sunk beneath it, and he was at length so reduced, that he was unable to leave his couch. Need I say, with what tender anxiety I watched by his pillow, and tended to his wants; but what racked me more than all was, that for several hours before his death, he was in a state of mental aberration and unconscious of my attentions or my presence. But a minute before he breathed his last, his senses returned;—he took my hand, pressed upon it his dying kiss, and solemnly breathing a benediction upon my head, resigned his soul into the hands of his Maker.

"It would be completely superfluous in me to attempt to describe my feelings upon this melancholy occasion; thy gentle breast, fair lady, must be fully susceptible to them; I hung over the corpse of my poor father, and it was with the greatest difficulty the Earl Harlingwood (for he was present) could induce me to leave the room and retire to my own chamber, where he sent to me my waiting-woman, and undertook the arrangements for the funeral obsequies. He tried to prevail upon me to retire to his castle until after the dismal ceremony was over; but nothing could persuade me to leave that place in which with my father I had passed so many years of comparative seclusion, and which now contained his cold remains. In this hour of trial, my lover did all that he could to soothe my anguish, and at length his arguments had the effect of ameliorating my sorrow, and enabled me to attend to see the body of my father consigned to the tomb of his ancestors.

"When the mournful ceremony was over, I retired to Harlingwood Castle, under the protection of the earl. Here I might say there was very little change in my condition, for my time was principally passed in the sick chamber of the countess, who received my attentions with the most unbounded gratitude, and many were the thanks she bestowed upon me. She was a most amiable woman, and bore her sufferings with the patience, and resignation of an angel. Unfortunate lady, my heart could fully sympathise with her; little had she known of happiness during the latter years of her life, being seldom free from pain, and entirely deprived of the means of enjoying those luxuries and pleasures, which her rank and station would have granted her the means of doing. But not long did she need my care; for some time past, her illness had daily increased, and it was very evident that she was fast approaching eternity. Two months only had elapsed after my becoming an inmate of Harlingwood Castle, when she was released from her earthly sufferings.

"Lord Alfred, who was doatingly fond of his mother, was almost inconsolable for her loss, but I could not help remarking that his father appeared to be but very little moved by the circumstance. This event, if possible drew my affections and those of Lord Alfred, more closely together; we had both of us lost a parent whom we had fondly loved, and we were, therefore, similarly situated.

"My father, it appeared had left the earl the sole guardian of myself and property, and he had left my future settlement entirely to his discretion, taking all power completely out of my hands, until I should become a wife. When the earl made me acquainted with these circumstances, I must confess that I felt the greatest surprise, and could scarcely credit what I had heard. It was couched in what I might term severe and despotic language, and placed upon me restrictions which were so unlike such as the affectionate nature of my father, I thought, would have dictated, that it seemed impossible they could have emanated from him. Not only had he left the earl my sole guardian, but he had also ordered that I should marry only the man whom he might think worthy of me, and that I should either submit to that, or be compelled to enter a nunnery for life, and the property at present entrusted to his care, in that event, with the exception of a handsome bequest to the holy house of which I might become an inmate, should become that of him and his heirs for ever.

"I looked at the earl with the most breathless astonishment, when he made me acquainted with this, and I noticed a singular expression in his countenance, when he beheld my searching glances, which gave rise to a painful suspicion in my breast, and increased the dislike which I had ever entertained towards him. Bitter was the anguish I felt, and many were the tears I shed, when I was alone. A dreadful thought took possession of my mind, and nothing could erase it. I suspected the earl of treachery, and firmly believed that the document called my father's will was a forgery. I considered it was absolutely impossible that my father could have left such tyrannical instructions respecting one, of whom he had been so doatingly fond, and whose whole study had been to alleviate his sorrows and to call forth the bright sunshine of joy in his heart. This idea having taken possession of my mind I plainly saw that I was marked out to be the child of sorrow, and regretted that the same day on which my father breathed his last, had not also closed my mortal career.

"Lord Alfred was also as much astonished at the circumstance as myself, and although he did not express the same to me, I could plainly perceive that he was likewise of a similar, if not the same opinion, as regarded the non-genuineness of the will. He, however, endeavoured to console me by giving it as his opinion that his father would never exercise, to its full extent, the arbitrary power that had thus been entrusted to him, and that he would not think of biassing my affections, when he found they were placed upon one deserving of me; on the contrary he said, that he was of opinion that he would be pleased when he learned that he (Lord Alfred) was the object of my choice, as it would accomplish all that was ordered in the will of Sir Willoughby.

"I sighed, and shook my head; and he could plainly perceive that I placed little or no confidence in his assertions, which were, I was convinced, far from being his actual opinions.

" ' But, my dearest Blanche,' he continued, let the matter rest for a short time, and then I will confess our love to my father, and ask his assent to our union. That will at once decide the business, and set all our painful doubts and surmises at rest; although I do not think that we need be under any apprehension as to the result.'

" ' Heaven send that thy ideas may be realized, dear Alfred,' I replied, but my looks evinced how small was the hope I entertained that such would be the case.

" In this manner three months passed away, and the earl behaved with great kindness to me; but still there was at times, a peculiarity in his manners which imparted to my mind a sensation approaching to terror and disgust. Lord Alfred now thinking he had waited quite long enough, and noticing my increasing suspense, determined at once to seek an interview with his father, and acknowledge the sentiments with which our hearts were inspired. He did so, and my worst surmises were confirmed. The earl had scarcely patience to hear him out, and flying into a great rage, commanded him, on pain of his displeasure, never more to mention such a subject to him, and to banish me from his thoughts, for I never could be his bride. I cannot do justice to the emotions of my lover on that occasion; in vain he remonstrated with, and supplicated his father; the rage of the latter was only the more increased. He bade him quit his presence, and never more to venture to enter it until he had learned obedience to his will.

" I now come to one of the most trying events of my life.

No 20

" Lord Alfred, after this treatment from his father, retired from the castle, and having sought an early opportunity of gaining an interview with me, he repeated a hundred times his asseverations of unalterable affection, and assured me that nothing while he had life should ever induce him to banish me from the paramount situation I had obtained in his heart; he also solicited from me a promise to the same effect, which, I need not say, I gave most cordially, at the same time I expressed my regret that he should risk the displeasure of his father, by opposing his wishes.

" ' Let not that idea trouble thee, my dearest Blanche,' he observed; ' when parents exercise an unjust authority they cannot expect obedience. I trust that I have ever done my duty towards my father, and so am I still prepared to do ; but I do not see how he can reasonably attempt to bias my wishes, when the object of my affections is every way so worthy of me, and such as even an emperor ought to feel proud to possess. Nay, more, I am determined, although by so doing I should gain his eternal displeasure, that nothing shall ever prevail upon me to submit to his caprices ; that fortune,—everything, I will readily sacrifice, sooner than resign my pretensions to thee ; and, although I should deeply regret, if I should judge my father wrongfully, it strikes me that he must have some powerful motive for his conduct, some sinister design in contemplation, or he would never so strongly oppose our alliance, which, I am perfectly convinced, would have met with thy father's perfect approbation had he been in existence.'

" I could not attempt to contradict him, for the same idea had previously occurred to me, and a terrible suspicion had been excited in my bosom, owing to certain peculiarities in the behaviour of the ¦ earl that had met my observation. Whenever he had met me accidentally, even before the death of my poor father, he had conducted himself in a manner that had caused me considerable surprise and confusion, although at the time I could not imagine from whence the motives could spring. I was very soon too fatally awakened to a full sense of his villany.

" With many tears and protestations of fidelity, Lord Alfred and I separated, he being compelled to join the standard of his sovereign. With heavy hearts, indeed, did we take our farewell of each other, for we foreboded that something was about to happen to create fresh cause of sorrow for us. I was present when Lord Alfred came to take leave of his father, and I could not help noticing, with the utmost surprise, the evident expression of satisfaction which beamed in his countenance on that occasion, and the impatience he evinced when Lord Alfred and myself were bidding each other adieu.

" ' Psha ! this is childish weakness,' he ejaculated, ' and must not,—shall not be indulged in. Blanche, betake thou to thy chamber, and leave this silly boy to indulge alone in his nonsense.'

" ' Father, returned Lord Alfred, with the utmost difficulty restraining his feelings within the bounds of decorum, ' surely thou canst not upbraid me for——'

" ' Enough of this !' interrupted the earl, ' and remember what I have said to thee.—I trust when thou dost return from the battle-field, thou wilt have learned that obedience to a father's will, which is one of the brightest precepts of our nature.'

"'I trust, my lord,' answered Lord Alfred, proudly, 'that thy son has never yet forgotten his duty; but I also trust that he will never learn to tamely submit to that which is dictated by injustice, tyrannical caprice, and oppression.'

"The earl frowned, bit his lips, and waving his hand peremptorily, we tore ourselves asunder, and my lover quitted the castle. I hurried from the room to my own apartment, the casement of which opened upon the turrets, and from whence I could view Lord Alfred depart. Never did he look so noble as when mounted upon his richly-caparisoned charger, and surrounded by the gallant knights that formed his train, he crossed the moat, and quitted the gothic castle ; but the deep melancholy with which his countenance was clothed, fully evinced the mental anguish he was suffering, and severely did my heart respond to the sentiments which inhabited his bosom. His eye caught my form, and removing his glittering casque, from which the white feathers waved proudly, he fixed upon me a look, and by signs bade me a farewell, which was so strongly impressed upon my memory, that it was continually present to my imagination ever afterwards. When the martial cavalcade had disappeared, I having remained watching it, until it was out of sight, I returned into the chamber, and throwing myself upon the couch, and covering my face with my hands, I gave full vent to my grief in a copious flood of tears. Alas ! too soon had I ample cause for grief ;—shortly was I doomed to suffer all that poignant anguish which my worst fears had prognosticated. But I am fearful, my dear lady, that thou wilt think me extremely prolix in this narrative."

"By no means," said Lady Marguerite, who had been listening to her with the most breathless attention ; " on the contrary, I feel more than usually interested by the recital, and sincerely can I commiserate with thee in the sorrows thou hast experienced. Pr'ythee, proceed."

Blanche obeyed.

"The day after the departure of my lover, I noticed a considerable alteration in the conduct of the Earl Harlingwood towards me ; he became more kind, and was attentive even to obsequiousness. He seemed to study my every wish, and expressed the utmost solicitude to render me happy. I saw they were the mere emanations of an hypocritical heart, and I felt more uneasy than I had before done. What more than all excited my suspicions was, that the earl most scrupulously watched my actions, and seemed fearful of my being out of his sight. He restricted my walks from the castle as much as possible, until I remonstrated with him upon the subject, and took every opportunity of which he could avail himself to be in my society. I frequently reflected upon this behaviour, formed conjectures upon it, and weighing it with other circumstances that had come within my knowledge, my mind became distracted with powerful apprehensions, and more than ever did I regret that Lord Alfred had quitted the spot. And then again the uncertainty as to whether or not he would ever again return, filled my bosom with the most acute pain. He might fall in the strife and deadly carnage :—and, alas ! what would then become of me ?—And, if even he should return from the battle-field, might not my worst fears long ere then be realised, and my body reposing in the silent tomb, the victim of a broken heart ?—This was no hasty or improbable idea ;—alas ! for me it was by far too reasonable. Many times did I reflect upon the document which had been shewn me as the will of my father, and the more I thought upon it, the more did my doubts of its authenticity increase. My poor father, so different in disposition, so mild,—so kind,—so indulgent,—so grateful to his unhappy daughter, could never have dictated such harsh, such unjust, such arbitrary measures towards her. Oh, no ; I could not believe it ; and if, then, there had been treachery on this point, what had I to expect from the future behaviour of the earl ?—I shuddered with horror when I thought of it. I trembled to dwell upon the probability of my worst fears being realized. Oh, how willingly would I have exchanged my condition for that of the humblest peasant, to have had with it content and liberty.—Liberty, I repeat ; for what was the life I was now leading, but one of the worst, the most painful species of slavery, since, not only were my actions fettered, but the purest dictates of my heart ?

" These feelings gradually gained such powerful ascendancy over me, that I could scarcely meet the earl without a shudder, or an open demonstration of the repugnance with which he had inspired me ; and what tended to add to my detestation (for by any milder term I cannot designate it), he daily became more offensively attentive, so that I was very seldom released from his society ; and there was a boldness in his manner, and a certain freedom of speech, that could not have any other possible effect, than to excite my most superlative disgust. If by chance I mentioned the name of his son, which I was generally cautious not to do, he would fly into a great rage, his passions being most ungovernable, and after giving utterance to the most unmanly invectives, would command me never to mention again to him the name of one, whom it was imperatively necessary that I should forget ; and it would take some time ere he could sufficiently recover himself to converse with any degree of temper or rationality. All these circumstances made a deep impression upon me, and caused my situation to become daily more painful and insupportable to me. But the confirmation of my worst surmises was about to take place.

" I had been one day walking in the gardens attached to the castle, and ruminating upon my untoward fate, when some one touched me on the shoulder, and turning round, I was alarmed at beholding the earl standing near me, and by his countenance, which was greatly flushed, it was evident he had been partaking freely of wine.

" All the fears and disgust, which his recent conduct had excited in my bosom, rushed vividly upon my mind, and noticing the excitement, from the effects of drink, under which he evidently laboured, apprehension in an instant took possession of me, and I endeavoured to avoid him. This, however, was futile ; and you may judge of my alarm, Lady Marguerite, when the hoary villain (for a villain it was shortly my fate to prove him to be,) threw his arms around my waist, and drawing me forcibly towards him, attempted to imprint a kiss upon my lips. This I contrived to defeat, and was retreating with indignation and disgust from the spot, when he hastily pursued me, once more seized me round the waist, and then, in tones of fearful boldness, he addressed me in the following words :—

" ' Beauteous Blanche, thou hast inspired in my bosom a passion as powerful as it is sincere, and now for the first time do I venture to unfold to thee the sentiments of my heart, and to solicit a return of thy love. Nay, thou need'st not frown, fair lady; opposition will not avail thee. I was prepared to meet thy scorn, but doubt not that in time I shall overcome thine icy coldness.'

" Disgust, fear, and indignation, for awhile choked my utterance, and tearing myself forcibly from his hold, I retreated to some distance, fixing upon him a look of mingled resentment and offended virtue, which for a moment or two seemed to awe him, and compel him to forbearance.

" ' My lord,' I at length exclaimed, in tones of the deepest reproach, ' this language from thee !—Suffer me to pass, and to retire to my own apartments.'

" ' Thou shalt not pass, maiden,' cried the earl, ' thou shalt not pass until thy lips have sealed my wishes. Thou mayest frown, and heap on me reproaches, but they will but add to the passion which hath taken possession of my heart, and urge me on to that, which by different behaviour thou mightest avert. For months these eyes, beauteous, too-lovely Blanche, have viewed thee with adoration, and I panted for an opportunity to be enabled to give utterance to my sentiments, and solicit from thee a return; that moment hath arrived, and now do I offer thee my hand, my heart, my fortune. Pause ere thou dost foolishly reject them, and remember that in spite of everything, I am determined, even at the hazard of my life, my soul, that thou shalt be mine !'

" He forcibly seized my hand as he spoke, in spite of my efforts to the contrary, and bending one knee to the earth smothered it with his loathsome kisses. How did my bosom swell with rage, shame, and offended modesty; and my apprehensions increased, when I noticed the vehement manner of the earl, and heard how determined he was to put his threats into execution. Alas ! what would become of me, without a soul near to whom I might look up for protection ?

" ' My lord,' I ejaculated, after a painful conflict with my emotions, ' release me, I command thee, or my cries shall alarm the inmates of the castle, and expose thee to thy vassals. Shame, shame on thee; thine age should have taught thee better; but more than all, thy promise to my poor dying father ;—is this the protection thou didst swear to him thou would'st afford me ?'

" ' Do I not offer thee the best of protection, damsel ?' returned the earl, releasing my hand, folding his arms, and gazing upon me with looks that caused the deep crimson blushes of shame to mantle in my cheeks ;—' the protection of husband of rank and power, and who is prepared to love thee with all the strength of the most ardent passion ? But since thou art pleased to remind me of the promises I made thy father, thou wilt likewise remember that by his will, I am thy sole guardian; that thou art wholly and solely in my power, and that thou must wed alone he whom I think proper, or forfeit thy fortune to me, and become the inmate of a convent for the rest of thy days. Think of this, girl, and choose between so terrible a fate, and an union with rank and power.'

" ' Oh, heaven!' I cried, clasping my hands together, ' could my poor father have been so cruel, so unjust, in his last moments to his only child, her who attended to his comfort for so many weary years, and upon whom he ever lavished the most unbounded fondness ?—I cannot—will not believe it!'

" ' Blanche, exclaimed the earl, passionately, and scowling fearfully, ' beware what thou sayest, lest thou shouldst turn my love to anger. Dost thou dispute the authenticity of thy father's will ?—Have I not the document in my possession sealed and ratified by him on his death bed ?'

" ' Some unfair means must have been adopted to extort that document,' I returned, with firmness; ' I am certain that my poor father would never voluntarily have bequeathed me to misery and anguish.'

" The earl bit his lips, and paced backwards and forwards for a few moments without giving utterance to a syllable; it was, however, quite evident that the boldness of my manner, and the answers I had given to him, had caused a violent commotion in his breast, and touched his guilty conscience.

" ' Blanche,' at length he observed, having by a powerful effort somewhat recovered his composure, ' the assertions thou hast made use of will only serve to exasperate me, and effect thee no service, while at the same time they are false and unjust. But it matters not; thou art in my power, and in spite of thine obstinacy, I will dispose of thee as I think proper.'

" ' Never, by heaven!' I exclaimed, with increased energy, ' poverty—a nunnery—any fate would be preferable to an union with thee! As the father of Lord Alfred I did respect thee, and was prepared to love thee as a parent, but now——'

" ' Hold, girl!' interrupted the Earl, fiercely; ' dare not again to mention to me the name of that disobedient beardless boy; I swear that he shall never be thine, and sooner than he should, I would myself, if he dies not on the field of battle, strike my dagger to his heart.'

" ' Oh, my lord,' I returned, with a shudder of horror, ' make not use of such dreadful threats. Is this the language a father should use in respect to his son? Shame, shame!—But thou wilt not persist in this conduct;' I continued, in softened accents; ' thou canst not mean what thou sayest; let me pass, I beg of thee, and I will think no more of this, which I believe only to be caused by the excitement of——'

" ' Fair, but scornful beauty,' cried the earl, with a determined air, and seizing my arm with a vehemence that hurt me,—' I again swear that thou shalt not quit this spot until I have exacted from thee a promise to——'

" ' Oh, help! help!' I screamed, struggling as much as possible to release myself;—' in the name of heaven, I appeal to the spirit of thy sainted wife, to protect me.'

" At the mention of his wife, the earl released me in a moment, and starting back with a shudder of horror, he covered his face with his hands, and groaned aloud. In an instant I seized upon the opportunity, and hurrying from the spot with the speed of lightning, I hastened into the castle, and retiring to my own apartment, I secured the door, and threw myself on my couch, completely overpowered by the violence of my wounded feelings.

" I need not, I am certain, lady, attempt to pourtray to thee the emotions that now agitated my bosom and distracted my brain ; I found myself placed in a situation of the most fearful description, in the power of a villain, and with no one near at hand, who would take any interest in my fate, or attempt to rescue me from the danger by which I was threatened. My thoughts immediately wandered to Lord Alfred, and my agony increased ten-fold, when I reflected upon the distance which divided us from each other, and the agony he would undergo did he but know the dangerous and painful situation in which I was placed, and the villany of his father. Our worst conjectures were confirmed, and it was very certain that the earl would run any risk, and would not hesitate to adopt the most desperate means, sooner than his wishes should be thwarted.— Alas ! what a dreadful prospect was now before me; what power had I to avert the evil ? Even were I to make my escape from the castle, whither could I flee ? —to whom go for protection ?—No one !

" The whole of that night I passed in the most indescribable state of agony; at times giving utterance to the most violent expressions of despair, and then on my knees imploring the protection of heaven, and calling upon the spirit of my father to save me from the cruel fate with which the earl threatened me.

" The following morning I became somewhat more composed, and was preparing to leave my chamber, when Geraldine, my waiting-maid, entered the room, and with a most melancholy expression of countenance, informed me that it was the earl's command that I should be kept confined to my own suite of rooms, and not allowed to leave them until he gave orders to that effect.

" ' Blessed Virgin !' I exclaimed, with fear and indignation ; ' am I then a prisoner ?'

" ' Alas ! it is even so, my lady,' said Geraldine, ' but I pray thee attempt to bear with it patiently, and trust to the protection of heaven. Deeply, most deeply do I sympathise with thy sufferings, and well do I read the motives of the earl ; but I trust his evil designs will be rendered abortive. Oh, my lady, think me not bold in my observations ; but I can never believe that thy poor father, my late honoured master, could have known the real character of the earl, or never would he have honoured him with his friendship, or entrusted thee to his protection.'

" I sighed mournfully, and by my looks showed Geraldine how wholly I acquiesced in her conjectures.

" 'The earl has ordered me to lock thee in, my lady,' continued Geraldine, ' and deeply as it pains me so to do, I have no other alternative but to obey; if I were to refuse, the task to wait on thee might be transferred to somebody else, who might not be inclined to pity thee, but on the contrary, be ready to further the earl's desires. And again, my lady, if I may make so bold as to offer thee any advice, I would impress upon thee the imprudence there would be in too rashly opposing the earl's orders, which might only provoke him to proceed to immediate violence; whereas, if thou dost act to the contrary, thou mayest awe him into forbearance, obtain time, and ultimately something may interpose to rescue thee from the danger by which thou art at present threatened, and to frustrate the wicked intentions of the earl altogether.'

" ' My good, my faithful Geraldine,' I ejaculated, while tears filled my eyes, ' I approve of thy counsel, and will adopt it. And now hope seems to whisper to me that something will happen to save me from the earl's villany. I will, at any rate, endeavour to meet my persecutor with fortitude, and surely that Almighty, whom I have never willingly or knowingly offended, will not suffer the base designs and machinations of the guilty to triumph.—Now, Geraldine, thou hadst best leave me, lest the length of thy stay should excite suspicion; I know thou wilt visit me as frequently as thou canst.'

" 'Aye, that I will, my lady,' answered the faithful girl; ' I shall shortly return with thy morning's repast, by which time the earl probably may have quitted the castle, and we may have an opportunity of conferring longer together. For the present, my lady, adieu, and the blessed Virgin protect thee !—Alas! alas! that I should ever come to this !'

" Thus sighing and wringing her hands, Geraldine left me, and in obedience to the orders she had received, secured the door after her. Not more than half an hour had elapsed, when I heard footsteps on the stairs, and immediately afterwards the key turned in the lock ;—I started up, thinking it was Geraldine returned; but when the door flew open, my disappointment and alarm may be imagined when the earl presented himself.

" The earl having closed the door after him, stood contemplating me for a few seconds with looks of boldness, while I could plainly read from the expression of his countenance the dark and villanous thoughts that were passing in his mind. I struggled with my fears as much as possible, and endeavoured to meet him with firmness and perfect composure, and I succeeded much better than I anticipated.

" As the earl folded his arms, and still did not offer to speak, I broke the silence by demanding in tones of indignation :—.

" ' My lord, probably thou hast come hither to explain to me the cause of this outrage—why am I detained here a prisoner?'

" ' Simply because it is my will,' he replied; ' thou dost forget, methinks, hat thou art under my jurisdiction, and must not question my conduct.'

" ' When that conduct is dictated by a spirit of tyranny and injustice, I will

question it,' I returned, boldly; ' I repeat that thou hast no right to make me a prisoner; what have I done to merit such a punishment?'

" ' Blanche,' said the earl, after a brief pause; ' it rests entirely with thyself; a word from thee and the bolts that confine thee shall be withdrawn immediately; but obstinacy will not only bring down contrary treatment, but will also not save thee from the fate thou wouldst avoid. I did fully reveal to thee my sentiments yesterday, and my determination to act upon them, and nothing whatever can alter my resolution. I offer thee my hand, rank, fortune—I would make thee my honoured bride, and lavish upon thee every happiness; then do not reject the proposal while it is yet in thy power. Of this, however, be assured, that here thou shalt remain confined until thou dost consent to become mine, or I drag thee by force to the altar.'

" ' Villain!' had almost escaped my lips, but I stifled my feelings as much as possible, and with a look and tone of the utmost resentment, said,—

" ' Thou hast told me thy determination, my lord; hear also my firm resolution—sooner will I die than live to endure a fate to me so detestable.'

" ' Obstinate, scornful girl,' cried the earl, in vain endeavouring to conceal the rage my opposition excited in his breast; ' mind that thou dost not repent this. But a little imprisonment may serve to alter thy tone. Were I to suffer thee to be at large, thou mightest perchance take it into thy head to elope from my custody; but I will not afford thee that opportunity. But think not that with the exception of confining thee, I either wish or intend to restrict thee in any of thy enjoyments; on the contrary, I would show thee by my kindness the sincerity of those vows I have proffered to thee. I would prove to thee, dearest Blanche, that I love thee to distraction; that I adore thee even;—here again, on my knees do I repeat to thee, fair maiden, the assurance of my boundless love; here at once do I lay my coronet at thy feet, and implore of thee to accept it. Dispel, then, those frowns of displeasure that so ill-become thy beauteous face; banish scorn and repugnance from thy gentle bosom, and accept the happiness I offer to thee.'

" ' My lord,' answered I, ' if thou wouldst not turn that respect I had for thee entirely to disgust and hatred, thou wilt cease thus to persecute me, and retire immediately from my sight. Oh, sir, reflect, I beseech thee, before thou dost proceed further. As the father of Lord Alfred, I would fain love thee as mine, but when——'

" ' Why dost thou again mention the name of that hated boy to me?' cried Harlingwood, passionately: ' I tell thee again,—nay, I swear that he never shall be thine;—thou art mine, mine, and no other. My mind is made up to it, and were all the fiends of hell to stand in my way, they should not prevent the accomplishment of my wishes !'

" The earl paced the room with hasty strides as he thus spoke, and the violence of his manner greatly alarmed me. I did not offer to make any observation, and was resolved not again to make any allusion to Lord Alfred, if I could possibly avoid it.

" At length his emotion being somewhat subdued, he took my hand, and in a voice of forced calmness, said,—

" ' Pardon me, lovely Blanche; the impetuosity of my passion at times forces me into expressions of violence, which I do not mean, and which I am afterwards sorry for. I do request thee to consider well the offer I have made thee, and complete at once my happiness and thine own, by yielding thy consent to become my bride. I will no longer intrude myself upon thee for the present, but will give thee due time to consider of it, and will expect thy answer in a week. Farewell, sweet maiden, until we meet again.'

" He pressed my hand with an air of respect to his lips as he spoke, and then after bestowing upon me a look of the most intense admiration, he quitted the room, and left me to myself.

" It would be a useless occupation of thy time, fair lady, were I to enter into a minute detail of the feelings that filled my mind after this interview, but fear and disgust were my most predominant sentiments; however, I knew that no good could possibly be derived by giving way to grief; I, therefore, on the contrary, endeavoured to compose myself as much as possible, and implored the aid of Providence to enable me to make a firm and determined resistance to the earl. One thing afforded me infinite satisfaction, which was, that I imagined from his observations, I should be released from the sight of him for a week, and in that interim I lived in hopes that something might transpire to induce the earl either to abandon his designs, or to restore me again to liberty, and rescue me from his power. Could I but manage to escape from the castle, I had come to the determination to seek protection and an asylum in some religious house, until I was out of his jurisdiction; and, in fact, any fate to me appeared preferable to that with which he threatened me. My thoughts were incessantly fix'd upon my lover, who was exposed to all the dangers and horrors of the sanguinary field of strife, and might ere now have perished; while, at the same time, should he be alive, how bitter, how very poignant would be his anguish, could he but know the misery I was enduring, and the fate with which I was threatened by the villany of his own father.

" My conjectures proved correct; I saw no more of the earl for the time he had given me to consider his offer, and Geraldine was my constant companion, and by the sympathy which she expressed in my misfortunes, greatly lightened me of my cares. Willingly would she have aided me to escape had it been in her power, but the earl had made use of such precautions, and had persons so continually upon the watch, that all chance of such an attempt was rendered abortive.

" As the day quickly approached when the earl would expect my answer, my apprehensions increased, but I tried to conquer them as much as I could, so that I might be able to meet him with that resolution and presence of mind which the nature of the subject required me to do.

" The earl was true to his appointment, and at an early hour in the morning entered my chamber, apparently elate with expectation. He entered into a long and fulsome rhapsody upon my beauty, and then at once demanded my decision. Now had the moment arrived which required all the firmness and intrepidity I could muster, and I succeeded by far better than I expected I should have done. I answered him mildly, but with decision, that honoured as I might feel by the offer he had been pleased to make me, I must positively decline it; because, were I to bestow on him my hand, it could never be accompanied by my heart. I could have told him that nothing could ever change the sentiments with which his son had inspired me; but I was fearful of exciting him too violently, and I, therefore, desisted. I shall never forget the rage of the earl when he heard my reply to his demand;—he stamped his foot furiously on the floor, bit his lips, and his countenance was so distorted with passion, that it was frightful to behold. He traversed the room fiercely for some moments, and was unable to give utterance to a syllable; at last he turned to me, and in a voice of half-stifled rage, he said,—

" ' And is that positively thy decision ?'

" I answered in the affirmative.

" ' Thou wilt not retract that decision ere it is too late ?' demanded he.

" ' I will not,' I answered with the greatest firmness, having completely conquered my fears.

" ' 'Tis well,' observed the earl, with fearful coolness,—' 'tis well,—then be the consequences on thine own head :—obstinate, headstrong girl.'

" He said no more, but with a look of fierce determination quitted the room, closing the door after him with a loud bang, and securing it on the outside as before. His behaviour seriously alarmed me, for I considered there was more to apprehend from it than if he had used any violent threats. The remainder of that day was passed by me in the most miserable manner, my mind being filled with alternate hopes and fears. Geraldine did not come near me the whole of the day, but as evening approached she entered the room with some refreshments, of which she induced me to partake; she expressed the greatest commisseration

my sufferings, but she did not seek for a moment to disown that there was but too
much reason to fear the worst from the earl, knowing so well as she did his determined disposition, and how little able he was to brook any opposition to his
will. Geraldine was compelled to leave me earlier than usual, having some particular business to attend to, and feeling thirsty, I took up the glass containing the
wine, of which I had before slightly partook, and took a hearty draught. I had
no sooner done so than a curious sensation came over me—my limbs tottered, my
head swam round, my eyes grew dim, every object in the room gradually faded
from my view, and sinking on the floor, I became insensible.

" On my restoration to consciousness, my astonishment and consternation may
be imagined, on finding myself in a vehicle, placed between two ruffians, whose
countenances were sufficient to excite the utmost alarm and disgust in my bosom.
The carriage was proceeding at a rapid rate, and the blinds being down, I had
no opportunity of judging in what direction we were going, or whether it was
night or morning. I had some faint recollection of what had taken place at Harlingwood Castle, and the insensibility which had immediately taken place after
I had partaken of the wine ; and it now seemed probable to me that some strong
opiate had been mixed with it, for the purpose of my being conveyed away
from the castle with greater facility and secrecy. These thoughts flashed in a
moment across my brain, and turning with a look of horror to my ferocious-
looking companions, I implored them, in tremulous accents, to inform me
whither we were going, and for what purpose I was borne away from the
castle. At first the men took no notice of me, and returned no answer to my
interrogatories, but upon repeating my supplications, one of them turned to me
and said,—

" ' It is useless your putting any questions to us, young lady, for you will get
no satisfactory reply. It is sufficient for you to know that you are in the power
of your guardian, the Earl of Harlingwood, by whose orders we act.'

" ' Good God !' I thought to myself, ' what can be his motives for removing
me from the castle, and whither are they taking me ? I am lost, I am lost, for
doubtless the earl has determined to put his diabolical threats into execution, and
there is no one that I know who can interpose to save me.'

" These were the reflections that passed in my mind only, for I did not attempt to give them utterance, knowing full well that I should meet with no pity
from the ruffians who had me in their power.

" The vehicle still continued to roll on its course at a rapid rate, and the men
maintained the utmost silence, not even exchanging a word one with the other.
By the howling of the wind I could hear that it was boisterous weather ; and
soon afterwards one of the men let down the blinds, when I found that it was
night, and that the wild tract of country over which we were travelling was but
dimly lighted by the lurid beams of the moon.

" We were at this time crossing a barren moor, and as far as the eye could
stretch, through the almost impenetrable darkness, no prospect could be more
cheerless. Not an habitation could be seen, and the place seemed to be little
frequented. Fit spot, thought I, for the perpetration of deeds of darkness ; and
as these ideas crossed my mind, my blood turned icy cold, I shuddered, and
looked at my companions with a feeling of uncontroulable horror.

"What part of the country we were in, I, of course, had no means of judging, nor the time we had been travelling; but it was evidently several hours, from the darkness which prevailed, and which led me to imagine that it was at least midnight. These ideas were followed by one that caused me considerable pain (for it is painful to be led to suppose those in whom we have placed our confidence, and whom we have believed to be our friends, have deceived us). When I reflected that it was from Geraldine I had received the wine, with which was doubtless mixed some powerful drug, I began strongly to suspect that she was acquainted with the plot, and had pandered to the base designs of the earl. Yet, on more mature reflection, I upbraided myself for entertaining such a suspicion, and entirely acquitted her of having any participation in the plot.

"I need not, I am sure, attempt to describe my feelings to you, gentle lady, as the vehicle moved on its way; I felt as if I were being borne to destruction, and, although it is hard to die in all our youth and freshness, death to me at that time would have been preferable to the terrible and certain fate which seemed to be impending over me. Alas! what would be the agony, the distraction of my lover, and his disgust at the cruelty of his unnatural parent, did he but know the situation in which I was placed. And yet he had foreboded evil, and had it not been for the duty he owed his king and country, nothing would ever have induced him to leave me. Alas! mine was a terrible fate, to have no one near at hand to interpose to rescue me from the guilty designs of a villain, whom it would be a libel on the human race to call a man. These thoughts, too, were succeeded by others of a still more painful nature, if possible; namely, the base means that had been resorted to to prevail upon my father to make so stringent and tyrannical a document, for I was confident that he never could of his own free will, or in his rational moments, consign his only child to the greatest possible misery. Thoughts like these filled me with the most indescribable horror, and added to the anguish I endured at the situation in which I was unfortunately placed, a situation from which I saw no prospect whatever of being released.

"The moor was several miles in extent, and during the time we were crossing it I did not see a single individual. It was one wide expanse of gloom and horror. Having crossed this, we entered a tract of country scarcely less dismal; it consisted of hills, intersected with ravines, down which, in the almost utter darkness which prevailed, we were in danger of being precipitated every moment. Not the least signs of a human habitation met my gaze, and despair seemed to surround me. I never remembered to have seen the men by whom I was guarded before, but their savage features and determined manners were sufficient to convince me that they were capable of perpetrating any deed, however monstrous; and that the earl should have such creatures in his pay, gave me a greater proof than all of his villany. Thus surrounded by danger, and in the power of one who was evidently familiar with crime, what hope was there for me?—I wrung my hands, and clasping my burning temples, sank back in the carriage, completely overpowered by the agony of despair.

"The men occasionally spoke to each other in under tones, but from what I could hear, the subject of their conversation did not at all relate to me, or to the place of our destination, and at length I became so completely engrossed by my own painful thoughts, as to pay little or no attention to them, although the boldness and freedom of their looks at first seriously alarmed and disgusted me.

" Several hours we continued to travel in this manner, never stopping on the road, and the scenery undergoing very little change. In fact, it appeared as if we had got into another country altogether, for the prospect had nothing at all of the beautiful and picturesque character of English scenery.

" We passed through but one solitary hamlet, the inhabitants of which seemed to be wrapped in sleep, for 1 did not perceive a single light in any of the casements of their miserable huts, nor did I observe any person stirring about ; and even if I had, I entertained considerable doubt whether they would have had either the will or the power to assist me ; I could, therefore, do nothing else than resign myself to my fate, looking up to the Supreme Being as my only hope of relief.

" At length the darkness gradually vanished, the first red streaks of dawn appeared in the eastern horizon, and the vehicle suddenly emerged into a scene of less wildness. The birds began to carol forth their sweetest notes to welcome in the day, and the hardy rustic might be seen plodding his way to his diurnal labours, with a countenance ruddy with health, and a brow upon which content and happiness had stamped themselves. Oh ! how I envied them their lot, and willingly would I have given up fortune and rank, to be free and undisturbed by care as they were. Several times I was half inclined to appeal to them, and solicit their aid in rescuing me, but the ferocious and threatening glances of the ruffians withheld me, and we proceeded in silence.

" At length the lofty turrets of a castle met my gaze, and it was soon evident that that was the place of our destination. It was blackened by time, and covered with moss and ivy. It was surrounded by a deep moat, and altogether presented the most impregnable appearance.

" Having arrived at the castle, one of the ruffians alighted, and blew three loud blasts on his horn, upon which the drawbridge was immediately let down, and we passed over, and entering at the gates, which were opened by an old, greyheaded porter of the most forbidding aspect, we passed through an extensive court-yard, and having alighted from the vehicle, I was ushered into a spacious hall, decorated with all the pomp of feudal splendour, and which, bearing the armorial trappings of the ancient house of Harlingwood, I was convinced that the castle belonged to that nobleman, and had an idea of what part of the country we were in ; but what could be the earl's motive for removing me thither, I could not imagine, as I should have been equally safe at Harlingwood Castle, and quite as securely in his power, as I could possibly be where they had brought me.

" After passing through several apartments, we stopped at the door of one, which opened on the western gallery of the ancient edifice, and here one of my conductors having unlocked the door, I was desired to walk in, which, having done, the door was closed upon me, locked and bolted, and I was thus left to myself.

" I looked around me, and found myself in a suite of handsomely furnished rooms, of lofty and commodious description; in one of which was placed a bed, which seemed to have been but recently placed there for my accommodation.

I threw myself upon it in despair, and covering my face with my hands, gave myself up entirely to despair.

"I remained for about two hours in this situation, without any interruption, when I heard the key turning in the lock of the door, and the bolts being withdrawn, and immediately afterwards an old woman, of wrinkled and repulsive appearance, entered, bringing with her refreshments, which she placed upon the table, and in harsh and disagreeable tones, desired me to partake, as I had had a long journey, and could, therefore, no doubt, find an appetite. My heart was, however, too full to eat, and turning towards the old woman with a look of supplication, I requested that she would inform me why I was brought thither, and whether the earl was in the castle.

"'As for why thou art brought hither, young lady,' replied the woman, 'I dare say thou knowest as well as I do, because thou art a fool, and hath refused to accept of the hand of the earl. Thou wilt see him thyself in the course of the day, and I do not doubt but that thou wilt then be taught that it is worse than madness to attempt to oppose the will of his lordship.'

"I turned from the old woman with a feeling of the most irrepressible disgust, and did not deign to make her any reply, but my bosom swelled with indignation, and it was with difficulty I could forbear the full expression of my feelings. Finding that I was not inclined to say anything more to her, the old woman almost immediately afterwards quitted the room, much to my relief, for I could not gaze upon her repulsive countenance without a sentiment of the most unbounded disgust.

"The words of the old woman had added to the anguish and terror which I had before experienced, and in a paroxysm of agony, I gave myself up entirely as lost. I implored the interposition of Heaven, and had scarcely arisen from my knees, when I heard some one at the room door, and immediately afterwards it was opened, and the earl stood before me.

"He gazed at me for a few seconds in silence, and an expression of triumph and exultation passed over his features; but soon afterwards he advanced nearer towards me, and in a voice of boldness, said :—

"'Welcome, fair Blanche, to St. Osbert's Castle. Thou, probably, did not anticipate such a journey, and thou mayest thank thine own obstinacy and contumacy that thou hast been put to the inconvenience of it. At Harlingwood Castle there were several obstacles to the completion of my project, but here there are none; and I now come to thee no longer to solicit, but to command. I will no longer be tampered with by the perverse opposition of a silly girl, but enforce that compliance which I have hitherto sued for; prepare thyself, Blanche; this evening makes thee my bride.'

"Overwhelmed with terror at the boldness and determination of his manner, I threw myself at his feet, and with clasped hands and streaming eyes, implored him to 'forbear, but he turned from me with indifference, and going towards the door, said as he opened it :—

"'Thou hast heard my determination; — that determination is unalterable. Adieu, till the evening, when I shall come to conduct thee to the altar.'

"Without saying another word, the earl bowed to me and retired.

"My feelings I need not now attempt to describe; I saw at once that all hope of escape from the fate with which the tyrant earl threatened me, was at an end, and that, situated as I was, in a place where I had not a single individual near me, who had either the will or the power to attempt to rescue me, I had nothing left but to make up my mind for the worst. My doom, then, was sealed. A few short hours, only, and I should be forced to become the bride of that man, whom, above all others, I now dreaded and detested.

" ' Ah, Alfred, dearest, most noble of youths,' I soliloquized, ' why art thou not at hand to rescue thy unfortunate Blanche from a fate so terrible? But, if thou wert, wouldst thou have the power to save me? Alas, no; thou darest not resist or oppose thy father's despotic will. Alas! alas! how great would be thy anguish, didst thou but know the misery to which I am at the present moment exposed. I am convinced, that even at the hazard of thy father's eternal displeasure, thou wouldst interpose to save me, and accomplish thy wishes, or perish in the attempt.'

" These thoughts, while they caused me much pain, at the same time re-kindled hope in my bosom, and a strange idea suddenly took possession of my mind, that something would occur to save me from the dreaded fate with which I had been threatened by the earl. Terrible were the sufferings I endured in the few short hours that intervened between the time at which the earl had promised he would return to force me to the altar, and never did it appear to pass more quickly away. Two or three times during the day, the old woman visited me to bring refreshments, and when she found me in tears, she would scoff at my anguish, and with many disagreeable additions, make use of such observations as :—

" ' Well, I'm sure; I should very much like to know what thou hast to fret about, young lady, because, forsooth, a nobleman of the highest rank and birth, wishes to make thee his bride. For my part, I think thou shouldst feel thyself highly honoured and delighted with the chance. However, it's no use fretting, or thinking anything about it; for have thee, the earl certainly will, and the preparations for the union are even now going on in the chapel of the castle.'

" I clasped my hands, and raised my eyes towards Heaven with a look of earnest supplication, as the old woman thus spoke, and mentally invoked the protection of the Supreme; and again did a beam of hope dawn upon my mind. Finding that I would not condescend to return her any answer, the old woman walked away, and I was again left to myself. But I am fearful, lady, that thou wilt deem me prolix, and I will, therefore, not detain thee any longer than I can help, by any unnecessary observations.

" At length the dull shades of evening fell upon the earth, and I suddenly heard a strange noise and confused bustling sounds in the castle. Persons seemed to be passing along the gallery in great haste, and the closing of different doors and other tokens, shewed that some unusual circumstance was about to take place. Full well could I understand the meaning of it; and my heart throbbed violently as the idea of my approaching fate darted upon my mind. In a few minutes afterwards, I heard some one advancing along the gallery towards the apartment in which I was confined, and the next instant they stopped at the room door. Next I heard the bolts being withdrawn, and the key turning in the lock; in a moment the door was thrown back on its hinges, and my dreaded

persecutor was in my presence, and eyeing me with looks of exultation and triumph.

"'Now, Blanche,' he exclaimed, advancing towards me, and forcibly taking my hand, ' art thou prepared to become my bride? I have come to lead thee to the altar.'

"'Ah, my lord,' I cried, throwing myself on my knees at his feet; ' surely thou wilt not be so cruel; thou wilt relent, and not force one to become thy bride, who can esteem thee as a friend, as a father, but who cannot love thee as her husband? Nature, justice, reason, all oppose it; and Heaven surely will not sanction such a deed.'

"'Psha! no more of this,' said the earl, ' I am sick of hearing such unmeaning trash; I told thee my determination in the morning, and it is seldom that I break my word. Come, to the altar,—to the altar.'

"'Oh, spare me! spare me!' I implored, as the earl threw his arms round my waist, and proceeded to force me from the apartment. But he was deaf to my entreaties, and the more ardent I became, so did his resolution appear to increase. He led me forcibly from the apartment, and in a state of almost unconsciousness along the gallery, across the gothic hall, and into the chapel, where I found a number of the earl's retainers assembled, and a monk waiting at the altar, upon which lights were burning. I looked around upon the different persons present, in the hope to see some of them pity me, and step forward to save me, but, alas! I looked in vain; they were all the servile creatures of

No. 22

the earl, and seemed to be highly pleased with the event, and gratified to think that they were allowed to be spectators of it.

"The earl led, or rather dragged me to the altar, and here I threw myself at the feet of the holy man, and in a voice of the most vehement supplication, implored his interference and pity.

"'Hear me, holy father,' I cried, 'hear me, while I declare that I am forced hither against my will, and that I object to become the bride of this nobleman. Oh, do not, I beseech thee, suffer me to fall a victim to ——

"'Proceed with the ceremony, monk,' interrupted the earl, peremptorily; 'heed not what this silly girl says; let the marriage be solemnized without more delay.'

"'Oh, mercy, mercy!' I shrieked, as the earl seized my hand, and with looks of the utmost impatience, motioned the monk to proceed. No one around, however, seemed to pity me the least in the world, and the monk obeyed the orders of the earl;—he commenced the marriage rites, and with the most un-utterable anguish I gave myself up to despair, when, suddenly the lights on the altar seemed to burn blue; a strange sensation of mingled horror and hope took possession of me, and the monk paused, as if his senses had all at once become stupified. The persons present seemed to experience the same mysterious feeling, and looked at each other with expressions of awe, amazement, and con-fusion.

"'What means this?' cried the earl, whose countenance had become ghastly pale, and whose limbs (in spite of the efforts he made to stifle his emotions) trembled violently;—'hath madness seized upon ye all, that ye stand there gaping, and with vacant stare? Why dost thou not proceed with the ceremony, monk?'

"The holy father re-commenced the ceremony, but, scarcely had he uttered a word, when a hollow and sepulchral voice which seemed to proceed from beneath the altar, cried :—

"'Forbear!'

"The monk became silent in a moment, and he was evidently much alarmed; while the earl trembled, and turning more ghastly pale than he had done before, looked eagerly around him upon the astonished and affrighted individuals present.

"'Who was it that spoke?' at length he demanded, in faltering accents ;—'who dared to give utterance to that insolent mandate? By mine honour, if I knew the knave he should pay right dearly for his impertinence.'

"'Hold, son,' said the monk, solemnly, 'it was no mortal voice that spoke! I refuse to unite thee with this maiden, Heaven is opposed to the nuptials.'

"'This, — this is beyond endurance,' exclaimed the earl, in a voice of the most ungovernable rage, 'hath madness seized upon ye all, I say again?—It is some base trick to frustrate my designs. Go on with the ceremony, I once more command thee, holy father; thou surely canst not be so weak and superstitious as thy words would infer?'

"Once more the monk partially conquered his emotion, and again he began the ceremony, and my situation and state of mind may be very readily imagined; scarcely, however, had he opened his lips, when the same awful voice which had excited so much alarm in the breasts of all present, repeated the word 'Forbear!'

a solemn strain of music floated on the air, and in a moment was seen standing between the earl and the altar, a shadowy female form, attired in long flowing robes of white. It had appeared to rise from the earth, and as every one stared aghast with consternation, and started back in amazement, it stood with one arm extended towards the earl, while the other was raised towards Heaven, as if commanding obedience in the name of the Most High.

"It was several moments before the earl was sufficiently recovered from his surprise and horror to give utterance to a word, but at length, in a voice of terror, he exclaimed:—

"'Speak, mysterious being, who and what art thou? Whence comest thou, and for what purpose?'

"'Behold!' replied the awful-looking visitant, in the same solemn and impressive accents as before; in an instant afterwards, the long white veil which had hitherto concealed her features was thrown aside, and what was the horror of every person present, when they beheld the spirit of the late Countess of Harlingwood standing before them. Her face was ghastly pale, and her eyes which beamed forth a supernatural expression that was awful to behold, were fixed upon the earl with a look of reproach, enough to freeze the blood in his veins with horror.

"'Shade of my Adelaide avaunt!' ejaculated the earl, in a hoarse voice, 'quit my sight, I cannot gaze upon thy ghastly features, once in life so lovely. Oh, hence! hence! to the charnel-house again.'

"Thus speaking, the terrified nobleman covered his face with his hands, and bent his knee to the earth. Again the music floated in one solemn burst of melody upon the air, and the phantom repeating the word 'Forbear,' vanished. The monk, alarmed, had made his escape from the chapel, and the other persons quickly followed his example, so that there was only myself and the earl left behind. For a short time, horror and astonishment had so enchained all my faculties that I could not move, and almost became unconscious; but when I beheld myself alone with my persecutor, and he in a state bordering upon insensibility, the thought of self preservation, darted with the rapidity of lightning across my brain;—there was no obstruction at that moment offered to my flight; the doors and avenues to liberty were open, and, therefore, seizing the opportunity which thus presented itself, with silent and cautious footsteps, but with the utmost precipitation, I fled from the chapel, and soon afterwards found myself in the court-yard. Fortunately, the drawbridge was down, and I passed over it without encountering any person, and ere many minutes had elapsed, I was treading the mazes of a deep wood, the gloom of which was almost impervious to the rays of the moon.

"The thoughts of liberty, and the fate from which I had so narrowly escaped, added speed to my footsteps, and I hurried on with the utmost rapidity, taking the direction of the Convent of St. Agatha, upon the protection of the holy sisters of which I determined to throw myself. Any fate seemed to me to be preferable to the one with which the earl had threatened me, and averse as I was to a life of seclusion, I determined to choose that rather than become the bride of a man who was so truly hateful to me. As for Lord Alfred, something seemed to whisper to me that I should never behold him again, and as I felt confident that no other man could ever engage my affections, if my fears were realized, what charms would the world any longer possess for me ?   None !

Those thoughts passed quickly in my mind as I hastened on my way, and entirely superseded every other. Frequently, however, I paused and looked back, fancying I heard the voices of persons in pursuit of me, but the pitchy darkness that prevailed, prevented me from distinguishing objects at the shortest distance, and I was at length enabled to persuade myself that I had only suffered my imagination to alarm me.

" From the Convent of St. Agatha, I knew I was distant about five miles, and could I but reach there before those who would, doubtless, be sent in pursuit of me, should overtake me, I knew I should be in safety. I con- tinued my flight for some distance without so much as venturing to stop ; but at last, completely exhausted and breathless, I was compelled to pause to rest myself, and leaning against a tree, listened attentively, ready to catch the least sound which might give me cause to apprehend pursuit. All, how- ever, remained still, save, at intervals, the wind whistling among the foliage, and after the lapse of a few minutes only, I resumed my flight with redoubled speed. Not far had I proceeded, when a heavy peal of thunder reverberated above my head, and soon afterwards the rain began to descend in torrents, and the forked lightning flashed its fury in the Heavens. I was fearful to proceed in such a storm, and yet to linger where I was, was to incur the utmost danger of again falling in the power of my dreaded enemy. The fury of the tempest terrified me, and in spite of the consequences that might ensue, I was con- strained to seek shelter in the ruins of an old castle that happened to be near the spot. Here I stood in a state of the greatest anxiety and apprehension, and every peal of thunder fell upon my ear with increased terror, while the flashes of lightning ever and anon, revealed to me the gloom of the place in which I now was. Many centuries had passed over these crumbling ruins, and its once proud and noble possessors mouldered with the dust, and were forgotten. Perhaps their grim shades haunted these dreary ruins ; what deeds of darkness might there not have been perpetrated within their gloomy pre- cincts. I felt a trembling seize upon my limbs, and my heart palpitated as these reflections crossed my mind, and I would have given anything could I have been able to resume my journey. But the storm increased in violence, until it became truly terrific, and did not seem likely to abate for some time. My present situation was a dangerous one, for every now and then some fragment of the ruins would fall, and the flashes of lightning which, at in- tervals, darted in at the different apertures, played across my eyes, and created my utmost alarm.

" But now another, and even more serious cause for apprehension occurred to me. Suddenly the voice of men, which seemed to proceed immediately from the outside of the ruins, smote my ears. A cold tremor came over me, and I was obliged to lean against a broken pillar to support myself. With breathless attention I listened, and was at last enabled to catch the following words :—

" ' Thou mayest proceed if thou likest ; but, by the mass, I would sooner encounter a legion of devils, than be exposed to the fury of this tempest for one ten minutes. I am wet to the skin already, and as these ruins seem to offer a chance of shelter, I shall e'en take up my quarters here till the storm is over, and let the lady go any where for what I care.'

" ' Plague on thee, Oswolph,' replied the voice of a second, ' what is the use of thou being so confounded obstinate ? If we tarry, the lady Blanche will escape, and we might as well hang ourselves at once, as to return to the castle without her. The earl is like a madman.'

" ' And e'en let him be so,' answered Roland, ' by all the saints in Christendom, I will not budge an inch farther while this storm rages in the manner it does.'

" ' Nor I,' observed another, ' I am of thy opinion, Roland ; but while we are standing talking here, we are getting wet through. Come along.'

" The men now moved towards the entrance of the castle ruins, and words could not convey an adequate idea of my terror when I heard the resolution they had come to. I gave myself up for lost, but with a determination not to be re-taken without an effort ; I concealed myself as well as I could, behind a portion of the ruins, and mentally imploring the protection of Heaven, I left my fate in its hands. The men entered the place, and even stood close to the part where I had hidden myself, and yet they noticed me not, for the darkness was impenetrable only for a moment when the lightning flashed. I was almost afraid to breathe, lest I should betray myself, but in that respect, the raging of the storm favoured my wishes.

" ' This is no pleasant place, by the mass,' observed Roland, ' but it is better than travelling through the storm'.

" ' Aye, aye,' said the third speaker, ' thou sayest right, Roland ; besides, I do not think there is much chance of our meeting with the Lady Blanche to-night. Indeed, I imagine that she has not left the castle at all, but that she has concealed herself in one of the secret chambers until she can find a fitting opportunity to depart ; what fools we must all have been, to have been so frightened in the chapel.'

" ' There thou and I differ,' said Oswolph, ' thou mayest be very fond of the society of ghosts and hobgoblins, but I must confess that I like them best at a respectful distance.—Ah ! what noise was that !'

" ' I heard no noise,' returned Roland.

" ' I thought I heard some one moving,' remarked the man, who had before spoken. ' This is a very likely place to be haunted by evil spirits.'

" ' Or robbers, more likely,' ejaculated Roland. ' What a passion the earl was in when he recovered from his fright, and discovered that the lady was gone.'

" ' Yes, and I fancy he will be in a still greater passion if we return without her,' rejoined Oswolph. ' For my part, I think the Lady Blanche was very silly to be so obstinate. What objection could she have to the earl ?'

" ' Two or three,' replied Roland, ' and, in my opinion, all of them very reasonable ones too. In the first place, she don't like him; in the next place, he is too old, and too harsh, for one of her amiable disposition; and, lastly, she loves our young master, who is a far better match for her; and as his affections are placed on her, he ought to have her. I say, what a way the lady would be in if she knew that Lord Alfred had returned from the wars, and that he is at present held in confinement by his father.'

" I could with difficulty repress a scream when I heard this; and while I was heartily grateful to Heaven that Alfred had escaped from the battle-field, yet the knowledge that he was made a prisoner by his father, and the cruelties he might be subjected to filled my bosom with the most violent grief."

" 'Thou mayest say that, Roland,' said Oswolph; ' but what is the reason of the earl's conduct?'

" ' Why,' answered the man spoken to, ' is it not clear enough? The earl is afraid that if his son was at liberty, he would contrive to get the lady out of his power, in spite of his efforts to the contrary, and marry her, to be sure. When he has made Blanche securely his, I do not suppose that he will keep Lord Alfred any longer confined. Well, after all, I shall not be sorry if the young lady does escape, and be enabled to frustrate the designs of our lord, for I do not like such unequal matches, neither do I approve of any person, especially a female, being forced against her inclination.'

" ' And I suppose it was that feeling which made thee so tardy in continuing the pursuit,' remarked Oswolph.

" ' As for that matter, I can't exactly say,' retorted Roland; ' but of one thing I'm certain, and that is, if I had been as foolish as thou wouldst have had me been, I should have got such a wetting, that I should not, in all probability, have recovered from for many a day. But, come, the storm has now abated, and I am ready to depart. We will take another direction, and make our way to the village, in one of the cottages of which the girl has most likely sought shelter; for it is not at all probable that she would travel far on such a night as this, if she has left the castle at all, which, as I have said before, I have my doubts of.'

" What a relief was it to me when I heard this proposition, and the assent that was given to it by the other two men, for now I could pursue my way to the convent without fear, as it was in a diametrically opposite direction. The three men directly afterwards quitted the ruins; and when I thought I had given them sufficient time to get away from the spot, I left the place of my concealment, breathed freely, and returned my thanks to Heaven for having so far escaped.

" The storm had by this time entirely ceased, the heavy clouds that before obscured the sky had passed away, and countless myriads of stars sparkled in the firmament. I left the ruins, and looked cautiously around me, but, as far as my eyes could trace, I could not behold a human being. I hastened along as fast as I could, and as I did so, the thought of Alfred having returned, and being confined by the earl, occupied my mind, and gave rise to a number of conflicting ideas. Could he but obtain his enlargement, I was fully convinced that he would let no effort remain untried to get me in his power; and I was resolved, at every hazard, when next we met, if we were ever destined to do so again, that I would consent at once to become his bride, and thus render the odious design of his father abortive. But where was he confined? And would not the earl use every precaution so as to render any attempt on the part of Lord Alfred to escape completely futile? These thoughts made me wretched, and I was glad when the convent of St. Agatha appeared in sight, for I was quite exhausted with thinking, and the unusual excitement and fatigue I had undergone.

" I approached the gate of the holy building, trembling, for I was doubtful of the reception we might meet with, my only reliance being that it was the same Lady Abbess who formerly belonged to it, and who had been the early friend of my poor mother. I knocked loudly at the door, and it was several minutes before I received any answer. At length a harsh, querulous voice demanded, in the name of the Holy Virgin, who it was knocking at that late hour, and what was the nature of my business? I informed the porteress (for so I discovered my interrogator was afterwards), and enquired whether the holy mother, Saint Agnes, was still the lady abbess?

" ' Yes, daughter,' answered the old woman, ' the blessed Virgin be praised, she is; what wouldst thou with her?'

" ' I pray thee inform her that the Lady Blanche seeks her protection,' answered I, ' and requests a few minutes converse with her, that she may explain the cause of her being prompted to such a step.'

" ' Tarry thou here, daughter, for a few moments,' said the ancient porteress, ' and I will attend to thy request.'

" Having thus spoke, I heard her depart; and while she was gone my anxiety and impatience became almost insupportable. At length she returned, opened the gates to me, and after scrutinizing me minutely, desired me to walk in, and she would conduct me to the abbess.

" The old woman conducted me to the refectory, in which the holy abbess was seated, and who arose on my entrance, and received me most courteously. She was a venerable woman, of the most mild and amiable aspect and demeanour, and frequently had I heard my father speak in the highest terms of praise of her; in fact, they had been at one period on the most intimate terms.

" ' Art thou Blanche De Mortimer?' inquired the holy woman, eyeing me with much interest.

" I replied in the affirmative.

" ' But I needed not to ask the question,' the abbess observed, ' for thy features so strongly resemble those of thy mother. Alas! unfortunate and guilty Adeline, little did I ever anticipate that thou wouldst have been so weak, so unguarded. Heaven pardon thee!—But, why should I mention this subject to thee, daughter?—Why thus inflict agony upon thine heart for the errors of thy parent; errors, that I sincerely hope thou mayest avoid.'

" Tears started to my eyes as the abbess thus recalled to my memory the agonizing recollection of my mother's guilt, and the blush of shame mantled in my cheeks.

" ' Nay, my daughter,' remarked the good abbess, noticing my emotion, ' I meant not to afflict thee, child. Say, why comest thou hither, and at this unseasonable hour of the night ?'

" ' Good mother,' I replied, ' I come to ask thy protection, and if thou dost refuse me, I am lost.'

" ' Ah ! what meanest thou ?' demanded St. Agnes, ' explain thyself.'

" In as few words as possible, I told her the treatment I had received from the earl, and the fate with which he threatened me, and she listened with the deepest interest, and with evident disgust at the conduct of my guardian. When I informed her about the will which the earl stated to be the document of my late father, she seemed greatly astonished, and remained silent for a few minutes apparently ruminating upon it ; at length she said,—

" ' This seems not like the conduct of the good Sir Willoughby ;—I cannot believe it ; some base deception has been practised upon thee, daughter, I am afraid, which Heaven, in its own wisdom, will ultimately unravel. In the meantime thou must not fall a victim to the earl, whom thou sayest thou canst not love. I was the early friend of thine unfortunate mother, and greatly esteemed thy late father for his numerous amiable qualities, and all the protection which I can afford thee, in the name of the Virgin, thou art welcome to.'

" ' Good, kind mother,' I exclaimed, ' how can I sufficiently express my gratitude for this ?'

" ' No thanks, daughter,' returned the Lady Abbess ; ' that which I have promised thee, is no more than a Christian duty we owe to each other. Bu the earl being thy guardian, can demand thy restoration to him, should he learn where thou art. I have no power to detain thee ; all, therefore, that we can do is, to endeavour to keep the place of thy retreat as secret as possible, until circumstances may occur which will leave thee no longer any cause to dread him. But, mark me, I cannot allow thee to remain here, unless thou dost consent to enter on thy noviciate, although thou canst at the expiration of that time, use thine own will whether or not thou wilt take the veil.'

" Again I thanked the abbess for her kindness, and after some little further conversation of no importance, she conducted me to a cell, where she gave to me her blessing, and quitted me for the night.

" I need not enter into the particulars of all that occurred to me at the convent ; suffice it to say, that I complied with the request of the abbess, and entered on my noviciate, being also resolved rather to pass my days in seclusion, than to yield to the wishes of the earl.

" My thoughts were, however, constantly fixed upon Alfred, and the uncertainty of his fate made me doubly wretched. Probably the earl, when he found that I had escaped him, would wreak his vengeance on his son, and at the present time he might be enduring the greatest sufferings. These thoughts

rendered me very miserable, and the more so as I had not the means of obtaining any information concerning him, and he would be in the same state of uncertainty as regarded me. I could easily picture to myself the anguish he was enduring, deprived as he was of the means of rendering me any assistance and protection, at a time when he would be certain I so much needed both. I could have been content to suffer much more myself, could I have been certain that he was at liberty; and well assured was I, that if he had been free, he would not rest until he had found out the place of my retreat, and placed me out of the power of the earl, his father, by making me his wife.

"The abbess and most of the nuns treated me with great kindness; but there was one to whom I formed a strong aversion from the first moment I beheld her. This nun was called Sister Bertha. She was a woman of about forty, of the most austere and repulsive manners, and a harsh forbidding countenance. She appeared to be a woman, however, of the most exemplary piety, for none were more severe in their penances, or so strict in adhering to the discipline of the convent.

"I could never look upon this woman without an involuntary shudder, and I shunned her presence as much as possible; for, in spite of all her apparent sanctity, I imagined I could see the hypocrite lurking beneath. I thought she viewed me with an eye of jealousy, especially when she saw

No. 23

the favour with which I was treated by the abbess, and I had no doubt I formed a just conception of her feelings.

"Sister Bertha was evidently more dreaded than esteemed by the pious sisterhood, and there were many who seemed to doubt her sincerity, although they feared to give utterance to their real opinions.

"Notwithstanding that I shunned this woman as much as possible, she would at times force her company upon me, and seemed to take a secret pleasure in throwing out insinuations at every opportunity, that were calculated to insult and annoy me ; but I took no notice of them, and could not imagine why she should treat me so, as I had never given her any cause for such behaviour.

"I had now been an inmate of the convent for about two months, and had heard nothing of the earl or my lover. A settled melancholy had taken possession of my mind, which the dull monotony of a convent was by no means calculated to banish. The good abbess tried all that was in her power to console me, and sought to remove all worldly thoughts from my mind, and to draw my attention to religion ; but how was it likely that I could forget my lover, or could listen to anything of the kind with any degree of patience, while I was in such a state of uncertainty as to the fate which had befallen him ?—It was madness to suppose such a thing.

"One evening after I had quitted the abbess, who had held me for some time in conversation, I was about to retire to my humble pallet, when I was aroused by hearing a knock at the door of my cell, and upon opening it, I was not a little astonished at beholding Sister Bertha.

"'The abbess wishes to see thee immediately,' said the nun, looking at me with a disagreeable expression, and speaking in an authoritative tone.

"'The abbess!' I repeated, with surprise ; ' why, I have but just left her.'

"'That matters not,' replied the nun, ' it is her will that thou attendest her now.'

"'Where shall I find her ?' I asked.

"'I will lead thee to her,' answered Sister Bertha.

"Wondering what the abbess could want, and feeling rather doubtful of Bertha, but yet afraid to disobey her, I followed her from my cell, and she took the way towards the chapel. When we had reached that sacred part of the building, I looked around, but could not see any one in the place ; but gazing towards the altar, by the lights which continually burned upon it, I imagined I beheld a dark shadowy form suddenly gliding past one end of it, but it was gone so quickly that I could not distinguish of what description it was. A feeling of apprehension came over me, and I paused.

"'Whither wouldst thou lead me ?' I demanded of the nun ; ' where is the lady abbess ?'

"'Thou seest she is not here,' replied the nun, in harsh, disagreeable tones; ' but, come, thou must not hesitate, but follow me.—This way,—this way.'

"As the nun spoke, she placed her hand on my arm, in a peremptory manner, and almost forced me onward. She led the way towards the altar, in the side of which I found a low iron door standing open, and which revealed a flight of narrow steps to me. The recollection of the shadowy form I imagined I had seen not a minute before darted upon my memory, and a sensation of dread took possession of me. Bertha observed my emotion, and seemed to exult in it. She held the lamp she carried above her head, and then told me to precede her down the steps.

"'Again I desire thee to tell me whither we are going,' I demanded;— 'whither do these steps lead to?'

"'Thou'lt see,' answered the nun, impatiently; 'but, come, no hesitation, the abbess will grow angry at the delay.'

"'Surely the holy mother hath chosen a strange place for the meeting,' said I. 'What can she have to communicate which requires so much secresy?'

"'I did not ask her,' returned Sister Bertha; 'but, doubtless, it is something of the greatest importance, and which immediately concerns thee. Come, girl, thou tirest my patience. Descend these steps; I will hold the lamp so that thou canst not miss thy footing, and then I will immediately follow thee.'

" I obeyed;—in fact, I was afraid to do otherwise, and having descended several steps, I looked back to see whether the nun was following me. At that moment she suddenly closed the door above me, and I was involved in complete darkness. Directly afterwards I found myself seized roughly by two persons, and was hurried along a narrow and dismal subterraneous passage.

" I screamed aloud and called for help; but one of the ruffians commanded me to silence on the pain of instant death; and not doubting but that they would put this threat into execution, I said no more, but mentally invoking the protection of Heaven I suffered them to proceed with me.

" This subterraneous passage was of great length, and when we had come to the end of it, we emerged into a kind of a cavern, and ascending some rough hewn steps, a secret door was thrown open (which I found to be formed in the huge trunk of an old oak tree), and I saw we were in the thickest of the forest. Here two horses were in waiting, upon one of which I was placed in front of one of the men who had seized me, and the other having mounted his steed, they clapped their spurs in their sides, and we went along with the greatest rapidity.

" It is surprising how I retained my senses, after being thus seized, and finding myself in the power of ruffians, whose very looks were sufficient to excite the utmost terror in the breasts of those who beheld them; and the speed with which we were travelling, was enough to take my breath away. To offer any resistance to the two men, I felt convinced would have been completely useless; and to scream for help in a place where we seemed to be the only individuals, would have been equally futile; moreover, it might only exasperate them to commit some desperate deed, which they would prebably not otherwise think of perpetrating.   I had not the least doubt but that the men were employed by the earl, who, having found out the place of my concealment, had, with the assistance of Sister Bertha, thus got me in his power again.   This idea was terrible enough, for I could not doubt but that the earl, to prevent all possibility of his being foiled again by my effecting my escape, would not only use the most prompt measures of immediately enforcing me to a compliance with his hated wishes, but also take care afterwards to keep me securely confined for the future.   I thought upon looking more narrowly into the features of the ruffians that I had seen them before, and had, therefore, not the least doubt but that they were the regular creatures of my persecutor, and that I had seen them at the castle.

"The wood was of vast extent, and a terrible gloomy-looking place.   Here any crime of horror might have been perpetrated, without any fear of interruption and detection.   They took, however, a contrary direction to that which led to the castle of the earl, from which I had so recently made my escape ; and it was, therefore, quite evident that it was their intention to convey me to some other place, and most likely from which there would not be the least chance of my effecting my liberation.   We continued to travel with unabated speed for two hours, during which time we did not meet with a single human being, and neither did the least signs of a habitation meet our gaze.   How my heart sank within me when I reflected on the horrors of my situation, and the uncertainty of the fate that was in store for me.   My bosom swelled, too, with disgust and indignation, when I ruminated on the treacherous conduct of Sister Bertha ; and I was at a loss to conceive why she should have imbibed such an evident enmity towards one who was a perfect stranger to her, and who had never, to her knowledge, seen her before they met at the convent.

"The horses being now almost jaded, and as we were in a most retired spot, it was agreed between the two ruffians that we should pause awhile to rest ourselves ; and having dismounted, they seated themselves on the grass— one on each side of me — took forth some refreshment from a wallet they had brought with them, and requested me to partake with them.   This, however, I, of course, declined, for my heart was too full to suffer me to think about eating ; and, with tearful eyes, I supplicated them to have pity on me, and to inform me whither they were taking me, and by whose orders they had seized me.

" ' Why,' replied one of the men, ' I do not see that we have any reason to conceal the truth, because thou wilt very soon know all ; we have acted by the orders of the Earl Harlingwood, to be sure ; and thou mayest make up thy mind, young lady, that thou wilt not escape from him a second time.'

" ' Escape !' quoth the other ruffian ; ' if the lady was not a fool, methinks she would not want to escape, when the earl hath made her such a noble offer. But these fine females have such strange notions, and if they were not to show a little customary opposition, they would, doubtless, be considered very unfashionable.   There was none of that nonsense in the courtship of me and my Mabel ; we had not known one another many hours before we fell desperately in love with one another—the next day I popt the question—she assented, and in less than a month after our first meeting, we were man and wife.'

" ' And the best way, too, Hugo,' returned the first speaker, with a laugh; long courtships generally make short lovings. And as for a woman being so confoundedly obstinate, when wealth, rank, and a title, is offered to them, I will maintain is complete nonsense. But come, the flask is empty, and the time draws on apace. If we delay much longer the earl will begin to grow impatient, and imagine that we have failed in our plot.'

" ' Oh, no, his lordship knows us too well to think such a thing as that,' returned Hugo. ' He can trust us, and that's more than he could say of some he hath got about him. However, as our horses seem to be somewhat refreshed, and it waxeth late, as thou sayest, it would be as well for us to resume our journey.'

" All hope for me was now at an end, and to expostulate with such heartless ruffians, would have been a complete waste of time. I sighed deeply as they assisted me again on to the horse, and having themselves remounted in the same manner as before, we resumed our journey at the same rapid pace we had previously gone.

" At length we emerged from the wood, and entered upon an open champaign country, lighted by the rays of the moon, which now peeped forth from behind the murky clouds that had before obscured it, and greatly enlivened the scene. After proceeding for some distance in the same manner, suddenly I thought I heard voices and the sound of horses' hoofs behind us. As a sudden ray of hope flashed across my mind, I turned my head round, and beheld four men, mounted on fleet steeds, who appeared to be in hot pursuit of us; and the next moment I plainly heard one of them call to the two ruffians who were bearing me away, in a commanding tone, to stop. How my heart leaped with astonishment, anxiety, and hope, and I mentally prayed to Heaven that the pursuers might really turn out to be my friends, and be enabled to rescue me from the two ruffians.

" ' By the Mass, we are pursued, Hugo!' exclaimed one of the men, who had beheld the four horsemen at the same time that I did;—' confusion! who the devil can these be ?'

" ' Clap thy spurs into thy courser's flanks,' replied the man who had been addressed; ' the odds are against us—away, away, the superior fleetness of our steeds may enable us to outstrip them.'

" The ruffian did as he was desired, and away flew the two steeds with the speed of the lightning's flash, and for a short time threatening to put pursuit at defiance. I am sure I need not attempt to describe to thee, fair lady, my feelings at this moment—the alternative hopes and fears which sprang up in my bosom, especially when I looked back and, as well as the light of the moon would permit, beheld the distance the pursuers were behind us. I never experienced such agonizing sensations before, and had it not been for the ruffian who rode the same horse on which I was placed, I must have fallen to the earth. Who the pursuers could be, I could not form any conjecture, and, perhaps, after all, they might turn out to be enemies instead of friends.

"At length, however, our horses being exhausted by the unusual exertions they had undergone, slackened their pace, and could not be urged forward at a faster rate, by all that the men could do by the application of their spurs. The curses and imprecations of the ruffians, when they found this, and that the pursuers were fast gaining upon us, were horrible to hear.

"'It's useless, Hugo,' said his companion;—'the game is up;—these confounded animals are completely jaded, and it is madness for us to think we can outstrip the fellows. However, it is not the first time we have had to contend with greater odds than this, and we will not relinquish our prize without a severe struggle. Guard well the lady, trust in thy good steel, and a resolute arm, and I do not yet despair of being able to make these men repent their doings.'

"Having thus spoken, the two miscreants prepared desperately for the combat, and awaited for the pursuers to come up. This was quickly done, and dashing up to them, the foremost one, in a commanding voice, exclaimed,—

"'Release that lady, villains! whom it is evident ye detain against her will;—release her, I say, or, by Saint George, we will cleave ye to the earth!'

"No sooner did I hear the tones—the well-known tones of that voice, than I screamed aloud with astonishment and overwhelming joy, and desperately springing from the hold of the ruffian, I threw myself deliriously into the arms of Lord Alfred Harlingwood!

"Yes, it was my lover! who having escaped from the confinement in which his father had so tyrannically and unjustly held him, had arrived at that critical juncture, to rescue me from the hands of my enemies. Overcome with the power of my feelings at this unexpected surprise, I fainted, and remember no more until I recovered my senses, and found myself in the parlour of a cottage, attended upon by a clean and kind-looking female, and with Lord Alfred hanging affectionately over me. The two ruffians who had seized me and borne me away from the convent of St. Agatha, were left dead upon the spot where they had encountered Lord Alfred and his companions, and the latter had afterwards conveyed me to the cottage I was then in, and which belonged to the mother of one of my lover's retainers. Words cannot do adequate justice to the transport of our feelings at this unexpected meeting, and for awhile we gave free indulgence to them, and returned our thanks to the Almighty for His goodness.

"My disgust exceeded all bounds when I heard from the lips of my lover the unnatural behaviour he had experienced from his father, and his rage and indignation exceeded mine even, when he was made acquainted with the cruelty of the earl's conduct towards me. But now that we had both been restored to one another, we determined that death should alone separate us. I remained for the present at the cottage of old Beatrice, and in three days afterwards

Lord Alfred led me privately to the altar, where I became his bride. When the ceremony was completed we retired to a distant estate, which Lord Alfred possessed from a relation, where we resolved to remain until we could either bring about a reconciliation with the earl, or I could obtain some satisfactory settlement about the document which the earl purported to be the will of my late father.

"The rage of Earl Harlingwood, when he heard what had taken place, was that of the enfuriated tiger, and for some days he did nothing but rave and storm, and invoke curses upon our heads. He expressed his determination to keep the whole of my property, which had been entrusted to his care, and likewise to disinherit his son. In addition to this, he declared that he would not rest until he had amply gratified that revenge which the circumstances I have been describing had excited in his mind. We paid but little attention to these threats at the time, thinking that when his passion had subsided he would relent, and forget the past; but it was not long ere we were too well convinced that we were wrong. The Earl Harlingwood contrived, through the agency of another nobleman, who was under great obligations to him, to accuse his son of some offence against the state, to his sovereign; in consequence of which, his estates were confiscated, and my husband outlawed. It was with heavy hearts we were forced to quit the castle of which we had been so unjustly deprived; and deprived of fortune, went forth as wanderers in the wide world, totally unconscious what course we should pursue. But yet, amidst all our troubles, we were supported by the consolation of knowing that our love for each other could suffer no abatement, and with the hope that, however gloomy our present prospects might appear, probably the time was not far distant when we should be restored to happiness, and those rights, which had been so unlawfully taken from us. Many troubles—many severe trials, however, were we doomed to undergo, which I will not detain thee by detailing; thou mayest be certain, fair Lady Marguerite, that it must have been something very severe that could have induced a nobleman of the exemplary character which I have only justly described my husband to be, to become the companion of robbers. Accident, as I have before stated, introduced us to Osmond and his gang, from whom we have experienced more kindness than we did from the inhabitants of the world. Lady, my story is at an end, and I can but thank thee for the patience with which thou hast listened to me."

Thus Blanche concluded her rather-long and romantic narrative, with which Lady Marguerite expressed herself deeply interested, and sympathized with the narrator in the many misfortunes her and her husband had encountered.

CHAPTER XVII.

" Bring all your force to bear,
  Gather the bravest from your ranks,
  A martial host combined,
  I laugh your power to scorn ;
  Here will I stand, and with my sturdy followers,
  Bid your utmost power defiance !"

                    THE REVENGE OF RODOLPHIN.

" THOU hast indeed suffered much in the school of adversity," observed Lady Marguerite, when Blanche had finished her story, " and hath but little cause to like the world or its inmates. But is the earl still alive ?"

" He is," answered Blanche, " and luxuriating in that wealth he hath so unjustly deprived me and his son of."

" Thou hast my compassion, Blanche," observed Lady Marguerite, " and I trust thou wilt believe me to be sincere when I make that assertion. But, alas ! my own misfortunes render me wretched, and the uncertainty of the actual purpose for which I am brought hither, and the dreadful anguish which my mother and my brother will endure at my mysterious disappearance, completely distract me. The words of Osmond, and which cast aspersions on the character of Lord Raymond, my brother, spoke a feeling of malignity and revenge towards him, that has filled me with dread, and the most conflicting and unsatisfactory conjectures haunt my imagination."

" If thy brother, lady," returned Blanche,—" if thy brother hath incurred the enmity of Osmond, I am extremely sorry for it, for the robber-chief is a most implacable foe. But I can answer that thou hast nothing to fear from him ; thou hast inspired him with love, and if thou hadst not even, such is the respect he bears towards the female sex, that he would not harm thee for the world."

" But he threatened me," said Lady Marguerite, " he hath hinted that unless I return his hateful passion, I have everything to fear."

" The impetuosity of his love may have led him to make use of observations that he did not mean," remarked Blanche ; " but didst thou not say, that Osmond had also assured thee that thou shouldst receive from him the most profound respect and attention, and that he would forgive thy brother all the injuries he alleges he hath received from him, if thou wouldst return his passion ?"

" He did," answered Lady Marguerite, " but thinkest thou that I could ever feel anything but hatred towards that lawless man, or that my brother would purchase his friendship at so dear a price ? As for his threats, my brother would only laugh at them."

" Did he know the power of Osmond, he would not, methinks, lady," said Blanche ; " how thinkest thou he hath been enabled to resist all the force of the law ?—Here, in our impregnable hold, we have been able to bid defiance to all the power which hath at different times been sent against us.—Resistance to the will of a man like Osmond, would be little better than madness."

"Alas! what then will become of me, with so dismal a prospect as this before me?" sighed Marguerite;—"Oh, Blanche, surely thou or thy husband will take compassion on me, and endeavour to assist me towards getting released from this alarming situation?"

"Lady Marguerite," replied Blanche, "I have before told thee that I am sorry to see thee in such a situation, and willingly, joyfully would I assist thee were it in my power. But in what way thinkest thou I might aid thee?"

"By apprizing my mother where I am confined," said Lady Marguerite, "so that they may adopt some plan or other to gain my liberation."

"That is not in my power, lady, or that of my husband," returned Blanche; "I have before told thee that we are all bound by a terrible oath to be faithful to our captain and each other, and death is the certain reward of those who break that oath. If thou wouldst take my advice, thou wouldst not appear so averse to the passion of Osmond, this might make him less urgent for the fulfilment of his wishes, and the delay which would thus ensue, would afford an opportunity for something to occur to restore thee to thy friends."

"Blanche, canst thou advise me to act the hypocrite?" demanded Lady Marguerite; "how, thinkest thou that I could for a moment, by any behaviour on my part, appear to encourage the sentiments of a robber, an outlaw, and a murderer?"

"Be cautious, fair lady, I beg of thee," said Blanche, "beware how thou speakest of Osmond, lest thou shouldst be overheard, and excite his vengeance towards thee. But I can duly appreciate the feelings that drew forth those expressions, and I once more repeat that I sincerely sympathize with thee, but it is out of my power or that of Ulric, my husband, to assist thee."

No. 24

" Then I have no hope but in the merciful interposition of heaven," ejaculated Lady Marguerite, solemnly; " but believe me, Blanche, that I do not blame thee ; under the circumstances thou hast mentioned to me, thou hast no power, though I doubt not, if thou hadst, thy will is good to serve me. But yet I cannot think that Osmond, when he sees the impossibility of making any impression upon my heart, will continue to persevere in his importunities; notwithstanding his lawless profession, and the many crimes with which his conscience is probably loaded, he seems to me to possess a certain innate nobleness of feeling, which will not suffer him to proceed to extremes in a case where a female is concerned."

" Thou dost him no more than justice, lady," observed Blanche ; " Osmond, in spite of his character, the life he hath chosen, and his apparent callousness to the feelings of humanity, towards the female sex especially, possesses a most noble and generous heart. And yet from all that I have heard, he hath had plenty of cause to make him hate them."

" Hath then the robber-chief been disappointed in love?" enquired Lady Marguerite, her thoughts being for a minute or two withdrawn from her own misery.

" I do not think there is more than one individual, lady, who is acquainted with Osmond's history;" remarked Blanche, in reply ; " but I have reasons to suspect that he hath received some heavy and lasting affliction from the source to which thou hast alluded."

" He seems not of lowly birth," said Lady Marguerite.

" No, lady, he is not," answered Blanche, " illustrious blood, I have always been given to understand, flows within his veins, and indeed his language and manners confirm the same."

" And is Osmond his real name ?"

" It is not;" returned Blanche, " but I know not what it is."

" And why doth he call himself the Avenger ?"

" Because, I have heard, that the person who was the cause of his misfortunes and subsequent degradation, still lives, and that he hath sworn to have ample retribution for the wrongs he is said to have done him."

" Holy Mary !" cried Lady Marguerite, " and he told me that my brother had been the bitterest foe he had ever known ; that from him he had to date his ruin —all his misery—the many bitter pangs he had for years endured ; the curse of blighted hopes, ruined fortune, name, and high estate."

" Ah, sayest thou so, lady ?" ejaculated Blanche, " then thy brother must be the secret foe against whom Osmond hath vowed a deadly vengeance."

" Impossible !" observed Lady Marguerite, " in what way could my brother ever have injured him ; and in what manner could they have formerly been connected ?—Besides, they have often met, and yet they appeared not to recognize each other, and had Osmond been anxious to obtain revenge, if his power is so great as thou hast stated, why did he not at once seek the gratification of the former ?"

" It is no easy task, lady," answered Blanche, " to divine at all times the motives which direct the actions of our captain, therefore, in that respect am I unable to answer thee. At any rate, Osmond hath offered thee the means of obtaining his forgiveness for thy brother, and again I advise thee not to be too precipitate in rejecting the same."

" Thou counsellest with a good intent, I do believe, Blanche," said Lady Marguerite, " but I am fearful, nay certain, that I shall not in this instance be able to follow thy advice; in fact, I consider that it would be the greatest imprudence in me to appear to give any encouragement to a passion it would be utterly impossible for me ever to view with any other feeling than that of aversion."

" Well, Lady Marguerite," remarked Blanche, " of course thou knowest best, and I sincerely hope that circumstances may not turn out so bad as thou dost apprehend. At any rate, I beg that thou wilt endeavour to compose thyself, and while thou remainest here, thou mayest depend upon my paying thee every kind attention in my power."

Lady Marguerite once more returned her thanks to Blanche, and they then proceeded to converse upon other topics, on all of which the latter evinced a perfect knowledge, and much intelligence, and Lady Marguerite became more prepossessed in her favour every minute. She regretted when the time arrived for them to separate for the night, and the idea of being left alone in that strange place, surrounded by the lawless wretches that infested it, filled her mind with terror. All the horrors and dangers of her situation rushed to her mind with full force, and the frenzied state her mother and Lord Raymond would be in, caused her more misery than anything she might have herself to undergo. But even more than all did the words of Osmond, the robber-chief, distract and perplex her. The hatred and revenge he had expressed towards her brother could not be misunderstood, and when she compared these threats with the hints Blanche had made use of, a sentiment of terror took possession of her feelings, which, in spite of all her endeavours to the contrary, she found it impossible to conquer. Could she but find some means of making them acquainted at the castle of the danger in which she was placed, she could not help thinking, in spite of the assertions of Blanche in respect to the power of Osmond, that Lord Raymond would, at the risk of his own life, find some means of rescuing her from the power of the former, and earnestly did she raise her supplications towards heaven, that something or the other might transpire to bring about that which she desired.

It was now getting very late, and Lady Marguerite, tired of thinking, and fatigued both in body and mind, fastened her room door, which was secured by a bolt inside as well as one out, and retired to rest.

Notwithstanding the novelty of her situation, and the fear and anxiety she was enduring, it was not long ere Lady Marguerite fell asleep, and she did not awake until Sol had gilded the western hills. She arose, and almost immediately afterwards a gentle tap at the room door announced to her the arrival of Blanche. Having withdrawn the bolt, Blanche entered the room, bringing in the morning's repast, and expressed her pleasure at the composure which Lady Marguerite displayed. Sleep had done much for her, and her mind was considerably more tranquillized than it had been before, and a faint ray of hope glowed in her breast.

" I am glad indeed to see thee so much better in appearance, dear lady," observed Blanche, " and commend thee for it. It is useless to give way to despair, which only unfits a person to encounter with firmness and resolution that which they may have to undergo. I would advise thee to prepare to meet Osmond, who, I believe, will demand an interview with thee presently."

This information filled Lady Marguerite with fear, and she expressed the same to Blanche.

"I again tell thee, lady," said the latter, "that thou hast no cause to dread the appearance of Osmond; his gallantry to the female sex is proverbial, and he is sure to treat thee with marked distinction, since he hath avowed for thee an ardent affection."

"Alas!" exclaimed Lady Marguerite, "have I not good cause to fear him, after the threats of vengeance he hath held out against my brother? Hath he not, also, expressed his determination to force me to become his bride? A robber's bride; the bare thought is horrible. Can I either forget that he was the man, by his own admission, who assassinated the unfortunate persons at the prison, to further the escape of Godfrey de Lacy? Oh, no; when I think of the human blood he hath shed, I cannot hear his name mentioned without a shudder of horror, and it seems to me to be impossible that he could ever be the noble and virtuous individual thou wouldst fain make him appear to have been."

"I have told thee the truth, lady, as I firmly believe," returned Blanche; "and much as thou art at present prejudiced against him, I do not doubt but that thou wilt, ere long, find him to be all that I have stated."

"I can find no excuse for his having torn me heartlessly from my home," remarked Lady Marguerite, "and endeavouring to force me to blast my fame, my happiness, and my prospects for ever, by an union with him."

"Certainly that was wrong," answered Blanche, "and must have caused thy friends much anguish; but then the violence of the passion, he hath, I dare say, imbibed for thee, must plead his excuse. But, hark! he approaches."

As Blanche spoke, a trembling sensation came over Lady Marguerite, for she heard a heavy foot fall on the stairs which ascended to the room in which she was confined, and she had not the least doubt but that it was Osmond. In another second, this suspicion was confirmed, for the chamber-door was thrown open, and the robber-chief stood before her.

He advanced towards her with the same respectful demeanour which he had displayed on their first interview, and having made a sign to Blanche to leave the room, he stood gazing at her for a moment or two with looks of admiration, and in silence; then endeavouring to take her hand, he said in tones of mildness:—

"Beauteous Lady Marguerite, I see that thou dost still view me with looks of scorn and repugnance, while, at the same time, my love for thee increases to such a degree, that methinks I could rather encounter any fate, than resign the hope of making thee mine. Nay, do not turn from me with that look of abhorrence; I know thou wilt call me a robber, and marvel at my presumption in offering my vows to thee. There was, however, a time when probably, even the high and noble Lady Marguerite St. Aswolph would not have thought herself disgraced by being wooed by he who now stands before her."

"Hadst thou ever been what thou wouldst fain boast," replied Lady Margueritce; "thou couldst never have acted as thou hast done towards a defenceless female, by tearing her away from her home and friends. But talk not 'to me of love; the word from lips like thine is odious. If thou wouldst not meet with punishment for the outrage of which thou hast been guilty, thou wilt immediately release me, and suffer me, unmolested, to return home."

" I have before told thee, lady," said Osmond, " that I bid defiance to all the force that can be sent against me. Many, ere now, who have made the attempt to oust me and my brave fellows from our stronghold, have had to pay dearly for their temerity, and so would it be if any further attempt should be made. No, lady; here thou must remain as long as it is my will to keep thee ; and as I have determined to make thee my bride, the prospect of thy deliverance is, indeed, very distant. But come, fair damsel, what is the use of this opposition ? Endeavour to conquer this aversion, and to look upon me with esteem, if thou canst not with love. Thou mayest think that a man, situated as I am, cannot be sensible to the tender sentiments I have avowed for thee ; but thou wilt find me sincere ; after what I have suffered, and the manner in which I have been served, I thought that I could never love again ; that the sentiment was banished entirely from my breast, and that vengeance held entire possession of its place ; but since I have beheld thee, beauteous Marguerite, I find that I had deceived myself, and that——"

" Cease !" interrupted Lady Marguerite, " to this language I must not, I will not listen. A robber, an outlaw, nay, a murderer,—for didst thou not confess thyself so on the trial of Godfrey de Lacy ? And thinkest thou that I can even esteem a man like thee ? Besides, hast thou not confessed thine enmity towards my brother, and threatened him with thy vengeance ?"

" Lady Marguerite, if thou didst know the cause I have had for this hatred, thou wouldst not marvel. It is to thy brother I am indebted for all my misery and degradation ; aye, thou mayest start, but I speak only the truth !—It was Lord Raymond that blighted all my hopes ; it was Lord Raymond that led me on to ruin ; it was Lord Raymond that made me what I am ;—a robber, an outlaw, and a murderer, as thou hast just called me, and——"

" Oh, no, no, no," interrupted Lady Marguerite, with much emotion, " that cannot be ; it is impossible ! my brother the cause of these misfortunes ; these horrors ;—thou must be mad to give utterance to such a thing ; how, in what way could he have been the cause ?"

" It suits me not at present to inform thee, lady," replied Osmond, " but I tell thee again, that I have spoken the truth, and have not exaggerated. Oh, lady, thou mayest think thy brother immaculate, but I tell thee, and good cause have I for saying so, that he is an hypocrite, and richly merits the retribution I have promised to bring upon his head."

" I cannot, dare not believe what thou sayest," said Lady Marguerite ;—" it can only be some base fabrication to frighten me into a compliance with thy wishes. Didst thou not tell me, robber, that one of thy principal motives for tearing me away from my home, was to gratify those feelings of revenge thou sayest that Lord Raymond hath excited within thee ?"

" I confess," replied the robber-chief, " that it was a feeling of revenge, which, at first, principally induced me to bear thee from the castle of St. Aswolph, but, afterwards, the power of thy charms completely subdued me, and what before was merely admiration, was heightened into the most ardent love. Lady, need I attempt to describe to thee the power thy beauty hath over me, when I repeat, that, for thy sake, I am even ready to abandon the darling wish of my heart ; the very idea of which, hath, of late years, I may say, formed a portion of my existence,—revenge?   Yes, sweet Marguerite, endeavour but to return my love only with esteem, and I am willing to swear, that all the injuries thy brother hath done me, shall be obliterated from my memory; love shall stifle all those feelings of malevolence that have for years raged within my bosom, and——"

"My brother would laugh to scorn the robber's boasted power," interrupted Lady Marguerite, in a firm voice, and with a look of the most ineffable contempt.

"He would repent were I to put his daring to the test," returned Osmond ; "but, come, this is a mere waste of words; I have told thee my sentiments, lady; I ask thee for a return ; there was a time when Osmond needed not thus to sue, when wealth and beauty were at his command, but he made the sacrifice to one who afterwards deceived him, cruelly deceived him. He thought, after that, that no woman could make any other impression upon his mind, save that of hatred. It was, however, fair Lady Marguerite who was destined to teach him different; fate hath ordained that she should re-kindle those sentiments that had so long laid dormant in his breast; let it, then, be her sweet task to endeavour to recal the robber-chief to what he formerly was. Thus, beauteous damsel, on my knees, do I urge my vows, and solicit of thee a return."

As the robber-chief thus spoke in the most impassioned accents, he bent his knee to the floor, and forcibly seizing the hand of Marguerite, he forced it rapturously to his lips, and devoured it with kisses. Shame, indignation, and offended modesty swelled the bosom of the maiden, and while deep crimson blushes suffused her cheeks, and resentment flashed from her sparkling eyes, she, with difficulty, released her hand from his hold, and retreating to the other side of the room, she exclaimed :—

"Desist robber, thy boldness but arouses my utmost wrath ! Leave me, and no longer insult mine ears with thine hateful protestations. Think not that thy vows can make any impression upon the mind of Lady Marguerite but that of the utmost scorn and detestation ! No, sooner than utter one sentence which might give thee encouragement, and must be so abhorrent to her feelings, she is prepared to suffer all that thy cruelty can inflict. No more ; I will not listen to thee ; the blood of the murdered is upon thine hands; crime weighs heavy upon thy soul ; thy presence excites my greatest horror !"

The robber-chief bit his lips, and traversed the room for a minute or two with hasty and uneven footsteps, then advancing once more towards Marguerite, the calm dignity and firmness of whose manner, however, completely awed him, he ejaculated :—

"Lady, these looks of scorn; these words of disdain will avail thee little; and may arouse my indignation, in which case, I know not to what lengths I might be tempted to go. I have offered thee fairly, at least, as fairly as circumstances will permit me, and by those offers will I abide, but——"

At this moment, there was a loud blast upon a bugle, and then followed a strange confused noise from below, which prevented the robber-chief from proceeding any further in his speech. The noise increased, and persons might be heard running to and fro in the greatest confusion.

"What can this mean?" cried Osmond, involuntarily laying his hand on the hilt of his sword, and looking towards the door, as he heard the heavy footsteps of some person ascending the stairs.

The following moment, there was a loud knock at the room-door, which Osmond having opened, one of the robbers presented himself.

"Captain," said the man, "thy presence in the cavern is immediately required; Orlando, in just passing through the forest on his way to our retreat, discovered a band of armed men advancing this way, and having secreted himself while they passed, he overheard the conversation of some of those who had led them, from which he learnt that this was the place of their destination!"

"Ah! sayest thou so?" exclaimed the robber-chief, unsheathing his sword, "then there is not a moment to lose! Doubtless, the intended attack is that which I have long expected, and for which we are so well prepared! By the mass! the daring foes shall soon have cause to repent! Osmond, the Avenger, will teach them such a lesson, that they will not easily forget. Is every man at his post?"

"He is, captain," answered the man, "and eager for the strife!"

"Away, then," cried Osmond, "I will follow thee immediately! Lady, we shall meet again, anon, when I have chastised the rash fools who have dared to undertake this enterprize!"

Thus saying, the robber-chief waved his hand to Lady Marguerite, and preceded by the ruffian who had been sent to apprize him of the circumstance, he made his way to the cavern. There he found his lieutenant and some of the principal of the gang assembled, and arming themselves for the affray, and having hastily buckled on his armour, Osmond hastened to the different places that needed most protection, and finding everything in fit condition for a desperate defence, he made his way to the battlements of the castle. Here, at first, he saw nothing but the tall trees waving their branches in the breeze; but, shortly afterwards, the rays of the sun fell upon the glittering pikes of the approaching assailants, and then he saw a number of men winding their course towards the castle, between the different avenues of the trees, led on by a noble-looking warrior on horseback, and who, as they advanced nearer, Osmond immediately recognized.

"It is the enemy I expected," he observed; "it is my detested foe, Lord Raymond St. Aswolph! The contest will be a short one, and I need not command every man to stand firm, and should defeat be our's, let us rather perish in the blazing ruins of this our retreat, than yield ourselves to their power!"

"We will stand by our captain, and perish rather than yield!" shouted a hundred voices.

"Enough, my brave fellows," cried Osmond; "I place the firmest reliance on ye; but I enjoin ye, one and all, to be careful not to harm Lord Raymond; he who forgets this mandate, dies!"

"We will obey!" exclaimed the robbers, and in an instant, at a signal from the robber-chief, the ramparts, battlements and every part of the impregnable edifice was filled with well-armed and desperate men, but so concealed, that the enemy could not behold them, and from the appearance of the castle, would be likely to imagine that the robbers were unconscious of their approach.

Feeling more confident of success from the apparent unguarded state of the

castle, Lord Raymond and his followers more quickly approached, and soon
arrived at the ancient and powerful edifice. What added not a little to the
astonishment of his lordship was, that the drawbridge was down, which had been
occasioned through some singular mistake of Osmond and his gang. Lord Raymond and his companions rushed across the bridge, and commenced battering
the ponderous doors, but no sooner had they done so, than they were saluted
with a terrific shower of arrows and stones, which stretched a number of them
dead, and with the most dreadful yells, the robbers were all in an instant, prepared to deal destruction on their assailants. This unexpected salute threw
the followers of Lord Raymond into the utmost confusion, more especially as
they had no means of retaliating upon the robbers, who were too well pro-
tected to suffer from the arrows of the besiegers, while they continued the
battle they had begun with overwhelming fury, and total defeat, in a very short
time, seemed to be inevitable.

With the greatest difficulty did Lord Raymond get his men to rally again, and
then a portion of them renewed their attack upon the doors, while others
rendered desperate by the unexpected reception they had met with, and
impatient to wreak their vengeance on their daring foes, climbed up the walls,
sword in hand, towards the battlements, but were dashed headlong into the
moat beneath, covered with wounds. The scene was altogether one of the
most bloody and appalling that could be conceived, and the groans of the dying,
and the shouts of the robbers, rent the air, and increased the horror of all around.
At length, the massive doors yielded to the violence of the assailants, and
bursting asunder, gave admittance to the castle, but no sooner had they attempted to enter, than they were met by another portion of the gang, and after a
desperate conflict, were repulsed with great slaughter on both sides !

Lord Raymond had now lost a number of his men, and the contest began to
assume a most alarming aspect, but determined not to be defeated without a
severe struggle, he again rallied his men, and once more, at their head, he
rushed into the castle, and the combat was resumed with redoubled fury. Again
and again were the assailants repulsed, and their courage began to fail them.
At this juncture, when Lord Raymond and his followers had again been driven
from the castle, the robbers from the battlements sounded a parley, and Osmond, their chief, appeared, and addressing himself to Lord Raymond,
said :—

"Lord Raymond St. Aswolph, thou and I art sworn foes, and I have determined
to wreak my vengeance on thee!—I have warned thee of it, but the time has
not come yet. Thou hast found already, methinks, that to conquer Osmond
the Avenger, is not quite so easy a task as thou didst at first imagine, doubtless ;
and thou wilt, if thou art mad fool enough to persevere in the attack thou hast
made upon me, find to thy cost, that Osmond, the robber-chief, sooner than
yield, would perish in the ruins of his castle. To save the effusion of blood on
both sides, I give thee fair warning. Thou mayest depart without fear of
interruption, but if thou art determined to proceed, thou must take the consequences, the extent of which thou canst not form the least idea of."

"Vain boasting villain !" returned Lord Raymond, "I am not to be frightened
from my purpose by the threats of a robber and an outlaw like thee. With

justice on my side, I do not doubt but success will crown my efforts, and by Heaven, I swear I will not rest until I have haunted thee from thy lair!"

"Rash fool!" cried Osmond, "behold, then, what the consequences will be, should fortune favour thee, and make thee conqueror. The same moment that gives thee victory, shall sacrifice the life of one, who, by the ties of blood, should be as dear to thee as thine own existence."

"Ah! what meanest thou?" demanded Lord Raymond, as a sensation of fear crept through his veins.

"Behold!" replied the robber-chief, and at that moment, he presented to the eyes of her awe-struck brother, the trembling Lady Marguerite.

It would be impossible to describe, as it ought to be, the horror which Lord Raymond evinced, when he thus beheld the realization of his worst fears; Marguerite in the power of Osmond the robber-chief! He was completely paralyzed, while Lady Marguerite with stretched arms, looked the very image of despair and terror. The robber noticed the emotion of his enemy with a look of exultation, and pointing towards the deeply-agitated damsel by his side, he added :—

"Now, what sayest thou, Lord Raymond St. Aswolph?—wilt thou accept the merciful offer I have made thee, or, by rashly persevering in this attack, bring destruction on the head of thy sister?"

"Desperate man!" ejaculated Lord Raymond, "what wouldst thou with that fair damsel? What cruel act hast thou in contemplation? Release her from thy power, and I swear not only immediately to abandon the attack, but never again to molest thee!"

"Nay, my noble foe, thou asketh me too much," observed Osmond; "Lady
No. 25

Marguerite must remain in my keeping, and by the mass I swear, that, shouldst thou be fortunate in the combat, with my own hands I will plunge her into the moat beneath me !"

"Oh, mercy ! mercy !—save me ! save me ! Raymond !" supplicated Marguerite in frantic accents.

"Take thy choice !" shouted Osmond ; "resume the battle, or depart, and save the life of thy sister !"

Lord Raymond paused a moment, uncertain which way to act, and gazed with intense agony upon Lady Marguerite. Already his force was greatly diminished ; and even should he prove successful, he had not the least doubt, from the desperate and determined character of the robber-chief, that he would keep his word, and the life of his sister be sacrificed. He also reflected that, should he abandon the present design, he might at some other time accomplish his object by stratagem, or additional force, and rescue the Lady Marguerite from the power of the villain ; he, therefore, at last, came to the resolution to withdraw with his followers ; and turning his gaze in the direction where Osmond was standing, he observed :—

"Osmond, I yield ; I take the offer thou hast made me, and withdraw with my men ; thou hast said that I have injured thee, and that thy vengeance is excited towards me, but how that can be, I solemnly declare I know not. At any rate, be that as it may I implore, thee not to let the innocent maiden in thy power suffer ; let her not be the victim of thy vindictive feelings. I implore thee this as a favour, and if thou dost but accede to it, I——"

"I want no promises, St. Aswolph," interrupted the robber-chief, "for I know that thou canst not fulfil them. Thou hast acted wisely in accepting my offer ; and hadst thou not done so, thou wouldst, most assuredly, have found me fulfil my promise. Osmond the Avenger is not a man to be trifled with, as thou wilt learn anon. Thou cravest of me a favour ; I grant it not to thy request, for again I tell thee that I have ample cause to detest thy very name ; but it is my own feeling which prompts me to act as thou dost suggest. Get thee hence, and tell the enemies of the robber, Osmond, that he not only despises but defies them all. That even though they crush his power here, if so, untoward fate should will it, he will still again arise in all his former strength, and dare their utmost to defeat him. Go, Lord Raymond St. Aswolph, and fear not till the hour of vengeance arrives, when Osmond, the Avenger, will have a subtle and ample retribution for the wrongs thou hast done him. There is but one can save thee. She stands here ; on her word thy life depends."

"Insolent slave !" muttered Lord Raymond to himself, his indignation rising almost beyond endurance at the tone which Osmond assumed towards him, at the same time that he could not control a certain feeling of dread at his words, and the mystery of his manner ; then turning his gaze upon Lady Marguerite, he exclaimed, aloud :—

"Farewell, dearest Marguerite, for the present I leave thee to the protection of that Almighty Being thou hast never offended, and who will not suffer thee to become the victim of the guilty power which now beholds thee. Farewell, and——"

"Brother Raymond !" shrieked Marguerite, clasping her hands, and fixing upon him a look of the most frantic and earnest supplication, "thou surely wilt not leave me thus, in the hands of those merciless, those lawless men."

"Bear the maiden hence," commanded the robber-chief, turning to his companions; "lead her to her chamber."

Osmond was obeyed; and Marguerite, complaining aloud, in hysterical wildness, was forced away from the battlements.

"Lord Raymond," said Osmond, "depart instantly, lest thou wouldst provoke me to that alternative which I would fain avoid. Comrades, on your lives, offer not to obstruct his lordship or his followers in their retreat, but unless he immediately hastens from hence, I will give ye the order to re-commence the strife, and then he will too soon learn that Osmond is a man of his word, and repent not accepting the opportunity I have afforded him."

It was with the greatest difficulty that Lord Raymond could restrain the rage that boiled within his breast; to leave his sister in the hands of such a man as Osmond filled him with the utmost agony; but he had no other alternative; and once more imploring the robber's forbearance, he gave the order to his men, and in a few minutes afterwards they were on their march from the castle, his mind filled with the most gloomy presages, and distracted at the unsuccessful result of the expedition.

But, if Lord Raymond's anguish and chagrin at the result of the attempt to capture the robber-chief and his daring gang, and the perilous situation of his sister were great, his anguish was exceeded, if anything, by that of Lady Marguerite, whose feelings, on beholding her brother, we have already described; when she was borne from the battlements by the orders of Osmond, and was conveyed to her own apartment, unable longer to support the terrors of her mind, she became insensible.

Having seen Lord Raymond and his followers vanish in the distant mazes of the deep-entangled wood, and left the battlements and every other part of defence properly guarded, Osmond and the remainder of the gang retired to the cavern in which they usually congregated, where, having collected the robbers around him, he thus addressed them:—

"My bold comrades,—victory hath again attended your irresistible, your unconquerable bravery; the insolent foe who would oust us from our stronghold, and annihilate us altogether, have, by ye, been defeated, and but for my clemency, not one would have survived to tell their shame to the world!— For this your captain thanks ye, certain as he is, that rather than be conquered, or see him fall into the hands of his enemies, ye would all of ye lay down your lives!"

Loud shouts, which made the vaulted cavern re-echo again, and cries of "Long life to Osmond, the Avenger!—Death to those who would betray him!" followed this address, and when the clamour had, in some degree ceased, Osmond continued in the following strain:—

"I again thank ye, my brave fellows, for this enthusiastic demonstration, and will take care to reward it as it deserves! But it behoves us to use redoubled precaution, now that the enemy has suffered this defeat, for, doubtless, they will muster in ten-fold strength to attack us, and we must also, too strengthen our forces, so that we may be able to meet and successfully resist any future attack that may be made upon us!—Our enemies little suspect the extent of our resources in the moment of danger!—And we will, therefore, be prepared to shew them that we do not boast without having full reason so to do!—It is my intention to summon to our aid, our faithful partizans, the Bandit Monks of St. Ethelbert, who, beneath the guise of sanctity, commit their depredations without suspicion; also the stalwart Archers of the bonny green-wood of Mercey, whose prowess and deeds of daring, have bid defiance to the law, and all the force sent again them!   With the aid of these, what can all the power of our enemies effect?"

"Nothing!" shouted a hundred voices;—"success to the Bandit Monks of St. Ethelbert, and to the Archers of the bonny greenwood of Mercey!"

" Pardon me, brave captain," remarked his lieutenant, "but methinks whilst thou retainest so fair an hostage as the Lady Marguerite St. Aswolph, there is but little cause to apprehend any danger!"

"From Lord Raymond St. Aswolph, her brother, I own there is not," answered Osmond, "but we have other and more powerful enemies, whom it is necessary we should guard against! But enough of this; I have told ye my plans, and I caution ye all to be wary and watchful! To-morrow, I intend to set apart for rejoicing at our victory, when, at the festive board, I will in-troduce to ye, my intended bride, the beauteous Lady Marguerite St. Aswolph !"

Loud acclamations followed this announcement, and then the robbers taking their places at the board, commenced their rude revelry with the following song of triumph, usually sung by them on occasions like the present :—

" Drink! drink!—'tis ours to laugh
    At gloomy care, at pale-faced woe;
Drink! drink!—cheerily quaff,
    We robbers only pleasure know!—
Round, round, again with glee,
    Let's be gay, let's be gay,
Shout! shout! for victory,
    Victory is ours huzza!
            Tiral la! tiral la!
Victory is ours—huzza!

Who would crush the robber's might?
    Who his hardy soul would scare?
Who can daunt him in the fight?
    Drink to them, despair! despair!
Round, round, again with glee,
    Let's be gay,—let's be gay;
Shout! shout! for victory!
    Victory is ours—huzza!
            Tiral la! tiral la!
Victory is ours—huzza! "

The chorus being ended, Osmond and his lieutenant put on the disguise of minstrels, and so completely metamorphosed were they, that it would have been utterly impossibe for any person to have recognized them, or to have had any suspicion of their real characters; then the former having ascertained that Marguerite had recovered, and was attended by Blanche, they set forward to learn the effect the late engagement had had on their enemies, and also to summon the Bandit Monks of St. Ethelbert, and the Archers of Mercey-wood.

There was only one among the gang who felt any repugnance at the conduct and designs of Osmond, and that one was Ulric, the husband of Blanche; and his discontent was yet but a spark, which it was uncertain whether it would ever expand into a blaze. Notwithstanding the little cause the outlawed nobleman had to like the world, there were moments when his heart shrunk with a feeling of disgust and shame at the life he was leading, and the wretches with whom he was associated; naturally virtuous and noble, his heart revolted with a sentiment of sickening horror at the sanguinary scenes he was often compelled to witness and mingle in, and he sighed to think that the cruelty of his father had driven him to such a course of life. Often had his merciful interposition saved the life of an unfortunate being, whom the robbers would otherwise have sacrificed; and, although many of them laughed at him for what they termed his foolish humanity, notwithstanding Osmond strictly enjoined them never to use violence but when they found it absolutely necessary for their own safety; Ulric's persuasions always had due weight with them, and he was a great favourite amongst them. But the chief cause of Ulric's regret and agony was, to see his wife, his still lovely and gentle Blanche, her who had been born to such different, such happy prospects, placed in this degrading situation, and frequently did he upbraid himself for having brought her into it. He, however, never mentioned his thoughts to Blanche, and always, when in her presence, disguised his real sentiments under a semblance of content he was far from feeling.

The account which Blanche had given him of Lady Marguerite and her perilous situation, with which he was so well acquainted, had excited his deepest interest and compassion, and the conduct of Osmond in the late battle, and the terrible threats he had held out to Lord Raymond, had created his utmost disgust. Fain would he have done all in his power to have assisted Marguerite, and aided her in escaping from the place of her confinement, but his oath bound him to fidelity to his captain and the gang, and he was fully aware that his own life would inevitably be sacrificed to their vengeance should he do so, and he was, therefore, compelled, much against his inclination, to abandon such a humane idea, and left to regret, more poignantly than ever, the hard fate and untoward circumstances that had placed him in a situation which excluded him from exercising the natural dictates of his heart.

But what more particularly excited Ulric's disgust, was the determination Osmond had expressed, to compel Lady Marguerite to become his bride; the bride of a robber, whose hands had been so often imbrued in the blood of his fellow-creatures, and who had no other prospect than a life of crime, and ultimately, an ignominious death. His intention, too, of having the lady present at the following day's revelry;—exhibited to the rude gaze of the gang, and constrained to listen to their ribald jokes, and witness their riotous debauchery, filled his bosom with a sentiment of the utmost indignation, which he could scarcely forbear the expression of in the presence of Osmond and the others; but, by a powerful effort, he stifled his emotions, well knowing what the consequence would be if they were observed, and that, if it did not bring down upon him the vengeance of the gang, would, no doubt, effectually prevent him from affording Marguerite any little assistance towards alleviating her misery, which he might have it in his power, and was resolved to do. To Blanche, however, he confided his real thoughts upon the subject, and begged her to assure the fair prisoner how deeply he sympathized in her misfortunes, and regretted that he had not power to rescue her from the thraldom in which she was placed, and the fate with which she was threatened, but which he sincerely trusted, that something would occur to prevent it.

We need not say how heartily Blanche responded to the sentiments of her husband, and how gladly would she have encouraged him to assist the unfortunate Lady Marguerite in escaping from St. Alwyn Castle, could it have been done without the terrible consequences that would accrue to them both, and had not the oath they had taken bound them in fidelity to Osmond and his gang; fearful, therefore, that Ulric might inadvertantly betray his real sentiments to the robbers, and excite their suspicions, she cautioned him seriously, which he, however, informed her was quite unnecessary, as he should take good care never to be off his guard. They then separated, and Blanche hastened to the apartments of Lady Marguerite, to whom she imparted what had taken place between her and her husband. Lady Marguerite heard her with a feeling of the deepest melancholy and despair, but, at the same time, begged that Blanche would express her gratitude to her husband for his sympathy, and inform him of her regret that fate had placed him in so degrading and painful a situation, and of her sincere wish that something would, ere long, take place to release him from it, and restore him to that station in society, from which oppression and cruelty had driven him.

It was some hours after the battle, and the circumstances that had taken place, ere Lady Marguerite could, in the slightest degree, compose her feelings, or listen with patience to the gentle soothings of the attentive and affectionate Blanche.

"Alas!" she ejaculated, "where is all that forbearance and deference to our sex, which thou didst lately give Osmond credit for possessing?—Did he not threaten me with death, had not my poor brother yielded to his commands?"

"True," returned Blanche, "but still I do not believe he would put such a threat into execution, and that it was merely uttered to alarm Lord Raymond. I really think that he is forcibly struck with thy charms, Lady Marguerite, and so far from consigning thee to death, would——"

"Compel me to become his bride, thou wouldst say," added Marguerite; "alas! death would, indeed, be preferable to that."

Blanche used all the arguments she could think of to soothe the unfortunate lady, but they failed in having the desired effect. She then took her lute, and played one of the most impressive airs she knew, but the sounds fell listlessly upon Marguerite's ear, and she at last desisted, and worn out with thought and anxiety, the fair prisoner retired to her couch, and shortly sunk to sleep, Blanche continuing to watch by her bed-side for some time.

CHAPTER XVIII.

" Confide in me, my lord ; I know
A secret pass will guide thee to his haunt,
And thou canst drive the villain from his lair !"

THE SANCTUARY.

WORDS cannot describe the anguish of Lady Celestine on the return of her
son, and when she was made acquainted with the perilous situation of
Marguerite. For some time she was in a state bordering upon madness ; and
it was only at last by the gentle soothings and persuasions of Ernnestine, who
deeply sympathized in her distresses, that she was restored to anything like a
degree of composure ; and then, when she thought of the power of the robber-
chief, who scemed to be almost more than human, repelling every force sent
against him, and bidding defiance to all, despair settled upon her heart, and she
gave her unfortunate daughter up for lost. Our heroine, who had formed a
sisterly attachment to Lady Marguerite, was greatly shocked and grieved when
she heard the account from Lord Raymond of her situation ; and, although she
assumed an air of confidence regarding her rescue, she was very far from entertaining any such sanguine hopes upon the subject. Lord Raymond, however, notwithstanding his late defeat, determined to lose no time in making another
attempt to rescue his sister, although he felt confident stratagem could alone
effect that object ; what scheme, however, to adopt, he knew not, and racked his
brain in vain to hit upon one.

There was another person who felt most keenly for the situation of Lady
Marguerite, and who was ready to sacrifice life, fortune, everything, to rescue her
from the power of the robber-chief ; that person was Sir Egbert de Courcy, who
had long felt the influence of her charms, and had received from the lips of Marguerite an acknowledgment of the return of his love.

Sir Egbert de Courcy was a gentleman every way worthy of the hand of
Lady Marguerite St. Aswolph ; noble in mind as he was in person ; brave, generous, and affectionate ; it is, therefore, no wonder that their sentiments should
become mutual. On the disappearance of the Lady Marguerite from the castle,
he had been from home, and was not aware of the painful circumstance until
the return of Lord Raymond from the unsuccessful expedition we have been describing. His indignation at the boldness of the robber-chief may be imagined, and
he vowed that he would rescue the maiden and punish the outlaw for his
audacity, at the hazard of his life.

" By the saints !" he exclaimed, " I will collect such a force that shall over-
whelm the villain, and annihilate him and his daring gang. Not only will we join
our forces, but I will seek assistance from the king if they should fail."

" Force against Osmond, is useless," said Lord Raymond ; " he bids defiance
to it : and, even should we be able to defeat him, that he would sacrifice the life
of Margueite, as he has threatened, is certain. By stratagem only can we effect
our object."

Sir Egbert paced the apartment for a few moments buried in deep meditation, then turning to Lord Raymond, he said,—

"Could we but contrive to find out a secret entrance to the castle of St. Alwyn, we might take the villain by surprise, and securing Marguerite, prevent the possibility of putting his diabolical threats into execution. That there are several secret entrances to the castle I know, but I am entirely ignorant of their locality. Could we only manage to get one of the gang into our power, we might, by threats or the promise of a reward, persuade him to guide us privately to the robbers' retreat, and we might effect our object with very little difficulty."

"Alas! Sir Egbert," returned Lord Raymond, "thou dost calculate too readily upon the means. The fellows are all sworn so faithfully to each other, that they would sooner perish than be guilty of such an act of treachery."

"She must,—she shall be saved!" cried Sir Egbert. "By Heaven! I will not rest until I have devised some plan to tear my Marguerite from the Avenger's power, and bring destruction upon him and his gang. Ah!" he added, as a sudden thought crossed his mind, "My esquire, Godfrey de Lacy,—he was taken by Osmond to his retreat in the castle of St. Alwyn, from whence be made his escape, and must, therefore, possess the knowledge we require. I will seek him immediately, and he shall be our guide, and the means of releasing the beauteous Marguerite from the outlaw's power."

"It is a lucky thought," returned Lord R.aymond, hope once more springing up in his bosom. "I marvel that it did not occur to me. Where is Godfrey?"

"He is not at present in the castle," replied Sir Egbert; "and, indeed, I cannot tell what hath come to him of late, for he is absent for hours, wandering in the woods, and when he is at the castle, he is gloomy and thoughtful, and changed in manners altogether. Hath his fair mistress, Ernnestine, offended him, I wonder?"

Lord Raymond made no answer, for the question caused anything but a pleasant feeling in his breast.

"We will this instant away to the wood, my lord," said Sir Egbert de Courcy, "where we shall, no doubt, find him. There is no time to be lost in this business; and I shudder to think upon the misery and degradation to which my beloved Marguerite is probably already subjected. Come, my lord."

Lord Raymond took the arm of the knight, and they hastily quitted De Courcy castle, and made their way to the wood.

While the events we have been describing in the last two or three chapters were taking place, Godfrey de Lacy had passed many bitter moments of agony, occasioned by the irresistible force of that feeling of jealousy which had taken possession of his bosom, and rendered all his moments miserable. The continued stay of Ernnestine at the castle of St. Aswolph, and the unabated warmth of the attention which Lord Raymond bestowed upon her, inflamed his mind to an almost insupportable degree; and there were moments when he could scarcely control his feelings within the bounds of reason, and when in the society of Ernnestine, frequently he behaved in such a manner as made her experience a sentiment of indignation, and she could not refrain from upbraiding him for his conduct in severe terms. Godfrey would listen to her in sullen silence, and then abruptly quitting her presence, retire to his favourite haunt in the deepest recesses of the gloomy wood, where he would pass whole hours in silent

meditation, and in feeding the cankerworm which he had suffered to prey upon his heart. Against Lord Raymond, he could scarcely refrain from exhibiting the most inveterate hatred; and that sentiment daily gained such strength in his bosom, that he from being open, generous, cheerful, and urbane, became morose, stern, and sullen, and the extraordinary change in his behaviour excited the utmost astonishment in the minds of all who knew him.

Sir Egbert and Lord Raymond found him wandering among those gloomy shades he was now so constant a frequenter of, with his eyes bent to the earth, wrapped in such deep rumination as to be perfectly abstracted from all around him. Sir Egbert spoke to him, but entirely absorbed in his own thoughts, he heard him not until he had repeated his name two or three times, when, looking up, and observing Lord Raymond, an expression came over his countenance which might have been easily understood, at least by the individual who had caused it.

"Godfrey," said Sir Egbert, "I have sought thee on a subject of the greatest importance, in which I require thine aid."

"It is only to tell me in what manner I can serve thee, Sir Egbert, and it is my duty to obey thee," said Godfrey.

"'Tis well," observed the knight; "I knew well how ready thou wouldst be to comply with my request. The Lady Marguerite thou knowest is at present in the power of the robber-chief, Osmond the Avenger, who appears to bid defiance to all the force that can be sent against him; and, although I do not doubt but that we shall be able to subdue the power of the daring outlaw, it would probably not be until he had fulfilled the threat he made to Lord Raymond, namely, to sacrifice the life of the unfortunate lady whom he has so brutally

No. 26

torn from her friends ; we must, therefore, at all hazards, effect her deliverance from his power by stratagem. Thou hast been a prisoner in the castle of St. Alwyn ?"

" True," returned Godfrey.

" Thou didst effect thy escape from thence ?" said Lord Raymond.

" I did," was the answer.

" And, therefore, thou must be acquainted with the means of secretly gaining an entrance to the castle ?" said Sir Egbert.

" I am, Sir Egbert," replied Godfrey.

" Ah !" observed Lord Raymond, " thou sayest so ; why, then, didst thou not offer thy services on the recent expedition, when by thy means the effusion of blood might have been spared, and Osmond and his gang easily conquered ?"

" Because I would not betray one who, however lawless his life, 1 have had reason to believe is my friend," replied Godfrey de Lacy.

" How !" cried Sir Egbert, " dost thou, then, acknowledge thyself the friend and colleague of these desperate men ?"

" I do not, Sir Egbert," returned Godfrey; " still will I not betray them. 1 now see what it is thou requirest of me ; it is to lead thee to the secret entrance of the robber's retreat ; but, deeply as I regret the situation of Lady Marguerite, I must decline to do the service thou requirest of me."

" Ah ! so bold ! Thou dost refuse to lend thine aid towards the restoration of Lady Marguerite to her friends, and, therefore, prove thyself to be the partizan of those whose lives are forfeited to the offended laws of the country ! —Beware, Godfrey !" said Sir Egbert.

" I am ready to take the consequences of my conduct," replied Godfrey, firmly ; " and though I am sorry to do anything in disobedience to thy wishes, Sir Egbert, in this instance, I must express my determination to be unalterable."

" Rash youth !" exclaimed Lord Raymond, " thou surely canst not know what thou art saying ;—is this thy boasted honour,—thy much vaunted humanity,. when thou knowest that an innocent damsel is held in the power of these merciless wretches, and threatened with a terrible fate, to refuse thine aid, when it is in thy power to put us in the way to save her ?—Thou must be mad !"

" Probably I may be !" retorted Godfrey, coolly, " and it is by no means pro-bable that I shall learn reason from Lord Raymond St. Aswolph."

" Insolent !" exclaimed Lord Raymond, passionately; " this is almost past endurance !—Is this the gratitude thou dost evince for the manner in which I have served thee ?"

" I thank thee, my lord, sincerely, for that which thou hast done for me," ob-served Godfrey, " and would fain return the obligation ; but I have expressed my determination, and nothing shall make me swerve from it. Heartily do I wish that Lady Marguerite may be restored to liberty ; but that which I am required to do towards effecting it, must be done by some other person than me."

" Godfrey de Lacy," said Sir Egbert, whose astonishment at the extraordinary behaviour of his esquire could only be equalled by his rage, " thou surely must be labouring under some strange delusion !—Thou hast given way to the gloomy thoughts that have occupied thy mind for some time past, until they have deprived thee of thy senses. Hath thy mind become completely insensible to every feeling of humanity, and honour; or dost thou presume to disobey the orders of thy master?"

"I am perfectly sensible what I am saying, Sir Egbert," replied Godfrey, "and, deeply as I regret the necessity which compels me, in this instance, I must decline the aid thou hast demanded of me."

"By the mass!" cried Sir Egbert, "this insolence is unbearable;—follow me to the castle instantly!"

"I am sorry, Sir Egbert," returned Godfrey, "that I cannot comply with that request, neither; I have business that calls me another way."

"Hold! mad boy!" cried his master passionately, but Godfrey had hurried away as he spoke, and was out of sight.

For a few moments Lord Raymond and Sir Egbert stood and gazed at each other in stupified amazement, at the extraordinary and unaccountable behaviour of Godfrey; and then having expressed their sentiments upon the subject, they made their way to the Castle of St. Aswolph to consult what was best to be done.

On their arrival there, Lord Raymond was informed that a stranger, habited as a monk, had been waiting there some time to see him, upon business, as he said, of the utmost importance, and seemed anxious to avoid his features from being seen, as he had kept his cowl carefully drawn over his countenance.

"A monk, and waiting to see me?" said Lord Raymond, with a feeling of surprise and awe, when he remembered the form he had seen in the vision, which had been raised by the power of Hal of the Glen, and the mysterious monk he had afterwards encountered; "accompany me, Sir Egbert, perhaps the errand he has come upon may concern us both."

Sir Egbert obeyed, and they made their way to the apartment in which the stranger was staying.

When Lord Raymond and Sir Egbert reached the apartment in which the supposed monk was waiting, he arose, and made his obeisance to the former, but he seemed dissatisfied that he should be accompanied by the knight. His figure was tall and commanding, and there was something in his appearance altogether, which plainly denoted that the character he appeared in was only assumed. He partly raised his cowl, only revealing the upper part of his countenance, sufficient, however, to shew that he was a man of about the middle age, handsome, but with a countenance deeply marked with sorrow. His eyes were dark and peculiarly penetrating, and he fixed them earnestly upon Lord Raymond as though he would read his thoughts, and ascertain whether he could confide in him. Lord Raymond was convinced that he was not the same individual who had appeared to him on a former occasion, which we have described.

"Holy father," said Lord Raymond, "what wouldst thou with me?"

"My business is with thee," answered the man, "and with thee alone."

"Sir Egbert de Courcy is my friend," said his lordship, "and whatever may be thy business with me, thou need'st not fear to mention it in his presence."

"Pardon me, my lord," returned the supposed monk, "but I would rather that what I have to communicate, should reach thy ear alone."

"I like not the mystery of thy manner," observed Lord Raymond; "who art thou?"

" Thy friend," answered the stranger.

" How am I to be satisfied of that ?" demanded Lord Raymond.

" My conduct shall prove it. Thou need'st not fear to trust me ; but, if the knight, Sir Egbert, doth not withdraw, I shall decline to impart that which I came here for the express purpose of doing. I would serve thee."

" How ?"

" Let Sir Egbert retire, and I will inform thee."

" I repeat that thou mayest trust him."

" Probably I may, but I would rather not run the hazard. The business I have come upon is of the utmost consequence, and thou wilt not blame me for the caution I have made use of, when thou art acquainted with it."

" My presence shall not be any obstacle to the business thou hast come upon, monk," said Sir Egbert, whose curiosity was, however, much excited by the manner of the stranger ;—" I will withdraw."

With these words, Sir Egbert de Courcy retired into an adjoining apartment, and Lord Raymond and his mysterious visitor were left alone.

" Now, holy father, if such thou really art," observed his lordship, " thy business ?"

" I am no monk, Lord Raymond," said the stranger, " suffice it to say that I am sincerely thy friend, and would assist thee in the accomplishment of a deed which, no doubt, at present, occupies thy thoughts, and upon which, I presume, that a great portion of thy happiness depends."

" What meanest thou ?"

" May I trust thee ?"

" Thou mayest, but why should'st thou doubt me ?"

" My life, and that which ought to be as dear to thee as life, depends upon your conduct, and, therefore, thou need'st not marvel that I should be so cautious," answered the man.

" I pledge thee my honour," observed Lord Raymond, " that, if thy intentions are just, to do all that thou canst wish."

" Enough ; I will take thy word," said the man.

" Who and what art thou ?" repeated Lord Raymond.

" It matters not for thee to know more than that I have already informed thee," answered the mysterious stranger, " namely, that I am thy friend, and would serve thee."

" Give me, then, the proof," demanded Lord Raymond.

" I will. The Lady Marguerite, thy fair sister, is at present in the power of the robber-chief, Osmond, the Avenger ?"

" True,—what of that ?"

" Thou would'st rescue her from it, but have not the means," said the man, " force thou hast tried, but without effect, and it is by stratagem thou canst alone hope to accomplish thy designs. To-morrow, it is the intention of Osmond to force her to become his bride, and, therefore, there is no time to be lost."

" My sister, the bride of the robber-chief !" cried Lord Raymond, in a tone of indignation, " by the saints, that shall never be. She must, she shall be saved !"

" She must," repeated the man, " but it can only be effected by my assistance."

"How so ? and why shouldst thou, who art an entire stranger to me, take such an interest in anything which concerns me ?" asked Lord Raymond.

" Because I detest the conduct of Osmond, in this instance, and the situation of the Lady Marguerite hath excited my sympathy," answered the man. " If thou wilt trust to me, I will conduct thee and thy friends to-morrow, by a secret passage, known but to few, to the retreat of the robbers, where, taking them by surprise, thou mayest succeed in rescuing thy sister from the situation in which she is placed."

"Aye ! sayest thou so, stranger ?" said Lord Raymond, in a tone of pleasure, " then thou wilt prove thyself to be indeed my friend ; but art thou sincere ?"

" I am," replied the man ; " wilt thou trust me ?"

" I will ;—I will ;" eagerly returned his lordship ; " but thy offer is so unexpected, that it completely overwhelms me. I fain would know to whom I shall be indebted for this kindness; a service which nothing can ever repay."

" My name I must decline to reveal," said the stranger, " I am a man, however, deeply oppressed with care, and have suffered severely from the injustice of those from whom I had the least right to expect it ; but I yet possess a heart which can sympathise in the distresses of suffering innocence. But I must begone. Thou wilt, then, avail thyself of the offer I have made to thee ?"

"With the most unbounded pleasure," answered Lord Raymond, speaking sincerely what he felt ; " but where, and at what hour shall I meet thee ?"

" To-morrow evening, when darkness hath veiled the earth ; in the forest, near the parricide's stone," answered the man ; " let thy followers be close at hand, and leave the rest to me !"

" Stranger, again I thank thee ;" said Lord Raymond, " I will do as thou directest me; but thinkest thou that success will attend us ?"

"That depends entirely upon the precaution thou usest ; thy firmness, promptitude, and determination," answered the stranger. "I will conduct thee to the place, as I have promised thee, and then thou must act as thine own judgment and the circumstances may dictate. Farewell, till we meet again."

Before Lord Raymond could make any reply, the stranger had quitted the room, and hastily retired from the castle, leaving him in a state of astonishment, which may be easily imagined.

Sir Egbert de Courcy, when he heard the stranger depart, hastened to rejoin Lord Raymond, so that he might be made acquainted with the nature of the business upon which the mysterious stranger had sought an interview with his lordship. When he was informed of what had taken place, the promise which the stranger had made him, his surprise was no less than that of Lord Raymond, and he was at a loss to conceive who the individual could be to take such an interest in the affair. Sanguine hope, however, was readily admitted to his bosom, and he looked forward to the following evening with the greatest impatience.

The joy of Lady Celestine and our heroine, was unbounded when they were made acquainted with the circumstance, but, at the same time, they could not help occasionally fearing that treachery was intended ; this apprehension, however, was strongly combatted by Lord Raymond, who was convinced from the stranger's manner, that he was sincere in what he offered, and there was a candour in his general behaviour, which was sufficient to do away with suspicion.

The astonishment and indignation of Ernnestine when she heard of the singular behaviour of Godfrey, upon the application which Sir Egbert and Lord Raymond had made to him, may be imagined without much difficulty, and she was completely at a loss to account for it. Such a refusal seemed so unreasonable, and was in such direct opposition to his general character, that had she been informed of his conduct by any other persons than his lordship and Sir Egbert, she could scarcely have credited it. Resentment at his unfeeling and dishonourable behaviour, filled her bosom, and she determined, when next she saw him, to demand of him an explanation, and to upbraid him severely for the remarkable manner in which he had acted.

As the reader may, probably, have guessed, the stranger who had visited the castle and offered his services to Lord Raymond, was Ulric, who, unable to conquer his repugnance to the conduct of Osmond in respect to Lady Marguerite, had come at last to the determination, at all hazards, to assist in effecting her escape from his power. This resolution he kept so secret, that he did not even divulge it to Blanche.

In the meantime, the misery and fears of Lady Marguerite were much augmented, since the defeat which her brother had sustained, and owing to the increasing boldness and importunities of Osmond, and she began to despair of being rescued from the fate with which she was threatened. What added greatly to her alarm was, the account which Blanche gave her of the arrival of the bandit monks, and the Archers of Merceywood at the castle, and the formidable state of defence it was consequently placed in; and it was with the utmost difficulty that the remonstrances and soothings of Blanche, could have the least effect towards alleviating her agony and terrors. At length, Osmond bade her prepare to become his bride, and fixed the time, when he expressed his determination that the ceremony should take place, a resolution which he publicly announced to his lawless companions, who received it with rude shouts of satisfaction.

We will not attempt to describe the anguish of Lady Marguerite upon this; she was, indeed, in a state bordering upon distraction, and entirely deaf to the expostulations of Blanche, who, it is needless to say, was very much affected, knowing, as she did, the determination of Osmond, and that he would not fail to put his threats into execution. Again and again, with clasped hands, and a heart tortured to distraction, she supplicated the protection of Heaven, and implored for death rather than to be doomed to that fate with which she had been threatened.

"My poor mother," she exclaimed, "how terrible will be thy sufferings when thou hearest of the unhappy, the dangerous, the degrading situation of thy child!—And thou, my brother, what can ever appease thine anguish? But thou wilt not rest, I am convinced thou wilt not, until thou hast devised some plan to rescue me, and I will not yet entirely despair. No, there is yet room for hope, however small it may be."

Little, indeed, was there any cause for hope, and when the morning dawned, which Osmond had informed her must make her his bride, its rays were entirely extinguished in her bosom, and she gave herself up for lost. She trembled at every footstep she heard, lest it should be the robber-chief coming to put his threat into execution, and at length her feelings were worked up to such a pitch, that they were almost insupportable, and the expostulations of Blanche were completely lost upon her.

In this manner, the morning past away, and Osmond did not make his appearance, but she was convinced from 'one circumstance, that his resolution was unaltered. When Blanche entered her apartments first thing in the morning, she brought with her a beautiful bridal dress, which she informed Lady Marguerite she had been commanded by Osmond to desire her to attire herself in.

Marguerite turned from it with a look of disgust, and a feeling of wounded pride and modesty which needs no description, and then said :—

" Take it away, good Blanche ; never will I consent to assume a dress so contrary to my feelings !—The bare thought of an union with that fearful man, strikes the most indescribable horror to my heart, and neither force nor anything else shall ever make me yield my consent to become his bride. No, he shall stretch me a corpse at his feet first."

Blanche could not offer anything in reply to this, but the assurances of her deepest sympathy, and the time passed on until the afternoon approached. They could, at intervals, hear a considerable bustle in the place ; persons were passing hastily to and fro along the different corridors and galleries, and everything gave alarming note of preparation. In the same manner, the afternoon wore away, and evening sat in, and still the robber-chief, much to the astonishment of Lady Marguerite, did not make his appearance. At length, however, she heard a hasty and heavy foot fall approaching along the gallery, which opened upon the suite of apartments in which she was confined ; her heart beat violently against her side ; a deadly chill fell upon her limbs, and convulsed her whole frame, and she was so violently agitated altogether, that she could with difficulty support herself ; she was not long kept in suspense, the room door was thrown open, and the next moment, Osmond, the robber-chief, stood before her.

He was very elegantly attired, and his whole appearance was so different to what it had previously been, that Lady Marguerite could scarcely believe it was the same. His tall and commanding figure was shown off to the best advantage, and there was a smile of joyful expectation upon his still handsome countenance, which, under any other circumstances, would have created interest and admiration.

He advanced towards Lady Margurite, who was too much bewildered and agitated to offer any resistance, and taking her hand, pressed it respectfully to his lips, while he said :—

" Beauteous Marguerite, Osmond comes to claim his bride ; this evening makes thee mine for ever !—But how is this ?—No bridal dress ?—No preparations for the ceremony ?"

" Stand off, robber !—outlaw !—assassin !" cried Marguerite, indignantly, and tearing herself from his hold ;—" thy touch ; thy sight is loathsome to me ! Marguerite become thy bride !—Oh, sooner would she die beneath the murderer's blade ; rather would she court that death with which thou didst threaten her to her brother ; any doom, however horrible, is preferable to a life of shame and degradation with thee !"

"Nay, sweet Marguerite," returned Osmond, in an insinuating tone, "me-thinks thou art too severe. Thou must not treat me with this freezing coldness, when I swear that thou hast full possession of my heart, and shall receive every affectionate indulgence and attention which thou canst wish for. It is true, that in order to stay the effusion of blood which would otherwise have taken place, I did threaten thee with death, unless thy brother did withdraw his forces, but thinkest thou that I could ever have perpetrated the deed ?—Oh, no, no ;—but, come, the priest awaits us ; my impatient feelings will not brook farther procrastination ; to the chapel ! to the chapel !—Attend us, Blanche !"

"Release me, ruffian !" screamed Marguerite, struggling violently in his grasp ; but her efforts were all unavailing ; and at length, overpowered with fear and emotion, the maiden fainted. Osmond then raised her in his arms, and commanding Blanche to follow to the chapel of the castle, he hurried from the place.

Ulric was true to his appointment with Lord Raymond, and the latter, accompanied by Sir Egbert de Courcy, departed together, their followers making their way in small parties, and by different routes, to prevent suspicion. They all met at the same time at the appointed spot, and Ulric was already looking among the trees near the mound on which the parricide's stone stood, disguised, as before, in a monkish dress.

" Thou art faithful to thy promise, stranger," observed Lord Raymond, " and thou seest that we are prepared. But thou dost not mean to deceive us ?"

" If thou doubtest me, Lord Raymond," replied Ulric, " return. Thou little deemest the risk I run in seeking to serve thee, or thou wouldst not doubt me."

" Pardon me, stranger, if I have wronged thee," said Lord Raymond ; " I will trust thee."

" Follow me, then, immediately," said Ulric, " we have not a moment to lose, even now, Osmond bears thy sister to the altar, to force her to become his bride."

" The daring miscreant !" cried Lord Raymond, " I will——'

" Silence !" cautioned Ulric, interrupting him, " there may be those not far off, who might overhear us, and then all would be lost. Are all thy followers here ?"

" They are," answered Lord Raymond.

" Quick, then," said Ulric, waving his hand, and bounding up the mound, on which was placed a rude cross, and near it, the parricide's stone.

" I shall want the aid of some of these men, to remove the stone," said Ulric.

Several of the followers of Lord Raymond immediately offered their services, and by their assistance, the huge stone was removed from its place, and revealed a trap-door. This was raised without any difficulty, and Ulric having brought with him a lamp, by its rays they beheld a winding flight of steps, which he began to descend, motioning Lord Raymond, Sir Egbert, and the rest to follow. This they immediately did, and on reaching the bottom, found themselves in a large paved vault, from which three different passages branched.

" Let thy men divide themselves ; a portion of them following us, and the others taking the other two passages," said Ulric ;—" they all lead to the chapel

of the castle, and by this arrangement, they will take the robbers by surprise and by throwing them into confusion, probably accomplish their defeat with much greater ease than they might otherwise be able to do."

" I like thy counsel, stranger," said Lord Raymond, " it shall be attended to."

The order was immediately given to the men, who, dividing, took the different passages, being compelled to grope their way along in the best manner they could, in the dark, after having received some necessary instructions from Ulric, he then led the way, and Lord Raymond, Sir Egbert, and the remainder of the men followed.

The passage which the latter party had taken, was of great length and winding, but at last they reached the end of it, and then found themselves in an extensive vault. They ascended a flight of steps at the farther end of it and passed under a low archway into an apartment of stone, and there Ulric paused, and in a low, cautious whisper, turning to Lord Raymond, said :—

" Thou seest yonder door ?"

" I do," answered his lordship, in an equally low voice.

" That opens by touching a spring, which thou wilt easily find, immediately behind the altar," said Ulric, " thou wilt, by listening, ascertain the most opportune moment, then rush boldly forth, and tear thy sister from the power of the robber-chief, and deal destruction upon him and his daring gang. I must now leave thee; act with determination and caution, and success is certain. Farewell, some time or the other we may meet again."

As he thus spoke, Ulric made a sign towards the door, and then hurried out by the same way they had come.

No. 27

Lord Raymond and Sir Egbert made a sign to their followers to be silent, and then advancing to the door, perceived the spring which Ulric had mentioned, and listened attentively to learn whether they could hear any sounds beyond the door.

We will now return to Lady Marguerite, who was borne to the chapel of the castle by the robber-chief, whose passions having gained a power above all controul, he determined to make her his bride, as he had threatened, on that very night. Blanche followed, in obedience to the commands of Osmond, and deeply did she sympathize in the unfortunate fate of Lady Marguerite, and mentally pray that something might take place to prevent it. Had she been aware of the conduct of her husband, how happy she would have been, and how readily could she have forgiven him for having turned traitor in a cause upon which the future happiness or misery of an innocent, virtuous, and beauteous female depended.

Lights burned upon the altar of the castle of St. Alwyn, and a venerable-looking man, dressed as a priest, was standing ready to perform the unlawful ceremony. The lights from the altar cast their lumens upon the gothic chapel, and the robust persons and determined countenances of the robbers assembled, gave to the scene altogether, a singularly wild and romantic appearance.

Osmond approached the altar with his insensible burden in his arms, and as he did so, she recovered, and opening her eyes, looked with a feeling of astonishment and terror upon the objects around her. For a moment her mind was so bewildered, that she had but a vague idea of what had taken place, or in whose power she was, but when she beheld Osmond gazing at her with a look o the most ardent passion and impatience, all the danger of her situation in a moment rushed upon her memory, and recovering her firmness, she looked at him with a feeling of the most ineffable hatred and disdain, and endeavoured to release herself from his hold. Osmond appeared to take little or no notice of Marguerite, and smiled in the most insinuating and encouraging manner upon her, then turning to the apparent priest, he said :—

" Priest, let the ceremony commence; I am impatient of any unnecessary delay."

" Oh, hold! holy father! if such, indeed, thou art," exclaimed the maiden, energetically, " I warn thee not to perform a ceremony which is unsanctioned by me."

" Heed her not," cried Osmond, " it is my will that it should be, and I will be obeyed. Proceed!"

" At thy peril priest!" shrieked Marguerite, struggling to release herself from the hold of the robber-chief.

" At thy peril, hesitate," commanded Osmond; " thou knowest me well."

The priest began the ceremony, but he had scarcely uttered three sentences, when three blasts upon a bugle were heard; the door at the back of the altar was thrown open, and Lord Raymond and Sir Egbert, with their followers, rushed forth, and darted impetuously upon Osmond and his gang, whilst the other two divisions of Lord Raymond's men poured forth into the chapel, and commenced the deadly work of strife with desperate determination. Sir Egbert and Lord Raymond rushed simultaneously upon Osmond, and he was so completely bewildered and astounded at the unexpected circumstance, that he could offer but a faint resistance; Marguerite was torn from him by her lover and her brother, and immediately upon recognizing them, she uttered a cry of frantic delight, and fainted.

Sir Egbert and Lord Raymond resigned their precious charge to the care of several of their men, with orders to force their way with all possible despatch to the wood, and to yield her up only with their lives; and then directed their attention to the defeat of the robbers, who, having partially recovered themselves from the confusion into which the unexpected attack had thrown them, prepared to resist their assailants with all that reckless bravery, for which they were renowned.

"Damnation!" cried Osmond, foaming with rage, — "betrayed! — What treacherous knave hath done this? Slaves!—will ye suffer our enemies to triumph thus? Prevent the escape of the Lady Marguerite, or perish in the attempt, and punish the daring intruders for their boldness!—On, on, I say, for vengeance, and Osmond your captain!"

With loud yells the robbers responded to the calls of their captain, and their companions having forced their way into the chapel, the battle became most sanguinary and terrific. But, in spite of the opposition against them, those who had the charge of Lady Marguerite, succeeded in reaching the secret entrance under the parricide's stone, and ultimately made their escape to the Castle of St. Aswolph.

Dreadful, indeed, was the scene of carnage which prevailed in the robber's retreat. The curses of the robbers; the yells of their assailants; the clashing of weapons; the groans of the dying, all combined to render the scene one of the most indescribable horror.

The fury of Osmond when he beheld his brave but lawless gang falling rapidly around him, exceeded all bounds, and he fought with a desperation which was almost resistible. He engaged with both Lord Raymond and Sir Egbert, and for some time with a skill and bravery, that they could, with the utmost difficulty resist, but when a portion of his gang saw that the enemy were gaining every advantage, and that he must be overpowered, they enclosed him and forcibly led him from the spot.

Heaps of dead strewed the pavement of the chapel, and the blood of the unfortunate victims flowed in all directions, but the cause of the assailants bore every prospect of being triumphant.

"Comrades!" cried Osmond, in a voice choked with the most inexpressible rage, "will ye suffer yourselves to be thus defeated?—On, on to them again! and rather sacrifice your lives than yield to defeat!"

Quick at the word, the robbers once more rallied, and for a few moments, fortune seemed to turn in their favour, but it was of short duration; the brave followers of Lord Raymond and Sir Egbert de Courcy, fought with a bravery unparalleled, and the robbers fell in numbers beneath the blows they dealt around them; a few minutes, and it appeared evident that the robbers must be defeated, and Osmond and the castle in their power, when suddenly there was a loud and appalling cry of fire, and quickly the flames were seen pouring into the chapel in all directions. Fearful of the consequences, and that they would all be immolated in the scene of destruction, and having succeeded in their principal object, namely, that of rescuing Lady Marguerite from the power of the robber-chief; Lord Raymond and his bold coadjutors now turned their direction towards making their escape, leaving the robber-chief and his gang to their fate. After some difficulty, they succeeded in reaching the passages that led to the secret entrance, and finally emerged from the mound, Lord Raymond and Sir Egbert then turned their eyes in the direction of the ill-fated castle, and beheld it in one mass of flames, while the appalling shrieks of those it contained, and who were unable to effect their escape from the devouring element, rent the air, and rendered it altogether, a scene of the most awful and impressive description. The following moment, the walls fell with a terrific crash; a dense cloud of smoke and sparks ascended to the heavens, and an immense pile of smoking ruins was all that remained of the once formidable and impregnable Castle of St. Alwyn, which had for so many years formed the retreat of the robbers.

Lord Raymond and Sir Egbert returned their thanks to Heaven for the triumph it had allowed them to obtain, and for the preservation of Lady Marguerite, and then bent their way hastily towards the Castle of St. Aswolph, anxious to know whether Marguerite had reached there in safety.

CHAPTER XIX.

"Amid the battle's deadly strife,
    Lorn and deserted now I go;
Reckless about my hopeless life,
    Since thou hast sealed my doom of woe.
But wilt thou drop the pitying tear,
    For he who thought he own'd thine heart;
For he who loved thee too sincere,
    And who ne'er thought from thee to part?"

WORDS cannot express the unbounded gratitude and delight of Lady Celestine and Ernnestine, upon the restoration of Lady Marguerite, a dozen times at least, they embraced each other, and their tears of thanks flowed so fast, that they were unable to give utterance to their feelings. There was one circumstance, however, which served to interrupt their pleasure, and that was their uncertainty as the result of the affair, and whether Lord Raymond and Sir Egbert de Courcy would, or would not return in safety, and immediately after the men had deposited Lady Marguerite in the care of her mother, they were despatched to their assistance. They met the victors on their way to St. Aswolph, and all returned together again. We will pass over the scene which followed; language must fail to pourtray it properly, and universal delight prevailed in the castle, for Lady Marguerite had made herself, by her amiable manners, universally beloved by every one.

No one felt more sincerely glad at the restoration of Lady Marguerite than did our heroine, but when the former heard of the conflagration of the castle, and supposed destruction of all it contained at the time, her grief for the terrible and melancholy fate of poor Blanche and her husband, was most unbounded, which feeling was entered into by her brother, Ernnestine, and all who heard it, when they were made acquainted with the kind manner in which Blanche had behaved to Marguerite, and the idea she entertained that it was none other than Ulric who had rendered such an inestimable service to them all, by revealing to them a secret entrance to the Castle of St. Alwyn, and had thus rendered their success certain. They despatched persons to the ruins to make every enquiry, and to see whether any assistance could be rendered to the sufferers, but not the least signs of a human being was to be seen, and nothing remained of the once formidable edifice, but a shapeless mass of blackened ruins; it appeared as if Osmond and the whole of his gang had perished, for the flames had spread with such rapidity, that all means of escape seemed to have been speedily cut off.

Lord Raymond and Sir Egbert felt gratified to think that they had destroyed those daring marauders who had for so many years infested, and been the terror of the country, but, at the same time, they could not help pitying the awful and untimely fate which, it appeared but too evident had befallen Blanche and her husband; and from the description which Lady Marguerite gave of the latter, they had not the least doubt but that the man to whom they were indebted for their secret admission into the Castle of St. Alwyn, was the same individual.

The circumstance caused a great excitement in that part of the country, and although the wealthy were heartily glad that they had at last got rid of that desperate gang which had so frequently lightened their purses as well as put them in bodily fear, there were many among the poor and humble who deeply deplored the fate of Osmond and his followers, in whom they had frequently found such generous friends.

But Osmond had not perished although it was with the greatest difficulty he escaped the terrible fate of his comrades, all of whom had fallen either beneath the swords of their assailants, or by the flames that destroyed the ancient and powerful edifice which had for so many years afforded then so formidable a retreat. The whole of the lower part of the castle was in one mass of flames, so that it was impossible for him to secure his retreat that way; and, indeed, the greatest portion of the upper part of the building was blazing away rapidly, and escape seemed to be almost impossible. With the greatest difficulty he reached the door through which Lord Raymond and his party had retreated, and hastened along the subterranean passage which led to the forest, but when he gained the steps that communicated with the trap-door over the secret entrance, his despair may be imagined, when he found it closed, and that it resisted all his efforts to open it. Lord Raymond had not only ordered his followers to fasten the trap, but to roll the ponderous stone over it again.

The madness of desperation now seized upon the brain of the robber-chief, and for a second or two he stood uncertain in what manner to act, but the suffocating smoke which made its way along the passage aroused him to action.—He determined not to fall without making a resolute effort to save himself. Even in that fearful situation, vengeance filled his mind; that feeling he had not yet been able to satiate, and he could not, dare not think of dying, until he had obtained the gratification for which he had so long been seeking.

Drawing his mantle across his mouth and nostrils, to prevent his inhaling the smoke, from the effects of which he was almost blinded, Osmond returned by the way he had come to the chapel, and then the scene was truly terrific. On every side an earthly hell was raging, and the roaring and crackling of the furious element, and the noise of the falling masses, were appalling beyond description.

All hope seemed cut off, but battling with the flames, the same as the shipwrecked mariner would with the raging waves, Osmond at last succeeded in reaching a flight of stone steps which led to the upper part of the castle, and in spite of their burning heat, he rushed hastily up them, and gained the room to which they led after being severely scorched.

The fire had reached this apartment, but the flames burned not so fiercely as in the other part of the fabric. Osmond rushed towards a lofty casement, which he dashed hastily open, and without giving a moment's thought to the danger of the leap, sprang from it into the court-yard.

He was stunned for a short time by the fall, but not hurt, and in a minute or two, starting to his legs, he ascended to the top of the wall, along which he ran until he reached the principal tower, to which he gained admittance, and having opened the gates, fortunately, found that the drawbridge was down, and consequently, he was quickly enabled to reach the forest. There he had not been many minutes, and had been compelled to pause, in order that he might recover himself from the effects of the excitement and exertion he had undergone, when he beheld the ruins of the castle fall, and nothing now remained to mark the spot where it once had stood but the walls of the court-yard and the towers by which they were flanked.

Osmond placed his back against the trunk of an ancient oak, and folding his arms across his broad chest, fixed his eyes mournfully on the smoking ruins; the proud and gothic edifice of which he had so long ruled the master, was destroyed!— Where too, were his bold associates?—Gone! gone!—and a pang shot through the heart of the robber which he had not experienced before for some time!—It was many years since he had found himself, as it were, alone in the world!—A curse, a heavy malediction escaped his lips upon the heads of those who had been the cause of the calamity, and then having once more fixed his eyes intently upon the spot where the Castle of St. Alwyn had stood, he turned away; darted hastily onward, and was soon lost in the deep recesses of the wood.

Amid the excitement which these circumstances might naturally be supposed to occasion in the breast of our heroine as well as the others, it could not be expected that the strange conduct of Godfrey in refusing Lord Raymond and Sir Egbert de Courcy the service they required of him, could be easily driven from Ernnestine's mind, and it caused her much uneasiness and perplexing thought. To what cause could she attribute it, but that of jealousy, and which had completely destroyed those feelings of humanity that had before so particularly characterised him?—And when this idea occurred to her, it occasioned a feeling of indignation in her breast, towards Godfrey, (who could thus, in spite of her solemn asseverations, still doubt her truth) which she found it impossible for her to subdue. But to act in that cruel and dishonourable manner towards a female, and that female the sister of the nobleman who had stood forward so pre-eminently as his friend in the hour of danger, was most unpardonable, and it was so unlike the general conduct of Godfrey, that she was half inclined to doubt its reality.—

The day after the restoration of Lady Marguerite to her friends, as Ernnestine had seen nothing of her lover, neither did Ranulph, his father, or Hubert Clensham know anything whither he had gone, she became very uneasy, owing to his mysterious conduct, and unable to remain in the Castle of St. Aswolph in so painful a state of suspense, she quitted the place with a determination to hasten to the residence of her foster parents, to consult with them what was best to be done, to ascertain whither Godfrey was gone, the motives for his singular behaviour, and what were his intentions. She went alone, although Lord Raymond wished to accompany her, and was proceeding along, buried in deep thought, when she was suddenly startled by beholding the shadow of a human form, reflected by the rays of the sun upon the green sward, and raising her eyes, she beheld Godfrey advancing towards her; his step was hurried but unsteady, and she noticed in a moment, the paleness of his countenance, although it was stamped with an expression of determination which plainly shewed that he had fully made up his mind to some desperate act. On perceiving Ernnestine, he started back a few paces, and seemed to be slightly confused, but he quickly recovered himself, and walking up to the maiden, he took her hand, looked for a few moments intently in her countenance, and then, in melancholy accents, said :—

"Ernnestine, we meet, probably, for the last time. Ere the sun hath sunk behind the western hills, he, who once flattered himself that he owned thy love, will be far from that spot where he first drew the breath of life."

"Once owned my love, Godfrey," repeated our heroine, the tears trembling in her eyes, and her bosom heaving with the various feelings that agonized it; —"oh, this is cruel. Tell me, Godfrey, how have I deserved it, and what is the meaning of this strange and unnatural conduct?"

"Unnatural conduct!"

"Ay, didst thou not refuse that service to Lord Raymond St. Aswolph and Sir Egbert de Courcy, thy master, which the common dictates of humanity should have prompted thee readily to have granted?"

"I did, and the motives that urged me to do so were such as, in my opinion, were sufficiently strong, and would prompt me to behave in a similar manner, were I now asked to do a like favour."

Ernnestine gazed at him with a look of astonishment, reproach, and incredulity, but he seemed fully prepared for the interview, and shrunk not beneath her glances.

"Can this be Godfrey de Lacy? he whom I thought the very soul of honour?" she exclaimed; "but no, no; thou canst not speak the real sentiments of thine heart; some wild infatuation hath taken possession of thee, and urges thee on to acts of madness."

"Ernnestine," returned Godfrey, "thou mayest blame me; thou mayest think me cruel, ungrateful, ungenerous; but the motives that guide my conduct are too powerful to be resisted. I have long struggled with the demon that rages within me; I have long endeavoured to stifle the thoughts that have gained possession of my mind, but in vain. Ernnestine, I come to bid thee farewell, probably a last farewell; and oh, may he, upon whom I have placed thine affections, love thee as fondly and sincerely as I have done."

" Godfrey," cried Ernnestine, in a voice of the greatest agitation, " do not distract me. He upon whom I have placed my affections—oh, heartless cruelty ;—oh, shameless injustice !—Godfrey, hear me."

" Dost thou not love Lord Raymond ?" passionately and impatiently interrupted the impetuous youth.

" I esteem him, Godfrey ; nothing more, as I hope for mercy hereafter."

" Esteem him !" reiterated Godfrey, in a tone of bitterness ;—" oh, what a mockery is that name. Ernnestine, thou dost deceive thyself; that passion, which thou callest by so wrong a name, is love, fervent love. I see it in all thy conduct towards my fortunate rival. In thine eagerness to be in his presence, in thy reluctance to quit the same roof beneath which he resides. Godfrey de Lacy hath no fortune, no chance of wealth, but that which he may acquire by his own exertions. St. Aswolph is rich, is noble, and hath a flattering tongue I tell thee, Ernnestine, that thou dost love him, and, moreover, that thou wilt become his bride."

" Godfrey de Lacy," said the blushing damsel, her feelings aroused to the utmost pitch of indignation by the manner in which the headstrong young man spoke, and the words to which he gave utterance, " thou couldst never have loved me, or thou wouldst not act thus. The poor girl, whose truth thou canst thus distrust, could never have possessed thine heart."

" Ernnestine," ejaculated Godfrey, after a brief pause, " thou mayest deem me cruel—thou mayest call me unjust—or thou mayest deem me mad, but I cannot banish the distracting ideas from my mind. Think not, however, that I will prove any obstacle to thy real desires ; no, fairest girl, my presence shall no longer disturb thee ; my mind is made up. I go from hence ; and while life's purple current still flows within my veins, although another shall possess thine heart, thine hand, my constant prayers shall be offered up to Heaven for thine happiness."

" Oh, whither wouldst thou go, Godfrey ?—Whither would this wild delusion hurry thee ?" cried our heroine in a voice almost choked by the agony of her feelings.

" To where the martial notes of the clarion shall mingle with the groans of the dying and the shouts of the conqueror," answered Godfrey; " to the battle field, where I perchance may win a glorious name, or meet an honourable death. Life for me hath lost its charms ; all, all now is a barren desert, dark and drear ; but I must away. Ernnestine, bless thee, bless thee, in whatever station of life thou mayest be placed, and deign in thine orisons sometimes to think of him, who, perhaps, may then be breathing his last upon the field of carnage. Farewell! farewell! farewell !"

" Thou shalt not leave me, Godfrey," shrieked our heroine, in frenzied accents, and clinging to him ;—" nay, nay, thou canst not, thou wilt no be so cruel."

" Unhand me, Ernnestine," cried Godfrey; " my mind is made up ; nothing can shake me from my purpose. Again, farewell, and every blessing attend thee. Should it be my fate to return from the strife, and I should win for myself

an honourable name and station in society, then, indeed, if I should find that
I have wronged thee, and that——but I dare not trust myself with the bright
vision. Adieu! and if we never meet again, adieu, adieu for ever."

" Hear me! hear me, cruel man!" exclaimed Ernnestine, deliriously ;—" oh,
God! oh, God!"

Godfrey de Lacy made no answer ; but fixing upon the poor girl one look of the
most intense agony, he tore himself away, and rushed with the greatest precipitation from the spot.

"Godfrey! Godfrey!" cried our heroine, with clasped hands and distracted
looks ; but he was gone ; and, overpowered by her feelings, she sunk upon the
earth in a state of insensibility.

Fortunately, in spite of what Ernnestine had said to prevent his accompanying
her, Lord Raymond was induced to follow her at a distance, fearful that there
might be some of the robbers, who had, probably, escaped from the destruction of
their retreat, lurking about in the wood, who might take advantage of her
unprotected state. He had seen the meeting between her and Godfrey, and
approaching nearer, and concealing himself from observation, he was enabled to
overhear part of the conversation which had passed between them. He now saw
at once the motives of Godfrey, in refusing to be their guide to the secret
entrance to the castle of St. Alwyn ; and although he could not flatter himself
that he at present possessed any more than Ernnestine's esteem, as she had
said, his sanguine hopes tempted him to believe that time would ripen that feeling
into one of a more tender nature in her breast, especially in the absence of
Godfrey, whose determination he felt the utmost satisfaction at. The agitation

of Ernnestine was so great, that he was several times half tempted to interrupt it, but was prevented by other feelings, and remained in the place where he had concealed himself until the departure of Godfrey and the insensibility of Ernnestine, when, rushing forth, he raised her in his arms, and after endeavouring, in vain, to recal her to animation, he fled with the utmost precipitation, in the direction of the castle, where, in a short time, he arrived, and consigned his beauteous burthen to the tender care of his mother and Lady Marguerite.

It was some time ere Ernnestine recovered her senses, and when she did, the parting which had taken place between her and Godfrey, was impressed upon her memory in such painful characters, that it did not seem likely would be easily obliterated. The mad infatuation which had evidently taken possession of his senses, while it offended the innate pride which she possessed, caused her the utmost astonishment, so foreign did it appear to the general conduct of Godfrey. Convinced as she was, that neither by thought or action had she given him any occasion for jealousy, she viewed his obstinate perseverance in doubting her sincerity, as cruel and ungenerous in the extreme, and fain would she have retaliated by driving his image from her heart, but love had fixed it too firmly there to be ejected. And now that she knew he had gone to the field of deadly carnage, and the probability that he would never return again, she became almost inconsolable. In spite of his behaviour, never did she feel more fully the strength of the affection with which he had inspired her, and she could have made any sacrifice for his sake. Great as was the injustice he had done her by the suspicions he entertained towards her, she could freely have pardoned him all, knowing as she did that it was the strength of his passion alone which originated them. That she entertained an uncommon esteem for Lord Raymond, she never attempted to deny to herself, for the sentiment sprang from the purest motives, and such as innocence need not to be ashamed to acknowledge, but the difference of their station in society, and the disparity in their ages; would have been sufficient to have subdued any other hopes and ideas in her breast which his numerous virtues and acquirements might otherwise have excited. Neither could she be blind to the interest which Lord Raymond felt towards her, and she had every reason to believe that Godfrey had not formed a wrong idea of his sentiments, but at the same time she entertained too high an opinion of the former, to suppose for a moment that he would attempt to dispossess him of those affections that had been so long devoted to him.

It was not without some difficulty that Lady Marguerite, who was constantly with her, could reconcile her to the circumstance, and lead her to hope that Godfrey would be enabled to brave the perils of the battle-field; that he would return in safety, and that future happiness would be their portion. She could not be blind to the real sentiments that Ernnestine had engendered in the bosom of her brother, and although she felt confident that the passion was an hopeless one, and one in which he ought, in honour, to endeavour to conquer, she could not but approve of it, and only regret the circumstances that formed the most insurmountable barriers to the consummation of his wishes.

At length, however, Ernnestine did somewhat regain composure, and endeavoured to think as Marguerite and her mother advised her. Nothing could be more affectionate than the attention which they paid her, and the anxiety which Lord Raymond evinced until she had recovered, was sufficient to satisfy them of the strength of the feelings with which she had inspired him if they had had no other reason. In spite of all his efforts to the contrary, Lord Raymond found it in vain to attempt to stifle his passion, and he could not but look forward to the absence of Godfrey with a feeling of hope, that in time he might be able to conquer the objections of our heroine, and gain possession of her hand and heart. Lord Raymond loved her not for her beauty alone, but for the inestimable intrinsic qualities she possessed, and a still more powerful, it might be called an indefinite feeling guided his thoughts and wishes. He could not gaze upon her without a sensation darting through his veins, which he felt himself at a loss to describe, and which at times moved him almost to tears. There was an expression in her eyes, especially when she smiled, and indeed in the general contour of her features, which so strongly reminded him of one, whom many years before he had known, and which had been the means of throwing a gloom over his future prospects, that he could almost imagine that being stood again before him, and the anguish it caused him, was of the most acute description. Ernnestine, with much confusion, frequently noticed this extraordinary emotion, and was unable to account for it in any other way than that she had excited an affection which he considered to be hopeless, in his bosom. The interest of Lady Celestine and her daughter, as has been shewn, was also drawn towards her in a most extraordinary manner, and they felt as if they were prepared to love her with the same ardent affection as if she had been related to them by the ties of consanguinity.

Ernnestine having recovered, and Lady Marguerite being restored to liberty, she considered, having noticed the increasing warmth of Lord Raymond's attentions towards her, that it would not be prudent to remain longer beneath the same roof, and, notwithstanding she could not help regretting the circumstances that compelled her to it, she expressed to her kind friends her determination to return home to Hubert Clensham and his wife, and resisted all their opposition to the same, although they tried every means in their power to persuade her to remain at the castle. They would not, however, suffer her to part until they had extracted from her a promise that she would be a visitor to them upon every opportunity whch presented itself

Of course no one regretted more keenly than did Lord Raymond St. Aswolph, the departure of Ernnestine from the castle, although they would be separated by such a short distance, and he could, if he thought proper, have an opportunity of seeing her every day. So powerful was the ascendancy which she had gained over his heart, that he could not bear the idea of being out of her presence even for the shortest space of time, and a presentiment took possession of his mind, which he strove, but in vain, to conquer, that something would occur which would render all the hopes with which she had inspired him, futile. Hopes! Yes,—notwithstanding all the obstacles that presented themselves, he had been unable to avoid encouraging them ; nor could he, with any degree of patience, make up his mind to abandon all idea of one day or the other being enabled to obtain her affections, and to make her his bride. The warmth of his manner on this occasion, fully convinced our heroine, if she had required any proof upon the subject, of the real nature of the sentiments Lord Raymond had imbibed towards her, and when she called to mind his many noble qualities, she could not help acknowledging to herself that he had excited in her bosom a feeling of the greatest interest; but yet it was a feeling of a very different nature to that which some persons might feel inclined to interpret it, and one which she was herself at a loss to understand. She returned to the "Flagon" labouring under a depression of spirits which needs no description, and which threatened, for some time, at any rate, to bid defiance to all the exertions of her friends to alleviate.

Ranulph de Lacy and Edith felt much uneasiness at the hasty determination of their son, and many were the dismal forebodings they entertained of the fate which would attend him; but they could by no means blame the conduct of Ernnestine, neither could they offer any excuse for the impetuosity with which Godfrey had acted, and at his ungenerous suspicions as regarded the sincerity of the sentiments she had confessed to entertain towards him ; yet, when they weighed all the circumstances in their own minds, and recollected the many and marked attentions that Lord Raymond had paid her, they could not be blind to his real feelings, and of the ample cause which Godfrey had to be jealous of him, although he should not, undoubtedly have suspected the truth of those vows which Ernnestine had plighted to him.

Weeks, months, many dreary months passed away, and still Ernnestine heard nothing of Godfrey, neither was she or his parents able to discover whom he had joined, although the place of his destination, of course, was well known to them. They could not obtain the least intelligence of him, and the anxiety and uneasiness of them all may be easily imagined. Sometimes they gave themselves up entirely to despair, as regarded his fate, concluding that he had fallen on the ensanguine field of strife, and at others, hopes would spring up in their bosoms that he was still alive, and would return in safety, and to acknowledge the injustice he had done Ernnestine by the suspicions he had entertained regarding her faith.

Hubert Clensham had always been opposed to the passion which existed between our heroine and Godfrey, for the reasons with which our readers are already acquainted, and he had sought by every means in his power to stifle it; not that he considered them unworthy of each other, but decidedly on the contrary ; when, however, the painful circumstances took place that more strongly testified the power of that passion, he became less particular about it, more especially as, from the number of years that had elapsed since he had heard anything of the stranger who had deposited Ernnestine when a child, in his care, gave him good reason to believe that he had either abandoned all thoughts of her, or otherwise was dead.

Although they had not thought proper to divulge the truth as regarded the mystery of her birth, and the manner in which she came under their protection, old Hubert and Maud had frequently inadvertantly let fall certain observations that excited her curiosity, and caused her to suspect that there was something more in connection with her than they thought proper to disclose, and she often questioned them narrowly concerning it ; while the evasive answers she got in return, rendered her more confident that her surmises were not without foundation. Of one thing she felt certain, namely, that she was not related to them, but who were her relations, or whether she had any living, and how it was that she had come under the protection of Hubert Clensham, and the parents of Godfrey, of course she was at a loss to form even the most remote conjecture.

Still week after week elapsed, and no intelligence was gained of Godfrey de Lacy, and the anguish of his parents and Ernnestine may well be imagined, especially when the gallant warriors returned from the field of battle, and he came not with them. To no other conclusion could they come than that the unfortunate young man had fallen, but those of whom they inquired, and who were the most likely to know, could not furnish them with any satisfactory answer upon the subject. Many and bitter were the tears that our heroine shed to the memory of the impetuous youth, and it was a considerable time ere her bosom would admit of the least consolation.

In the meantime, Lord Raymond was unremitting in his attentions towards Ernnestine, and they were of that kind which left her no longer room to doubt what was the nature of his real sentiments towards her; indeed his passion had so powerfully increased, that he found it utterly impossible for him to conceal it from the beauteous object who had inspired it; and when the return of the army took place, and there seemed to be but little doubt of Godfrey having been slain, he considered that he had no necessity any longer to keep his love a secret from her, and he, therefore, made to her a confession in the most glowing language, and energetically endeavoured to prevail upon her to become his bride, willing to waive all objections arising from the difference of their rank, thinking as he did, that no sacrifice could be too great to obtain so rare a treasure.

Our heroine heard him without any expression of surprise, for she had long been prepared for it, but although she warmly gave utterance to her feelings of gratitude for the honour he did her, and could not help really experiencing the most profound esteem for him, she declined the offer he made her.

Lord Raymond received her answer with considerable emotion, and tried all his powers of persuasion, but without effect, and he, therefore, ceased, for the present, to urge his suit, although he did not entirely despair of success at some future period.

In this manner two years passed away, and although Lord Raymond had again urged his vows, they were declined by our heroine, although not with the same resolution as she had done before, a circumstance which strengthened his lordship's hopes, and he trusted that he should ultimately succeed. Time had now had the effect of mellowing the grief of Ernnestine, but nothing could ever lessen the regret she felt at the headstrong passions that had induced Godfrey to take the course he had, and which had brought about such an unfortunate result. Lord Raymond still persevered in his addresses, in which he was aided by Lady Marguerite and her mother; but our heroine needed no such pleaders to induce her to regard his lordship with the greatest esteem, and could she have been certain that Godfrey was indeed no more, she would not have hesitated in encouraging his love. At length, however, when six months more had fled, and still the fate of Godfrey remained unknown, all hopes of ever again seeing him became extinguished in her bosom, and she delighted Lord Raymond by admitting that he had made a deeper impression upon her than any man she had known with the exception of her late lover, and referred him to her friends, whose consent if he could obtain, she would not offer any obstacle.

On the wings of hopeful expectation, Lord Raymond hastened to Ranulph and Edith de Lacy, but to his astonishment, they informed him that they could say nothing upon the subject, and that the passion their unfortunate son had imbibed for Ernnestine had never been sanctioned by them, as they had not the power to do so. His lordship with much surprise, inquired whether Ernnestine had not been brought up almost entirely under their protection, and whether she was not related to them? The latter question they declined answering, but referred him to Hubert Clensham.

Mine honest host of the "Flagon," expressed his hearty thanks for the honour which Lord Raymond had intended to his *protege*, but like Ranulph and his wife, he informed him that he had not the power to sanction his addresses to Ernnestine, and moreover, that he must request he would not persist in a suit of which he could not but approve, although he had no power to encourage it, and which, if he persevered in urging, would, in all probability, not only involve him (Hubert) and his family in trouble, but might also be productive of much unhappiness to his lordship.

Lord Raymond looked astonished; the words of Hubert were completely incomprehensible to him.

"Why," he exclaimed, "hast thou not the power to sanction my addresses? Is she not thy relation? Art thou not her only protectors, and, consequently, the only persons who have any power over her actions?"

"Do not, I beg of thee, my lord," said Hubert, "do not press me to that which I cannot answer; but endeavour to stifle this unhappy passion which I fear me can never be gratified by the possession of the object which hath inspired it."

"But thou wouldst have given thy consent to an union between Godfrey and Ernnestine," said Lord Raymond.

"Not at present, my lord," answered Hubert, "they must have waited until such time as I had the power of granting my assent; and I am willing to give thee the same promise, my lord, should the power ever be delegated to me."

"Thou speakest in problems, Master Hubert," observed Lord Raymond, "but I am willing to accept thine offer, and trust it will not be long ere this mystery is explained, and I shall gain the consummation of my wishes."

With these words, Lord Raymond quitted Hubert, and hastened to our heroine to inform her of the bad success which had attended his application.

Ernnestine heard the account given by Lord Raymond of his interview with her supposed relatives with much astonishment, both on account of their rejecting so wealthy a suiter, and the mystery of their manner. She had, however, frequently noticed circumstances in the behaviour of Hubert Clensham and his wife, as also in that of the parents of Godfrey, that had excited her amazement, particularly when she questioned them about her parents, a subject which they always sought to evade, and there were times when it caused considerable speculation in her mind, and she was often inclined to conjecture that they were not actually related to her. And now the reception which the suit of Lord Raymond, and the observations they had made, more than ever strengthened these surmises.

"It is strange," she ejaculated, after she had listened to the statement of his lordship; "there is some mystery in this which I cannot fathom."

"There certainly is a great deal of mystery in the circumstance," said Lord Raymond, "and to me it is a most painful one. The only conjecture I can form is, that thou art not related to those that have brought thee up, Ernnestine."

"But if not related to them, why should they take such an interest in my fate, and bring me up with so much care and affection?" said our heroine.

"Probably they have been well rewarded for doing so, my dear Ernnestine," returned Lord Raymond, "and to do them justice, amply have they merited any reward they may have received."

"Oh, yes, they have indeed," exclaimed Ernnestine, her heart overflowing with gratitude, when she recalled to her memory the innumerable acts of kindness she had experienced from them; "the closest ties of consanguinity could not possibly have rendered them more assiduous and affectionate. But this idea has taken such strong hold of my thoughts, that I cannot rest satisfied until I have questioned them upon the subject. I will immediately make the inquiry."

"I commend thee for that resolution, dearest Ernnestine," said Lord Raymond, "and if they really feel for thee that love which they have always professed for thee, they will not hesitate to yield to thy importunities. Alas! Ernnestine, no one hath more occasion to regret this secret than myself, since by it I am doomed to a state bordering upon despair. Without thee, Ernnestine, I feel that life would become to me a dreary blank, a void, from which no future happiness could spring; and I am presumptuous enough to think that thou, my Ernnestine, canst not look upon the uncertainty of the consummation of my wishes with indifference."

Ernnestine looked up in his lordship's face with an expression of melancholy sweetness, and the deep blushes of maiden coyness that suffused her cheeks, spoke a more powerful language than words could have done. Suddenly, however, the image of Godfrey started before her mental vision; her bosom heaved with agony, and she was unable to restrain the tears that gushed spontaneously to her eyes, and streamed down her cheeks. Lord Raymond looked at her for an instant with a feeling of sympathy and regret, and then taking her hand, he said—

"Well, I can read thy thoughts, lovely Ernnestine, and think not that I will attempt to depreciate them. It is but natural that the strength of first love, although the object that hath inspired it is no more—but forgive me, Ernnestine, I know the subject causes thee the most poignant agony, and Heaven knows that I would not cause thee a moment's pain. Nay, painful as would be the task to me, did I think that thou could'st not accept of my hand without the sacrifice of the least portion of thy peace of mind, instantly would I absolve thee from the promises thou hast made me, and endeavour to view thee only in the character of an affectionate, a dearly beloved sister."

"Oh, my lord," returned our heroine, "pray forgive me this weakness; but I know thou wilt. In spite of every effort, memory will cling to the object which first inspired our youthful affections; but—I have told thee my sentiments—I have not disguised a thought from thee, and when I again tell thee that, after the unfortunate Godfrey, there is no other man that hath or can hold so warm a place in mine heart's affections as thyself, thou wilt—"

She paused, and was unable to finish the sentence. Lord Raymond raised her hand rapturously to his lips, and devoured it with kisses.

"Ernnestine," he ejaculated, "dear Ernnestine, I could not, I did not doubt thy truth; and this last acknowledgment endears thee, if possible, more closely to mine heart than ever. I cannot describe the feeling with which thou hast excited me! It is not only love, but something deserving of a more powerful name. All my thoughts, my wishes, my affections, my hopes, are drawn towards thee. Each pulsation thou feelest, I feel. I seem to breathe the same breath as thou dost. I imagine that thou art a portion of myself; that we are already united, and to be divided from thee and still live would be impossible."

"The same feeling, my lord—the same indescribable feeling—animates my breast," replied Ernnestine. "It is not the same sentiment that throbbed my heart for Godfrey, and yet it is one, if possible, more powerful. I love thee not only for thy virtues, but because an instinctive voice seems to whisper me it is my duty so to do."

"Strange, unaccountable feeling!" ejaculated Lord Raymond, "what can it mean?"

A hollow laugh at that moment smote his ear, and Ernnestine, terrified, clung closer to him, and following the same direction as his eyes, she beheld standing near them, with his cowl drawn over his face, the tall figure of a friar. It was but an instant, however, that they were permitted to see him, for waving his hand in a menacing attitude towards Lord Raymond, he darted forward, and was soon lost from their view, and before Lord Raymond had recovered from the astonishment, not unmingled with a feeling of awe, into which his appearance had thrown him.

"Who can that mysterious man be," said our heroine, who was at first very much alarmed, but shortly regained her composure, "and what purpose could have brought him hither?"

"Twice or thrice before hath that figure crossed my path," observed Lord Raymond, "and even dared to utter threats in my ear. Ah!—Osmond, the robber-chief, the change which I saw exhibited to me by Hal of the Glen, exactly corresponded with that of him and this mysterious monk. And then their stature, their features, their voices, all resembled each other so closely, that—"

"What meanest thou, my lord?" said our heroine, with astonishment depicted in her countenance.

"That the man we have just seen is Osmond, the robber-chief," answered Lord Raymond.

"Impossible!" ejaculated Ernnestine; "have we not every reason to believe that Osmond perished with his daring associates in the flames that destroyed the castle of St. Alwyn?"

"He may have escaped," returned Lord Raymond, "and the fear of being detected and brought to punishment, would have been sufficient to have induced him, if even he had no other reason, to remain for awhile concealed."

"Oh, no, my lord," said our heroine, "I do not think that is probable. Besides, thou sayest that this apparent monk hath used threats to thee, and—"

"And, therefore," added Lord Raymond, "doth it render my conjecture the

more likely; since Osmond made use of the same threats to me, and also to Marguerite, when she was in his power, as thou hast heard her say."

"But why should Osmond so have threatened thee, my lord?" asked Ernnestine, "how couldst thou, prior to the attack which thou didst make upon his retreat, have excited his vengeance? and if thou hadst, surely he had plenty of opportunities of putting his designs into execution, so often as he hath been near thy person."

"That, my love," replied St. Aswolph, "is an ambiguity which I cannot solve; but that this grey friar and the robber chief are one and the same person, is so powerfully impressed upon my mind that I cannot divest myself of it; some mischief is brooding, and I must be watchful and wary that the machinations of the guilty do not succeed. But come, Ernnestine, let us hasten to the castle, for there may be danger in remaining where we are. I cannot suffer thee to return home without being attended by those who may protect thee from any harm which might otherwise befal thee."

Ernnestine, who could not question the prudence of his step, suffered his lordship to take her arm, in silence, and accompanied him to the castle of St. Aswolph, frequently looking back, and expecting again to encounter the tall figure of the mysterious grey friar.

Lord Raymond made his mother and the Lady Marguerite acquainted both with the result of his interview with the friends of Ernnestine, and the adventure with the mysterious monk. The first circumstance caused in their minds as much surprise and regret, as it had occasioned Lord Raymond and our heroine, and they could not but agree with them that there was considerable mystery attached to the conduct of Hubert Clensham, and Ranulph and his wife,

No. 29

and they warmly approved of the resolution which Ernnestine had come to question the former narrowly upon the subject. The appearance of the monk also caused them much astonishment and alarm, especially when they were told by Raymond of the former meetings he had had with the same mysterious being, and the threats he had held out to him, and they were unable to come to any satisfactory conclusion upon the subject.

By the urgent persuasions of Lady Celestine and her daughter, Ernnestine was prevailed upon to remain at the castle till the morning, a domestic being despatched to the house of Hubert Clensham, to inform him of the same, and the reason; and the remainder of the evening was passed in conversing upon the circumstances of the day. In speaking of the former meetings which Lord Raymond had had with the apparent monk, and the threats he had made use of to him, the agitation of the former was very evident; he frequently seemed totally abstracted from everything in deep thought, often sighed deeply and appeared to be suffering from some painful reminiscence recalled to his mind; but when his mother and Lady Marguerite questioned him more closely, his emotion increased, and he begged of them to desist, and requested of them permission to leave the room for a few minutes to recover himself. This only served to increase their anxiety, but seeing the emotion it caused him, they reluctantly dropped the subject, hoping that time would unravel the mystery to their satisfaction.

In the morning, Lord Raymond, who had regained his composure, attended by several domestics, accompanied our heroine home, and after a short time passed in conversation with Hubert and Ernnestine, he returned to the castle. That day our heroine had resolved to question Hubert upon the subject which so completely engrossed her thoughts, and he broached it himself, by informing her of the application which Lord Raymond had made to him, and the answer he had been compelled to return him.

"How, sir," ejaculated Ernnestine, with unfeigned surprise, and fixing upon Hubert a penetrating look, "are not thou and my foster parents the only protectors I have ever known; the only relatives that I have in the world? who then hath a right of disposing of my hand if thou hast not?"

"Ernnestine, my dear child," said old Hubert, much agitated, "I repeat that I have not the power so to do, or how willingly would I give my consent for thee to become the bride of one so worthy of thee, as the noble Lord Raymond St. Aswolph."

"What meanest thou, my more than father?" ejaculated the astonished Ernnestine; "there is some mystery in this, which I cannot fathom."

"The greatest misery is threatened to me and mine, should I do so," answered Hubert.

"By whom, and from what motives? Oh, tell me, I implore thee?" interrogated our heroine.

"By one whom I know not," answered the old man.

"One whom thou knowest not?" said Ernnestine. "I cannot understand thee; for Heaven's sake explain thyself? this suspense is insupportable."

" Ernnestine," said Hubert, after a pause, during which he endeavoured to collect himself for the task, " I fear thy suspense will be little alleviated by that which I can reveal to thee. There is a secret connected with thee, which I was enjoined not to disclose until thou hadst arrived at the years of maturity. That time hath now come, and I think it my duty no longer to keep thee in ignorance of the extraordinary circumstances that placed thee under my protection. Ernnestine, thou art in no way related to me, or Ranulph and his wife!"

" Gracious Heaven!" cried our heroine, starting from her seat in a state of the most violent emotion, " is it possible? who then are my relations?"

" I know not," answered Hubert.

" My parents," gasped forth the trembling maiden, " Who are they? Do they still live? and why was I abandoned to the care of strangers?"

" Calm thy agitation, Ernnestine," said Hubert Clensham, " and listen to the strange story I have to tell thee."

" I will—I will—" hastily ejaculated our heroine, " but pray be quick."

Old Hubert went to the door to see that there were no listeners, and then drawing his chair closer to that of Ernnestine, detailed all the particulars with which the reader has been made acquainted at the commencement of this narrative.

With the most breathless attention Ernnestine listened to this extraordinary recital, and when Hubert had come to the conclusion, she clasped her hands vehemently together, and raising her eyes towards Heaven, stood for a few moments in speechless astonishment.

"Oh, God!" she at length exclaimed, " how wonderful are Thy ways!—but alas! how little cause for satisfaction have I at this disclosure, since it shews to me the utter misery of my state; deserted by my parents, burthened upon the bounty of strangers, and knowing no one upon whom I have the slightest claim!"

" Ernnestine, dear Ernnestine; child of my adoption," exclaimed the poor old man, pressing the weeping damsel to his heart, and the big tears rolling down his furrowed cheeks, " say not so;—thou art still mine;—still the child of thy foster parents, while the current of life flows within their veins."

Ernnestine tried to speak, but the power of her emotions, the tumult of thoughts that rushed to her brain, choked her utterance, and she returned the ardent caresses of the good old man, with all the fervour that her bounding heart prompted.

" Alas !" ejaculated our heroine, after a pause, " would that I had never been made acquainted with this secret, what anxiety would it have saved me. Parents! oh, they were unworthy of the name,—or they never could have abandoned me in so heartless a manner."

" Say not so, Ernnestine," observed Hubert Clensham, " judge them not too harshly;—stern necessity may alone have driven them to such a course."

" Oh, what necessity could be so stern as to induce them to desert their offspring?" sighed Ernnestine.

" Perhaps, thy life was sought."

" Oh, no, no," returned our heroine, hastily ; " thou sayest I did not appear
to be more than eighteen months old when I was left so mysteriously to thy care,
and who cou!d be monster enough to seek the life of such an infant ?"

" Ernnestine," replied Hubert, " there are monsters in the world, whom motives of interest will urge to the perpetration of any crime."

"Ah ! thine observations, dear Hubert, have suggested an idea to my mind,
which did not occur to it before ;" said Ernnestine, ; " the letter, too, that was left
with thee, also, thou sayest, stated that I was of noble origin ? —Hast thou
that letter still in thy possession ?" eagerly inquired our heroine.

" I have, my child," answered old Hubert,—" for so must I still continue to
call thee ;—1 have preserved it, with the utmost care, thinking it might some day
or other be the means of bringing about a discovery of thy birth."

" Oh, pray let me then see it;"—said Ernnestine, in a tone of impatience.

" 1 will," answered the old man ; and he hastened to a little box which he had
placed in his own private cabinet and carefully locked, and taking out the letter,
presented it to the anxious maiden. She glanced over it with a look of the utmost
curiosity and the deepest interest, and then proceeded to peruse the contents
aloud ;—

" The child entrusted to thy care is of noble origin, but by a strange chain of
events, which time, may, perhaps, reveal, she is placed in thy charge, with a hope
that thou wilt acquit thyself fairly, (which thou art enjoined to do,) or thou mayest
repent thy refusal when too late. Mark ;—the writer of this hath power to injure
as well as to aid thee ; he is disposed to do the latter, and, for thy service receive
the purse of gold left behind. A like sum shall also be forwarded thee on the same
day of the month, every year, for the trouble thou mayest be at. Thou art requested to bring her up with the most studious care and affection, and do not let
her know but that she is thine own relation, until such time as circumstances
may render it necessary, or thou mayest. receive instructions as to the same.
Thou mayest call her Ernnestine. Remember these injunctions, and obey."

" This letter throws not any light upon the subject," said our heroine, after
she had two or three times read it ;—" the characters are written in a male hand
evidently, and the commanding tone in which it is couched, pleases me not.
Thou sayest the stranger who brought me to thy house, was noble and commanding ?"

"He was," replied Hubert, " and a more handsome countenance I have seldom gazed upon ; but his features were impressed with a deep melancholy."

" Thinkest thou, that thou should'st know him again, dear Hubert ?"

" I cannot say that I should, my child;" replied the old man ; " for so many
years have elapsed since the mysterious circumstance took place. But, I had
almost forgotten to tell thee that which strengthens my belief that it was
only to save thee from some terrible fate, that thy parents were induced to take
the step they did."

" Oh, tell me, what was that ?" eagerly inquired Ernnestine.

" After I had admitted the stranger, and I saw the smiling and beauteous
little innocent he had with him," said Hubert, " myself and Maud naturally
evinced considerable surprise ; which he perceiving, informed us that thou wert

the victim of tyranny and cruelty, and that he was endeavouring to save thee from a terrible fate."

"Ah!"—ejaculated Ernnestine, "that doth, indeed seem to confirm thy surmises;—the melancholy appearance of the stranger, too;—should he have been my father!" and at the thought, her bosom heaved with a sensation she had never before experienced, and her eyes lighted up with an expression of mingled delight and sorrow.

"It might have been," observed Hubert, "but still something seems to whisper to me that he was not."

"But hast thou never seen the stranger since that night?" anxiously inquired our heroine.

"Never," answered Hubert.

"And the money which was promised to be remitted to thee yearly for my support?"

"1 received the same sum the following year;—it was left for me in this very parlour;—it was the last."

"Strange," ejaculated Ernnestine; "but yet doth that make it appear that my parents entertained no care for me, after they had once got me off their hands."

"Oh, no, misfortune may have rendered them incapable of fulfilling their promise, my dear child!"

"Or death," solemnly observed our heroine, and tears, which she was unable to restrain, rushed to her eyes. Hubert again snatched her affectionately to his bosom.

"Dear, dear Ernnestine," he exclaimed, "weep not, weep not; should Providence ordain that the mystery of thy birth should never be unravelled, in myself, Maud, Edith, all thou wilt ever find the same fond friends that we have hitherto been to thee; and when the cold grave shall receive this aged form, thank Heaven I have wherewith to——"

"Oh, cease, cease, dear Hubert," sobbed the deeply affected girl;—"long, long may it be ere that melancholy time arrives. But Lord Raymond—"

"Thou lovest him?"

"I do; but," and the maiden hid her blushes in the old man's bosom.

"But, as thou didst love the unfortunate Godfrey?"

"Oh, no, no," cried Ernnestine, weeping bitterly at the remembrance of that headstrong and ill-fated youth who had wholly possessed her heart; "not as I loved him — but with a different feeling ;—a feeling I cannot describe, yet equally powerful ! But, alas !—how hard is my fate!—Every hope—every prospect that my fond imagination cherished, blighted ;—what is there for which I should wish to live ?"

Ernnestine sunk in a chair, and covering her face with her hands, gave way to the violence of the grief which distracted her bosom. Hubert gazed at her for a few minutes with an expression of the deepest sympathy, then paced the room apparently wrapped in profound thought. At length, turning to our heroine, he took her hand gently, and said :—

"Ernnestine, my love, thou seest from the letter which I have shewn thee, how I am restricted from disposing of thy hand."

" I do;—I do," eagerly replied our heroine, "but surely the long silence of those who, probably have a claim upon me, ought to be sufficient to do away with all such scruples, and——"

" I know what thou wouldst say," interrupted Hubert, "and have been seriously thinking on the subject; say, Ernnestine, wilt thou agree to a proposal that I have to make to thee ?"

" Anything, my more than parent," replied our heroine, her eyes sparkling with renewed hope, " anything thou canst propose to me, I feel it is my duty to comply with. Nay, should'st thou command me to bid Lord Raymond despair, sooner than I would cause thee any unhappiness,—painful as it would be to me, I will yield without a murmur to the decree."

" Good, kind girl;" cried the old man, embracing her with the utmost tenderness, and kissing her cheeks ;—" but no, my love, I will not exact any such a promise from thee ; it is a cruelty which I feel, whatever may be the consequence of my conduct to myself, I could not inflict upon thee. I would ask thee to wait for one year only before thou again requesteth me to bestow thine hand upon Raymond, and if before that period no one appears to claim thee, I promise thee that I will no longer withhold my consent."

" Promise thee, dear old man," sobbed the delighted Ernnestine, returning Hubert's warm caresses with equal ardour, " there is nothing that I could refuse thee !—Oh, what a weight of sorrow hast thou removed from my heart. Strictly, cheerfully will I obey thy wishes !"

" I knew thou wouldst, my child," said Hubert, " my gentle Ernnestine, I was certain could never refuse anything to that being, to whom, by the will of Providence, she was in infancy consigned. Enough, enough ; wipe the tears from thine eyes and endeavour to be happy."

Ernnestine looked up in Hubert's venerable countenance with a sweet smile of affection beaming through her tears, and there was more expressed in that one look, than a volume of words could have described.

" And yet there is one thing more that I would request of thee, Ernnestine," said Hubert, after a brief pause.

" Name it, dear Hubert," she demanded, anxiously, " thou hast but to speak thy wishes to command obedience."

" When thou mentionest this interview to Lord Raymond, as doubtless, thou wilt," replied Hubert, " I must beg of thee to enjoin him strictly to keep it confined to his own breast, until the allotted time hath expired, when all may be explained."

" I will do so," returned our heroine, " and fear not but that his lordship will faithfully comply."

At this moment, Maud and Edith made their appearance, and the conversation dropped, Ernnestine conquering her emotion, so that she might not attract their attention, and thus occasion any further conversation upon the subject for the present. Old Hubert, however, made them acquainted with it at another opportunity, and likewise the resolution he had come to, of which they expressed their approbation, although, at the same time, a pang of the most intense sorrow and regret shot through the heart of Edith when she thought of her son, and the ardent affection which she knew had existed between him and the gentle maiden whom fate seemed to have ordained, should become the bride of another.

The next day Lord Raymond hastened on the wings of anxiety to meet Ernnestine at their usual trysting place, impatient to hear the result of her interview with Hubert Clensham. Our heroine recounted to him every particular, exactly as it had occurred, and the promise which Hubert had exacted from her. We shall not detain our readers by attempting to describe the feelings of Lord Raymond as he listened to her, and his joy was equally powerful when he heard the reasonable request which Hubert had made. The despair which had previously began to settle on his heart was banished, and hope and happiness once more shed their influence over him.

" Yes, dearest, loveliest girl !" he cried pressing her fervently to his heart, " thou wilt be mine. Kind hope whispers to me that nothing will interpose to prevent our fates being united together !"

A loud laugh of derision made them both start with astonishment, and Ernnestine clung to Lord Raymond with terror. He looked round, and beheld peering between the foliage at their back, the head of the mysterious monk who had before alarmed them; his cowl being drawn nearly close, concealing all his features, but just suffering his dark and piercing eyes to be seen, which were fixed upon Lord Raymond with a look of the most mysterious meaning. It was but a moment only, and, with another loud laugh, it vanished.

" Again, mysterious being, dost thou appear to me !" exclaimed Lord Raymond, hastily drawing his sword ;—" stay, I command thee. I will know who and what thou art, and thy purpose with me !"

He rushed behind the trees, sword in hand, as he spoke; but the monk was gone, and he returned hastily to Ernnestine, who was so much alarmed at the circumstance that she could scarcely support herself. Lord Raymond endeavoured to calm her fears, and immediately conducted her towards home; where, after some discourse upon the singular event, they separated, and he directed his steps towards the castle, indulging in the reflections to which it was naturally calculated to give rise.

CHAPTER XX.

" No one his face had seen, a veil
Of mystery hung upon his actions,
Dark, and unfathomable !"   THE CHIEFTAIN.

ABOUT this period a great sensation was caused in that part of the country in consequence of the actions of a mysterious individual, who had received the appellation of the *White Knight*, on account of his always appearing in white armour, and mounted on a milk white charger. His figure was tall and powerful, but no one had seen his face, always appearing with his visor down. His name, residence, and real character were equally unknown; yet he was met with in all situations, and at all hours, and had been known to perform deeds of prowess that would seem to give him almost a supernatural power, and the skill with which he wielded his glittering falchion never failed to defeat those whom he encountered. At tilt or tournament the *White Knight* was always sure to appear, and he never failed to surpass every other competitor in the chivalrous sports. He ever appeared in a good cause ; he had once saved the life of the king when attacked by robbers ; and wherever any outrage was endeavoured to be committed, he was almost always sure to make his appearance to protect the injured party.

This mysterious being had caused the utmost curiosity, and many were the conjectures that were formed about him ; but all endeavours to discover his real character had hitherto failed.

Vain had been all the endeavours of persons, whose wonder was excited by this extraordinary individual, to discover who he was, or where he resided, and although many had been set to watch him, and to pursue him, he invariably contrived to elude their utmost vigilance. The king had requested his name, after he had rescued him from the daggers of the robbers, but he declined to furnish him with it, and having seen him in the safe custody of his attendants immediately galloped off as fast as his swift courser could bear him. No wonder, therefore, that all these circumstances should cause especial wonder, and that the *White Knight* should become the universal theme of conversation all over the country.

In the back parlour of the "Flagon," there nightly assembled a select few of the principal inhabitants or tradesmen of the neighbourhood, to converse on the passing events of the day, and to toast in deep potations the health of Ernnestine de Lacy, the "Fayre Mayde of the hostelrye," and the light of our heroine's glances, which ever beamed with kindness, was sufficient to exhilarate the spirits of these goodly bacchanals to such a degree, that they were apt to forget there was such a word as temperance in the English language, though, by the by, it is uncertain whether, at the period of which the history treats, the word had been very clearly extended, or more strictly practised than it is at the present day. Albeit, the frequenters of the little back parlour before mentioned, from the deep libations in which they were in the habit of indulging, were certainly no particular friends of it, either in theory or practice.

The little back parlour was kept exclusively for the assemblage of the select few, Master Hubert Clensham occasionally joining them, and at all times being a welcome companion, for, when their conversational powers flagged, his favourite song of " More Sack," which he sang as merrily as he had been in the habit of doing twenty years before, never failed to raise their spirits, and to set them in a humour which was likely to prove most profitable to the promoter of their hilarity.

Notwithstanding the precaution which Hubert had used to keep the attachment of our heroine and Lord Raymond a secret, by some means, this little clique of jolly individuals soon became acquainted with it, and considerably to his annoyance, it became the principal theme of their conversation in their evening meetings afterwards, and the health and happiness of both Ernnestine and his lordship were pledged so often, that many of them were brought to that state of blessedness, as to be compelled to take up their lodging for the

night at "The Flagon," much to the alarm and anxiety of their wives and families, and the censure of "mine host," who had to bear the blame, although
innocent of the sole cause of their misconduct.

It was a few weeks after the circumstance which we have related in the previous chapter, that the same party were assembled as usual, and Hubert was
in their company. The conversation, much to the relief of the latter, turned
upon the *White Knight,* and the wonderful deeds he had performed, and each
arrogated to himself a sagacity above his fellow, in forming a conjecture as to
who he was, and his real character. One set him down for some great prince
in disguise; another for a madman; a third for a foreign spy; a fourth for an
evil spirit, and a fifth for the very devil himself, and attributed his good actions
merely to the artifices said to be practised by his satanic majesty, the better to
ensnare and secure his victims. Words ran high, and the argument did not
appear likely to be brought to any satisfactory conclusion, when, in the midst
of it, a heavy footfall was heard approaching the room, and before they had
time collect themselves, the door was thrown back on its hinges, and there
stalked into the middle of the apartment a tall figure, so completely enveloped
in a huge mantle, that not a portion of it could be satisfactorily distinguished,
and the countenance was entirely concealed from observation by the mantle being
drawn over the head.

The company trembled with astonishment and consternation, and Hubert was
so confused and surprised, that he was unable to move from his seat, or to ask
the stranger the cause of his intrusion. The guests turned each very pale, and
the terror was not a little increased, when the mysterious-looking object indulged
in a long and sonorous laugh, which reverberated through the building, and then

No. 30

stalked up to the head of the table, at which the individual who considered himself the principal of the party was seated, laid his hand upon his collar, and although he was a stout, burly man, unceremoniously ejected him from his seat, with as much ease as if he had been an infant, and ensconsed himself in it.

The company again looked at each other with increased amazement, and the chattering of teeth and knocking together of knee-pans, became very distinctly audible, whereupon the mysterious stranger once more gave vent to a laugh still louder than the one before. There was now a general move among the affrighted guests, and one by one skulked off, until Hubert was left alone with the mysterious unknown.

Several moments elapsed, and Hubert Clensham remained in his seat, staring vacantly at the stranger, and unable to give utterance to a syllable, but at length the latter made a bit of a movement in his chair, and then a loud and deep-toned voice from under the cloak, exclaimed :—

" Master Hubert Clensham !"

Hubert crossed himself devoutly, mentioned as many names of the different saints in the calendar as he could repeat in about a second and a half, and then said :—

" Heaven preserve me ! marry, and that is me."

" Hubert Clensham !" repeated the stranger.

" What art thou, man or woman, devil or mortal?" demanded Hubert, regaining his usual firmness, a latent idea crossing his mind, that, after all, it might only be one of his neighbours, who had a mind to have a joke at his expense ;—" and why dost thou come hither thus disguised, frightening all my best customers away ?"

" That was the very thing I wanted to do ;" replied the unknown.

" Thou art very kind, truly ; but what was thy reason for wishing to do so ?"

" For the simple reason that my business was with thee alone."

" But if thy purpose is not a bad one, why dost thou not reveal thyself ?"

" Because I have a wish to remain concealed."

" I like not thy manner, and——"

" Hold !" exclaimed the mysterious stranger, grasping Hubert's arm, as he was about to hasten from the apartment, with an iron gripe ;—" I mean thee no harm. Ernnestine——"

" Ah ! what knowest thou of her ?"

" More than thou dost perhaps imagine. It is now about eighteen years since she was consigned to thy care by a young man who sought shelter in thine house."

" Ah !" exclaimed Hubert, starting, and looking more narrowly at the unknown, " how knowest thou that ?"

" No matter. A letter was left with her, in which thou wert strictly enjoined to protect her, being the victim of tyranny and cruelty. It also informed thee that her origin was noble."

" Oh, stranger," said Hubert, anxiously, " thou evidently dost know everything relating to the poor damsel ; in pity, then, to her, I beseech thee to reveal this long hidden secret, and——"

" Not yet,—not yet," interrupted the unknown ; " circumstances will not permit it. She loves Lord Raymond St. Aswolph."

"True,—true—but how knowest thou that?"

"Lord Raymond would make her his bride," continued the stranger, without heeding the question of Hubert; "I have authority to tell thee that thou mayest encourage his suit, and on the day of their nuptials, I promise thee that the secret of the maiden's birth shall be revealed. Remember, none other than Lord Raymond St. Aswolph must be the husband of Ernestine de Lacy!"

Having giving utterance to these words, the unknown hastened from the room before Hubert had recovered from his astonishment ; he, however, quickly followed him, and overtook him at the threshold, where the amazed guests were assembled, and were gazing with looks of the most unfeigned astonishment and awe at a beautiful milk white charger which stood at the door. When they beheld the unknown approach, they fell back with terror depicted in their countenances, and he strode with a stately air from the house, sprang upon the courser's back, and clapping his spurs in its sides, away it flew with the speed of lightning. When he had got to some distance from the house, he threw aside the mantle in which he had been concealed, and there was a simultaneous shout of surprise arose from the beholders, followed by exclamations of,

"The White Knight! The White Knight!"

It was, indeed, that mysterious being who had sought an interview with Hubert Clensham, and before he had time to recover from the astonishment into which the discovery had thrown him, he was out of sight.

The bacchanals looked at one another vacantly, but they were all too much flabbergasted to make use of any observation. There was a subject for their evening discussions! Here was a thing to talk about!—They had actually been in the very company of the veritable, *bona fide* White Knight, the mystery of whose conduct was at that time creating such an extraordinary sensation all over the country! But they recollected it with feelings of horror ; for that he was not a being of this earth, they now one and all agreed. But what could he have come there for ?—And what had passed between him and Hubert ? They must be made acquainted with all the particulars. They walked back to the parlour, thinking that Hubert would follow them, but in that they were disappointed, for Hubert was too much astounded by the circumstances of the evening, to subject himself to their idle scrutiny, and retired to his own private room, where he found old Maud, who, having been taking a comfortable nap in her old arm-chair for the last hour, was ignorant of what had occurred. Hubert quickly made her acquainted with what had taken place, and the amazement evinced by the old woman was as great as may be expected.

"Blessed Virgin!" she ejaculated, "how thou dost surprise me, Hubert! —But art thou certain it was the real, right down earnest White Knight?"

"Positive, Maud," replied her husband.

"And that he talked to thee in the manner thou hast described to me?"

"Word for word."

"Wonderful! wonderful!—This, then, must be some relation to her ;—her father, take my word for it ; and he is some great nobleman,—perhaps a duke or a prince, in disguise ; and our dear, dear Ernnestine will turn out to be a fine lady!"

Tears of joy ran down the poor old woman's cheeks, as these flattering surmises darted upon her imagination, and Hubert was as deeply affected as herself.

"Only to think, too," continued Maud, "only to think that the injunctions he gave thee should so well agree with our wishes, and those of Ernnestine. Oh, how delighted will his lordship be, when he is made acquainted with it!"

"But I think it would be advisable not to let Lord Raymond know anything at all about it," said Hubert, "and I must, therefore, request thee, dame, to be silent upon the subject."

"Well, well! I will do as thou wishest me, Hubert," said the old woman, "but oh, dear! I shall be all impatience until the day of the nuptials of our dear child and his lordship, when the mystery of so many years will be unravelled, and we shall be made acquainted with who Ernnestine really is, and all the particulars about her parents. But, bless me, where can the dear child tarry? —It is getting late, and hark how it rains."

"Yes, it is a rough night," said Hubert, going to the casement and looking out; "but I do not mind the weather, so get me my cloak and hat, and I will go forth in search of her, though, doubtless, she is at the castle, and will stay all night."

Maud gave her husband his hat and cloak, which he put on, and taking a stout oaken staff in his hand, he quitted the inn.

Ernnestine having paid a visit of benevolence and charity to a poor, sick cottager, where she was detained until the evening, was crossing the wood with an intention of going to the Castle of St. Aswolph, which was nearer than her own home, as the sky had become overcast, and portended a coming storm, when she was suddenly alarmed by hearing a shrill whistle, and before she could look round to ascertain from whence it proceeded, she found herself in the rude grasp of a couple of ruffians, whose appearance betokened them to be robbers. She screamed loudly for help, but the fellows making use of the most revolting language, proceeded to force her along, and after struggling with them until she was quite exhausted, she was on the point of swooning, when, suddenly a loud and commanding voice reverberated through the wood, calling upon the wretches to forbear.

"Hold! hold! dastard miscreants, hold, on your lives!" repeated the voice, and the heavy sound of horses' hoofs were heard approaching. The robbers started, and involuntarily resigned their hold of our heroine. At that moment a horseman clad in glittering mail, and mounted upon a snow white steed, was seen to emerge from a deep wilderness of trees, and falchion in hand, galloped fiercely up towards the spot.

"The White Knight! the White Knight!" shouted both the ruffians in a breath, and turning immediately in a contrary direction to that in which he was coming, they fled with the utmost precipitation.

Ernnestine was so astonished, that she was completely rivetted to the spot in which she stood. The mysterious knight approached her with his vizor down, and dismounting from his steed, took her hand gently, and with an air of the utmost respect. She could not help feeling a sensation of dread while in the presence of the mysterious being, and she shrunk back.

"Nay," ejaculated the stranger, in a tone of reproach, "the fair Ernnestine de Lacy hath no cause to fear the White Knight. Most happy am I to have been the means of rescuing you from danger."

"Noble stranger," said our heroine, recovering herself, "whoever thou art, I heartily thank thee for thy kindness."

"Danger may still lurk at hand, fair damsel," said the White Knight, "and if thou wilt accept my proffered services, I will conduct thee to the Castle of St. Aswolph, whither, I presume, thou art going."

Ernnestine became more surprised at the knowledge which the mysterious knight evidently possessed of her, and her intentions, and in spite of all her efforts, she could not conquer the feeling of awe which his appearance had occasioned her. To entrust herself to the care of a stranger, and that, too, one of so much ambiguity, was she considered, not only dangerous, but imprudent; and yet, how could she refuse? or, if his designs against her were evil, she had no power effectually to resist him. The knight seemed to penetrate her thoughts, and repeated his assurances.

"I will but convey thee to the portals of the castle," he said, "and will then leave thee. Wilt thou not trust me, lady?"

Ernnestine made no answer, but suffered herself to be lifted on to the saddle; the knight mounted behind her, and setting forward at the full speed of his fleet courser, the Castle of St. Aswolph soon appeared in sight. Having reached the gates he dismounted, and assisting our heroine to alight, he blew a loud blast on the horn, and then turning to Ernnestine, he bent one knee to the earth, took her hand, pressed it to his lips, and before she could withdraw it, he placed upon her finger a curiously-wrought ring. In an instant afterwards, he bounded on the back of the horse, waved his hand to our heroine gracefully, and before she could recover from the surprise and confusion into which his remarkable conduct had thrown her, he was out of sight.

Ernnestine remained transfixed to the spot, filled with the most indescribable astonishment at the singularity of the adventure, and gazed into the wood in the direction which the mysterious white knight had taken, completely bewildered and amazed by his manner and the words he had made use of; but much more at his last action, which was so sudden that she had not time to return the ring, which to accept from a stranger she considered was not only highly improper, but might be fraught with danger. She looked at the ring, which was a very handsome one, and curiously worked; and when she took the whole of the circumstances into consideration, she could not help thinking that there was more intended in this simple event than might appear at first sight, and that the mysterious stranger was thoroughly acquainted with her she could not entertain the least doubt, from the familiar tone in which he addressed her; and a variety of strange thoughts were beginning to crowd upon her brain when the portals of the castle were opened, and she was admitted.

She made her way immediately to the apartment in which Lady Celestine, her son, and daughter, usually sat, and found them all three there assembled. They arose on her entrance, and welcomed her with their usual kindness; but immediately noticing the agitation of her manner, they requested an explanation of it. Ernnestine, in as few words as possible, explained to them the adventure she had met with, and their wonder may very well be imagined.

" The White Knight," ejaculated Lord Raymond, while a slight scowl passed across his brow. " In vain have I racked my brain to endeavour to imagine who he is ; and yet, if I were inclined to be superstitious, much as his noble deeds are vaunted, I should have ample cause to look upon him with caution, if not dread."

" Ah ! what mean you ?" demanded Lady Celestine.

" No matter—no matter," said Lord Raymond, recollecting himself. " Thou wouldst only smile at me were I to mention particulars ; and, indeed, I am ashamed that I should have deigned to give the subject a second thought."

" At any rate," observed Marguerite, " we should feel greatly indebted to the gallant stranger for having rescued Ernnestine from the ruffians ; and I hope we may some time have an opportunity of personally returning to him our acknow-ledgments."

" Aye," observed Lord Raymond, who had been deeply immersed in thought upon the subject; " but why art thou looking so intently at thine hand, Ernnestine ?"

" I have not yet told you the whole of this mysterious incident," replied our heroine; " on leaving me, the stranger suddenly placed upon my finger this ring, and——"

" A ring !" interrupted his lordship, a glow of anger and astonishment crimsoning his cheeks,—" strange, unparalleled effrontery ! Let me see it."

He took Ernnestine's hand hastily as he spoke, and removed the ring from her finger ; but the moment his eye fell upon it his countenance changed, and the extreme emotion he betrayed filled them with the utmost amazement. He examined it minutely, and, as he did so, his cheeks became pale and red by turns, and his form trembled violently. He walked to the other side of the apartment with his eyes still fixed upon the ring; and, after a pause, he exclaimed, in a voice which evinced the great emotion of his mind :—

" By Heaven ! it is the very same. I cannot be mistaken ! What can this event portend ?—and how, after the lapse of so many years should it——"

He paused, and returning to his seat became for a short time buried in thought, and unmindful of the astonishment and curiosity which the singularity of his behaviour had excited.

" What is the meaning of this, dear Raymond ?" at length said his mother ; " why does the sight of that ring cause in thee so much agitation ?"

" Mother," replied Lord Raymond, " question me not; at present I cannot answer thee. This ring—oh ! never did I expect to see it again ! And the mysterious stranger—oh ! who can he be ? how could it have come into his possession ? and what could have been his motive for placing it on the finger of Ernnestine ? When will the marvellous events that so rapidly succeed each other be satisfactorily explained ? Ernnestine, this ring must remain in my possession."

" And what can be thy reason for wishing to retain it, Raymond ?" eagerly inquired Lady Celestine.

" Oh, a most powerful one," replied his lordship. " I would not part with it again for mines of wealth. Thou canst have no idea of the important matters, at least to me, which the possession of this simple bauble may be the means of bringing to light."

" The ambiguity of thy words and behaviour, Raymond," said Lady Celestine, " alarm me. Oh! why not explain ?"

" Not now; not now !" returned Lord Raymond; " but the time may not be far distant, when it will be in my power to divulge everything. Would that I could ascertain who this White Knight really is. But I will not rest until I have done so."

Lord Raymond then made an excuse to retire from the room for a short time, and left the females to converse upon the mysterious circumstance, and to endeavour to form a conjecture as to the cause of the violent agitation which his lordship had betrayed on seeing the ring. Various were their surmises upon the subject, but each was equally unsatisfactory; but Lady Celestine and her daughter could not help believing that it was connected with that event which had depressed the spirits of Lord Raymond for so many years, and through which secret they were never able to penetrate.

In a short time, Lord Raymond returned to the apartment, and, although he evidently endeavoured to appear more composed, he could not succeed in concealing from the eyes of all three of the females, that his mind was still very unhappy.

" Ernnestine will remain at the castle to-night, I presume," said he ; " and I will despatch a vassal to her friends, to apprise them of her safety."

" No," said our heroine, " the storm has subsided, and I have a particular wish not to defer my return home till the morning."

" Of course, then, it would be useless my attempting to persuade thee further, my love," said his lordship, " and I am, therefore, prepared to accompany thee."

Our heroine immediately arose to depart, and, attended by his lordship, quitted the castle.

On their way home, Lord Raymond questioned Ernnestine more particularly about the White Knight, and the words he had spoken to her, but she had already told him everything.

" But, when he placed the ring on thy finger, dear Ernnestine," he inquired, " said he nothing then ?"

" Not a word," replied our heroine.

" And couldst thou not observe his features ?"

" His visor was down, and, therefore, I could not."

" And had no means of judging whether he was old or young ?"

" Certainly not ; although, from his figure and active bearing, I should imagine the latter," answered Ernnestine.

" By Heaven, I will by some means discover him !" exclaimed Lord Raymond; but he had scarcely given utterance to the words, when the snorting of a steed was heard near them, and looking up, by the broad light of the moon, they beheld, standing before them, looking like a spectre, or a statue of marble, the mysterious subject of their discourse. Ernnestine clung closer to Lord Raymond, and could not help giving utterance to an exclamation of terror, and his lordship was so taken by surprise, that he had not the power of moving or speaking.

"Thou wilt know who I am ere long, Lord Raymond St. Aswolph," said the White Knight, in a hollow voice; "the discovery thou art so anxious for will be made, and thou wilt then have cause to tremble. Mark me! mark me!"

"Mysterious being!" cried St. Aswolph, "that comest in such suspicious form, who art thou, and why should I tremble at thee? If thou art my foe, reveal thyself, and give me an opportunity of affording thee satisfaction."

A loud and scornful laugh was the only answer which was returned to this demand, and the White Knight, galloping with the speed of lightning from the spot, was out of sight in a moment.

Ernnestine was filled with terror at the threats which the white knight had uttered towards Lord Raymond, while he was so much surprised, that he was unable for a short time, to speak a word, or to offer to move from the spot which they were standing.

"I seek in vain to fathom this," he said, at last, "unless this White Knight as he is called, is some wild character, acting alone from caprice, and a wish to sport with the terrors of others. He may, however, have reason to repent his humour some day or other."

"Whoever he is, and whatever may be the motives for his actions," said Ernnestine, "he certainly has succeeded in rendering himself an object of wonder and awe."

"He is some base impostor," cried Lord Raymond, warmly, "and should we ever encounter each other again, and under more favourable circumstances, I will learn who he is, or perish in the attempt."

"Oh, my lord," said Ernnestine, alarmed, "beware of what thou dost; thou mayest have a more powerful and dangerous enemy to contend with than thou dost imagine."

"Why should I fear one whom I know not?" said St. Aswelph; "and yet the ring," he continued, "how could that have fallen into his possession?"

"Come, my lord," observed Ernnestine, seeking to arouse him from his lethargy, "the night air begins to blow cold; prithee let us hasten on our way to the inn, and leave the unravelling of this ambiguous affair until some future period."

Lord Raymond once more took her arm in silence, and they hastened from the spot. They shortly afterwards reached the "Flagon," where both Hubert and Maud were very glad to see them return in safety, and he scarcely allowed them to be seated, when he detailed to them all the particulars of the visit of the White Knight, and the injunctions which he had given him. This more than ever added to the surprise of our heroine and Lord Raymond. It was very evident that the White Knight was fully acquainted with the history of Ernnestine, and that he had good reasons for taking such an interest in her fate; but yet he had said that he was the friend of Ernnestine, and his

conduct proved him to be so, but his injunctions that none other than Lord Raymond should become the husband of our heroine, seemed so completely at variance with the threats he had held out to the former, that it was quite impossible to understand them.

"And hast thou no recollection of the stranger?" inquired Lord Raymond of Hubert.

"How could I, my lord," answered Hubert, "when his features were so entirely concealed from view?"

"Dost thou not think it likely that he is the same man who brought Ernestine to the inn and left her in thy charge?" interrogated his lordship.

"It may be," answered Hubert; "but still I had no recollection of his voice."

"Oh, I'm certain the White Knight is no mortal man," ejaculated Maud, "or he never could perform the deeds he does. Why, is he not here, there, and everywhere, and all at the same moment?"

"Psha! if he is a devil, dame," said Hubert, "he is a very good sort of a one, for he is noted only for noble actions. Did he not preserve Ernestine this evening from the robbers, and—"

"Yes, yes," answered Maud, impatiently interrupting him, "and did he not afterwards threaten his lordship, which I cannot conceive to be a very noble action, marry can I not? especially as Lord Raymond is so generally and deservedly esteemed; for who is there, I should like to know—"

"There, there, my good dame," interrupted his lordship, who was not at all willing to hear his good actions vaunted; "we shall not be able to fathom this mystery to night, depend upon it; and although he did threaten me, he cannot seriously be mine enemy, or he never would urge my union with the beauteous Ernnestine. We must endeavour to wait patiently until the day of the nuptials, when we shall see whether or not he will keep his promise by unravelling the secret which so deeply interests us all."

Although Lord Raymond affected to be satisfied upon this subject, he was very far from really feeling so, and shortly afterwards took his departure from the inn, and directed his steps towards the castle.

He walked forward in a pensive mood, ruminating upon what had taken place within the last few hours, and was just penetrating through the deepest recesses of the wood, when he felt his arm suddenly arrested, and in an instant beheld Hal of the Glen standing by his side.

CHAPTER XXI.

" Dread, unlook'd-for, like a visitant
    From th' other world, he comes as if to haunt
    The guilty soul."
                                        T. Moore.

THE eyes of the sorcerer were fixed upon the countenance of Lord Raymond with a glance of fire, which seemed to penetrate to the very soul, and made him tremble involuntarily beneath their unearthly influence, and a demoniacal and malicious grin o'erspread his frightful features, which could not fail to inspire the beholder with horror. Lord Raymond looked up to him as he stood in the broad glare of the moonlight, and endeavoured to speak, but could not; and at length Hal of the Glen, after a fiendish laugh, which made the wood re-echo again, said :—

" Lord Raymond, we meet again; once more I cross thy path; why dost thou tremble in my presence ?"

" Sorcerer !" cried Lord Raymond, as the mysterious and awful being released him from his hold; " why dost thou again obstruct me ? — What would'st thou with me ?"

" To bid thee beware of the White Knight; to beware of the Grey Friar !" answered Hal.

" Ah ! fiend, if such thou art," cried Lord Raymond, " tell me why I should fear them ?"

" Because they are thy mortal foes."

" For what reason ?" demanded his lordship; " if thou hast the power to answer me, tell me who they are, and why should I fear them ?"

" I have before warned thee to beware of them," returned the magician, " but time alone must unravel who they are; that time quickly approaches, and that which will then be revealed to thee, will make thee wretched for ever, if thou dost not avoid the misery into which thou art about to plunge."

"Demon or mortal, whichever thou art," cried Lord Raymond ; "thou mockest me! Why am I selected to be the victim of thy sorceries?—Begone! I will not listen to thee!"

"Thou wilt repent not having done so!" said Hal of the Glen, turning to depart; "I tell thee again thou standest on the brink of a precipice down which, if thou plungest, perpetual misery to thee is inevitable. I go, proud lord; thou scornest my warning, and, therefore, let the White Knight triumph in the success of the scheme he hath wrought for thy destruction!"

"Stay! stay! mysterious, awful being," exclaimed Lord Raymond, as Hal of the Glen was about to quit the spot ;—"stay! whatever thy purpose, I will once more listen to thee!"

The magician laughed awfully, which was returned in a hundred echoes through the deep-entangled wood.

"Torture me not," ejaculated his lordship, as an indefinite feeling came over him ;—"tell me, if thou canst, how I may avoid the evils thou dost prognosticate to me?"

"If I canst," repeated Hal, "dost thou, then, still doubt my power?"

"No, no, I will trust thee; but keep me not in suspense. Tell me, how am I to avoid it?"

"By not making Ernnestine thy bride ; by retracting the vows thou hast made to her!"

"Retract my vows! Forget Ernnestine! Never!"

"Then take the consequences; and curse thy mad impetuosity when it is too late;" said Hal of the Glen, and his eyes gleamed yet more fiercely than ever.

"Impostor!" exclaimed Lord Raymond; "thou would'st deceive me, and urge me to abandon the only earthly happiness upon which my hopes are fixed."

"Rash fool!" thundered forth the voice of the magician, "I tell thee if thou dost persist in uniting thyself to Ernnestine, thou wilt bring upon thyself the most inexpressible misery, and she will afterwards curse thee, and look upon thee with horror and disgust."

"Impossible!" cried the distracted Lord Raymond, "what but bliss the most unspeakable can attend a union with the beauteous Ernnestine?"

"Wilt follow me to the glen, and I will shew thee?" returned Hal.

"I will; lead on," replied Lord Raymond, and drawing his sword, he made a motion for the sorcerer to proceed.

"Attend me, then, and if thou canst, satisfy thy doubts," said Hal.

Lord Raymond folded his ample cloak closer around him, and Hal having once more turned to look at him, plunged into the deepest recesses of the wood, with a rapidity which rendered it difficult for the former to keep up with him. Ever and anon the awful and mysterious being paused, to enable his lordship to approach nearer to him, and then he again started off at his former speed, his gaunt form seeming to skim over the earth without his feet touching the ground; and as he burst through the different openings in the wood, the broad light of the moon reflected upon him with a ghastly and supernatural effect. Several times Lord Raymond was compelled to pause to take breath, and he was frequently half-inclined to turn back, when a loud laugh from Hal would seem to mock his fears, and again he pursued his way, with a determination to proceed with the singular adventure to the close, regardless of the consequences that might result from it.

At length they reached the glen, and there the darkness was so impenetrable, that he lost sight of his awful conductor, and again paused, unknowing which way to proceed. This delay, however, was only brief, several blue and sickly lights danced before him, and he once more saw the form of the magician, who motioned him on, at the same moment a number of unearthly voices sang the following words :—

> " Follow, follow, through the glen,
>   Seldom trod by mortal men ;
>   Follow, follow, through the gloom,
>   If thoud'st hear thy future doom.
>   Follow, follow, fear avaunt,
>   Dare the wizard's fearful haunt.
>   Fear not fiend, or goblin sprite,
>   Stalking 'mid the gloom of night.
>   Let resolution onward goad,
>   Fear not snake, or slimy toad.
>   Follow, follow, through the glen,
>   Seldom trod by mortal men !"

Lord Raymond was prepared for the terrors that followed these words, and boldly he plunged on his way, amid the most dreadful shrieks and howling, the hideous grinning of terrific phantoms that flitted around him, and all the other fearful paraphernalia which had characterised his former visit to the awful haunt of the sorcerer.

At last he arrived at the deepest recesses of the glen, where Hal performed his mystic orgies, and having formed the magic circle, Lord Raymond stepped boldly into it, and the incantation commenced.

Around and around the blazing caldron the magician danced in the most wild and frantic manner, waving his wand above his head, and muttering strange unintelligible sounds, and as he did so, Lord Raymond heard the following words sang by a number of demoniacal voices :—

> " Again, again the magic spell
>   We weave, the future to foretell ;
>   Round again the caldron go,
>   And in its flames the charms how throw !
>   A nail from murderer's finger torn,
>   Hair from monkish beard shorn,
>   Lizard's blood, and adder's sting,
>   In the caldron quickly fling !—
>   Round again the caldron go,
>   And in its flames the charms now throw !"

At the end of every line of this wild incantation, the magician threw something into the caldron, and each time the flames blazed higher, and the noises in the glen became more terrific ; but Lord Raymond having recovered himself from the first shock, remained standing, firm and undaunted in the magic circle, and watched the actions of Hal of the Glen with the utmost attention and anxiety. At length, a loud peal of thunder rolled above his head, the lights all became extinguished, and the noises ceased. Lord Raymond felt a curious sensation creeping through his veins, followed by a fluttering of something around him. He kept his eyes fixed upon the spot where Hal had stood, and suddenly a pale light seemed to issue from the earth at the back of the glen ; solemn music was heard, and Lord Raymond the following moment beheld the magic mirror, whose power the magician had consulted on his former visit to the glen, and before it stood Hal waving his wand, and giving utterance to words of mysterious import, but quite unintelligible to his lordship. He fixed his eyes anxiously and intently upon the mirror, and in a short time the mist which had before obscured its surface disappeared, and Lord Raymond beheld the interior of a gothic chapel, exactly resembling the one in the Castle of St. Aswolph, fitted up as if for the performance of some solemn ceremony. A priest was standing behind the altar, and towards which, directly afterwards, two figures approached, followed by bridesmaids and others, and Lord Raymond recognized in the bridegroom, an exact representation of himself, and in that of the bride, Ernnestine. They knelt before the altar ; the ceremony was performed without interruption, and Lord Raymond's bosom was swelling with extacy when he thus beheld the realization of his wishes foretold in the vision, when, in an instant, a piercing shriek was heard, and there rushed between them a female form, whose well-remembered features filled the mind of the gazer with horror, and tearing them asunder, she exclaimed :—

"Incestuous wretch ! she's mine ! thine !—And thou art accursed for ever !"

At the same moment two more figures appeared in the magic mirror, one of which tore Ernnestine to his bosom, —it was Godfrey de Lacy! The other was the White Knight, who, raising his vizor, revealed a countenance which Lord Raymond had never expected to behold again, and pointed with a fiendish smile of triumph, first at Godfrey and Ernnestine, and then at the woman, who had first appeared after the celebration of the ceremony.

"Fiend ! sorcerer !" shouted Lord Raymond, unable any longer to restrain the expression of his emotions ;—"what means this ?—Let me understand this mysterious visoin !—I——"

The charm was broken—loud thunder pealed through the glen—forked lightning flashed around—the mirror and every other object faded from the sight, and immediately afterwards Lord Raymond was left involved in total darkness.

He felt a choking sensation at his chest; a dreadful pain shot through his head ; his brain seemed to whirl round ; his limbs tottered beneath him, and he sunk in a state of insensibility to the earth.

How long he had thus remained he had no means of forming the least conjecture, for when he again became conscious, he found that the glen was still involved in the same impenetrable gloom. He felt deadly cold, and his limbs were completely benumbed—so much so, that some time elapsed before he was able to rise from the earth. He did, however, manage to do so at last, and tried to grope his way out of the glen ; but this was a task of no ordinary difficulty, and it was some time before he could accomplish it. When he reached the wood again, he found that the shades of night were fading away from the horizon; and, apprehensive of the terrors which his long absence from the castle would be sure to occasion his mother and sister, he was hurrying forward, when his way was obstructed by a tall figure, and looking up he again beheld the mysterious monk who had so repeatedly before crossed his path. His cowl was drawn close over his face as usual ; and, in his usual attitude, with his arms folded across his chest, he stood as if he was gazing with a sentiment of exultation and hatred upon Lord Raymond.

Wound up to a pitch beyond all endurance, Lord Raymond exclaimed—

" Tormentor, that with mysterious solemnity so often appearest before me, to distract and bewilder my senses, again art thou here ! Reveal thyself and thy purpose, or dread the vengeance of one whom thou hast frequently threatened !"

To this the mysterious monk only replied by a loud laugh of derision, and still retained his position unmoved.

" Insolent wretch ! darest thou mock me ? By the saints, then, I will know who thou art; I will force the secret from thee."

He drew his sword as he spoke, and rushed fiercely upon the monk, who met him with the most extraordinary coolness ; wrenched the weapon from his grasp, and, seizing him in his arms, dashed him violently to the earth, without any apparent exertion on his part. Burning with rage and shame, Lord Raymond with much difficulty raised himself from the earth, and looked around him, prepared to make a second attack upon his unknown foe, but he was gone.

" Confusion !" he exclaimed; " gone ! Am I for ever to be made the sport of a wretch who seems to delight in and mock at my rage and suffering?"

Again he looked around him, but could not see anything of the monk. His sword was left behind upon the grass, which he picked up and sheathed ; then, filled with a variety of feelings of the most painful description, he quitted the spot, and went on his way towards the castle of St. Aswolph.

On his arrival at the castle, as might have been expected, he found his mother and Lady Marguerite in a state of great anxiety at his absence, and his return was a most important relief to their minds. Of course they were anxious to be made acquainted with the reason of his being away from the castle the whole of the night, and could see from the paleness of his countenance, and his agitated manner, that something particular had occurred to disturb him ; but he did not satisfy them as to the real circumstances that had happened to him, and made some excuse, the best he could think of at the moment, to account for his absence, and although they were far from being satisfied, it was all they could elicit from him.

The extraordinary scene he had witnessed in the glen, and the visions conjured up by the supernatural art of Hal, made an extraordinary impression upon the mind of Lord Raymond ; and he in vain endeavoured to banish them from his thoughts, still less was he able to comprehend them. He racked his brain in vain, and now regretted that he had been prevailed upon by Hal to visit the glen, and to mix himself up with his infernal sorceries and incantations.

He determined not to mention a word of the adventure to Ernnestine, well convinced as he was how greatly it would alarm her, and with this resolution he struggled violently to overcome his emotions, so that he might not betray, by the agitation of his manner, anything which was likely to excite her curiosity.

There was, however, more difficulty in fulfilling this resolution than he had at first imagined, for such was the effect that his singular and impressive adventure had made upon his mind, and so deeply did the remarkable prognostications of Hal of the Glen prey upon his mind, and also the encounter he had had with the grey monk, that they kept him in a constant state of agitation. Who the latter individual could really be, and the motives for his extraordinary conduct, he was at a loss to conceive; but, in spite of all his efforts to the contrary, he could not help thinking on him with a feeling of the most unconquerable dread, and was determined to leave no means untried to discover who he was, and to unravel the mystery of his conduct.

The whole of that day he passed at the castle, keeping principally to his own room, for he was too much agitated to enter into the society of his mother and sister, and he was fearful to see Ernnestine, lest he should not be able sufficiently to conquer his feelings to keep concealed from her the circumstance which we have been detailing.

As we have before observed, Lady Celestine and her daughter were both very much disturbed by the mystery of his lordship's behaviour, and felt convinced that something had occurred to him; but they were fearful of questioning him, thinking that, in all probability, it would but increase his agitation, and throw him into one of those paroxysms of intense grief they had frequently witnessed some years before, soon after his return from abroad, and the occasion of which they had never been able to fathom; and that his present emotion sprang from the same source, they were fully disposed to imagine.

Although Lord Raymond did not leave the castle, he sent a domestic to "The Flagon," to enquire after Ernnestine, and to make an excuse for not seeing her that day, giving, as the reason, that he had some particular business to attend to; and with this message, of course, our heroine was satisfied.

"But am I not weak to let this wild adventure disturb my mind?" he soliloquized, as he traversed his apartment, and after his mind had been for some time brooding upon the circumstances; "why should I think seriously upon the predictions of this Hal of the Glen, as he has chosen to call himself, who may be an impostor, after all, taking advantage of the credulous, and delighting in distracting their minds? But no," he added, after a pause, "he cannot be an impostor. No mortal man could perform the things that I have seen him do. The visions raised by his awful incantations ought to be sufficient to convince me of his supernatural powers, and to make me place the firmer reliance upon his prognostications. And the frightful phantoms I saw in the glen—all—all strengthen that conviction which I now feel it impossible for my mind to reject. Who, then, is this mysterious monk? Is he the same individual as the White Knight? and if he is, why should he thus continually obtrude himself upon my presence, and threaten me with his vengeance? There was but one man who—but why should I think of him? the cold grave has long since confined his mouldering remains; and even had he been living, I feel certain that were we to meet again, instead of his proving my enemy, I should be able to convince him how much he wronged me by his suspicions, and how severely I have suffered for any indiscretion of which I may have been guilty. Oh, Marian, Marian!"

Here his lordship's agitation became so violent that he was unable to proceed, and traversed the apartment, beating his breast, and at intervals muttering incoherent sentences, that sufficiently proved the mental agony he was undergoing.   At length he threw himself into a chair, and, leaning his head upon his hand, he gave himself up entirely to the intensity of his dismal thoughts.   He brooded over the past events of his life—events which he had kept secretly confined to his own breast; and at times, he reproached himself for the imprudence of which he had been guilty, and then partially reconciled his mind by endeavouring to believe that there were many extenuating circumstances, and upon that point he at length succeeded in becoming more composed than he had been for some time.   His thoughts then reverted to Ernnestine, and the trouble which was predicted to himself if he were to persist in making her his wife; but the utter improbability of this ever being realized was so strong, that it was impossible for him to think upon it with any degree of patience.

"Ernnestine be the cause of bringing misery upon my head !" he exclaimed ; "never !—it could not be !   It is a base libel upon her gentle and virtuous nature to encourage such an idea for a moment, and I will drive it from my mind.   Ernnestine, thou shalt—thou must be mine, and I will brave the consequences, whatever they may be !"

No sooner had Lord Raymond spoken the latter words, than again that loud, scornful, and almost unearthly laugh which he had heard in the morning, smote his ears.   He started to his feet with astonishment, and, gazing in the direction from whence it had proceeded, no language can describe his amazement and agitation, when he beheld, standing at no great distance from him, the tall figure of the mysterious monk.

He was fixed in his usual attitude, with his arms folded across his chest, and so closely was his cowl drawn over his face, that all that could be seen were his large, black, and powerfully-expressive eyes, that were fixed upon Lord Raymond with a look which we are completely at a loss to describe.

His lordship was quite paralyzed at this unexpected appearance, and stood gazing with a vacant stare upon the monk, unable to move, or to utter a syllable.   The mysterious visitor seemed to enjoy his astonishment and alarm, and once more he laughed, in a voice of derision and exultation.

He had entered the room by a sliding panel, which opened with a spring, and which he had not again closed; but in what manner had he gained access to the castle, and by what means could he have become acquainted with the apartment in which Lord Raymond was, and the manner in which to effect his secret entrance ?—These were the thoughts that darted upon the brain of Lord Raymond in a moment, and before he could utter a word; but these were questions that he would afterwards find a difficulty in solving to his satisfaction.

"By Heaven !" he cried at last, "this must be some wild delusion !   My eyes must deceive me !   Again dost thou present thyself to me, mysterious being !   Man or devil !—reveal thyself; I am ready to encounter any horror rather than endure this suspense."

"For awhile longer, Lord Raymond St. Aswolph," said the monk, in a deep and hollow-toned voice; "for awhile longer thou must endure thy suspense; but,

fear not, the mystery will be shortly unravelled, though not much to thy satisfaction!"

"Strange, ambiguous man, if man thou art," exclaimed Lord Raymond,
"again I ask thee, why dost thou so often appear to me?"

"Because I delight to torture thee," replied the monk.

Lord Raymond placed his hand upon the hilt of his sword, but another loud
and scornful laugh from the awful visitor arrested his purpose.

"Idiot!" cried the supposed monk, "keep thy weapon in its sheath; thou hast
already seen its inutility when opposed to me. It is not thy life I seek, or I have
had plenty of opportunites of accomplishing my wishes, and thou wouldst long
ere this have been an inmate of the tomb. No! I seek a more terrible revenge
than that; my vengeance could not be satiated by thy death alone."

"And why shouldst thou seek to revenge thyself upon me?" demanded Lord
Raymond, still remaining fixed to the spot on which he was standing, and gazing
upon the monk with a feeling of awe which he found it impossible to conquer.

"Because I am, and have reason to be thy mortal enemy," answered the
monk; "beware, Lord Raymond, thy time is coming—quickly coming! And then
it will be my turn to triumph and exult over the misery—the shame—the maddening torture I shall see thee endure."

The monk made a move towards the secret entrance as he spoke, waving his
hand in a menacing manner towards his lordship.

"By Heavens! thou shalt not quit this place until I know who thou art!" cried
Lord Raymond, acting upon the impulse of his excited feelings, drawing his
sword, and rushing towards the mysterious man. The former was about to dart

upon him, when he seized his arm with an iron gripe, and wresting the sword from his hand, dashed it to the floor, and, laying hold of Lord Raymond with the same ease as he had before done in the morning, he laid him prostrate.

Burning with indignation, Lord Raymond arose again, as quickly as the shock he had received would permit him, but the fictitious monk was gone, and closed the panel after him.

"Even at the very hazard of my life !" cried St. Aswolph, " I will pursue thee."

He touched the secret spring as he spoke, and dashing through the aperture, bounded like lightning through the suite of rooms beyond, the open doors of which pointed out the way the monk had fled. When he arrived at the end of the gallery, he thought he caught a glimpse of his person, turning the angle at the bottom of the staircase, and hastily descending, he looked around him, but could not see the least signs of him ; and not knowing which way to proceed, and thinking of the uselessness of his doing so, as he had no doubt but the object of his pursuit had gained the outside of the castle by that time, he abandoned it.

He made his way to the old and faithful porter at the gate, and inquired whether he had seen any person answering the description of the monk pass in or out. The old man seemed surprised at the question, especially when he noticed the agitated manner of his lord, and immediately replied in the negative, with which answer Lord Raymond was satisfied, and concluded that his singular visitor knew of a secret entrance to the castle, by which means he had been enabled to make his appearance before him, without the knowledge of any other person, and without any fear of his retreat being cut off. He returned to his chamber in a state of mind which may easily be conceived, and soon became immersed in a strain of reflections of the most bewildering description.

CHAPTER XXII.

" And wailing shrieks were heard
    When the black mantle of the night was spread
    Around. And the owl screech'd,
    And ghastly phantoms were seen to glide
    In the pale moonbeams, 'mid
    The crumbling ruins of that dreary pile." —ETHELRIDA.

IT was night, and the party of gossippers we have before described as frequenters of the back parlour of the hostelrie of Master Hubert Clensham, were assembled as usual, with the exception of one individual, whose absence was considerably missed by them, as he happened to be the most important and talkative personage amongst them ; and upon an average being capable of drinking about as much as three of them, the landlord was one who had not the leats cause to regret that he was not present.

Various conjectures were formed, and it was at last concluded that the absentee was ill; and they had just proposed that a deputation should depart straightway to his residence, when the door was suddenly burst open, and the person about whom they were so much concerned, rushed in, pale, trembling, and his teeth chattering in the most violent manner. He sunk into a chair, and staring about him, his knees knocked together, and, in fact, he presented one of the most perfect pictures of terror that could possibly be imagined.

His associates stared at him in amazement, and then they all together enquired what had happened to alarm him in such a manner. He made several efforts to reply, but they were all ineffectual; he opened his mouth very wide, looked remarkably stupid, and found it impossible to give utterance to a syllable.

"In the name of all the blessed saints in the calendar, Gregory," repeated Hubert Clensham, "what has happened to thee? What hath occurred to scare thee thus?"

Gregory once more opened his mouth, and made an effort to return an answer to this interrogatory; but he failed, and, if possible, looked more frightened than ever.

"Something particular must have taken place to cause Master Gregory to be, in such a condition as this," said another of the company.

One who, in spite of the state of suspense and curiosity into which they were all thrown by this remarkable circumstance, ventured to surmise that he had met his wife, knowing that she was a bit of a termagant; and a fourth party thought that perhaps he had encountered the White Knight, who they now all set down for a supernatural being; but none of their conjectures appeared to be right.

"Oh, friends! oh, dear! oh, dear!" at last Gregory found power to exclaim; and they all opened their ears, anxious to learn the whole particulars of the cause of his emotion.

"What's the matter, man?" asked Hubert, impatiently. "Have thy senses left thee?"

"Oh, no, good Master Hubert," answered Gregory, "my senses have not left me, although I have had enough to make them."

"What do you mean? Why don't you explain?" asked three or four voices at once.

"Oh, dear! I will never pass that way again; I will never more venture near that place, if I should get half the kingdom," said Gregory.

"What place are you alluding to?" asked Hubert Clensham.

"The ruins of the castle of St. Alwyn," said Gregory; "the late retreat of Osmond and his gang. Oh, dear! oh, dear!"

"What have the ruins to do with your alarm?" inquired one of the party.

"What have they to do with it!" cried the terrified man; "why, everything. Oh! such a sight, I shall never forget it to my dying day!"

"What, have you seen something?"

"Seen something! The Holy Virgin keep me from having such another sight, and from hearing, also, the fearful sounds that I have done this night. My dear friends, as true as I am a sinner, the ruins of St. Alwyn Castle are haunted. I have seen a—a—"

"A what, Gregory?"

"A ghost!—Oh, dear!"

"A ghost?"

"Ay, I am certain that it is either a ghost or a devil; or else the ruins ar haunted by a whole legion of evil spirits. I really do think that the ghosts c all the robbers who lost their lives when the awful conflagration took place haunt the ruins. Oh, dear!"

"The saints preserve us! you don't say so, Gregory!" exclaimed the othe guests, looking more terrified than they had done before.

"But I do say so," returned Gregory, "and I think so too. If they had acte right, they would have razed the ruins to the earth, and erected a monastery o the site; that would have driven all the hobgoblins away, I'll warrant."

"Well, well, but thou hast not yet told us what thou hast seen," said Hubert.

"I shudder with horror when I think of it," returned Gregory, looking roun the room, as if he feared and expected to behold some frightful object.

"Well, do tell us the particulars of this adventure, and then we shall b better able to judge how far it is true, or whether you have suffered your ow timid imagination to overcome you," remarked one of the individuals who wer present.

"My timid imagination!" cried Gregory, becoming rather incensed—"wha do you mean by that? I will let you know that I have all the courage whicl mortal man ought to possess; but I do not pretend to be particularly partial t the society of hobgoblins and evil spirits; and if that is your taste, you will fin plenty of company to your mind, I have no doubt, at the ruins of the castle of St Alwyn."

"Come, a truce with this waste of time," remarked Hubert Clensham; "what is the use of quarrelling upon this subject? We do not suppose that thou would'st tell us an untruth, Gregory; but we thought, perhaps, thy eyes migh deceive thee. But thou art such a while before thou wilt satisfy our curiosity that it is quite enough to put us out of all sort of patience."

"Well, then," said Gregory, after he had refreshed his "inward man," ir order to give himself more courage for the task he had alloted to himself, "al of ye draw your chairs closer to mine and listen to me."

His friends and associates did as he desired them: and then, having for abou the hundredth time taken a survey of the room, fearful that his eyes might en- counter some ghastly object, he began:—

"You must know," said he, "that it was very particular business which called me to the vicinity of the ruins, or you may rest assured that I should not have gone near them; for the castle of St. Alwyn was not any favorite place of mine before its destruction, neither, I dare say, was it that of any person present. The business I went upon occupied me longer than I expected it would have done; and it was night and pitch dark before I started from the house of my friend, and as I should be compelled to pass the ruins, I did not feel myself very comfortable, and that's speaking the truth, although I should not have minded so much if I had had a companion. You know that it is a particular lonely spot where the castle formerly stood, and even by daylight it is by no means in- viting; and by the time I arrived there it was very dark indeed, and I could not see any person near me. Well, at length I reached to within a few yards of the dreaded place, and was endeavouring to quicken my pace, when suddenly my footsteps were arrested, and my whole soul bound up in horror, when a noise which I cannot describe, and which seemed to proceed from at least a hundred demons, smote my ears, and froze the very blood in my veins."

" God bless us !" cried two or three of the alarmed listeners at once ; " are you sure you were not deceived, good Master Gregory ?"

" Certain," replied Gregory ; " of course I am ; and if I were to live for a hundred years, I should never forget it. It was such a sound ; oh ! awful ! I endeavoured to hasten from the place, but I was fixed, rivetted to the earth, and my eyes, although I would fain have averted them, involuntarily became fixed upon the ruins. The tower, which remains almost entire, seemed to be lighted up with a supernatural fire ; and, as I looked, I could swear that more than once or twice I saw hideous forms flitting past the different broken casements ; but so deep was the feeling of horror which crept throughout my veins, that I found it impossible to move from the spot. While I thus stood, an appalling shriek vibrated in my ears ; I turned my head hastily round, and, as I live, I saw—oh—oh—oh !"

The guests drew their chairs closer to each other ;—their countenances bespoke the most intense anxiety and fear ; their faces became very pale, and a chattering of teeth might be plainly distinguished.

" Wh—hat did you see ?" faltered out the anxious and frightened guests ; and yet they were fearful of being informed of the nature of that which Gregory had either seen, or imagined he had seen.

" Oh ! it was dreadful," said Gregory, after a pause. " Close by my side stood a tall figure in white, and its countenance, which was ghastly pale, bore upon it all the horrors of the charnel-house ; and then its eyes, oh, I—"

" The Blessed Virgin protect us !" cried the guests, crossing themselves, and then the chattering of teeth, and knocking together of knees, became louder than before ; " but are you sure it was a spectre ?"

" Oh, yes," answered Gregory, " quite certain, and that it was the phantom of a woman. Oh, it was so horrible, and she did look so frightfully at me, and then, uttering another piercing shriek, it glided from my sight ; and by the light of the moon, which had just before peeped from behind a dark cloud, I saw the spectre glide into the tower, and soon afterwards re-appear at one of the casements, surrounded by a supernatural light, at the same time that I heard a repetition of the wonderful and terrific sounds that had before so greatly alarmed me. I rushed from the spot, and made my way precipitately to this house, and nothing should ever induce me to go near the ruins of the castle in the broad daylight again even, no, not if I were to be made King of England."

There was a long pause ensued after this recital, and the guests looked at one another with an expression of countenance which plainly shewed the fear with which it had inspired them.

" Marry, but that is a most extraordinary account, Master Gregory," observed Hubert, at last; "so extraordinary, indeed, that I can scarcely credit it, and am inclined to believe that thou hast suffered thy fears to deceive thee."

"Psha!" testily exclaimed Gregory, "how very unbelieving thou art, Master Hubert. I tell thee, believe me, or believe me not, I saw it as plain as I see thee now, and such an impression thou mayest be sure it made upon me that I shall never be able to efface the circumstance from my memory, and I could almost fancy that the awful spectre was standing before me now."

"Oh,—oh,—oh!" groaned out all the guests simultaneously, and getting still closer than ever to each other;—"don't, Master Gregory, don't."

Still was Hubert Clensham very sceptical upon the subject, and he could not bring his mind to believe but that Gregory had only imagined that which he now stated positively to have seen and heard. This was, however, a most awful and important subject for the party to discuss, and it occupied the whole of the evening, and until they had worked themselves up into a state of such extreme terror that they were almost afraid to look around them, and dreaded the time when they must separate for the night, arriving, although they were all going in the same direction, and would, therefore, be company for each other. The lateness of the hour, however, compelled them at last to break up, and they quitted the house, keeping very close to each other, and fancying every sound they heard, if it was only the whistling of the wind amidst the foliage, was some dismal and unearthly moan, and conjuring up all kinds of shapes to alarm them.

As may be expected, this strange and awful adventure was soon spread all over the neighbourhood; and, prone to superstition as most persons were in those unenlightened days, every credit was almost universally attached to it. At length a party of gentlemen, including Sir Egbert de Courcy and Lord Raymond, as the report of the haunted ruins became more current, formed a resolution to watch and inspect them, in order that they might ascertain the truth or falsehood of the rumour, and also to endeavour to find out whether or not it was the work of some impostor, or impostors, for some sinister purposes. The same noises were heard, and the same form appeared to them, and exactly as Gregory had described them, and they endeavoured to seize the supposed spectre, but in an instant it vanished, and shortly afterwards re-appeared at one of the casements of the tower, surrounded by a blue light, and its ghastly countenance seemed to grin at them with the most unnatural exultation; but a moment, and it was gone; but in that moment Lord Raymond had seen enough to fill his breast with the most powerful feelings of terror and emotion. He had fixed his eyes intently upon the ghastly and cadaverous features of the phantom, and they recalled to his memory a being he would fain have effaced from his recollection altogether. A deadly sickness came over him, and he could scarcely support himself.

Notwithstanding the gentlemen were all of them positive that they had not deceived themselves, and really believed that the form they had seen was not of this earth, they resolved not to let any opportunity pass of unravelling the mysterious and awful truth; they, therefore, agreed one amongst the other having brought with them the necessary articles for obtaining a light, to search the ruins all over.

Lord Raymond would rather not have accompanied them in this part of the business, after the shock his feelings had sustained; but fearful that his friends might by any chance misconstrue his motives, he raised no objection. A torch was speedily lighted, and the whole party immediately crossed the old drawbridge, which had not yet been destroyed; and without meeting with any opposition or obstruction, they entered the tower, which we have frequently before mentioned. Their entrance disturbed several owls, who had taken up their residence therein, and they set up a dismal screech, as though to warn them to depart and abandon their design. This was, however, the only noise that disturbed them; and, perceiving nothing to excite their alarm, they proceeded over the different delapidated apartments, without encountering any object whatever, and at length they arrived at the door of that room at the casement of which they were confident that they had seen the phantom standing. It was wide open, but no one was in the room, nor did there seem to be the least signs of any one having been there. There was not a single place about the ruins that they missed examining, at least that they were acquainted with, and they left them, feeling satisfied that there was too much reason to believe in the place being haunted by some troubled spirit, and agreeing that the sooner the ruins were removed the better.

Notwithstanding, however, this opinion, no steps were taken to pull them down, and they remained a terror to the neighbourhood, and to all persons who had occasion to pass near the spot. Lord Raymond frequently reflected upon the mysterious circumstance; and although he endeavoured to persuade himself that he had suffered his imagination to deceive him, he could not succeed in driving away the impression the features of the supposed spectre had made upon his mind; and this event, added to the singular behaviour and threats of the mysterious monk, and the White Knight, and the prognostications of Hal of the Glen, notwithstanding the near approach of his nuptials with Ernnestine, occasioned him many hours of uneasiness. But the time was nigh at hand when the mystery was to be unravelled.

CHAPTER XXIII.
" Hence, horrible shadow!
Unreal mockery, hence!"—SHAKSPERE.

THE consternation caused by this mysterious circumstance amongst the persons who frequented the little back parlour of Hubert Clensham's hostelrie, has been before described; and it was increased by the alarming reports that were daily being made by individuals who stated that they had been led accidentally near the ruins, and had seen the spectre of the woman as she had appeared to Gregory, and those gentlemen who had visited them for the purpose of ascertaining the truth or falsehood of the rumour. Such, indeed, was the terror created by the event, that the cottages in the immediate vicinity were quickly deserted, the simple peasants imagining that they would be spell bound were they to reside in the locality.

That the report was not false, was very evident from the corroborative testimony of various individuals, who had seen it, and upon whose word the utmost reliance might be placed; but whether it was a spirit, or some wretched maniac or impostor, who had taken up her residence there, and adopted the plan for the purpose of alarming the neighbours and rendering her retreat the more secure, they had not yet been able to ascertain, but it will not be wondered that in those days of ignorance and superstition, the generality of the people should firmly believe in the former.

Gregory, when they met together in the evening at the " Flagon," never failed to broach the subject; and every time that he reverted to it, it was to add something to the horror of his description of what he had seen, and to protest the most implicit faith in the supernatural character of that which he had seen. And his auditors were all of them ready enough to believe his statements, however extravagant they might be, and, therefore, it is no wonder that the alarm in the neighbourhood became so great.

Several weeks passed away, and Lord Raymond, in the society and affections of our heroine, had almost forgotten what he had recently seen at the ruins of St. Alwyn Castle, and the other events, his meeting with the White Knight, and the mysterious monk, and the threats which they had held out to him; although when they did recur to him they caused him the utmost uneasiness, and defied all his efforts to unravel them.

Ernnestine, however, felt far from satisfied at the mystery of his manner, and frequently questioned him upon the different events that had recently taken place ; but more especially as to the cause of his agitation on seeing the ring which the White Knight had placed on her finger, and his detention of the same. He always evinced more emotion on this question being put to him than any other, and evaded it as well as he possibly could ; and Ernnestine, seeing the anguish it caused him, at length forbore to refer to the subject, although she was so anxious to have the mystery unravelled.

And now the day which was appointed for the nuptials of Sir Egbert de Courcy and the Lady Marguerite rapidly approached ; and the greatest preparations were made to celebrate it with the utmost magnificence. All the nobility for miles around were invited to be present at the ceremony, and to partake in the festivities that were to take place on that occasion; and it was determined that the gates of the castle of St. Aswolph (in the chapel of which the marriage rites were to be solemnized,) should be open to all who chose to come, whether high or low, rich or poor. Ernnestine was to be the bridesmaid to Lady Marguerite, and never did she look forward to any day with more joyful anticipation, which she hoped would consummate the happiness of her whom she had every reason to love with the same warmth of affection as if she had been her sister.

The chapel of the castle, and the grand banquetting hall, were fitted up in a

style of the utmost splendour for the happy event; and the munificence of the noble family of St. Aswolph, and Sir Egbert de Courcy was never more liberally displayed. For weeks before every person had been on the tip-toe of joyous anticipation, and the wedding day was looked forward to as a general holiday in the neighbourhood ; and it was resolved that the festivities should be prolonged for several days in tilt and tournay, and other noble sports.

Sir Egbert was very much esteemed, for there were few gentlemen that could surpass him for the goodness of his heart, and his other noble and generous qualities; and the amiable and philanthropic disposition of Lady Marguerite had endeared her to every one who knew her—therefore they had the blessings and good wishes of all for their happiness, and joy seemed certain to crown that auspicious event.

Ernnestine was almost constantly at the castle previous to the union, and in fact she was already looked upon as one of the family, betrothed as she was to Lord Raymond, and conciliating by her numerous virtues the love of them all and every person who knew her.

A few evenings before the day appointed for the union had arrived, Lord Raymond having been called away from the castle upon business, Lady Marguerite and our heroine rambled forth together ; and attracted by the fineness of the weather, and indulging in pleasing conversation, thus wandered on, heedless of the course they were pursuing, or of the lapse of time, until they were aroused by the shades of night falling upon the earth, and looking around them to see the place to which they had strolled, they were surprised to find themselves in the immediate vicinity of the ruins of St. Alwyn Castle.

No. 33

Although Ernnestine and her fair companion placed but little belief in the supernatural, the wild stories they had heard about the spectre which was said to haunt the ruins, and which had been authenticated by Lord Raymond, Sir Egbert, and others, naturally created their alarm; and on finding themselves so near the place to which so many horrors were attached, they felt a most powerful sensation of dread stealing over them, and were immediately about to turn away to retrace their footsteps to the castle, when they were suddenly startled and appalled by piercing shrieks, that seemed to proceed from the delapidated tower, and in a moment lights blazed from every casement, and a number of strange and indistinct forms appeared to flit past them. They were both transfixed to the spot, and looked in each other's faces with terror, but were unable to utter a syllable, or to move. A brief pause ensued, and then the shrieks were repeated, and resounded loudly through the forest, and were reiterated in fearful echoes around.

"The holy Virgin protect us!" exclaimed Marguerite. "What can be the meaning of these unearthly sounds? Is it not strange that we should have unconsciously directed our footsteps hither?"

"Oh! let us begone," returned our heroine, "my heart sinks with terror. Come, come, let us not delay a moment, for we know not what danger may be impending over us while we remain here."

Ernnestine took the arm of her terrified companion as she spoke, and they were about to hurry from the spot as fast as their legs would permit them, when another shriek as appalling as the others they had heard, reverberated in their ears, and turning themselves suddenly round upon the impulse of the moment, by the light which the moon now shed upon the earth, their alarm may be readily conceived when they beheld standing within a few paces of them the figure of a female clothed in white, and whose countenance was ghastly pale, while her eyes were fixed with an awful expression upon them. The spectre, for earthly being it did not seem to be, was perfectly inanimate, and might have been taken for a marble statue, had it not been for the penetrating glances that darted from its eyes; but although the pallid hue of death was upon its countenance, there was something peculiarly beautiful in its cast of features, which fascinated while at the same time it awed the beholder.

Horrorstruck, Ernnestine and Lady Marguerite clung to each other, and were incapable of moving from the spot, and their eyes became rivetted on the mysterious and awful form before them.

At length the spectre seemed to fix its eyes intently upon the countenance of our heroine, and as it did so, it appeared to be moved by some powerful and extraordinary emotion, the chest heaved, and the features became animated as with life. It advanced nearer to them, and as a feeling of awe thrilled through their bosoms, they involuntarily sunk on their knees, and the phantom, if such it really was, raised its arms above the head of Ernnestine, as if invoking a benediction upon her.

An indescribable feeling superseded that of terror in the bosom of our heroine, and she once more ventured to raise her eyes towards the countenance of the spectre, and beheld it lighted up with an expression that charmed her to look upon. Another moment, and she felt her arm grasped, and she was raised from the earth. It was the grasp of a mortal hand, in which the life-blood flowed warm, and convinced that she was not now in the presence of a supernatural being, Ernnestine gave vent to an exclamation of astonishment, and the mysterious being seemed to be about to throw her arms around her to embrace her, when suddenly a loud voice cried " Forbear !"— and the tall figure of the Grey Monk stepped in between them, Ernnestine and Marguerite shrinking back with terror.

"Away! away!" exclaimed the monk, addressing the strange being, and waving his arm in a commanding manner ;—" the time has not yet come. Beware !"

The mysterious woman, for such she evidently was, fixed one more fervent look of affection upon our heroine, and then turning away in the direction of the ruins, she disappeared with astonishing rapidity.

Ernnestine and Marguerite now felt more terrified than they had been before, when they found themselves in the presence of the Grey Friar, whose designs might be of the most evil description ; and Marguerite was more especially alarmed, when he seized her by the arm, and she saw his black and piercing eyes fixed upon her countenance, in a manner which made her tremble.

"Fair Marguerite of St. Aswolph," he said, in a peculiar voice, the tones of which were sufficient to make the hearer shudder ; "thou tremblest, and well mightest thou, didst thou but know in whose presence thou now standest. Did I but feel inclined to gratify the wishes I once indulged, how easily might I now bear thee away, and hold thee securely in my power. But the designs I had once against thee, I have now abandoned, and my thoughts are directed to another purpose. Go thy way, therefore, and fear not interruption from the Grey Friar, although thy brother may well dread his vengeance. Ernnestine, I caution both thou and Lady Marguerite, not to mention this circumstance exactly as it has occurred, but to endeavour to keep up the impression that the form thou hast seen is that of a supernatural being. Farewell ; we shall often meet again, and the time is not far distant when thou shalt know who I really am, and when every mystery will be explained."

As the monk spoke, he snatched a hand of each of them, and raising them to his lips, kissed them vehemently, then rushing hastily from the spot, he quickly disappeared, leaving them in a state of the utmost astonishment and bewilderment.

This extraordinary event had taken such an effect upon them both, that they could not offer to stir from the place on which they were standing for several moments after the supposed monk had departed; but at length Ernnestine being the first to recover herself, laid hold of the arm of her companion, and hurried her away without speaking a word.

They were not long in arriving in sight of the Castle of St. Aswolph, and it was not till then that Ernnestine and Lady Marguerite could give expression to their feelings. They paused to take breath, after the speed with which they had been walking, and then our heroine turning to her companion, said :—

" Oh, Marguerite, what a remarkable adventure is that we have met with this night ;—it is one of that mysterious description, which I find it impossible to fathom, and which the more I think of it, serves to involve me still further in doubt, anxiety, and uncertainty. That singular being, which now we are convinced is mortal, didst thou not notice the extraordinary emotion she evinced when she saw me ; and the glances of affection and agitation which she fixed upon me, as she leant over me, and invoked a blessing upon my head ?"

" I did, Ernnestine," answered Lady Marguerite, " and never did I behold anything more impressive ; and her countenance which had before excited our terror, looked lovely in the extreme. Who can she be, and what can induce her to behave in the singular manner she is now doing, and to take up her abode in the old ruined tower ? That monk, too, I cannot think of him without a feeling of horror, and especially after the threats he has held out against my brother, and the frequency of his appearance to him, and under such strange circumstances."

" He told us that the time was approaching when these ambiguities would be explained, and I am all anxiety for its arrival," said our heroine, " although, at the same time, I have a secret dread that the explanation will bring misery to some of us."

" From the words he uttered, and the commanding tone in which he spoke to her, it is evident that the mysterious woman and himself are in some way connected," observed Lady Marguerite.

" True," returned Ernnestine, " and probably she is the victim of his cruelty and oppression. But I think, Marguerite, that it will be better for us not to mention anything of this occurrence to Lady Celestine, your brother, or Sir Egbert, after the warning which the monk gave us, and I tremble at the bare idea of incurring his displeasure."

" I agree with you, Ernnestine," replied Lady Marguerite, " and will not divulge a sentence ; my brother is fully aware that he has an enemy in this unknown monk, and, therefore, there is no necessity for our putting him on his guard."

" I trust that the evil designs of that strange being, whatever they may be," remarked our heroine, " may be frustrated. But, is it not singular, Lady Marguerite, that, although your brother, Sir Egbert, and the other gentlemen who accompanied them, saw the woman who has this evening appeared to us enter the old tower, and immediately followed her, they were unable to see anything of her in the building, although they searched every part of it most minutely, they could not see anything of her, nor discern the least signs of the place being inhabited ?"

" That was remarkable," said Lady Marguerite ; " but she might have escaped by some of the underground passages immediately on their entrance."

They had now reached the castle, and they, therefore, dropped the conversation ; although, as may be expected, it had made a very powerful impression upon their minds.

Lord Raymoud and Sir Egbert, who had returned, were rather surprised at the length of their absence from the castle, but as they did not evince any emotion or alarm, they had not any suspicion that anything of an unusual nature had happened, and that the fineness of the evening had merely induced them to prolong their walk.

Ernnestine remained that night at the castle, and slept in the same chamber as Lady Marguerite, and when they retired to rest, they again conversed upon the extraordinary adventure they had met with, but were quite unable to form the slightest probable conjecture as to who the supposed phantom and the myste-rious Grey Friar really were; and the more they discoursed upon it, the more bewildered did they become.

At length tired of talking upon a subject which they found it utterly impossible to unravel, they gave it up, and retired to rest.

The time passed rapidly away after this adventure, and at length the auspicious day which was set apart for the nuptials of Lady Marguerite and Sir Egbert de Courcy arrived.

CHAPTER XXIV.

" Oh, listen to my minstrelsie,
Ye lords and ladies bright,
The while I sing of gallant deeds
Perform'd by stalwart knight.
The deeds perform'd on battle field
Shall fill the minstrel's song;
And how his prowess he display'd
At tilt and tournament."—OLD BALLAD.

ALL was gaiety and bustle in the neighbourhood of the castle, and at an early hour of the morning it might plainly be seen from the unusual activity of the inhabitants of the different cottages on the wide domains of St. Aswolph, that something of an extraordinary character was about to take place. There was no distinction of personages invited to celebrate the auspicious event in festive mirth, but from the peer to the peasant, all were alike at liberty to enjoy them-selves according to their stations and tastes. The preparations were upon the most extensive scale, and the hilarity which prevailed seemed to be the har-binger of future happiness to the fair bride and bridegroom.

In the castle itself the scene was not less animated than that which prevailed without. The lovely bride, and her still more beauteous bridesmaid, our gentle heroine, who had remained at St. Aswolph Castle for a few days previous, left their chambers at the first blush of " grey-eyed morn," and soon afterwards the different noblemen, knights, and ladies, who had been invited, arrived, all attired in the most elegant manner, and the bridal procession shortly after-wards moved on its way to the chapel of the castle, a number of beauteous maidens preceding the bride and bridegroom, strewing the way with flowers.

They reach the chapel—the ceremony is over, and Lady Marguerite and Sir Egbert de Courcy are united in the indissoluble bands of matrimony, and then the guests return to the grand hall, where mirth and revelry were destined to hold their undisputed sway.

The festivities for the poorer classes, as we have before stated, were upon the most unlimited scale, and the humble hinds seemed determined to enjoy the diversions provided for them to the fullest extent. Booths were erected, which were filled with traders from various parts, imposing paltry glittering baubles on the simple clown, who bought for his mistress the tinsel finery, and thought her charms more brilliant when decked with their false lustre; roasted oxen and sheep smoked on various parts of the plain near the castle of St. Aswolph, of which, as the hungry peasant partook, he blessed the bride and bridegroom, and also invoked the greatest happiness on the family of St. Aswolph, and drunk long life and prosperity to them all in bumpers. Dancing, wrestling, tumbling, and dexterous leaping and jumping, attracted the gaping crowd, who did not think proper to engage in the sports; while throwing the sling, aiming the swift arrow at a mark, running, and all manner of athletic sports, engaged the adventurous youths, who, by their skill and dexterity on that day, won many an unguarded heart.

Nor were the sports of the noblemen of a less pleasing nature; care was not permitted even to peep within the walls of the castle of St. Aswolph that day, and every person seemed to endeavour to outvie his fellow in demonstrating his happiness. The sumptuous feast—the notes of "minstrelsie," and the fantastic mazes of the dance, each came in for their full share of patronage, and the " galliard measure" had seldom been done more justice to than on that occasion.

At night the hall was one blaze of splendour, and the festivities were kept up even till Sol began to show his face over the eastern hills.

The three successive days were devoted to the tilt and tourney, and much gallant sport was anticipated, owing to the number of brave knights and noblemen that had come from all parts, to do honour to the nuptials of Lady Marguerite, and Sir Egbert de Courcy.

Sir Egbert and Lord Raymond were allowed to be equal if not superior in all manly and athletic exercises to any of their competitors; but on this occasion, elate with anticipated triumph, and expected happiness, the bridegroom and Lord Raymond waited at an early hour on Lady Marguerite and Ernnestine, and with rapture they kissed their fair hands, as they each adjusted an elegant scarf, enriched with their beloved names, across their shoulders.

Never was the appearance of Sir Egbert and Lord Raymond more noble or commanding, and they excited universal admiration from all who beheld them. The former was encased in bright silver armour, studded here and there with diamonds and other costly jewels, and from his casque nodded a plume of blood red feathers. The latter's mail was a bright green, whilst waving gracefully in the wind from his glittering helmet was a plume of snow white feathers.

Lady Marguerite, (who, of course, was the queen of the tournament,) and Ernnestine, (who looked more lovely on that occasion than she had appeared for some time before,) were conducted to the place appointed for the pageant, and took their seats, amid the loud shouts of admiration from the persons assembled. There the scene was one of the most imposing and magnificent that can well be imagined. Many gallant knights there were assembled in superb accoutrements, the blandishment of love wore the mask of war, and some of England's most peerless beauties were seated in the spacious galleries around. Ernnestine was seated by the side of Lady Marguerite on a costly throne, and all eyes were directed in enthusiastic admiration towards her and the fair queen of the tourney. At their feet the trophies won were laid—the wrested sword, the broken plume; the discomfited knight, brought as prisoner, received emancipation from their lips, and vowed they left them more enslaved than ever.

Sir Egbert de Courcy was mounted on a large white war-horse, that neighed and pawed the ground as proud of his gallant burthen, and without a saddle, firmly erect, seated only on a rich saddle cloth, entirely covered with flowers or gold embroidered over it; the lining was of scarlet.

Lord Raymond was superbly mounted on a beautiful chesnut charger, who seemed impatient for the sport, and his bearing was no less noble than that of Sir Egbert.

The first and second days of the tournament passed off gallantly, and Lord Raymond and Sir Egbert, either by courtesy or real superiority of ability, surpassed their fellows, and at length they remained the undisputed heroes of the field.

The third day dawned from the Heavens, and a lovely one it was, the bright sun shining in all his golden glory, the sky unchequered by a single cloud; the air fresh and balmy, and all around seeming to be inspired with the most unbounded happiness. The assemblage of the knights was even greater than it had been on the two previous days, and everything promised a gallant day's sport.

It commenced, and as they had done before, Lord Raymond and Sir Egbert came off victorious in every contest. At length, after there had been a pause of some minutes, the former once more threw his gauntlet down, and the heralds sounded a loud blast upon their trumpets;—a second blast; but still no one appeared to accept of the challenge,—but scarcely had the third escaped the brazen throats of the heralds' trumpets, when, from amidst the noble host assembled, there issued a warrior, clad in glittering steel, and mounted on a coal black steed, and riding fiercely into the ring, he accepted the challenge.

There was a murmur of admiration run through the throng, at the noble appearance of this knight, (who bore on his shield a burning heart, with the motto of "Faithful till death," inscribed in characters of gold upon it,) and even Lord Raymond could not help gazing upon him with a feeling of approbation, not unmingled with awe.

Ernnestine shuddered, and as she fixed her eyes upon the knight of the burning heart, whose vizor was down, an indescribable sensation came over her,— she turned ghastly pale, and seemed as if she was going to faint; but a few words from Lady Marguerite, whose confidence in the skill of her noble brother was unshaken, aroused her, and she made a desperate effort to stifle her real feelings, in which she partially succeeded.

The attack seemed to promise an easy victory to Lord Raymond, for his unknown adversary appeared to be governed by most infuriate rage, while he, on the contrary, was cool, collected, and most intrepid. A short time, however, soon altered that opinion; the lances of the combatants met each other with terrific violence, and the knight of the burning heart unhorsed Lord Raymond who fell to the earth with a fearful crash, at which the shouts of the host around rent the air.

The victorious knight immediately alighted from his steed, and approaching the prostrate and almost insensible Lord Raymond, and tearing the scarf from his shoulders which the fair hands of Ernnestine had placed there, he whispered in his ear :—

" Raymond St. Aswolph, we shall meet again, but it must be in mortal combat !"

He then hastily remounted his charger, and riding up to the throne where sat the Lady Marguerite, her mother, and our heroine, from the hands of the former he received the precious gift, and turning hastily to Ernnestine, he snatched eagerly her hand, pressed it vehemently to his lips, and remounting his steed, followed by his esquire, he galloped away, with the speed of lightning, and was out of sight before any of the beholders had recovered from the state of astonishment into which the whole circumstance had thrown them.

Several persons immediately flew to the assistance of Lord Raymond, who was so much stunned by the violence of the fall he had received, that he was unable to raise himself from the ground. He was borne directly to his chamber, and the sports abruptly terminated. His sister and mother were quickly at his bedside, and administering to his hurts; but great as was the bodily anguish he suffered, his mental was much greater, at the thoughts of defeat, and that it should have been by an unknown knight.

Ernnestine was greatly troubled in her mind at this incident, and there was something in the general bearing of the knight of the burning heart, which, without being able to account for it, filled her bosom with a mingled sensation of awe and admiration. She longed to know who he was, but there seemed to be no chance of her wish ever being gratified, and she, therefore, gave up the idea.

CHAPTER XXV.

" Oh, could I but forget how fair she was,
    What vows of love she pledged with mine,
    Then might my hatred for thee cease !
    But no !—Love says it shall not be,
    And one or both of us must die !"—The Avenger.

Some weeks after the marriage of Sir Egbert de Courcy and Lady Marguerite had elapsed, and Lord Raymond had perfectly recovered, but still he could not forget the circumstance of his encounter with the knight of the bleeding heart, and the more he reflected on it, the more did his indignation increase.

" He told me we should meet again," he soliloquized, " and that the combat must then be mortal ; from that, it appears evident he is my enemy. But let fortune once more throw him in my way, 'tis all I wish ; I will then know who he is, and amply averge myself for the defeat which I suffered."

It was a few evenings after this, that Lord Raymond was returning through the wood, towards the castle, when suddenly emerging from some of its most

deep entangled mazes, he heard the sound of horse's hoofs approaching, and he had only time to draw his glittering falchion, when a warrior mounted upon a noble steed galloped up to him, and by the light of the moon, he beheld the Knight of the Burning Heart.

"Ah! by the mass, well met!" cried Lord Raymond, "this is a circumstance I have long been anxiously wishing for. Thy name, Sir Knight?"

"Conquer me, and know it," replied the latter, drawing his sword;—"Ernestine or death!"

"Ernestine or death!" reiterated Lord Raymond in furious tones, and their steeds neighed and snorted, alarmed at the sound of their terrible and enraged voices. There was not another moment's delay, but they both rushed furiously to the strife, and most fearful, indeed, was their first onset, but deceived by the uncertain light of the moon, they passed by each other several times without a blow taking effect. This added more to their rage, but it was all useless; in vain they cut and thrust, parried and passed; their horses, alarmed at their own shadows flitting before them, started and trembled, thus baulking their riders' strokes. Fruitlessly they spent their strength, till completely worn out, they both desisted, and gazed sternly upon each other for a few seconds in silence.

"The combat is useless to-night," at last exclaimed the Knight of the Burning Heart;—"but wilt thou meet me at the first streak of day?"

"I will."

"Where?"

"On this spot!"

No. 34

" Enough.   When ?"

" To-morrow morning !"

" Be it so."

" But thou wilt not play me false ?"

" By the honour of a true knight, I will not," was the answer.

" I will take thy word.   I shall come alone."

" I will also be unattended."

" 'Tis well," returned Lord Raymond ; " by the first blush of day, then——"

" We meet again."

" In mortal combat !"

" For Ernnestine or death !"

" For Ernnestine or death !" responded Lord Raymond, and as he gave utterance to these words, the Knight of the Burning Heart clapped his spurs into the flanks of his fiery courser, and plunged into the deepest recesses of the wood, disappearing almost immediately, and leaving Lord Raymond to recover from his astonishment, and to retrace his steps to the Castle of St. Aswolph.

As he hurried on, his mind became entirely occupied in reflecting upon the singularity of the circumstance, and the mysterious behaviour of the Knight of the Burning Heart.   Who could he be, and what motives could guide his conduct?   He had shewn himself to be his most inveterate foe, and yet Lord Raymond racked his brain in vain to endeavour to imagine to whom he could possibly have given such cause for hatred.   Added to the mystery of the White Knight, and the grey friar, it was a circumstance which entirely bewildered and distracted his brain ; and he felt as if he was the victim of some infernal spell.

" Yet," he soliloquized, as he proceeded, " why should I thus meet in deadly combat a man who professes himself to be mine enemy, and yet is afraid to reveal himself?   He has pledged his honour not to act with treachery towards me ;— yet what dependance ought I to place in the promise of a man whom I know not, and who has chosen to act with so much mystery ?—I will meet him in the morning, but I will not go unattended, so that I may be prepared for any danger which may threaten me.—And yet,—would not that appear like cowardice ?— Would he not think I feared him ?   He would, and I will, therefore, meet him alone, and brave the consequences."

By the time he had come to this determination, he had arrived at the castle.

The event at the tournament had caused the greatest uneasiness and excitement in the breasts of Lady Celestine, Marguerite, and our heroine, but more particularly the latter, and the defeat which Lord Raymond had experienced from the Knight of the Burning Heart, had caused much speculation in their minds, but they were quite unable to form even the slightest conjecture as to who the young stranger was.   Lord Raymond, fearful lest he might cause them any alarm, had forborne to mention the words which the unknown knight had made use of towards him, after he had unhorsed him in the manner we have described ; but he was unable to conceal from them the agitation under which he laboured, which, however, appeared to them to be much more violent than that which would be occasioned by the chagrin which must be consequent upon his defeat.   Ernnestine had marked the peculiar demeanour of the young knight, for such he appeared to be, as far as could be judged by his person, throughout the whole event, but more especially on his receiving the scarf, inscribed with her name, the vehemence of his manner, as he pressed her hand to his lips, and the sensation which had crept over her at that moment, she had never been enabled to banish from her bosom since. The feeling with which she was imbued was a mixture of awe, mystery, and pleasure; and she could not help feeling a dread yet an anxiety to behold him again. She had frequently mentioned it to Lord Raymond, but he was evidently anxious to evade the subject, and, although his conduct appeared strange and inexplicable to her, as she saw that it caused him so much uneasiness, she did not press it, notwithstanding, she had a presentiment that it would be the forerunner of some painful events to them.

Singular dreams had also haunted her pillow since the day of the tournament, and the scene had been several times re-enacted in her imagination. In fact, from that day, the mysterious Knight of the Burning Heart, had been ever present in her thoughts, and she in vain endeavoured to conceive why he should have created such an extraordinary interest in her bosom.

The prolonged absence of Lord Raymond from the castle, on the evening when he encountered the Knight of the Burning Heart, and which we have just been describing, had caused much uneasiness to the three ladies, and fearful lest some accident might have befallen him, they dispatched a couple of domestics in quest of him, but they, having taken a different route to that which he had pursued on his way home, missed him, and did not arrive for some time after he had reached the castle.

Although he tried all that was in his power to disguise the excitement which the combat he had had with the unknown knight, and the appointment they had made in the morning had caused, his uneasiness could not escape their penetrating eyes, and they would have questioned him upon the subject, but a peculiar look from him stayed their tongues, and having changed the topic of conversation, he gradually became more composed, and by the time the hour had arrived for them to retire to their chambers, he was much more collected than might have been anticipated. But although he appeared so, he was very far from experiencing a composed state of mind, for he was still rather irresolute how it would be advisable for him to act, and whether he should actually keep his appointment with the Knight of the Burning Heart, unattended, after what he had said about his being his mortal foe, although he could not conceive why he should be so, or who he actually was. He knew not but that he might mean treachery, and he was more than once half inclined to have two or three of his retainers secreted near the spot where the hostile meeting was to take place, to rush out to his assistance, should he need it; but then again the idea of shewing the least symptoms of fear, prompted him to abandon such a project, and he finally determined, at all hazards, to go alone.

"Yes," he said, "I will dare everything; there was something in the manner of the unknown knight, and the tone in which he spoke, which induces me to believe that he is an honourable foe, and would scorn to take any unmanly advantage. I will meet him, and may Heaven protect me, as I firmly believe my cause to be just. This event may be the means of elucidating all the many mysteries by which I have for some time been tormented and bewildered. 'Ernnestine or death,' that motto will nerve my arm, and render me doubly powerful in the combat."

Lord Raymond, however, slept but little that night, his mind was too intent upon the combat which was to take place in the morning, and which, from the samples he had already experienced of his unknown adversary's skill and prowess, convinced him would be a desperate one, to suffer him to court the drowsy god ; and long before the grey mists had disappeared from the horizon, he was up, and having buckled on his armour, he stole cautiously from the castle, fearful of being seen by any of the inmates, and having mounted his favourite steed, rode off in the direction of the place where he and the Knight of the Burning Heart had encountered each other on the evening before. His fleet courser soon bore him thither, but he found that the knight had not yet arrived.

He dismounted from his horse, and leading him to the thicket, he there determined to remain and watch, which he could do without being observed himself, and if he saw anything which might lead him to suppose that the knight meant to play him falsely, he might easily depart again unseen, and thus frustrate his designs.

He had not stood there long, when he heard the sound of horses' hoofs upon the turf, and immediately afterwards, as well as the obscure light would permit him, he saw the Knight of the Burning Heart gallop up to the spot alone. He was armed in the same manner as he had been on the two former occasions when they had met, and was encased in the same glittering suit of mail, with his vizor down, so that Lord Raymond had no more chance than before of seeing his features.

The knight looked around him, and seemed disappointed at not seeing Lord Raymond, muttering some incoherent sentences to himself ; but his lordship having satisfied himself that he was unaccompanied by any one, did not keep him long in suspense, but advancing from the place where he had been standing, he greeted him.

"Ah !" exclaimed the Knight of the Burning Heart, " 'tis well ; you have not, then, broken your word."

" Lord Raymond St. Aswolph never does break his word, Sir Knight ;" returned Raymond, haughtily. " But art thou still resolved not to let me know with whom it is I am about to contend ?"

" I am ;" answered the Knight of the Burning Heart ; "as I before told thee, defeat me and know."

" Thou art a man of mystery," observed Lord Raymond, " and I know not how I can be thine enemy."

" Thou wilt have the mystery solved ere long, mayhap," returned the Knight of the Burning Heart ; " thou lovest the fair Ernnestine ?"

" I do."

" Art thou willing to resign all pretensions to her hand ?"

" Never !"

" Thy doing so is the only way by which this combat, which must end in the death of one or both of us, can be avoided."

" Death, then, rather than resign the hand and heart of her to whom my whole soul is devoted."

" Be it so, then, Lord Raymond," said the stranger, in a determined tone ; " Ernnestine or death !"

" Ernnestine or death !" repeated Lord Raymond ; and having mounted their steeds, they advanced nearer towards each other. It was yet too dark to see each other sufficiently distinct enough to commence the combat, and they, therefore, agreed to await the first streak of day. By mutual consent, they stood at fifty paces distant from each other, nor stirred, nor spoke ; but laying the bridles gently on the necks of their horses, with folded arms they watched the eastern sky, while the unconscious beasts calmly partook of such green herbage as the spot on which they stood afforded.

At one and the same moment they hailed the dawn, and gathering up their reins, they drew their shining swords, and uttering the name of Ernnestine, advanced furiously against each other. Every moment the increasing light gave energy to their strokes, and the rays of the rising sun added fire to their rage. Soon the brittle swords were shivered to atoms ; they then had recourse to their battle-axes. The feathers that waved on the helm of the Knight of the Burning Heart were scattered to the winds, and his broken vizor fell, but left not his features exposed to view, as they were concealed beneath a black mask.

Fired at the stroke, he aimed at Lord Raymond's casque ; that, too, gave way, and over his brawny shoulders fell the dark locks which had always been so much admired by the fair sex. His noble countenance shone with avenging ire ; his mild eye bore the hue of the basilisk.

The sound of an approaching horseman now met their ears; they looked around, each at the moment suspecting treachery, but they saw nothing to strengthen that supposition. Their expiring vigour was renewed by this little excitement. Seizing their lances, they first retreated some paces distant from each other, then, whirling their horses round, they advanced impetuously forward. Useless was the scaly steel meant to protect the breasts of their noble steeds; such was the force with which they threw their deadly weapons, that at one and the same moment, each animal received the point of a lance in his breast. Shrieking with agony, the horses fell to the earth, and their riders rolled on each other. Disarmed of sword, battle-axe, and lance, nothing remained but the dagger ; panting and bruised, they still sought to continue the contest, and wrestled on the ground.

The scarf, with the name of Ernnestine embroidered in gold, which rested on the heart of the unknown knight, attracted the eye of Lord Raymond ; he extended his left hand, with the intention of seizing the envied prize,—in his right he grasped his dagger. The Knight of the Burning Heart held off his hand with one of his, and with his dagger threatened vengeance with the other.

One knee on the ground, and with uplifted daggers, both struggled unconquered ; but at length, Lord Raymond, by a sudden movement, succeeded in getting the Knight of the Burning Heart underneath him, and was about to plunge his deadly weapon into the unguarded bosom of his unknown foe, when a loud voice from behind him shouted "Hold!" and at the same moment he was seized by the arm and dragged violently to the earth; he looked up, and to his astonishment beheld the White Knight standing by his side.

The Knight of the Burning Heart, who had been panting from exhaustion, beheld him at the same moment, and rising gradually upon his feet, he stood apparently anxious to hear what the White Knight would say, although it was evident that they knew each other.

"Hold!" repeated the White Knight, in an authoritative tone of voice;— "this combat must cease." Then turning to the Knight of the Burning Heart, he added:—

"Instantly begone, and remember thy oath. Lord Raymond St. Aswolph is reserved for my future vengeance, and thou wilt then have an opportunity of gratifying thy revenge in a much more ample manner than his death could now afford thee. Away, I say!"

The Knight of the Burning Heart muttered some words that did not distinctly reach the ears of Lord Raymond, and having fixed upon him a glance of mortal hatred, he bowed to the knight, and hurrying from the spot, was soon hidden from the sight.

The White Knight did not speak another word, but waving his hand in a menacing manner, he disappeared, leaving Lord Raymond astonished and paralyzed to the spot.

After the lapse of a minute or two, Lord Raymond partially recovered himself from the confusion into which he had been thrown, and then bursting through the thicket, he looked eagerly around him to see whether he could observe anything of the two mysterious knights, but they had both vanished, and he turned astonished and disappointed to retrace his footsteps to the castle.

"Confusion!"—he exclaimed, as he walked along, "fiends surely have conspired together to keep me in a continual state of mystery and excitement. Who can these singular beings be?—My bitter enemies they certainly are, but why they are, or what cause I have given them to be so, I am at a loss to imagine I must, and will adopt some means to discover them, and to guard myself against the evil designs they have evidently in contemplation against me."

He walked slowly on towards the castle, for he was completely worn out with the fatigue he had undergone in the combat, although neither himself nor his antagonist had received a wound, and the state of his mind may very well be imagined. Fearful, however, of causing any alarm in the bosoms of his friends, he was anxious to conceal his emotion from observation, and, therefore, before he arrived at the castle, he tried all he could to put on an air of composure in which he was more successful than might have been expected after the event which we have been describing. It was now very evident that the White Knight, the Knight of the Burning Heart, and the female form which had created so much alarm in the neighbourhood of the ruins of the former retreat of the robbers, were all connected together, and that they had some nefarious design against him, which he was fearful they would at some future period succeed in effecting, if he did not contrive some immediate and ready means of counteracting their plans ; and he resolved to have persons constantly on the look out to surprise them, and once in his power the mystery would at last be elucidated, the characters of the parties made known, and all farther danger from them be destroyed.

He had never been able to banish from his thoughts for any length of time, the remarkable behaviour of the mysterious woman, and the impression which the familiarity of her features had made upon him. Although the glance he had at them was only transient, it was long enough to enable him to take a minute survey of them, and he could not again get them from his thoughts. The nature of the reflections which they gave rise to in his bosom, caused him the most poignant anguish, but the real nature of his thoughts will be disclosed at a future period. One thing, however, he at last determined on, and that was to make Sir Egbert acquainted with the circumstance, and with a sufficient number of followers to make an entrance into the ruins, and see whether they could not discover the person, or persons, who might be there concealed. He regretted that he had not done this before, as, from the fact that the noises in the ruins had been discontinued, there was very good reason to suppose that they had been abandoned, and if such was the case, he had in all probability, missed an opportunity which might never occur to him again, of unravelling the mystery, which was to him the source of so much annoyance and alarm.

It was yet so early in the morning, that it was not likely that any of the inmates of the castle would have arisen, and, therefore, it would not be known that he had been away, although he had noticed with some uneasiness, that, in spite of all his endeavours to prevent it, the agitation of his manner on the previous evening after his encounter with the Knight of the Burning Heart, had not escaped the observation of his friends, notwithstanding they had not mentioned anything to him.

Having reached the castle, where he found that the inmates were still at rest, he quickly disarmed himself, and put aside his heavy mail, and appeared in his ordinary dress, and by the time that the morning repast was ready, he had sufficiently recovered himself to appear at the table with every sign of composure.

As soon as the meal was over, the ladies having left the room, Lord Raymond immediately made Sir Egbert de Courcy acquainted with all the particulars of his recent adventures, as we have detailed them, and asked his advice upon them, and the intention he had formed regarding the searching of the ruins of the castle of St. Alwyn. Sir Egbert was very much astonished at the account which Lord Raymond gave him, and remained silent for a moment or two afterwards, reflecting upon it.

"I regret that you did not make me your confident in this affair with the mysterious Knight of the Burning Heart," said Sir Egbert ; "for I might have suggested some means of surprising him, and getting him in our power, and then all which we are anxious to know, would most likely have been unravelled, and the whole of the persons by whom you have been so much annoyed, discovered, and the schemes they have evidently, and by their own admission, in contemplation against you, frustrated."

"It may not yet be too late," said Lord Raymond;—"it is my intention to have persons continually on the look out, so that one or other of the party may be surprised, and thus bring about the result we desire."

"But an excellent opportunity has been lost," returned Sir Egbert, "and you acted with great imprudence in accepting of the appointment of the Knight of the Burning Heart, who might have meant treachery, and your life have been placed at his mercy."

"But the manner in which he behaved, shewed that such was not his design," said Lord Raymond; "in truth he is a brave fellow, whoever he is, and it will take a strong and skilful arm to defeat him. But what sayest thou to my proposition respecting this mysterious woman?"

"Thy account of that event surprises me more than all," replied Sir Egbert; "but art thou sure thou wert not deceived?—And that it was really not a supernatural being?"

"Positive of it," replied Lord Raymond; "how could I be mistaken, when her hand grasped my arm, and she gazed steadfastly in my face?"

"And the features, thou sayest, seemed familiar to thee?" said Sir Egbert.

"Oh, yes, they were indeed!" returned St. Aswolph;—"they reminded me of one, who—but I cannot trust myself to speak upon that subject now. At any rate, I am determined to be satisfied upon this ambiguous affair, and, of course, Sir Egbert, I may calculate upon thy aid."

"Certainly," answered the latter, "but I am fearful that it will not be attended with any satisfactory result; as, from the discontinuance of the noises in the ruins, it appears that the persons, whoever they might be that resided there, have quitted the place."

"I confess," said Lord Raymond, "that I am partly inclined to be of the same opinion; still, it will be more satisfactory to me to ascertain the truth, and if there is no one secreted there, I propose that the ruins be razed to the ground, to put a stop to any future annoyance, and to do away with the superstitious terrors of the persons residing in the locality."

"I agree with thee on that point, Lord Raymond," observed Sir Egbert; "but when shall we put our design into execution?"

"The sooner the better. It is useless to delay;" replied St. Aswolph.

"To-morrow morning, then."

"Ay; as soon as daylight peeps, we will away together, and take with us a chosen few, in case of danger."

This point arranged and settled, the two friends separated, and Lord Raymond having sufficiently revolved all the circumstances that had happened in his mind, became more composed, and began to think that they would terminate more satisfactorily than he had at first anticipated. The being who principally occupied his thoughts was the mysterious woman, whose remarkable likeness to one with whom was connected some of the most painful circumstances of his life; and the reflections they naturally gave rise to were fraught with the most poignant anguish. But should they discover her in the ruins, and she should prove to be the party he thought upon, what a wonderful revolution it would work in his fate, and the secret which he had so long kept locked within his own breast would be divulged. But no, it could not be, he again ruminated; that being, he

had very little doubt, had long slept within the silent grave; if she had not, i was not at all unlikely that all would have been unravelled, and everything arranged long before.

Tired with reflecting, Lord Raymond joined the ladies, and, by dint of great exertion, he appeared more cheerful than he had been for a day or two before.

In the morning, before daylight, Lord Raymond and Sir Egbert left the castle, attended by several of their retainers, taking with them implements to batter in any impediments that might present themselves to their search; and taking the way which was the least frequented, they were not long in reaching the ruins. They found everything, in appearance, as they had seen it on their former visit; the drawbridge was down, and, therefore, they crossed the moat, and entered at the portal, the door of which was standing wide open, without any obstruction. All was silent, save the whistling of the wind, or the flapping of the wings of the bats that were disturbed by their entrance, and fluttered wildly above their heads. Still Lord Raymond could not help feeling a sensation approaching to dread, as he entered that gloomy place, and he looked around him ever and anon, expecting, yet fearing to behold once more that form which had created so much uneasiness in his bosom. But no such object was destined to meet his gaze; there was not a single portion of the ruins which was not most minutely examined, without anything being discovered, and nothing which seemed to denote that any person had inhabited them for some time: and, after having satisfied themselves that they had not missed any part in their search, they quitted the ruins, and having dismissed their attendants, left the place, and walked slowly on towards the castle, conversing upon the subject, and Lord Raymond

No. 35

being in much better spirits after the result of their examination. A few days afterwards a number of workmen were employed, and soon every vestige of the ruins of the castle of St. Alwyn was entirely removed.

CHAPTER XXVI.

" The bride was fair as opening day,
    And noble was the knight;
And many were the prayers that joy
    Should on them both alight.
But little thought they on that day,
    Their bliss would soon be o'er;
Or, that the vows they'd plighted, must
    So quickly be no more."—THE BRIDAL.

SWIFT flew the time, and at length, it wanted but a few days to the time appointed for the union of our heroine and Lord Raymond St. Aswolph; and, as it approached, the mind of Ernnestine became greatly tormented with a variety of conflicting emotions and strange forebodings, and her anxiety need not be wondered at when it is remembered that on that day it had been promised that so many mysterious circumstances should be elucidated. The secret of her origin, and who were her parents, it had been stated should be revealed; and it was, therefore, only reasonable that she should look forward to such a day with the greatest impatience.

Lord Raymond, anxious as he was to become united to that beauteous maiden who had taken entire possession of his heart, could not at times help feeling some strange presentiments, when he recollected the observations that had been applied to him at different times by the Grey Friar, the White Knight, and others; but he endeavoured all he could to shake off these dismal ideas, and to look forward to the auspicious event only as the certain consummation of his every earthly happiness. That was a task of no easy accomplishment, and, in spite of all his efforts, in the midst of his greatest happiness, the same melancholy ideas would obtrude themselves, and render him miserable. For the last two or three months, however, Lord Raymond had not met with any adventure which was calculated to cause him any uneasiness, and nothing more had been seen of the mysterious beings who had so frequently crossed his path, and filled him with anxiety and perplexity.

The preparations that were making for the nuptials, and which were commenced some weeks before the day appointed for the union, were even upon a more extensive scale than those that had been got up on the occasion of the marriage of the Lady Marguerite and Sir Egbert de Courcy, and it was expected that the company would consist of all the principal of the nobility and gentry, who were invited to do honour to the lovely bride and her noble bridegroom.

The foster-parents of our heroine, poor old Hubert Clensham and Maud, were in perfect extacies as the time approached, at the idea of their *protegée* becoming Lady St. Aswolph, the bride of so noble and virtuous a man as Lord Raymond; but there were times when to the former it was not unaccompanied with the most poignant feelings of sorrow, when they reflected on the fate of Godfrey, who would otherwise have stood in the situation of his lordship.

At length the day, so "big with fate," arrived; the day on which so many wonderful revelations were to be made, and which was to make such a remarkable and unexpected change in the circumstances of many of the actors in this romantic drama.

We will not occupy our space by giving a detailed account of the magnificent and extensive preparations that had been made for the ceremony, for even the most elaborate description could not do justice to them, and imagination can but faintly picture them. Yet, notwithstanding the near approach of that moment which would make her the bride of a nobleman whose numerous virtues had excited her warmest affections, Ernnestine could not help feeling a melancholy presentiment of something which was about to take place to mar their happiness, in which feeling Lord Raymond evidently shared. But he endeavoured by every means in his power to banish the doubts and apprehensions from his mind, and appear cheerful and happy, in which he succeeded much better than he had at first expected.

Most beauteous, although pale, did our heroine appear, and great was the sensation she excited among the persons present; every one of whom shewed by their looks the admiration which they felt for her, and how heartily and sincerely they wished her every happiness.

All the kind friends of Ernnestine, were present, and Hubert Clensham felt not a little delighted on the occasion; yet he was not without some strange misgivings, that their joy was about to suffer some interruption, and more especially when he recollected the words of the mysterious White Knight, and the promise that he had made, that on the day of the nuptials of Lord Raymond and Ernnestine, the secret of the latter's origin, and every circumstance connected with her, should be divulged; and he awaited in the greatest suspense the solemnization of the ceremony.

At last the particular moment arrived! The favoured guests filled the gothic chapel; Lord Raymond and our heroine knelt before the altar; and Hubert, Maud, Ranulph, and Edith, with the mother of Lord Raymond, Sir Egbert, and Lady Marguerite, stood around them, and the ceremony commenced. All was as still as death in the chapel on that occasion, the only sounds being heard were the solemn tones of the priest, and the responses of Ernnestine and Lord Raymond.

The ceremony was over, Ernnestine had become the bride of Lord Raymond St. Aswolph, and their friends were about to congratulate them; when, suddenly, a loud and thrilling exclamation rung through the sacred building, and came like an electric shock upon all the persons present, who directed their eyes towards that part of the chapel from whence the sound appeared to issue.

A death-like chill came over the frame of Ernnestine, and she clung fearfully to Lord Raymond, who was scarcely in a less state of trepidation than herself.

" Hold !—Forbear !" shrieked a female voice, and the next moment, rushing along the aisle towards the altar, was seen a woman, who, from her dress and demeanour, Lord Raymond immediately recognised;—it was the supposed phantom of the late ruins of the Castle of St. Alwyn. Her hair hung loose and dishevelled about her shoulders, and her face was ghastly pale. Lord Raymond trembled as she approached, and Ernnestine, notwithstanding her astonishment and terror, felt a sensation of awe and veneration stealing over her.

There was but an instant for thought;—the next, the mysterious woman knelt at the feet of Lord Raymond, and clasping his knees, looked frantically up in his face. The persons present were thunderstruck, but not a word was spoken by any one. Lady Celestine and her daughter's astonishment and suspense may be imagined. As to Lord Raymond as he fixed his eyes upon the countenance of the woman, his face became ghastly pale; his lips quivered, and he appeared fixed as a marble statue with terror and amazement!

"Raymond! Raymond!" ejaculated the woman, in a voice half stifled with mental agony;—"dost thou not know me?"

"Gracious Heaven!" exclaimed Lord Raymond, in a voice of the most indescribable agitation; "can this be reality, or are my senses leaving me?—Marian, and living!—No—no—I am going mad!—And yet, that face!"

"Raymond!" cried the woman, in hysterical accents, "thou art not deceived; it is the guilty, but penitent Marian, who kneels before thee; once the possessor of thine heart;—thy wretched, distracted *wife!*"

Wife!" screamed Ernnestine, and she sunk senseless on the pavement of the chapel.

Language must fail to do adequate justice to the feelings of astonishment that filled the minds of every one present, especially Lady Celestine, her daughter, and the friends of our heroine;—they gazed at the careworn, but still handsome being who yet knelt at the feet of Lord Raymond, and clasped his knees, and awaited to hear his answer; but he seemed to be turned to stone, and gazing vacantly upon the woman before him, and who had announced herself by so tender a title, he was for some time incapable of uttering a syllable.

"Wife!—wife!" he at length articulated, wildly;—"but no—no—it cannot be—it is mockery all;—you are but a spirit, and—and—wife!—Ernnestine is now my beauteous bride; and ——"

"*She is your daughter!* — My child! — Yours!" cried Marian, in a voice which made the place re-echo again! "Nay, spurn me not from thee!—It is Marian that kneels before thee. Ernnestine De Lacy, as she has hitherto been called, is thine own daughter!"

Lady Celestine no sooner heard the words that Marian gave utterance to, than he screamed, and immediatly fainted, and together with Ernnestine was about being conveyed away from the chapel, when Marian started to her feet, and rushing between the persons who were about to bear them away, she exclaimed:—

"Hold! a mother claims the right to enfold her long estranged child to her bosom, and to implore the forgiveness of Heaven for having abandoned her in her nf ancy!"

"Woman, for the love of Heaven! dost thou, indeed, speak the truth?" demanded Sir Egbert.

"Before the sacred altar of the Most High, I swear I do!" solemnly answered Marian.—"Let Lord Raymond deny it if he can!"

"She speaks the truth!" groaned Lord Raymond. "Great God! thy ways are wonderful!"

"My child! my child!" exclaimed Marian, clasping our heroine frantically to her bosom, and kissing her pale cheeks rapturously, while Lord Raymond, with clasped hands, and upraised eyes, seemed completely paralized to the spot. The persons present had all flocked around, and the expression of astonishment with which they gazed upon the remarkable group, formed a scene of the most extraordinary description.

Ernnestine now slowly recovered, and opening her eyes, and passing her delicate hands across her temples, she gazed wildly and vacantly around her. She found herself clasped in the arms of Lord Raymond, who had snatched her from the embrace of Marian, and was weeping tears of mingled anguish and extacy upon her.

"Where am I?" she exclaimed, in delirious accents ; "what place is this, and for what holy ceremony has it been decorated?—Ah!—I see now!—The whole dreadful truth flashes upon my brain!—Raymond, deceiver!—His wife!—Oh, God!"

"My child! my child!" ejaculated Lord Raymond, clasping her more fervently than before to his bosom; "oh, look up,—speak to me; it is thy father who enfolds thee to his heart!"

Ernnestine looked at him, and then at Marian, wildly, for a moment, and then uttering an hysterical laugh, she once more fainted in the arms of Lord Raymond St. Aswolph. He motioned to some of the attendants, for he could not speak, and they bore her and the Lady Celestine from the chapel to their own chambers.

While this was passing, Marian, whom the reader must recognize as Lady St. Aswolph, was standing with clasped hands, and her eyes raised towards Heaven, with an expression of countenance in which awe, misery, and joy were blended, and the deepest attention and interest of every one was directed towards her. Suddenly, however, she started, and once more throwing herself at the feet of Lord Raymond, she looked imploringly up in his countenance, as she exclaimed :—

"Raymond!—lord—husband, if such I may be still permitted to call thee ; oh, wilt thou not pardon thy guilty, but repentant wife, and suffer her, ere she dies, to be again enfolded to that heart, where once she reigned supreme?—'Tis the last request she will ever make to thee ; grant her then that, and she is prepared to make her peace with God, and die!"

Lord Raymond looked at her for a moment, as if he would penetrate to her very soul : the full tide of affection then rushed once more through his veins, and flashed from his eyes ; and, with an exclamation of rapture and astonishment, he threw his arms around her, and pressed her to his heart, and wept upon her bosom like a child.

"Traitress!" shouted a loud voice at that moment, which startled every person present. Marian extricated herself hastily from the embrace of her husband, as the well-known tone vibrated in her ears, and had no sooner done so, than she uttered a piercing shriek of agony, and fell, bleeding, with a wound in the side from an arrow, into the arms from which she had only the instant before withdrawn herself.

"Ah! who hath done this bloody deed?—Where is the murderer?" ejaculated several persons, looking around them.

"He is here!" replied the same voice which had before spoken, and immediately, from behind one of the large pillars that supported the lofty roof, bow in hand, appeared the mysterious Grey Friar, who had so often crossed Raymond's path, and walked boldly into the midst of them, and confronted the former; but his cowl was down, and no one could behold his features. His appearance inspired a feeling of awe, and the individuals around involuntarily shrunk back.

"She hath deceived me, and robbed me of half that revenge I have been so long panting to obtain," continued the false monk; "and her fate is merited. Raymond St. Aswolph, thy mortal foe stands before thee;—the time hath now arrived when the secret thou hast been so anxious to know shall be revealed to thee. Marian hath told thee the truth, although her lips should not have spoken it, and I only granted her life upon condition that she did not reveal herself, or make thee acquainted that she was still living. That girl, to whom thou hast been united, is thine own daughter, the child whom I found in the forest, and committed to the care of Hubert Clensham. I could have long since gratified my revenge by sacrificing her life and thine; but I had another and deeper plan, which yon dying woman, who contrived last night to escape from my power, hath thwarted.—Eternal curses light upon her soul for it!—I had planned to make thee guilty of incest, and after a few days to have revealed to thee the whole of the facts as thou hast heard them now, and left thee to all the horrors of remorse and unspeakable agony, which such knowledge must have imparted to thee. But I am foiled, and that by—"

"Monster!" interrupted Lord Raymond; who, as well as the other individuals, seemed, as it were, spell-bound to the spot on which they were standing, and were unable to move or to offer to seize the mysterious man.

"Nay, thou mayest spare thy compliments," replied the apparent monk, with the utmost coolness, "I heed hem not. Thou hast frequently demanded to know who I am.—Behold!"

He tore away his monkish garb as he spoke, and to the astonishment of every person, the White Knight stood before them. A simultaneous exclamation of surprise escaped them when they saw him, and Lord Raymond now discovered that the surmises he had all along entertained, that the mysterious monk and the White Knight were one and the same individual, were confirmed.

"Thou hast yet to know further of me," ejaculated the knight, and raising his vizor, the well-known features of Osmond, the robber-chief, who had been supposed to have perished in the conflagration of the Castle of St. Alwyn, were disclosed to them. He stood for a minute or two, and appeared to enjoy the astonishment they experienced; then advancing closer to Lord Raymond, he took off his casque, removed the dark wig, and large false whiskers, that had hitherto served to disguise him, and St. Aswolph staggered back with amazement depicted in his countenance, and in a hollow voice exclaimed:—

"Gracious Heaven!—It is Lord Ethelred!"

"Yes, I am that injured nobleman, who hath so long been near thee as the robber-chief,—the White Knight, and the Grey Friar," said Lord Ethelred; "I am he from whom thou stolest that which deprived me of fortune, fame, and happiness!"

"'Tis false!" answered Lord Raymond. "It was by Marian both thou and I wert deceived."

"Liar!" cried Lord Ethelred; "but I waste words with thee!—The revenge I sought hath been thwarted, but still will I have thy life's blood!—Die!"

As Lord Ethelred spoke, he suddenly drew forth a dagger from his belt, and rushing upon the unguarded St. Aswolph, would have plunged it in his bosom; but at that moment, his hand was arrested by two or three of the persons around, and in spite of his violent struggles to release himself, he was secured, and was being dragged away from the place, when Lord Raymond ejaculated:—

"Bear the misguided man to one of the chambers of the castle, and keep him closely confined, but harm him not!"

"Slaves! unhand me!" shouted Lord Ethelred, foaming with rage; "I will not accept of mercy from the hated St. Aswolph! Release me, I say!"

But he appealed and struggled in vain; he was carried from the chapel into the castle, and confined in the north tower; the unfortunate Marian having been previously borne to a chamber, where a monk attended her, and dressed the wound she had received, which he pronounced to be mortal.

The guests who had been invited to partake of the festivities on the occasion of the nuptials of Lord Raymond and Ernnestine, now dispersed, completely bewildered and astonished at the singular events that had so unexpectedly occurred, and were likely to serve them to talk about for some time to come.

CHAPTER XXVII.

"Woman, that fair and fond deceiver,
How prompt are striplings to believe her;
How throbs the pulse, when first we view
The eye that rolls in glossy blue,
Or sparkles black, or mildly throws
A beam from under hazel brows.
How quick we credit every oath,
And bear her plight the willing troth;
Fondly we hope 'twill last for aye,
When, lo! she changes in a day.
This record will for ever stand,
'Woman, thy vows are traced in sand.'"—BYRON.

WE will now proceed to explain those mysteries which the reader has, no doubt, been long anxious to have solved, and which will bring this eventful narrative to a close.

In the early part of this story, we stated that Lord Raymond St. Aswolph, although unmarried, was about forty years of age, he being the eldest offspring, and only surviving son of the Earl and Countess St. Aswolph. We also mentioned that he had been abroad from a youth, and that on his return to England, he was oppressed with a deep melancholy, which his mother and sister vainly endeavoured to ascertain the cause of. Lord Raymond never before had any secrets from his mother ; but in this one instance, he knew that he had acted imprudently, and, although he dreaded not to encounter her reproaches, he was fearful of causing her some unhappiness, and was, therefore, resolved to keep the secret of his grief locked within his own bosom.

It was during the time that he was in France, and when Lord Raymond was a very young man, that he became acquainted with Lord Ethelred Fitz-Aubrey, who was about the same age as himself, and in many traits of his disposition, being like him, they contracted a friendship for one another.

Lord Ethelred's real character was, however, composed of inconsistencies ; he was brave and generous, but passionate, and frequently obstinately opposed to conviction. He was ardent in his friendship, but once offended, he was a most implacable enemy ; and the cool, persevering, and deliberate manner in which he would seek the gratification of his revenge, has been shown by the circumstances recorded in this narrative.

His father, the Earl Fitz-Aubrey, who at that time was living, possessed all the inconsistencies and eccentricities of his son's disposition, one of which was exemplified in a most unreasonable and tyrannical manner by the arrangement he made for his son's future settlement.

The Earl Fitz-Aubrey, in early life, had contracted a very warm friendship for Sir Arther de Covington, who, marrying young, was left a widower, with an only daughter. As a proof of his friendship towards him, the Earl Fitz-Aubrey contracted a marriage between their two children, the young Lord Ethelred, and Marian de Covington ; and, in order that this contract should be fulfilled when they should arrive at years of maturity, the earl, in a fit of madness,—for it could have been nothing else which could have induced him to come to such an unjust and cruel determination,—ordered in his will, that if Marian should marry any other man, the whole of his (the earl's) fortune and estates should go to his nephew, and that Ethelred should be left without a single coin.

Sir Arthur was covetous enough to accede to this arrangement ; and as the children grew older, they saw no reason to think that it would be a matter of regret to either of them, for being brought up together, as brother and sister, they early imbibed an affection for each other, and when they were made acquainted with the contract, so far from expressing any disapprobation of it, they evinced the greatest pleasure at it, and were anxious for the period to arrive when their fates would be united.

Marian was a lovely girl, and as she increased in years, her mind became well stored with various accomplishments, but she possessed many intrinsic blemishes, that afterwards most unfortunately displayed themselves.

At the age of fifteen, Sir Arthur thought it would be better that they should be separated for a few years, in order that they might the better pursue their

studies, and accordingly, Marian was sent to France, and placed under the care
of a female relative, who behaved to her with the kindness of a mother.

Lord Ethelred had not beheld Marian for more than four years, when Sir Arthur was taken suddenly ill, and died in a few hours, and it was agreed between
the earl and his son, that the latter should go over to France with the melancholy intelligence to Marian, and to invite her to England to take up her future
residence at the castle, and under the protection of the earl.

Lord Ethelred did this, and once more beheld his betrothed, who had now
grown into all the full loveliness of woman, and received him in a manner
which convinced him that her sentiments were unchanged.

Lord Ethelred resolved to stay a few months in France, happy in the society
of his lover, and it was there, and at that period, that Lord Raymond and
him first became acquainted with each other, and Lord Ethelred introduced him
to the beauteous Marian.—Fatal introduction !—Little did they imagine the consequences that would result from it. Lord Raymond and Marian no sooner beheld each other than they loved, and with all the passionate ardour which two
warm and susceptible hearts are capable of loving.

At length a circumstance took place which brought about an explanation of
affairs sooner than would otherwise perhaps have happened. Lord Ethelred
received intelligence from England of the dangerous illness of his father, who
was not expected to live, and it, therefore, became necessary that he should
immediately depart thither, and the time of his return would, of course, be
uncertain.

Some weeks elapsed, and although Lord Raymond would fain have kept away
from the place where Marian resided, she was a magnet whose attraction he

No. 36

could not avoid. She ever received him with the utmost demonstrations of pleasure, and seemed sad when he was about to leave; in fact, her every look and action plainly showed that the sentiments he had so unfortunately imbibed, were returned by her.

In a month after the departure of Lord Ethelred, Marian informed him that she had received intelligence that the Earl Fitz-Aubrey was no more, and took the opportunity of remarking that the letter was a very cold one, and Ethelred did not so much as mention any time when it was likely he should return to France.

Another month passed away, and still Lord Ethelred did not return, neither did Marian hear anything from him; but she had now become entirely callous upon the subject, as Raymond occupied her whole thoughts.

One day when Lord Raymond paid a visit to Marian, she met him with an expression of countenance which convinced him she had something particular to impart to him. Her face seemed flushed with indignation, but still there was a sinister expression in her piercing eyes, which showed plainly that she felt a malevolent pleasure in that which she had to inform him of. She presented him with a letter, which she requested he would read, and she sat and watched his countenance narrowly while he did so, apparently most anxious to see what effect it would have upon him.

The letter purported to come from Lord Ethelred, and was certainly of a most extraordinary description. It stated that, owing to an alteration in his sentiments, and a different arrangement which his late father had made in his will, he had thought proper to release her from the vows she had made to him, and that henceforward, if they should meet, it must only be as friends. Lord Raymond read this letter with astonishment, and did not wonder that Marian should express so much indignation. It was the foerunner to all the misfortunes he was afterwards destined to undergo. Lord Ethelred having thus broken off the intimacy himself, he saw no reason that he should not pay his addresses to the fair being who had captured his heart, and he, therefore, candidly revealed his mind to Marian, and with the approval of the lady under whose protection she was living, they became acknowledged lovers; and, led on by the impetuosity of his passion, he made Marian his wife.

When they had been married about six months, Lord Raymond's duties to his king called him away, and they parted most affectionately, he leaving Marian at the time *enceiénte*. He was absent some time; but judge his astonishment and horror, when, on returning home, he found that Marian had deserted it, soon after her confinement, taking her infant with her, and without-leaving the least idea of whither she was gone, or her reasons for such extraordinary conduct. Too soon, however, was the unfortunate Lord Raymond made acquainted with the fatal truth. Marian had left a letter behind for him, and on breaking the seal, and hastily glancing at the contents, he groaned aloud, and his senses immediately left him.

Fearful that her husband would discover her guilty conduct, and dreading to encounter his indignation, she had fled, informing him that it was her intention to bury herself in a convent for the remainder of her days, together with her child, and that he must never hope to hear of, or see either of them again.

She confessed to him all her errors, from which it appeared that, induced by the violence of the love with which he (Lord Raymond) had inspired her, she had secretly connived with the cousin of Lord Ethelred, who was anxious that his union with her should never take place, as in the event of that, the fortune of the late Earl Fitz-Aubrey, would go to him, and he had employed persons to way-lay Ethelred, and to convey him to a place of security, until she could forward her designs, and should have become the wife of Lord Raymond. She also acknowledged that the letter purporting to come from Lord Ethelred, had been forged by her, with, of course, the same object in view.

While in this state of agitation, and apprehension, she heard from the relative of Ethelred, whom we have before mentioned, that the latter had effected his escape, and had been to him, where, upon learning what had taken place, he had become completely distracted, and vowed the most terrible vengeance against Lord Raymond, whom he believed to have acted so base and treacherous a part towards him, and to have been the cause of his seizure in England, in order that he might the better execute his nefarious plans.

When the wretched Marian heard this, fearing to encounter the presence of Ethelred, and seeing no chance but that Lord Raymond must become acquainted with all the particulars of her guilt, as we have before stated, she fled with her child, and made her way to England, resolving to make all the atonement she could, and to live for the remainder of her days in seclusion. She disguised herself, and for some time resided in an obscure retreat, but at length her money being quite exhausted, and reduced to a most pitiable condition from want, and the bitter upbraidings of a guilty conscience, she resolved to immure herself for the rest of her days in a convent, and with that design, she quitted the place where she had dwelt, with her child, which, in a moment of desperation, she had determined to leave at the castle of St. Aswolph, with a note, stating who she was, and consigning her to the care of her father and his relations. Her courage, however, failed her, and in a moment of madness she left her in the forest where she was afterwards found by Ethelred, then known as Osmond the Avenger. She then made her way to the nearest nunnery, where she was admitted, and passed many years in sorrow and penitence, augmented greatly by the uncertain fate of her child. She was somewhat consoled, however, by hearing that her husband was alive, and had escaped the vengeance of Ethelred, who had not been heard of since he left the castle of his treacherous relative, accompanied only by his faithful attendant, Hugo. The course pursued by Ethelred, has already been related, and it now only remains to be explained by what extraordinary means Marian, after the lapse of so many years, again fell into his power.

After his escape from the burning ruins of the Castle of St. Alwyn, the robber-chief retired to another part of the country, where he still nourished his scheme of vengeance against Lord Raymond, and enacted those parts in the characters of the White Knight, and the Grey Friar, that have been recounted. The nunnery in which the guilty Marian was secluded, happened to be situated close by, and one night, it being accidentally destroyed by fire, Marian made her escape from the flames, and miraculously encountered Ethelred, who bore her away from the spot to his retreat, where he was half inclined to sacrifice her immediately to his vengeance; but a second thought arrested his hand, and he spurned her, determined to make her subservient to his future schemes against her husband, although she confessed the whole of the guilty plot of which she had been the authoress, and entirely acquitted Lord Raymond of having the remotest share in it; but he would not believe her, and felt a pleasure in torturing her by informing her of the existence of her daughter, and of the abominable scheme of vengeance he had determined upon. For better security he removed her to the ruins of the Castle of St. Alwyn, and retired there himself. There he forced her to assume the disguise she did, and invented those supernatural appearances, that succeeded so well in frightening away any intruders upon his retreat. On the night, however, before the union of Lord Raymond and Ernnestine was to have taken place, she managed to escape, and determined to make her way to St. Aswolph Castle, and reveal everything; but she lost herself in the forest, and wandered about until the morning, when she made her way to St. Aswolph with all the precipitation she could, but was unable to reach it until after the ceremony had taken place. What followed has been shown.

It may appear necessary to state, that the Knight of the Burning Heart, as he was called, was only an accomplice of Ethelred's, employed to further his evil designs, and to increase the perplexing mystery in which his actions were shrouded.

CONCLUSION.

With what unspeakable rapture did our heroine feel herself clasped to the heart of her father;—with what transport did Lady Celestine and her daughter embrace so dear and near a relation!—and how unbounded was their gratitude for the miraculous manner in which the disclosures were brought about, and Lord Raymond and his daughter saved from a fate which it was too dreadful to think upon!—We must draw a veil over the scene!

The unfortunate and misguided Lady Marian died before the morning, after embracing her daughter and her husband, and receiving an assurance of forgiveness from their lips, and many were the tears of commiseration that were shed at her melancholy fate. Her errors were forgotten in the tomb, and prayers to Heaven for the pardon of the Almighty, were frequently offered by those to whom her guilt had been productive of so many miseries.

Two hours after Ethelred had been conveyed to the place of confinement, by the orders of Lord Raymond, two of the vassals of the latter who had the care of him, entered the room, where they found him stretched upon the floor, a stiffened, blackened corpse. Certain of the fate which would be awarded to him, he had taken a subtle poison which he had had concealed about him for another purpose, and thus terminated his guilty career.

*   *   *   *   *

Several months had elapsed since these events had taken place, and the different actors in the drama were almost entirely restored to tranquillity, our heroine supremely happy in the love of her dear relations, and those friends who had been her protectors; when one day, as Lord Raymond and his daughter were seated in the blue chamber, a page made his appearance, and informed his lordship that a strange knight requested an interview with him and his daughter.

On their entrance, his back was turned towards them. His figure, which was clad in a splendid suit of mail, was tall and graceful. On hearing them move in the apartment, he turned hastily round, and they then perceived that his vizor was down. Ernnestine trembled. The next moment the knight approached, and bent one knee to the floor before Lord Raymond and his daughter:—

"My lord,—fair Lady Ernnestine," he said, "an humble supplicant craves your pardon, and ——"

"Good God! that voice!" ejaculated our heroine, clinging for support to her father;—"it is ——"

"That of one who once was dear to thee, lady," replied the knight, and raising his vizor as he spoke, Ernnestine screamed, and fell insensible in the arms of her father.—It was Godfrey de Lacy!

"Oh, my lord," he cried, in a voice of the greatest emotion;—"see to thy lovely daughter;—the shock has been too great for her!"

"Godfrey de Lacy, and alive?" exclaimed Lord Raymond with the most indescribable astonishment.

"Yes, my lord; it is indeed true; but oh, say, canst thou forgive me for—"

"No more, no more!" interrupted Lord Raymond, seizing his hand;—"thou art forgiven, and I hail with delight the miraculous circumstance which has restored thee to thy friends."

Ernnestine on her recovery found herself clasped in the arms of that lover whom she had believed to have been long since no more! He had achieved glory in the field of battle!—Had been honoured and rewarded by his sovereign with title, rank, and wealth! and, after having been taken prisoner, and endured a long and painful captivity, had returned to his native country admired by all who knew him!

*   *   *   *   *

We have little more to add in conclusion:—the sentiments of Sir Godfrey as was now his title, and Lady Ernnestine were unchanged;—and Lord Raymond having cordially given his assent, the union of the lovers was solemnized with much pomp three months after the return of Sir Godfrey to England. On the morning of the union another surprise of a most agreeable nature awaited them. Osric and Blanche, who had escaped from the flames which destroyed the Castle of St. Alwyn, made their appearance at the castle. The father of the former was dead, and stung with remorse, he had repented of his crimes, and made a full confession of all his guilty transactions, and they were restored to rank and fortune.

To say that every happiness attended all the individuals that have appeared in this narrative, may suffice in conclusion;—Sir Godfrey de Lacy and Ernnestine had a numerous family, and Lord Raymond lived long enough to see the his grandchildren possessed all the virtues of their parents; and were admired and esteemed by all who knew them.

Lady Celestine survived several years after these events, and then died as she had lived, with the blessings and prayers of those to whom she had ever been so generous a benefactor; and her numerous virtues lived in the memory of many a grateful being.

Sir Egbert and Lady de Courcy enjoyed a long life of uninterrupted happiness, surrounded by a virtuous family.

Poor old Hubert Clensham and his wife lived but a short time after the circumstances we have recently been recording, and the venerable couple were deposited in the family vault of St. Aswolph, at the request of Lady Ernnestine, and their many amiable qualities and the care and affection with which they had attended the poor foundling, were cherished in the memory of our heroine and all those so dear to her, as long as they lived, with feelings of unbounded gratitude.

The parents of Sir Godfrey de Lacy resided with them for many years at the Castle of St. Aswolph, and were surrounded by every comfort and enjoyment that wealth and virtue could bestow.

THE END.

LONDON: Published by E. LLOYD, at the Office of "The Penny Sunday Times," 231, Shoreditch.

www.ingramcontent.com/pod-product-compliance
Lightning Source LLC
Chambersburg PA
CBHW081146020726

47504CB00009B/2020